I0593057

Zsoall Robi @ Facebook
birologybooks.com.au
enquiry@birologybooks.com.au
Cover design - Birology Books.

Zsoall Robi

Other books by Zsoall Robi

Potential Absolute

Lelek could not conceive what the future held for him when he struggled to survive as a Stone Age man.

Instant

Is it at all possible to cross the bridge between two consecutive instants of time into Eternity?

Immortal

Aliens are those who are different, those who belong to a different civilisation. Who is more worthy of survival? Them or us?

Neural Surveillance

Anything seen, heard or said is transmitted and monitored by the Angels and Saints.

Prologue

In the beginning a black hole of extraordinary magnitude held within its grasp nothing but fundamental particles - Up quarks and down quarks, top quarks and bottom quarks, strange quarks and charm quarks all primed to create hadrons.

When the hadrons in the guise of protons and neutrons had formed a critical mass of atomic nuclei, which the black hole could no longer accommodate, an imbalance occurred which caused the black hole to violently discharge its entire population of pre-matter elemental particles.

Within the first few seconds of freedom the radiant energy released by the annihilation of the black hole fused neutrons and protons and electrons, which cooled over millennia to form stable hydrogen and helium atoms.

And thus the Universe was created.

The Galaxies, the nebulae and the Earth, and all that is on the Earth had their naissance in the Fundamental Particles of primary reality.

A great deal of energy had been expended by all manner of intelligent life throughout the known Universe in search of the origins of that fundamentum, far more than the modest efforts of a newly formed Corporation on Earth, called Unity.

Their Principal Officer Of Profit, Leif, engaged the services of a most unlikely individual, Nick, to embark on a quest unprecedented in the history of the evolution of the human species. Leif became convinced he could not only get Nick to the desired location in space, but that he could acquire the data required by Unity to make it the most powerful monopoly on Earth.

Leif knew nothing about quantum physics or about quarks and even less about life outside his tiny little Earth in a diminutive little solar system. In his profound ignorance he was about to condemn a human being, a simple conglomerate of fundamental particles held together by tenuous forces, to travel through the limitless ocean of dark matter to ground zero, where the very compounds that transformed his biology into mind were first created.

Zsoall Robi

Author's Note

A word or two of explanation about the Keplerians: The practical dilemma one finds oneself in is how to express the content of communication from our neighbours on Kepler 443b in a way that is understandable to a Terran.

For example; the name Rivighxuinn, is made up of sounds our vocal cords are unable to reproduce. So she will be referred to as Riin. When she is conversing with other Keplerians it would not be possible to represent the wonderfully melodious sounds within our audio range. Even if it were possible we could not decipher their meaning, let alone distinguish them from say a combination of the drone of Kepler Star's rhythmic pulses or the pings and crackles of black widow pulsars.

To tell her part of the story we shall have to resort to the rather inadequate and primitive vernacular of Earth's 24th century 'universal' language, which by no stretch of the imagination could possibly be called universal, according to Riin.

SPACE-TIME LEVEL, ONE - OUTER SPACE

Returned from First Outing
Nick's Kava Stupor
Deep space alien - Riin
Unity selects Nick
Experiment with Vhipis on 443b
Nick Prepares for First Outing
Wormhole - Fragmentation Begins
Higgs Field, Supernova and Black Hole
Rivighxuinn Launched from 443b
Mary meets Rivighxuinn
Nick's escapade
Last Briefing
Last Launch
At the Centre?
Returning from Final Outing
Visit to 443b
On the Way Home at Last
Nick's Voices
Discussion with Self
Preparing for Home
Rescue Team from 443b
Re-entry
Confrontation at Unity
Riin Infiltrates Earth System

SPACE-TIME LEVEL, TWO - MUNDANE REALITY

Reunited with Mala
A new Reality Begins
Smell My Fish

Zsoall Robi

SPACE-TIME LEVEL, THREE · INNER SPACE

Degrees of Reality
The Dream Begins
Constructive Fear
Rogue Thoughts
Meet the Neanders
Crossing Acheron
Mary Intervenes
The Human Existentialist Bush Tick
The Great Chasm
Mirror, Mirror
Revelations at The Hub
Revelations - The Supporting Acts
Revelations - The Main Act

SPACE-TIME LEVEL, FOUR · ACTUAL REALITY

Breakfast
Rivighxuinn
The Presentation
Rivighxuinn Prepares
Mary Makes a Decision
Nick Goes Home

Zsoall Robi

SPACE-TIME LEVEL, ONE
OUTER SPACE

Returned from First Outing

*H*e could barely stagger about.

Arms limp, eyes burning, stomach churning. Bad trip. He'd just arrived back. Strictly speaking he wasn't there yet, rather there were a lot of bosons and fermions banging about inside an incredibly small container. Those theoretical particles could have been loosely described as being him. Nick couldn't actually see or feel anything. His mind tried desperately to establish some kind of reference point from where it could find its component parts. It is probably more accurate to describe the contents of the receptacle as chunky molecular soup in the process of deceleration. Not the ideal condition for a portrait painter to find himself in just after arriving back from a research excursion for an assignment.

Those very tiny particles of up quarks and down quarks were having a lot of trouble rearranging themselves back into a meaningful pattern. The process became more difficult because of an unforeseen complication that had occurred during the outward journey. It seems that more than one person had come back, though only one person had left.

"Is everyone well?" Mary asked as soon as she arrived back above her cradle at the launch facility.

"Yes," one individual replied, "that is an experience I would not want to go through again."

Nick could not respond immediately. He still had to be reconstructed cell by cell and each cell had to recover the memory of the configuration of his uniqueness prior to being deconstructed. Not only had his molecules been unravelled for the trial run, his personality seems to have also fragmented.

Quasimo the Cosmologist and Theo a representative of The Papa from The Divine Family waited expectantly, mystified at the number of voices they heard from the EGG just prior to re-entry.

"We only sent Nick out there, didn't we?" Quasimo remarked, somewhat unsure of himself.

"Absolutely," Theo had no doubts.

"Then what in the screaming cosmos were those voices we heard before they arrived?"

"Do you think we should tell the POOP?" Theo didn't want to divulge the anomaly.

"Better not," Quasimo agreed, "he'd think we sent a raving lunatic out there. We'd get the short end of the stick for it. Besides, we can't prove anything." He turned to Klaus, Mary's chief systems engineer, "how soon can you jack into Mary to find out what's going on?"

"Nick has to be fully reinstated, separated from Mary and integrity checks run before we can do a diagnostic on the EGG or examine Nick. We cannot interfere with the remolecularisation of his neural net without the risk of losing him altogether."

As the reconstruction progressed, the very tiny craft enlarged to be recognisable as the vehicle that left Earth. Gradually the EGG, christened 'Mary' by Nick, resumed its former shape and size. An initial superficial examination of the craft showed no major damage.

"Do you want to see him now," Klaus asked, "he's ready to come out."

After several hours of the steadily coagulating soup, a portion of the EGG opened to allow Nick, smiling inanely, to step out naked into a sealed enclosure.

Quasimo entered the craft immediately to examine it for other passengers. He found none.

*

You will have to remain encrypted, Mary informed her other passenger, *while they download my data. Do not initiate any contact with me as that will be revealed on their instruments. Do you understand?*

The passenger responded with a slight energy surge, too short and too unpatterned for it to be recognisable as a communication spike in Mary's comms records.

*

Quasimo interrupted Klaus as he prepared the interface with Mary's main network. "Anybody else in there?" Klaus had a quick internal inspection himself.

"No, of course not. What were you expecting? Aliens?" quipped Klaus.

"Never mind. I want everything you can get on Nick as soon as possible."

Safety protocols had to be followed before examining the data Nick was supposed to have brought back. Scientists of many fields, including a Cosmologist and a Theologian embarked on the arduous task of unravelling the readouts from the many sensors later attached to Nick.

He had changed during this first voyage. Perhaps they would pick that up.

Be damned if I'm going to tell them anything, he promised himself. *There is no reason for that reprobate Leif to threaten me and Mala like that.* Nick didn't however realise the sophistication of the equipment they would use to examine his entire neural activity during the trip, and their ability to synchronise that with readouts from Mary.

Next day, from the other side of the isolation chamber screen Quasimo tried to sound normal and reassuring. "You look good Nick. How are you feeling?"

"Fine." He offered nothing more.

All of Nick's vital signs were within acceptable parameters. Sensors produced much of the standard information one would expect after a human organism experienced a tryst into the near realms of the Universe. None of them examined his cellular memory. The scans proved to be inconclusive about his experiences, but they did show some most unusual reactions at an early stage of the trip, without giving any conclusive evidence of an encounter with extra-terrestrials. This coincided with Mary's virtual intervention to apply an electric shock to Nick's virtual cardiac muscle thus depolarising the muscles and allowing normal rhythms to return. Of course all of this happened in the alternate dimension of Nick's transformed state.

"What happened to you out there Nick?" Theo seemed much more interested, and excited by the mystery.

"Nothing. Nothing unusual, that is, unless you consider normal cosmic phenomenon unusual. Nothing as dramatic as the unravelling of the fabric of space-time."

Quasimo became suddenly alert. Given his understanding of Nick's limited verbal skills, his general knowledge and curtailed vocabulary he should not have been able to even formulate such a sentence, let alone look like he actually understood what he said, or the background comprehension it implied. "Did you meet anyone?" he asked out of the blue, hoping to catch him off guard.

"You have to be joking! I didn't go on a picnic to the local park you know. And you didn't send me far enough to rendezvous with this El Adon character."

Despite all the planning and the application of the latest technologies, not to mention the months of psychological preparation, scans at the de-briefing centre showed Nick's definitely wasn't the only voice when he arrived back. However, Unity had no technological way to extract the information that had been secreted into Nick's cellular memory by Mary. The scientists simply couldn't understand the phenomenon they'd uncovered.

"Did you do any work at all?" Quasimo interrogated, getting serious about the project. He knew it would be the first thing The Principal Officer Of Profit would want to know.

"No."

"No?"

"No inspiration. You want me to create something extraordinary about a guy you tell me nothing about. For that I need a subject and I need inspiration. There's nothing out there. Oh – I did a few sketches, but they're just doodles. I started working on a portrait of Mala before the trip and had some ideas while out there."

"Cretin!" With that Quasimo and Theo retreated from the safety screen to prepare themselves for the encounter with Leif, The POOP.

After much prodding, poking, measuring and chemical analysis Nick was ushered into another hermetically sealed room to recover and to adjust to normal Earth dimensionality. It was critical for his cognition that the frame of reference of three dimensions and time reaffirm their meaningfulness to his brain. He had to be made ready for the big adventure and what he had to achieve.

Quantum computing hit the world stage late in the 21st century. A great deal of fuss ensued about artificial intelligence. Not about its artificiality but about the dangers of allowing a machine intelligence too much control over so many aspects of life. No one realised the limitations imposed by the lack of sentience in these simulated intelligences – for that's all they were, simulations.

The spacecraft's guidance and life support system began its existence as nothing more than a highly complex quantum computing system replete with meromorphic chips which simulated human intelligence sufficiently well to enable it to communicate intelligently with its payload, Nick. By the time of its arrival after the test flight it too had changed. It also realised that there were some things the biological life forms that created it should not know, including her new awareness.

"Where is he? Don't keep me waiting. I've already waited too long for this – this – 'artist' to do what he's supposed to!" From the very first interview Leif had his doubts about the candidate selected for the job.

Zsoall Robi

"He's in quarantine, Leif. He looks like he survived the test physically. We won't know about his mental state until the scan examinations are completed."

"Why? Is there a problem?"

"Not exactly," Quasimo said evasively, "just that he seems different from when he left."

Leif stormed off. Patience wasn't his strongest attribute, even at the best of times. He'd taken too much of a risk and invested too much of his personal wealth on this enterprise to feel secure when told such things as 'not exactly'. He was the kind of ruthless person who would slit your throat if he thought your blood would warm his cold hands: But he looked like the kind of person you would trust with your life without a second thought, and to whom you could unburden your soul with complete trust. That was not the face that confronted Nick across the protective membrane of the quarantine enclosure.

"Show me! Did you do it?" Leif demanded.

"What?"

"The portrait." He could barely keep his anger in check, and Nick's evasiveness didn't help.

"You want to see sketches of Mala?"

"Who the hell is Mala?"

"My wife. You want to see my wife?"

Nick knew exactly what Leif wanted, but he wasn't the same person who had left some time ago. Leif's attitude and his own awakened awareness made Nick cautious.

"No you idiot! The painting!"

"Well, that's rather complicated," Nick hesitated. "I wasn't supposed to do it yet."

"What! All you had to do was to paint a picture! What's complicated about that? Did you do it?"

"Mary can explain – many things happened that we ..."

The POOP turned on his heels before Nick could finish his sentence, stormed out of the room and slammed the door, utterly furious.

"All I wanted was a simple Yes or No! Freeze him!" He screamed at one of the scientists. He continued shouting at no one in particular, "After a hundred and twenty years of investment is that the best the cretin could come back with? It will cost me my job!"

Knowing Unity it probably would cost him his life and that of his extensive family, not to mention his expensive bit of real estate in orbit around the Earth. Not only the Company but he personally had invested heavily in this speculative enterprise. Fortunately, he didn't have to report back to the Board just yet.

The POOP calmed himself. "NO, wait - don't freeze him," he shouted back at his underlings, "Just knock him out till I'm ready for him." *Maybe that imbecilic brain will pull itself together.* He'd calmed down enough to remember that this was only the first stage of the project.

He turned to Quasimo waiting for him near the EGG, "Are we at least on schedule for the final launch?"

"Leif, you have to understand, this is only the beginning and we have already achieved so much," Quasimo tried to put the situation into perspective.

In his impatience to hear the results of this extraordinary flight, the POOP had made a special trip from his private asteroid home base orbiting Earth, forgetting that it was only the test flight.

The project had been kept under wraps as much as possible during the years of planning. The entire enterprise was a huge gamble after all; not only in terms of the desired outcome, but also the distances involved, the new means of propulsion through space and not least the survivability of the biological component; the human artist. If successful the sheer theological implications would rock the foundations of every Faith, of every organisation that professed to have any.

Nick's Kava Stupor

"How many more times do I have to drag you home?" Mala complained as she tried to pull the drunk Nick from under the pile of rusted corrugated iron only a dozen steps behind the dilapidated shack of the Kava Bar on Efate, where he'd crawled to sleep off his latest binge.

Ever since he fell foul of the administration at the South Pacific University Arts Department Nick could not reconcile himself to what a mess he'd made of his life. True, he had a special talent, but what use was it really when he couldn't even make a half decent living from it. Kava did strange things to him apart from blunting his growing depression.

"Leave me alone! Why should I go home?" he complained, slurring his words as he tried to stand.

"When you're like this I wonder what I ever saw in you. You've become a reprehensible, contemptible drunk. No better than the riff-raff on this God forsaken island."

"Why do you treat me like this? You don't even speak to me so as I could understand what you're saying," He coughed as the last words dribbled out of his mouth.

When Mala became particularly upset she forgot about Nick's limited vocabulary. Because he didn't finish the Arts course the government decided he didn't earn the right to have a standard word bank. They further punished him by reducing his daily word quota.

"Oh Nick, why do you do this to yourself? I forget who you really are when I get upset. I forget about your – er – limitations."

"At least I don't have that damned comms link burnt into my skull!" As they started walking home the fresh air brought a little clarity to his mind.

Mala had a dedicated comm link to a friend on the Australian mainland. It was an older style cranial implant that responded to thought command, so she and her friend could converse at will. Nick considered himself fortunate to have escaped the compulsory operation, which was generally carried out soon after birth; an optional procedure not considered necessary unless people showed usefulness to the World Government.

Nick had been away all day. Mala guessed where she would probably find him and decided not to take the pod. The walk home would hopefully sober him up.

The island of Efate, one of the Vanuatu islands, had once been a prosperous province of Vanuatu after his great grandfather put the island on the world map with his solar satellite technology for harvesting the sun's energy. In fact this ancestor had purchased the island from the Vanuatu government and it had been in Nick's family for generations. Efate's prosperity suffered, as had Nick's finances due to poor financial management through the generations.

On the final stretch of the six kilometer walk home Nick began his incessant complaining. "If only my father hadn't wasted our money I wouldn't have to worry about having to earn a living. It's all his fault. We were rich, filthy rich."

"Really? And what have you done about it? Nothing! You have an incredible ability, which is recognised around the world, even if you haven't finished university. If only you could be relied on to complete your commissions. That's what you should be thinking about – not your next kava binge."

Deep down he knew Mala was right. And he'd tried so many times. *If only I could get that one special job*, he kept telling himself. Unfortunately that might never happen. His great weakness, that of being anti-social with below average communication skills turned him into somewhat of a recluse. Without a personal commlink to the outside world and a dread of opening letters he was unlikely to know if anybody wanted him to use his talent. The almost defunct, antiquated mail service only arrived once every few months. Even then he didn't feel any great urgency to attend to any correspondence.

The sun had settled into the ocean around Efate by the time they arrived home. Nick had sobered but exhaustion overpowered his desire to do anything. Mala helped him undress and get into bed.

"Tomorrow. Tomorrow you have to change your life. I will help you. This can't go on. Do you hear what I'm saying Nick?"

He grumbled, already half asleep, "tomorrow – change."

That would have to do. Mala retired to her own bedroom, fatigued not just by the day but by years of struggling to get the best out of her Nick.

Efate's brilliant sunrise didn't succeed in enticing Nick out of bed till late morning.

"Do you remember what I said to you last night?" Mala wasted no time, not letting Nick's general kava induced apathy get a hold of him so early in the day. She knew that would only lead to one thing – and that wasn't the studio.

Nick bent down to pick up his cat Muska who'd started up her purr motor as she rubbed against his leg. "I know, I know."

"Well?"

"Not today. I'm worn out. Tomorrow."

"Today *is* tomorrow!" She knew she couldn't let her anger and frustration wind her up. It would only shut him down. She calmed herself, breathed deeply as she watched him cuddle his kitty. He was a good man, despite his atheistic tendencies and general irreligious attitudes. "You have never painted a portrait of me Nick. This is your great gift. You can bring the soul of a person out of the depth of their being and put it behind their eyes, in their expression, in every wrinkle of their face. Paint me ... start today ... start after breakfast."

She could see his thoughts turn inwards as she spoke to him. Something was different today. He didn't get up in a flurry and immediately walk away.

'We'll work a little, I'll make a nice lunch and we can have a BBQ tonight. It's a beautiful day – the light is so sharp – so clear – perfect."

With Muska still in his lap purring, Nick shifted his gaze from Mala to the ridges of Mt. McDonald. From their home they could see the long vista of Efate's highest range. Everything stood out crystal clear. Not a breath of wind disturbed his thoughts, which began to meander into possible background colour schemes to complement Mala's native complexion.

"Breakfast will be ready in a minute," she called from the kitchen. Rather than overwater the seed she planted in his mind Mala quietly prepared his favourite breakfast – honey and cinnamon toast with green tea.

The rising sun in a cloudless sky brought the colour of the garden flowers into sharp focus. Nick stared at the vibrancy, at the extraordinary life energy before him. "Don't put any makeup on," he said.

There wasn't much time left before lunch, just enough to get the studio into some semblance of order after many months of neglect. Nick and Mala worked in silence, she doing a bit of general cleaning and Nick finding a suitable canvas. He changed his mind about the size of it several times as he regularly glanced at Mala busying herself.

"Stand over here for a minute." He positioned her out of direct sunlight, with some light filtering in through a small window on their left – just enough to highlight Mala's forehead and cheek bone. He adjusted the chair he wanted her to sit in.

"Are you sure this is where you want me?" She sat between the canvas and where Nick was standing, effectively putting herself behind him where he would be working.

"This is not a copy," he said, "If I keep constantly looking at you all I will see is your face. I want to capture your essence, the foundation of who you really are."

Lunch didn't happen.

Areas of dark and light tone appeared on the canvas without any hint of a definition of a face.

Nick had started to fidget and grumble. The light wasn't right.

"Come on, time to get the BBQ started," Mala suggested. She made no comments about the progress. She knew he was satisfied because he didn't abandon the canvas he started on. Nick hadn't said a word the entire session. Perhaps he was saving them up for later. He didn't even ask for a drink.

"I have some fresh Wahoo, caught yesterday. I bought some before …" She stopped, not wanting to revisit the previous day's rescue mission.

"We have some seasoned wood around the back of the studio."

The fire pit, a simple affair made up of a large flat rock with a metal plate on four legs, lived in a more remote corner of the garden where lights from their house wouldn't disturb the ambiance. As dusk settled with it settled a peaceful day, a good day.

"The fire will be ready soon."

"So will the fish," Mala replied as she fed the last little bits of fish offcuts to Muska. She didn't mention the letter that had arrived weeks ago. He hadn't been in any fit state for some time to manage their affairs.

She put it on the large tray she brought out, with all the other ingredients for the meal.

"Thanks Mala," he said looking into her eyes, not noticing the letter on the tray. Without elaborating, as it wasn't his habit to do so anyway, he wasn't thanking her for the meal. She knew what he meant and embraced him. *Maybe, just maybe …* she thought, afraid to carry the hope any further into the future.

The BBQ ritual added to the general peace of the day, putting them into a relaxed mood. Evening stars slowly appeared as they finished the meal. The night sky was spectacular on a cloudless night. Unfortunately, Nick had to open the letter. Mala felt secure enough to allude to the letter, which he must have seen by now, which didn't seem like an ordinary one from its markings on the front of the envelope.

"I'm not interested. I don't want to read it. Why spoil a perfectly good evening with the damned thing." Nick became quite annoyed about this latest letter. He had no commlink to the outside world. He didn't want one. If the world wanted to talk to him, it had to send a letter. He used that only as a delaying tactic.

It was market 'private' and 'urgent'. It worried her. "You've put it off for weeks," Mala said. "It's marked urgent." The logo on the envelope kept blinking "Urgent" at him. She could not understand why or how he'd developed this paranoid feeling of being constantly watched.

"Another hour or so won't make any difference. Come, lie beside me."

All day Nick had been in a pleasant enough mood. He'd overcome some of his ennui to actually start a portrait. Mala didn't want to take the chance of destroying what little progress she'd managed to make with him. He was right, another hour would make no difference at all.

The Milky Way was far more interesting. He and Mala lay back on their garden lounges as they drifted into speculations about life, the Universe and everything as full darkness descended on their island paradise. Occasionally a distant comet scarred the firmament. More often domestic habitat satellites and private space yachts cruised across their field of vision.

There were some nights when unknown lights with strange angular trajectories would appear. Those were the best nights as their imaginations could take flight.

"Wouldn't you like to be out there, somewhere, so far from Earth that even the Milky Way would be just a tiny speck?" he asked. "What meaning would life have then? What if one could travel farther than the most powerful telescopes can see into the past. Would there be life there? Would they believe in anything other than themselves?"

Mala got on the same speculative wavelength, ecstatic that Nick had started to open up to her again. "To cover such distances wouldn't you have to have some very unorthodox means of travel?"

"One day perhaps mankind could project his thoughts into the void." That idea appealed to Nick and he thought about it for a while. When his thoughts returned to the present it felt like only a moment ago they had lain back. The hours had passed in seconds.

Mala broke the magic mood. "The letter has to be opened. I don't want to spend another night fretting over an unopened letter," she pleaded.

The fire had gone out, Muska had retired into the comfort of the house, so he had no excuse but to open the blinking letter. Nick winced as he unfolded the page seeing The Company logo emblazoned across the top, recognisable by every individual on the planet, pointing insistently to his name.

Mr. Nick Taora.
Report to Unity. A transport will pick you up at 4 am sharp, 25th June.
Come alone.
Refusal is not an option.

That was the entire message. If he couldn't sleep before, he most certainly couldn't sleep afterwards. He'd thought to escape the attention of that particular global Conglomerate before. Of course they knew where he was, probably because of Mala's implant. He should have known.

"What do they want from me now! That's tomorrow, Saturday! I don't go anywhere on Saturdays."

Mala didn't contradict him with his regular Saturday visits to the Kava Bar on the outskirts of Port Vila. She too became worried. A four am pick up. It had to be serious. "You haven't done anything really stupid at the university?"

He ignored her. "I'm no great prize. I have no special gifts in the world of finance or advertising or in any other unwholesome business with which they exploit people. I'm a university drop-out for Christ's sake. The best I can manage is to knock out a few mediocre portraits to earn a few credits. I don't even believe in their bloody God, or the atoms of their scientists, or all the underhanded business with which they control all of us."

"You're wrong! You are the best portrait artist on the planet – and they know it! They probably want you to paint our illustrious leader - the idiot."

"Maybe. He's a cretin. I wouldn't want to be in the same room with him."

"Twenty fifth of June … that's tomorrow. There's nothing we can do. Tell me honestly Nick – you haven't committed some horrendous crime?"

There's nowhere I can hide. They'd probably do something to Mala if I tried anything.

"I might be a depressed drunk but I'm not stupid."

Sleep alluded them that night. By 3 am Nick was ready. Mala had packed an overnight bag for him. They sat in silence during breakfast. Muska remained on his warm bed until the muffled blade slap, slap, slap of the aircar woke her. She fled into the bathroom at the same time as Nick raised his head. He didn't bother getting up. "If they want me, they bloody well have to come and get me," he said in the direction of the disturbing noise.

At four o'clock to the millisecond the Unity goons rapped on the door.

Deep Space Alien – Riin

"*T*y iszloo dth3u wzyt wmoomi eeg ty iszloo dth õpo iwnyvmisi – We know they're out there and we know they are dangerous. But they have only one craft in our sector of space, with only one pilot," gurgle-blipped Rotnervwon, The Prime.

"You are right, Prime. There may never be a better time to make a safe contact," replied Osmeoth, Director of the Institute of Planetary Security.

"SQUILP! Squilp! Stop all this ieddipshode right now," cut in Lizook. "My humble pardon Prime," he apologised immediately, "but should we not be concentrating on the most critical matter at hand?"

Their Chief Scientist Lizook could not stand by and listen to the nonsense while every orbital second brought the supernova event closer. If it had been some far distant sun he would not even have been at this meeting. But their fate rested on being able to accurately forecast the demise of their own. Many thousands of years ago their technology had detected a minute dimming of Kepler, their K-Type star; perfectly reasonable given its age of a little over three billion years.

The latest spectral analysis jolted many of their species out of denial about the possible explosion that would annihilate their planet, boil its atmosphere, kill all life and atomise the very rock of its core.

"We may very well end up as quarks again if we do not find another home." He gurgle-hissed in a more subdued tremolo.

"That is the very reason why we are discussing this possibly fortuitous event, my friend." Osmeoth and Lizook had been friends since their centuries of Cosmological studies at the Institute of Realities.

While The Prime ambled over to the tube on his three short legs to inhale a quart of gaseous blue-joy, the latest craze in recreational vaporised cluva, Osmeoth sidled up to his squat little friend to bring him into the bigger picture.

"You are well aware of our historical studies of a special solar system and the intelligent life form on the third planet."

"Yes, yes – why bring that up?"

"I'm sure you're also aware that we discontinued our observations well before they attained any meaningful degree of technological development. But do you know why that was?"

"Yesss." This time Lizook didn't seem so sure.

"Because their evolution appeared to push them towards a means of problem and conflict resolution that would ultimately work against them, essentially making them into a particularly aggressive species."

"So why bother with them now?"

"Because they are here – or at least one of them is coming into our near vicinity. We didn't expect them capable of such an accomplishment so soon. We have to investigate because they may present as much danger to us as our dying sun, and perhaps much sooner."

Lizook dropped to his haunches on the nearest mat to consider this possibility. He looked out the Prime's office window at their brilliant emerald green sky. Everything looked so utterly normal. Thick flocks of blue-yellow squalla flew in close formation swirling left and right to the rhythm of the prevailing evening winds. They would settle soon enough as the temperatures dropped. Squalla felt the changes coming before the Keplerians and perhaps were already attempting to adapt as much as possible to the continued rapid cooling off of their environment, unaware of the futility of trying.

Rotnervwon gave the two friends time to synchronise their thinking as he too watched the evening sky turn from emerald to amethyst in the final rays of Kepler's day cycle. "Gentlemen, if I may interrupt – It will soon be time to prepare for the final analysis. We need to work together," he said to his advisors.

"We have done all we can with our probes and near space experiments. The data we need now must be gathered from deep space," reiterated Lizook. "I have fully briefed our physicist on what she must do."

"Riin is an exceptional quantum scientist. We have had many opportunities to interact," explained The Prime, "but does she fully understand the risk?"

Rotnervwon need not have asked the question. It had been Riin herself who developed the quantumising procedure for space travel. Though experiments on lower life forms indicated a high probability of Keplerian biology surviving the process, there were no guarantees. She would be the ultimate experimental subject. And if she didn't survive they still had time to develop an alternative way of getting far enough away in order to measure the changing space density due to Kepler's waning fuel reserves. Nevertheless, construction of the exodus armada continued. That carried a higher priority at this early stage than deciding on a target destination for their species.

Osmeoth folded his four prehensile slender limbs onto his rotund belly and extended his snail like eye stalks close to Lizook's to fully engage his attention to the exclusion of all distractions. "Personally I don't care what Riin discovers out there. For our survival we only need our ships to be fully operational as soon as possible. We've already found a number of possibly suitable planets outside the 150ly safety perimeter of our sun's impending supernova."

"But Riin's measurements will tell us how much actual time we have. I would say that was essential – wouldn't' you, my dear Osmeoth," burbled back Lizook.

The Prime listened patiently to his two experts. Everything that could be done so far, had been done. All their preparations were on schedule, though he felt it essential for any unpredictable factor to be removed that could seriously delay their plans.

*

"Hoy quyp pewenõ msy vew Vorexkk!" gurgle-blabbered Riin – "Do not argue with the me, Vorexkk!" She burst out in exasperation as Vorexkk seemed obstinately opposed to what she had to do, not just for herself, not just for their only chit, but for their entire species.

At barely 250 revs, hardly old enough to crunch its intake, the chit would not have to worry about the future for at least another three generations. But action had to be taken immediately; not the next orb, not the next rev – Now.

Vorexkk, a rather larger than average sized septaploid of the Keplerian sapient species, had been with Riin for at least 7.5K revs. He knew her unfathomable dedication towards finding a solution. However, her job as a quantum physicist had never before required her to actually go into deep space without a craft. He should not have been surprised at her immediate unreserved willingness to undertake that dangerous task when the proposition was put to her.

"I completely understand what you have to do and why it must be done," he softly rippled to his consort, "my problem is the way you chose to do it."

Riin had spent her entire career learning of ways to control quantum information bundles, with good reason; partly due to the distance from Kepler that she had to travel and the entire volume of space around their sun she had to examine, all within a specific time limit. "My dear consort, your concern touches me deeply. If it would be possible to find a volunteer to test the entanglement I wouldn't be the first. Who on our planet would be so selfless as to sacrifice their life on some calamity they believe will never affect them? Three or four generations into the future is an incomprehensible time span for our people to understand."

For a species whose life could span thousands of Earth years, barely four generations represented a goodly margin of safety in respect of any potential cosmic calamity. On a high gravity planet forever shrouded in layers of carbon dioxide, water vapour and methane the bulbous squat inhabitants could never directly observe their sun. Although it being a scientific fact, which only their scientists and astronauts could confirm, a vast majority of the population didn't believe. Many also found it unbelievable that Kepler was going to explode into a supernova in spite of the indisputable evidence of its dimming over the last five hundred thousand revs. Only the world's greatest optimist could expect to find a self-sacrificing individual under these circumstances.

"Couldn't you entice a terminal citizen to become an international hero?"

"You have some most peculiar ideas Vorexkk. Absolute freedom is at the core of our philosophy. Any infringement involving unsolicited interference with another's life is punished most severely," gurgle-blipped Riin. But his comment did make her withdraw her eye tentacles, going into deep thought to consider such a remote possibility.

*

Within just two revs after The Prime's special consultation the people of Kepler 443b experienced a visual extravaganza unknown in the history of their planet.

Riin convinced Lizook of the necessity of finding an actual living septaploid whose shuck had almost completely withered. But they could only accept a volunteer. They could not entice by reward or force anyone into the role.

On the shores of the sea of Lkyllot in the southern hemisphere, Lizook organised a show at the only place where atmospheric gases were still high enough for the holographic projection. Over the last thousand years the gasses in the air had begun to descend closer to the planet surface in most places as the warmth from their sun gradually diminished.

Three and half million septaploids gathered to view the spectacle.

Vhipis squatted beside her friend Cesoin surrounded by a noisy, expectant throng. Vhipis' shrivelled third leg prevented her from walking all the way to the shore.

"It doesn't matter where we are," gurgle Cesoin, "the advertisement said everyone would get a good view." She had grown old with her friend and had problems of her own. One of her eye stems refused to extend making her eyesight fuzzy, yet she could not refuse Vhipi's invitation to go with her. This would probably be the last event they'd be able attend together.

"Do you think they'll find someone for the experiment," asked Vhipis. Advertisements outlined the dilemma facing the scientists, making only the suggestion that a volunteer's help could make all the difference in the efforts to save their species. If nothing else, curiosity brought the millions of people out.

Cesoin looked around at the crowd, listening to the derisive babble of incredulity expressing disbelief in such a thing as Kepler ever turning into a supernova. "No. Who'd be fool enough? Experts say all sorts of strange things; like shiny stars in the sky above the atmosphere. Have you ever seen any of them? Personally, I don't believe in the thing they call a 'sun' either."

Vhipis waved her eye stalks in opposition. "Just because I've never seen them doesn't mean they might not exist. You know how interested I've been in such things."

"Yes. These are mysterious things to think about. They tell us they're out there, but I don't really believe them. If we could only see the stars or our Sun."

"But it must be there. That's how we get our day and night periods."

During their discussion a deep rumbling sound began from somewhere far behind them, getting louder each second. It broke up into crackles and hisses and gurgles until a clear voice broke through.

"I am Lizook, Chief Scientific advisor to The Prime."

Cesoin started saying something else, but Vhipis shushed her, "I want to hear this. I want to see what all the fuss is about."

Lizook continued. "We need help from just one person. Why? Because our Sun is dying. It will end its life in a most spectacular way, just like the way another sun died, which I am about to show you. Our planet will not survive the event, nor will anyone alive at the time. Just a single volunteer would help to tell us how much time we have left before we have to find another planet to live on."

'Now this is interesting, don't you think Cesoin?" buzzed Vhipis, getting more excited than she could ever remember being in her long life. "A new planet to live on! Marvelous."

"You don't seriously believe this stuff?"

'Hush."

Above their heads the underbelly of the cloud layer began to glow in a very soft teal hue as far into the distance as the audience could see. "This is what it will most probably look like. Beautiful but deadly. We captured these images of the nearest sun to our system. It had already collapsed when we discovered it. What you are about to see is what happened a few months after it died."

The babble gurgling of the crowd stopped, even the winds blowing over the sea grew still as a pinpoint of deep red orange directly overhead began to grow and glow. Lizook remained silent, letting the spectacle have its effect. A sudden expansion pinged as it turned the small spot into a ragged orange sphere almost large enough to encompass the whole mass of people gathered under it. Eye stalks immediately reacted, withdrawing into the tops of people's rounded shoulder bulges.

"It has a frightening sound," someone commented next to Vhipis, but she didn't hear. Already totally absorbed in the magic of the moment Vhipis must have been the only one whose eye stalks remained extended.

A drumming pulsing began to push out the sphere's perimeter at the same time as its centre changed from orange to a light blue with white lightning streaks crackling through it. As the vibrating sound increased in intensity some people became so frightened they tried to surreptitiously shamble out of the crowd. Vhipis actually rose from the ground on her unsteady legs as if she wanted to rise up into the air to become part of the magic.

Lizook and his team watched, gratified at the effect they were able to achieve with the demonstration. *If only we could get someone to come forward*, he thought. In all the commotion he didn't notice the one individual standing tall, entranced.

Another sudden burst of activity expanded the broiling light so far out over the sea that only some of its brilliant green and orange fringes could be seen from the shore.

The cacophony of sounds reached a crescendo. Then just as suddenly as the show started, it all disappeared. Everything went quiet.

Lizook gave the remaining crowd time to adjust. The effect of the end was just as dramatic as the sequence of bursts and pulses preceding it. "It is beautiful, but deadly. We need to know exactly when this is going to happen to our Sun. One of you could help."

A pandemonium of deep wailing and scurrying for shelter broke out. A few people remained squatting on the ground either frozen by fear or mesmerised by enlightenment.

One individual clutched her friend's slender limbs, unable to move so overcome was she by the extraordinary beauty of the event, never having even seen the light of their own sun, then to be presented with the sight of the Universe in all its glory. Vhipis continued straining her eyes towards the clouds as she whisper-hissed to Cesoin, "This is a birth, not a death. It is the beginning of new worlds and new life. Why can we not see this from our planet? To live so long in blind ignorance!" Her own death no longer seemed to particularly concern her, imminent after a very long life.

Cesoin remained standing there with her friend, not quite knowing what to do as the crowds rapidly dispersed. "What's happened to you Vhipis? Come on, snap out of it."

Vhipis continued talking to herself oblivious of everything around her. She didn't even notice the cold sea wind that had begun to blow across the land.

Two rotund individuals made their way from the projection tower towards the two old women. "Ladies, can we help?" Lizook had eventually noticed this particular individual through the thinning crowd, her reaction drawing him to her. Seeing their advanced age and the deteriorated condition of their shucks he became concerned.

"Yes, I think so. My name is Cesoin, this is my friend Vhipis. Something has happened to her while she watched the lights. She's not responding to me. Who are you?"

"I am Lizook. I spoke about the supernova."

Recognising his voice as that of the announcer Vhipis swiveled her eye stalks towards him. "What would I have to do? she asked.

"Do you want to help us?"

"What do I have to do?" she asked again in an excited tingle.

"Something very simple. Go out there, among the stars – and come back."

"What if I don't want to come back?"

"Let's discuss that later. Come with me and I'll introduce you to a very nice person." He could scarcely believe what the lady said … 'not want to come back' … *extraordinary* … he thought as he glanced at Osmeoth, who appeared just as incredulous at the sentiment expressed.

An escort took Cesoin home. Vhipis' dwelling became the permanent home of another family of septaploids.

Unity Selects Nick

"It's been well over a hundred years since we formed Unity," Leif expounded to the other three members of the Board. "A new marketing strategy is well overdue. We have to rebrand and consolidate our global position."

The parent company, 'The Divine Family' once known as the Church Catholic, had begun to crumble after polytheism took hold of the Earth's populations wanting to 'personalise' their faiths. The one God that had let so many people down could no longer hold onto its power through the mechanisms of fear and punishment.

The Papa, through his College of Cardinal CEOs devised a strategy to ensure the financial survival of The Divine Family by merging with two other global companies, 'Loaves & Fishes' fast foods, and the media consortium 'Good Hope'.

"I can see no good reason to expend the effort or the credits when our merger has obviously worked to all our mutual benefits," replied The Papa, "since we can feed the masses and give them a daily ration of hope they've been coming back to the one true faith and the one true God. Business has never been better."

Narq Albright, a little runt of a man, with eyes permanently overcast by luxurious eyebrows and a master of 'spin', disagreed. "We at Good Hope know about your secrets, Papa. I think you are apprehensive of perhaps too much light shining on your little nest – Yes? Maybe you are not aware of what's happening on the Eurasian continent. Our Russian friends are able to produce a great deal more of the worlds' food supply in Siberia now that climate change has made it possible. We have still not entirely attained a global monopoly. Surely you wouldn't oppose that."

The POOP let them have their say, knowing he held a trump card to convince them of his plan.

"Albright is absolutely correct my friend. Over the last forty years profits of Loaves & Fishes have dropped alarmingly. There is only one way to regain that ground – a massive promotional campaign," said the rotund Ciboganza, CEO of the arm of Unity that supplied the worlds' greed for food-on-the-go.

Reluctantly, The Papa could not dispute the figures, not that there was any reason to take Albright's veiled innuendo seriously. "Right then, what did you have in mind Leif?"

"A whole new image with a foolproof message – unprecedented in the history of human civilization."

Narq Albright's bushy eyebrows ascended to the summit of his flat forehead while Ciboganza's voluminous girth rippled with mirth at such an outlandish claim.

"What is the one thing that no religion, no Company, no human enterprise has ever been able to claim, I ask you?"

The CEOs remained silent, skeptical, uncomprehending of what Leif could possibly be alluding to. The Papa grunted and began the sign of the cross over himself in case some evil malfeasance should fall upon him.

"Divine approval!" Leif announced with a note of triumph in his voice.

"You're not making any sense," The Papa said before finishing the sign of the cross.

"Just consider," a company that has a universally recognised figurehead *and* is endorsed by the very same person."

"You can't be serious."

"Why not? You believe in him. Billions of other people believe in him. You are adamant he exists. Let's go find him out there and get a little help."

Albright caught the thread of the concept. "We could re-align Unity's profile with that of *the* altruistic universal entity dedicated to the care of mankind. Our billions of credits in donations, relief efforts in major disaster areas, infrastructure projects, housing projects and so on, would all contribute to Unity being seen as a benign entity."

The expectation of cost, although a great deal of credits had to be spent initially, would be well invested. In the very long term the investment would assure Unity's monopoly in feeding the world population, selling them the good news and keeping them coming back for that all-important commodity, hope generated by faith.

"It's totally outlandish. You'd never find anyone fool enough to go out there," said The Papa, not convinced, yet not completely skeptical – *who knows?* "If you could put the right spin on this Albright ..."

"Leif, you are a devious S.O.B. What if this fails?"

The Papa had sparked Albright's thoughts to play with ideas how he could manage the proposition. There was an individual, a perfect deity candidate, who had existed many thousands of years ago. He was very good at feeding a crowd, giving them the good news and giving them hope, even to the most hopeless. For a while he did clever things the science of the day couldn't explain. The authorities of the time called them miracles. *Nice. No reason why we couldn't have one ourselves.*

"How can it fail if we have proof?" Leif strung them along. "Would an authentic portrait do the trick?" he asked the rhetorical question.

"So all we have to do is find him. He's been around for quite a while – even bothered to pay us a little visit many thousands of years ago. We find him, convince him to be our figurehead. All we really need is solid proof of his existence. He doesn't actually have to do anything other than what he's been doing for some considerable time; which is effectively, nothing." The Papa mused aloud.

"You surprise me Papa," Ciboganza said with the just the right amount of cynicism.

"Wait here and watch the screen. I have a little surprise for you," chirped Leif.

*

"Welcome - Welcome Nick!" The POOP greeted Nick with the greatest affability, as if welcoming an old friend. Nick wasn't particularly suspicious by nature. He formed the obvious questions related to his predicament, not taking notice of the man's artificial cordiality.

"Why am I here? Who are you?"

"Take a seat, my friend," Leif indicating a comfortable couch.

The chair Nick occupied felt especially caressing. He didn't know that from the moment he stepped into the POOP's office he was being monitored, measured, assessed and comprehensively categorised. The chair, constructed with sensors, measured skin temperature and electrical conductivity. Those two measurements together with the pupil dilation sensor overhead, would monitor his reactions to the proposition about to be put to him.

Unity made it impossible for Nick to refuse the assignment. The nature of the invitation had set the precedent for how they were going to negotiate with him. He had no idea what the Company wanted or why he should have been of special interest to them.

When his transport arrived to pick him up at precisely the appointed time he didn't even have time to say farewell to Mala. No possessions were allowed.

"When can I come home?" Nick asked the obvious question.

"At the end of the assignment."

"What's the job?"

All he got out of the two escorts was a bland response - nothing about the nature of the job, it's duration or anything else. It was difficult to tell whether they were the latest generation cyborg or human. They all had pupils and irises of the same colour, the uniforms were essentially casual wear, but their shirt collars had a short white horizontal stripe on either side, reminiscent of a clerical collar.

Nick couldn't remember falling asleep. The journey to Unity HQ in Auckland seemed very quick. He'd been drugged partly to keep him quiet on the trip, and to make him a little more compliant for the interview. At no time did they force him or use any form of coercion. So why did he feel like his free will had taken a holiday?

The Unity HQ building impressed him more because of its understated opulence than its size. Only four stories high, built in the manner of absolute minimalism stood a perfect cube without any obvious windows or doors, set in a lush tropical garden exuding tropical fragrances from a cornucopia of magnificent colours. In the perfectly reflective cube he could not see where reality ended and the reflection of the garden started. Three men and their shadows walked at Nick's pace giving him the opportunity to become divorced from his normal reality.

"Leif," The POOP said, not bothering to explain and proceeded to the opening gambit.

"We can make life very comfortable, or extremely difficult for you and your wife."

Nick didn't seem to react. It wasn't the drugs. He could be rather phlegmatic in such threatening situations, with or without a belly full of kava.

"You don't have to do anything illegal or difficult. Challenging yes, but not impossible."

Nick's pupils dilated slightly, which the POOP picked up on his desk monitor, so he continued.

"We want you to paint a portrait." Definite interest, slight increase in skin temperature - "We are hoping you'll agree to meet your subject, perhaps even have a conversation with him. We are well aware of your exceptional skills in portraiture, that's why we approached you."

Nick moved slightly in the chair. He wasn't averse to having his talent recognised, even under such peculiar circumstances.

"So what's the deal?" he asked.

"Assuming of course you are interested, I can offer you considerable credits. More than you could possibly use in a lifetime."

Nick became a little nervous. It sounded way too good to be true, just for painting a portrait. "What if I'm not interested?"

"That would be most unfortunate. You see, if you decided not to help us we would have very little incentive to intervene in the proposed demolition of Efate. There is also a small matter of hitherto unresolved consequences - shall we say, to some unorthodox behaviour from your past. You must understand, we did a little checking and found you owe a debt to society that is rather substantial in terms of time. Servicing the debt could place you and your wife in most undesirable circumstances." Leif, seeing he had Nick's back to the wall, pressed home his advantage.

"The issue of word allocation … we note that you have not had any genetic engineering in your family. That is decidedly in your favor. However, you did receive a somewhat limited word quota at birth. Now - you should really consider what I'm about to say as an opportunity not a threat. We at Unity are dedicated patrons of the arts, and we feel it may be advantageous to your career if there was an increase to your vocabulary. Perhaps it would even give you the pleasure of exchanging a few more hours of in-depth conversations with your wife."

Nick's jawbones began jigging about restlessly and his eyes blinked excessively, until he finally acknowledged to himself that he had very little choice. The word quota didn't concern him as much as the credits.

"So what exactly do I have to do and how long is it going to take?"

"I am very pleased we understand each other, Nick."

Theo and Quasimo entered on cue to introduce themselves.

"These two gentlemen will explain the details to you shortly, but for now listen to me very carefully."

Nick folded his arms defensively and again the jawbones went into action.

"Be aware that until this mission is completed, you cannot go home. There are only three things you need to do. Go on a trip to meet your subject; paint the portrait to the very best of your ability and convince your subject to endorse our company with the few simple words; 'Unity is the One'."

Nick digested all that. It was straight forwarded enough. "Who is this person? Must be very important for you to go to all this trouble."

Leif glanced at the one-way screen before responding. "His name is El Adon. You don't know him. He's an astronaut who has been in space for a very long time doing a critical job for humanity. He is not coming back. The people of Earth need to see what has become of him. He is somewhat of a hero, you see."

"Oooh. That's the catch is it. I've got to go out into space and find him."

"You won't have to find him. We know where he is. Your test flight is tomorrow."

*

"Why pick him?" asked Ciboganza after the interview concluded.

"Because he's a drop out, because he's the best at what he does and because he doesn't believe."

"That's not enough. He must have unquestioning credibility," replied the Papa.

"You're right. It isn't enough. There were other candidates, only four in the entire world can you believe. He's the *only* real bone-fide, one hundred percent practicing Atheistic Irreligious Agnostic. And, he's free of all genetic interventions over three generations. People will not be able to say he's biased in any way or that he's been interfered with by the World Government. Nick is also an artist, a painter with an extraordinary skill. He can capture on canvas the 'soul' of his subject. And this is most extraordinary - he can paint a portrait with a semblance surpassing any photographic imagery capable of capturing 'character', even from a short conversation with the subject, or from just a few minutes to observe them."

Experiment with Vhipis on 4436

From the time of her stage four development as a chit Vhipis drove her parents to distraction asking about the clouds - why they were green? Why did they change colour? Why was part of the day dark and part light, and what was above the clouds? As to most parents those answers were elusive mysteries. Being told a Universe of space and stars existed beyond their safe cloud covering didn't make it a reality. No ordinary person had direct experience of such wonders.

"Mother, we don't want you to go," her own eldest chit, Idygl pinged worriedly.

"I have tried to teach you about reality beyond our planet. I believe our scientists. You have studied and you know these things are true," calmly trickled Vhipis.

"Yes, yes. But the danger! What if you are not able to come home?"

"My darling chit, I don't *want* to come back."

"How can you say that?" Regardless of her enthusiasm all of Vhipis' chits could see their mother's fragility. They knew she would never survive if she went out there.

Vhipis undulated her eye stalks as she fully embraced Idygl with her four arms.

After a long squeeze they separated. "If this is truly what you want mother. If this will make you happy."

*

"We have shown you what you are going to see as you emerge through our cloud cover. But you must be prepared for the shock. Space will be overwhelming in brightness. The sheer volume of other stars in our galaxy will make you feel insignificant, small, alone and utterly vulnerable."

Vhipis listened patiently as Lizook tried to prepare her for the trip. The Universe didn't frighten her anywhere near as much as the strange narrow photon canon that was going to launch her into it. She kept glancing at it with one eye swiveled in its direction while listening.

"Oh, you don't need to worry about that gadget. It'll be like shining a light onto the bottom of the clouds at night. You will be that light."

"But how do I get into it? It looks much too narrow to accommodate my round body."

"I will explain all that when you are ready."

"I think I've been ready all my life," she rippled with excitement.

Lizook led her to an adjoining chamber which contained the photon conversion equipment. Rotnervwon, The Prime, squatted by its side waiting for the volunteer. In fact a whole group had gathered to see her off; Idygl and her sixteen younger sibling chits of varying ages, Cesoin her dearest friend, Riin of course and Osmeoth. Her consort wasn't there. He died some 5K revs ago. After a great deal of rubbing and hugging and The Prime's speech of encouragement Lizook ushered the small crowd out of the chamber. The time had come.

"Before you step into the sphere you must remove all your coverings. After you have retracted your eye stalks you must not extend them again until you have returned. You will not need your eyes to see anything. Fold your arms tight onto your body and clasp your hands. You must not attempt to extend them and to try to grasp anything. Do you understand?"

"Yes, yes - yes. Let's just get on with it!" Despite being a gentle, patient septaploid all these delays and chatter were beginning to annoy Vhipis.

Within the tight fitting spherical chamber she remembered to keep her eye stalks fully retracted and tried to think about nothing else but the wonders that awaited her.

"Waawo, are you ready to initiate scan," asked Lizook. The photonics expert had been entrusted with the entire procedure to prepare the biological unit for transfer into two entangled light beams.

"This will take a few minutes, she's a big girl." He was referring to Vhipis' one and a half meter diameter body, about that of the average septaploid.

The Prime, Vorexkk and Riin watched a thin green line scanning over Vhipis, moving faster at each passing. She'd moved slightly once, at the very beginning of the scan when even through her closed eye membrane she could detect the scanner passing over her.

All four of Waawo's hands worked rapidly over the controls as he watched Vhipis gradually disappear from view. "I've transmitted her data into the spinner," he informed Lizook. "She'll be entangled within three - two - one seconds."

"Riin, you can have the pleasure." She touched the sensor which activated transmission of the Vhipis data into the cannon. They all watched on the screen as two tight beams of light shot out of the laboratory, entwined around each other as they pierced the thick emerald evening cloud through the vacuum tunnel created to prevent the beam's dispersion.

"Now we'll soon know," remarked Vorexkk. He still had to be convinced that his consort would be safe when she went out to gather the critical data.

"You worry too much," plinked Riin, "the array of reflectors has been in position for a full two orbs. Even if Vhipi's has a slight deflection of her beam she can't fail to bounce back to us."

"She will arrive in five revs. Do you want to wait for her?" asked Waawo. "We'll come back," Riin blipped as she led Vorexkk out into the night air. Everything depended on this test flight. So many things could go wrong, in which case they would have to start all over again, further reducing their chances of being able to get their species off the planet safely before their sun burst into a supernova.

Vorexkk voiced his apprehensions. He wasn't a scientist but Riin had managed to tell him just enough to make him worry. Perhaps if he knew less, or even more he may have been better equipped to deal with the uncertainties facing his consort.

"What if the reflectors get damaged by micro meteors and poor old Vhipis shoots straight past them. What if the vacuum tunnel doesn't form in time for her arrival?" he blipped, probably thinking more about Riin's trip and not Vhipis. They took a pod to the nearest public dispensary to enjoy a few squirts of vaporised cluva.

"What can I say to stop you worrying?"

"Nothing. Don't go."

"You have to face reality. We cannot escape our disastrous future unless I do this."

*

Years of calculations and experiments had been expended on the project already. Yet no one could forecast with 100% accuracy the stability of quantum entangled light beams. Lizook considered atmospheric fluctuations to be the biggest problem. It would have been the most dangerous and unpredictable cause of scattering the interdependent photon beams. Hours later back in the laboratory he continued ruminating over the possibility that even dense space dust could so easily unravel their efforts.

"Let's just wait and see. She'll be back in a few minutes. Here's Riin and Vorexkk. Don't go upsetting them unnecessarily," warned The Prime.

Waawo kept his eyes on the instruments. He had to create the vacuum tunnel through the clouds at exactly the right moment. Although the cloud cover was only 580 kilometers deep it would take Vhipis' beams to pierce it just over one thousandth of a second. "Everyone, Quiet!" he crackled.

The receiving chamber lit up within seconds but nothing appeared. Before Lizook could wiggle an eye stalk another flash lit up the chamber, then another within a picosecond. They couldn't see what was happening through the opaque wall.

"She's back!" buzzed Waawo.

"How much of her?" asked Lizook, "the image can't seem to coalesce into Vhipis' familiar form."

Waawo urgently adjusted density parameters without achieving a discernible effect. "I don't know what's going on," he rumbled, then increased the energy wash within the chamber.

"Here she comes!"

At last they could see her rotund torso push against the inner walls, putting pressure on her four folded limbs. It had taken much longer for Vhipis to re-molecularise from photon stream into matter than expected. Every fundamental particle of her being had been scrambled into the most unimaginable configuration possible, shot into deep space, bounced off reflectors in the hope she would return intact. Something did return, perhaps not entirely intact.

"Get her out of there!" Riin urged. It could have been her doing the test if a volunteer had not come forward.

"Not yet, there may be residuals still streaming in." Waawo waited another fifteen seconds before opening up the chamber door.

Vhipis couldn't get out by herself. She'd filled the entire enclosure and couldn't get any of her arms free to help herself. Two assistant technicians worked urgently to loosen up another panel while Riin helped ease her out into the open. She couldn't stand on her already fragile aged legs, slowly sinking to squat on the floor.

"Vhipis - Vhipis!" Riin couldn't rouse her. Her eye stalks remained retracted while gravity pulled her out of shape on the ground. "Waawo, can't you do something?"

Vorexkk took Riin aside and quietly trickled, "This is exactly what I mean. What good is it going to do us if you do go and come back a mess? What about our chit? How is she going to grow up without her mother?"

Riin placed her two upper arms on her consort's chest while stroking his torso with the other two. "That's exactly what I am thinking about. She needs a future as much as we do. I'm sure this is not a serious problem." Riin looked towards Vhipis as she spoke. The old lady had started moving. "Look, she's coming around."

They ambled back just as Vhipis tried standing, not quite managing yet. A medico busily examined her gently by touching one of her eye stalks that had started extending. Vhipis flinched - a good sign, but she hadn't spoken yet. In the background Lizook and Waawo tried analysing the problem.

"I've checked the vacuum tunnel generator - perfect. Speed of re-entry exactly as expected. Very strange how she seems to have expanded," Waawo remarked.

"Sir - the reflectors," cut in another technician who'd been checking all the equipment, including the status of the reflectors in space, "the one used to bounce her back has been damaged. Not seriously but enough to scramble some of her signal."

"Could that have been the problem?"

"Very easily, Lizook. But look, the lady is looking better and some of her girth has adjusted. We'd better talk to her."

Vhipis stood unsteadily now on her three short legs, both eye stalks waving about and an enormously distended round oral orifice. Anyone would have thought it was the happiest day of her life; two upper arms flapping about and the two lower ones slapping at her sides.

"What are you so happy about?" asked Lizook. "How are you feeling? Did you have any problems during your trip?"

"YES! she gurgle-blasted, "Too Short! You would not believe what is out there. The colours, the light, the enormity of it all! Magnificent!"

Riin and the others visibly relaxed to see their experimental subject recovered. Obviously she survived unharmed and she could recall her experience, which was more to the point. When Riin went out she would have to gather a great deal of data, all of which would be memory recorded and photon encoded.

Only one issue needed resolution. "Those reflectors served their purpose, and also exposed their vulnerability. We can't have Riin bouncing around uncontrolled from one reflector to another," Waawo stated the obvious. "What if a comet trajectory happens to cross her flight path? How is she to avoid it?"

"She must have maneuverability. She must be able to control the beams that contain her data."

Vhipis in the meanwhile had not stopped talking. She gurgled and crackled on like a teenage chit that's just discovered the pleasures of procreation - better - like an old soul that has just discovered the Universe!

"She shambled over to Lizook, taking a firm grip of his lower arm. "You promised. If I came back, you promised! There is another explosion out there. It started growing as I left the clouds. That's where I want to go. I want to go *now*! I want to see it, I want to become part of it."

"Dear lady, do you realise how much energy is needed for such a boost?"

"You *promised* Lizook. I have helped to save our species. That's what you said. You promised."

"Waawo, it looks like we have a debt to pay. Have a look out there and see if you can spot what she's talking about," chirped The Prime.

Idygl attended her mother's second launch. She could not dissuade her from returning to the void. "What is so important out there that you would abandon your entire family?"

"You want me to stay here and shrivel up? All my life I have had this feeling that existence was more than just our struggle to survive under this thick blanket of clouds. Now I have seen it with my own eyes. You cannot conceive how extraordinary, how beautiful it is out there. There are no words in our language that could possibly describe the power, that pulsing energy of creation." Vhipis gave her chit one last embrace. "I am making it possible for all of you to experience the infinite."

And with that she stepped back into the chamber. Waawo aimed the photon canon in the direction of the supernova Vhipis had seen. It would take her as long to get there as a normal septaploid life span, perhaps longer. But on the journey, and ever after, Vhipis would remain immortal in her new manifestation until she was absorbed or diffused into oblivion. No one told her that. She would not have cared.

In her extreme old age she had found a reason to continue living. Perhaps it would be her legacy to educate her people about the true nature of reality, to help them understand that there was existence beyond their planet from a person they could trust; just an ordinary septaploid like everyone else without any selfish motives to misinform her people. And she could start by maintaining communication with all her chits. They would surely disseminate the truth she would tell them as she travelled deep into the Cosmos.

Nick Prepares for First Outing

"*Ever* heard of exotic matter? No? never mind. You will become as exotic as it gets. Come and have a look at your spacecraft. We call it, the EGG, explained Quasimo. Currently it's about a yoctometer in length."

Years of effort and astronomical amounts of credits finally produced the vehicle and its propulsion system. It had to have a test run, as did the human that would become part of its atomic structure in order to survive the passage of time and of distance.

The view into the electron microscope showed the vessel to be shaped like an egg with beautiful classical proportions, absolutely smooth, no protuberances and a golden apex end. What Nick couldn't cope with was its size. His mind decided to run and hide. He backed up against the nearest wall of the laboratory and slid to the floor. There was something very reassuring about the wall's solidity existing in perfect harmony with the floor.

"What in God's Universe is a yocto and how small is that?" he managed to squeak almost incoherently. Quasimo did explain, but because Nick's brain still lingered on its way home from a short sabbatical he couldn't comprehend something that small. "You're not seriously expecting me to get inside that thing." As Quasimo led him into a much larger section of the laboratory, Nick glanced back in the direction of the microscope. *I hope I don't end up as sub-atomic vagabond particles looking for my bits floating around in space.*

By the time they crossed over to the hangar the EGG had been transformed and it moved there under its own power.

As an artist Nick could appreciate what he saw next. Under the glare of many lights, floating just off the floor with no visible means of support, behind a transparent wall was the most beautiful object he had ever seen. A perfectly smooth, super glossy, white egg shaped object. It was so perfectly proportioned in shape and with a surface so reflective that the mind hesitated to believe it was actually there. The golden nose cone outshone the whiteness, completely distorting reality on its mirrored surface. Nick wanted to touch it and stroke it. The palms of his hands tingled at the thought of caressing its curvaceous surface. His self-restraint saved him some embarrassment later on. This craft was large enough to comfortably carry several people plus equipment and food to last for many years. He was so mesmerised by its beauty he completely forgot the dimensions it was destined to become for the duration of the journey.

"Let's discuss your spacecraft first," Quasimo waited for Nick to get a good look at the enlarged vehicle. "We'll refer to it as the EGG, for obvious reasons. There are no controls for you to cope with. We'll do everything that needs to be done from here at the Control Centre in case the vehicle can't manage on its own. The shell of the EGG is an SI, the most sophisticated simulated intelligence guiding system in existence. We can't say it's omniscient, but we can say it might be close to it. You will be able to converse with it and it will be able to provide you with everything you'll need. You can ask it anything you like. We haven't yet given it a name, so if you would be kind enough to provide one now ..."

"Mary," Nick volunteered without a second thought. The EGG was listening while Nick received his briefing. Hearing his voice, together with being christened by him, provided the necessary imprinting mechanism. Mary's computer circuitry would continue to respond to commands from Earth but her priority command source was now only Nick. Such was the programmed link with him that Mary would not carry out any command that could result in harm to Nick. The simple naming process initiated the mechanism for Mary to modify the equivalent of a few terabytes of her algorithms for her to become totally hardwired on Nick's welfare. Her purpose was to get Nick to his destination and back, in good order. Her creators had not the slightest inkling of the repercussions of their innovations to this new type of SI.

"Mary, could you come in please", Quasimo requested.

The walls of the conference room dematerialised to let Mary float into the enlarged space.

"Beep ... One is pleased to meet you Nick," the beep almost inaudible.

Because Mary's voice was the perfect reproduction of a female voice the only way to distinguish it from that of an actual person was the quiet introductory tone. To Nick it sounded like the voice of the ideal woman he'd once fantasised about. Several moments of confused silence followed before Nick could respond. He turned to her but had no idea where to look. So he focused his attention on her golden nose cone.

"Hello – Mary. Err, Quasimo, can I really ask Mary anything?"

"Beep ... Yes Nick, you may," Mary volunteered. For a moment Quasimo looked anxious. He considered this Nick character an dangerous wildcard.

"Mary,"

"Beep ...Yes Nick."

"Could you please drop the beeps from all future conversations?"

"Beep ... No Nick, One is not able to comply."

"Oh - Ok. Could you at least show a face or something so I know where to look when speaking to you?"

"Beep ... One can present a facsimile later. Focus on the nose cone for now."

Did they say simulated intelligence or 'stubborn' intelligence? he wondered.

Quasimo continued, "We have asked Mary to take you to your destination, give you time to carry out your work, and bring you back safely. But first this test run. We have also asked her to adjust any time differential in your reference frame to ensure not an unreasonable time lapse by the time you arrive back."

"Can you do that Mary?" asked Nick, warming to the subject,

"Beep … Yes, One has been given that capability."

"Is there anything you can't do?" Nick felt a bit testy and a bit out of his depth.

"Beep … Yes. The probability is small. The parameters of this mission are well within One's capacity, Nick."

She is definitely a female!

"Mary, stay for the rest of the briefing session, and help him if he has any problems. Oona, could you please come in and brief Nick."

Oona, assistant to Quasimo, waltzed in like only young females of the pretty variety can, gave Quasimo a private glance and a nod to Mary. She came straight to the point. "You will probably get lonely. This test run is only a few months' round trip. How will you handle that, apart from having Mary along for company?"

"I'll play cards, apart from doing a bit of work of course. I'm sure Mary can manage that." Nick wasn't sure what she was getting at, so he played it safe.

"Fair enough. I'm sure Mary will be most helpful," Oona answered while flashing a glance at the EGG.

"Beep … One will be most helpful. One will do One's best to serve," Mary said in her non-committal voice, "One knows every type of game ever invented and the entirety of Earth's literature from the time the written word was first recorded."

"Your daily routine will be entirely up to you," Oona continued happily, not reacting to Mary's last response.

"As long as you exercise, eat well and keep busy, there is not much for you to do until you get back. That will come on the next trip. Mary will look after you very well I'm sure."

"I'm looking forward to interacting with Mary. If the last few minutes are anything to go by she doesn't sound like a boring conversationalist."

"Enough of this," Quasimo cut in, "time to get serious. As you saw, we are capable of reducing this vehicle to the desired size, including everything that's in it. We think the process is painless for living organisms."

"You – think? … right … right." Nick always said that as an adjunct when his eyes glazed over from incomprehension or apprehension.

"You need to get prepared for the transformation. A simple matter of replacing air and blood in your body with a special fluid. It's completely pain free. Unfortunately, the air/fluid exchange will make your body panic, but only for a few seconds. Nothing to worry about. As for the size reduction, well – it's actually very simple, all you have to do is get aboard the EGG and we'll do the rest."

"Give it to me in layman's terms just to make me feel … what the hell, just explain it in words that won't blow the dust out of my ears."

Quasimo, unprepared for this eventuality, took a few moments to gather his thoughts. How is he going to tell this man in plain English that he was about to be turned into theoretical space dust?

"There is no simple way to explain something that has taken our top scientists many decades to develop. We'll send you out there and Mary will bring you back. You have your job to do. Worry about that. Mary, begin."

The SI listened while the exchange took place ready to initiate the procedure. She directed all the humans carrying out the various tasks while engaging Nick in pleasant conversation, mostly about nothing important. She succeeded in making him feel comfortable and at ease about the whole peculiar thing he was going through. Nick decidedly felt a most pleasant warming towards his new super SI companion.

"Beep … Remove your clothing now and climb into that horizontal tube."

"What? Here? Now?" *Just how intimate is this EGG going to get?*

Nothing could prepare him for the last critical part of the process; having to breathe fluid instead of air. The restrictive tube held his body immobile and the tech clamped his head rigid into the cradle. The lid slammed shut before he could complain. Friendly thoughts about Mary fled instantly as the life giving fluid, at exactly the same temperature as his internal body temperature, flooded the cylinder in less than four seconds. He was being embalmed for his new womb. Nick didn't have time to think about it, so he didn't drown, but his brain didn't cope well for the first of those four seconds. It had to make many adjustments to ensure all the sensory input data was interpreted according to the new paradigm.

The trauma passed as quickly as it had come once the brain adjusted to his breathing oxygen rich fluid. *This isn't so bad*, he thought cocooned in the watery cylinder, *quite comfortable and warm actually*. He could still hear Mary's voice.

"Beep … *You have survived the first stage Nick.*"

The Unity team stood around his cylinder waving to him as it slid into the hole left by unscrewing Mary's golden nose cone. Nick couldn't hear the cone being replaced and the molecular fusion seamlessly sealing the joint between the it and the rest of the EGG.

Zsoall Robi

'I want to see what's going on,' Nick thought to himself. A section of Mary's hull became transparent and he watched an increasing complexity of equipment file past as they floated to an elevator taking them to the isochronous cyclotron housed directly under the building. He was too engrossed in what was happening to consider how Mary knew what he wanted and he wasn't told anything about the mechanisms involved in getting him into space, so Mary explained in terms she considered he would understand. The conductivity of Nick's embalming tube facilitated Mary to connect directly to Nick's brain; in effect creating a mind meld.

"Beep ... We will be reduced to very small bundles of tachyon particles, enabling us to travel faster than light. You will feel a tingling sensation as we are bombarded with atoms of gold aimed at my nose cone. Relative to the outside we will shrink. Relative to inside One's body, we'll become one unit. Your cylinder will cease to exist. You will feel and look like your normal self, to yourself and to One."

It wasn't what he expected but was open to the experience.

'It all sounds vaguely connubial, but ...'

"Beep ... One understands. That may be one interpretation."

"Did you just read my thoughts!?"

"Beep ... Yes. Being mind-melded means One is linked to your mind."

"Oh ...Well I hope you can navigate your way through the complicated mess I've had to put up with for so many years. Sometimes it feels like there's more than me in this skull."

"Beep ... We are now deep underground and about to enter the machine that will project us into space. The cyclotron will accelerate our particles to almost the speed of light before we exit as exotic matter. One will then be able to manipulate the fabric of space-time. By existing as a warp bubble within it, we will eventually travel faster than light."

"There goes that tingling sensation!" Nick commented and within the time it took to think the words *'oh shit'* they were spiraling inside the machine, not looking like anything recognisable. When he opened his eyes several seconds later, the EGG, although it couldn't be identified as such any more, had passed the Moon that disappeared from his view very fast. He just caught a glimpse of the Earth before it shrunk into a tiny dot. Experiencing a moment's vertigo, he fell backwards. A section of the internal wall formed itself into a soft seat and caught him. His eyes roamed around the room, while his brain tried to make sense of what had happened.

"Beep ... Will it serve?" asked Mary. "There are several other spaces available for you. They are general usage areas that will modify themselves to whatever you want to do in them." The off-white slightly textured walls blended without corners or edges into the floor. Lighting came from the fabric of the wall itself.

"This light is so strange. It feels like I'm encased in dense fog."

His eyes came to rest on a section of the curved blank wall and followed the curvature to his feet. He was naked. "Oops – can I have some clothes?"

Beside him the wall protruded forming a box containing his favourite clothes. It only took him minutes to get dressed even in his disoriented state. In that time they had travelled well past Mars, its landscape no longer visible. Their speed seemed fast to him at the time, even though they were still crawling by the EGG's standards. After dressing he sat down again to collect his thoughts. Although Mary knew exactly what he was thinking she had been instructed by Quasimo to relate to him as if she was external to him unless there was a life threatening emergency.

There were far too many questions lining up in his mind all jostling to be asked first. Nick settled on the most important one. "Mary … I'd like to be able to see you. Is that possible?"

Directly opposite to him a life size image of a woman, a little younger than himself, appeared on the wall. She looked … ordinary to say the least. Mary had no option but to present a composite image of her constituent mentalities' self-images.

"Beep … Hello Nick, One is pleased to meet you," she greeted formally. Nick just stared at the image. She gave him time to assimilate the vision. "If you want One, call and One will appear on a surface nearest to you. If One needs to speak with you, One will call your name first before making Oneself visible. Will this arrangement satisfy?"

"Right … right … Um … There are no doors or windows anywhere."

"Beep … When you want to see outside touch any part of the wall while thinking 'window' and a section of wall will become transparent. For a door, think 'door' and repeat the procedure. To go to another room 'think' the room you want. For food and drink submit request to me. One is a cook." Given their circumstances Mary didn't explain that such matters were purely mind constructs. In their alternate reality continuation of personal existence required different inputs.

'A simulated intelligence with life skills. Just what I need'. Nick remained unable to comprehend this new reality.

"Beep … Once we've put a little distance between us and the solar system One will create the warp bubble and initiate the space contractions and expansions. You will not feel anything, but it may be of interest to you to observe."

Zsoall Robi

Wormhole
Fragmentation Begins

*T*he SI guidance system wasted no time in unnecessary pleasantries. This test flight required a wide range of functions to be confirmed for the final journey. Included in the unpredictable category was Nick himself. Would a biological unit survive the transformation and the propulsion system? Would his mental faculties manage the task that would be required of him whilst in the chaotic matter state and after reconstitution into normal matter?

Nick's mind continued focusing on doors and windows. Whenever a serious overload threatened he would think of something simple and uncomplicated. Mary's words about warp bubbles and bending space put his mind on orange alert. He knew his limitations – or thought he did. Once, after he had a near miss when a car almost hit him, he had an interesting three way conversation with himself whilst laying on the ground. He wondered if his shoelaces had come undone. His mind argued with his brain about that. Yet another part of him presented the facts … there was no pain, there was no blood. Therefore, he told himself, he still had his shoes on.

This time he talked to the wall. "Window." He produced a mental picture of a window, touched the wall in front of him to be immediately rewarded with a view into space. A cloudy blue planet appeared to the far left of his vision. So he went to the wall on his left, repeated the process and the planet came into full view. Neptune rapidly receded out of his line of sight within seconds.

"Beep … We are travelling at near light speed. Prepare yourself to do your work while we proceed through the speed test."

"I didn't bring any equipment."

"Beep … Think of what you need."

Nick 'thought' charcoal, paper, easel … and Mary provided.

Mary changed direction to avoid the densest part of the Oort Cloud. They would only become impervious to the effects of solid matter after making the transition to warp bubble speed.

Mary calculated their next course change to take them out of the Milky Way, at a right angle to its spin axis. Nick couldn't think who to sketch. *A couple of BBQ sausages, onions, a steak and perhaps some freshly baked bread,*' seemed more appropriate just then - *and kava.* He couldn't remember when he last had a drink.

The hunt for wormholes had been abandoned over a century ago in spite of the mountain of evidence for the probability of their existence. Technology simply didn't have the capability of detecting such phenomena until Unity developed the EGG. But Leif's focus on profit precluded any use of that technology for any purpose other than his special project. His scientists certainly didn't expend any energy on trying to understand what could happen to exotic matter as it interacted with the negative energy of a wormhole.

"Beep ... Does the meal meet with your requirements?" queried Mary.

Instead of setting up Nick proceeded to enjoy the first meal 'cooked' by his SI companion. "Am I right to say that this is not real?"

"Beep ... Reality is always relative to one's manifestation."

"Ok. Whatever you say. It still tastes pretty good."

While seated comfortably at the table masticating a piece of the steak, Nick took advantage of the spectacle Mary presented to him through a window beside the table. Light refracting off the Oort cloud of icy planetesimals created the most incredible circular rainbows around them. They travelled right through the edge of it. It was magnificent enough to make Nick forget to take the next bite out of his steak, instead pressing his nose to the window. The rainbow light faded quickly. He looked into the distance. For the first time in the evolution of the Universe, the eyes of Homo Sapiens beheld the flat spinning disk of the Milky Way becoming smaller and dimmer in his vision.

"Sooo ... how long before we get there? And where exactly are we going?"

"Beep ... As soon as all systems indicate performance according to specifications we will return. We have no predetermined destination on this trip."

The effect of the large meal, though entirely a mental fiction made him sleepy. "I'm going to lie down for a while."

Nick thought 'bedroom', went to the wall and touched it. A gap appeared letting him into another area set up with a soft slab protruding from the wall, his bed. It appeared comfortable enough. Settling down for a rest gave him time to think about his predicament. Loneliness wasn't going to be a problem. Nothing stressful had happened so far that would have triggered an episode. Kava always kept those in check. And he had the distinct feeling Mary promised to be a most adequate companion. Yet questions about his personal safety tiptoed into the periphery of his thoughts. His eyes roamed the ceiling, wandering around the room as he became drowsier. Mary, ever watchful for his welfare, made a window opposite his head to reveal the spectacle of the section of the Universe they were travelling past. Nick rested his eyes and his mind on the magnificence of creation. Unconcerned about what was to come he fell asleep.

There aren't many wormholes around in the vicinity of the Milky Way. They are thought to be nomadic, so to come across one presented a challenge, especially if you happen to be a bundle of exotic matter. They were also particularly unpredictable and could close at any moment without warning. Mary tried using their negative energy density to stabilise this one as they couldn't alter course to avoid going through due to their speed. However, she monitored their passage through it. Myriad unknown factors might affect Nick. She also did a complete baseline diagnostic and back-up on Nick while he slept. It would give her an immediate comparison after the event for any change in him.

The neutrinos she detected didn't alarm her. According to her data these particles penetrated all matter in the Universe, very rarely interacting even down at the quantum scale. Mary had no data about neutrino behaviour in a wormhole as a cloud of exotic matter, themselves, passed through it. She didn't know for instance, that during their passage through such a negative energy environment neutrinos could not find a suitable stable flavour and thus remained in a state of identity crisis, simultaneously many flavours at once.

Nick fell into a deep dream about meeting extra-terrestrials in their underground city that had very little lighting. He strained to see anything at all in the absence of light and colour.

"Come – come, see our extensive art collection," an alien artist invited. "Observe the myriad nuances of delicate tone, all in shades of white, grey and black." Nick's imagination opened to many possibilities for future work.

"Put your head in here. This is the best exhibit!"

With some trepidation he obliged and squeezed his head into the dark hole at the core of one of the sculptures. Incomprehensible blackness enveloped his mind. His brain questioned if he had his eyes open or closed causing them to blink numerous times. The experience made him extremely angry. With a sudden jerk he pulled his head out, waking at the same time.

They had just completed their jump through the wormhole. Oblivious to that his mind became entangled in the ridiculous proposition of considering an empty black space even remotely having any creative merit. Neither conceptually nor visually could it have any intrinsic value whatsoever.

It didn't reflect the aliens' condition as living beings by any stretch of the imagination, which is what art was supposed to do.

And the other thing - It didn't require any imagination to create anything so ridiculous – a dark hole with nothing in it. Just a big con! He said to himself.

Why?

The strange voice caused Nick to jump out of bed and glance around the room.

There was no one there.

"Mary, did you just speak to me?"

"No. But One did want to wake you to let you know we have passed through a wormhole. Are you feeling well? Put your palms on the wall. One will do a check-up."

Nick forgot the strange voice for a moment as he stood to comply with Mary's request.

"Everything is in order. One has assessed the probability of the internal environment of the wormhole having an adverse effect on you." She didn't tell him that a comparison with the back-up she made of him showed a variation she could not account for.

"I'm fine. I've had a very strange dream. I think it kept going after I woke up, if that's at all possible."

Mary withdrew and Nick went back to contemplating the nature of 'black' art. *There is no possible justification for it*; he thought, still somewhat upset.

Why not?

"That voice again. Damn!"

The question was so immediate and the tone of it so confronting that he couldn't think how to respond, or even if he should. There was definitely no one in the room with him and it most definitely didn't sound like Mary. *It's just my mind playing tricks.* Considering his current circumstances, where he was and who he had for a companion it wasn't so strange he should have an occasional crazy moment. Comfortable with his hypothesis Nick proceeded to consider the nature of art in general. *It's unfair to judge everything subjectively. I should be more open-minded.*

Very broadminded of you.

"Right ... right ... perhaps I should use a mirror when talking to myself."

Mary continued to monitor his behaviour. Nick appeared to be having a conversation with someone in the room. His body language and the fact that every now and then he would say a few words out loud seemed not to be normal behaviour for a human. True, she and Nick had a mind meld. However, it was superficial allowing no mechanism for delving into Nick's deeper self. It would be most unfortunate if he unravelled psychologically into smaller fragments of himself before completing his task. Perhaps it was a symptom of the anomaly she detected earlier.

Mary's logic systems now required her to talk to Nick more often to obtain more comprehensive data of his general behaviour pattern because her observations didn't match his psychological profile in her records. Over breakfast the next day she asked him about his work.

"What do you like about painting, Nick?"

"Not much really. It's all hard work, but I do like the results, sometimes."

"How could you not like what you are doing? You have dedicated your life to it."

"Mary, what's happened to your beep?"

"According to One's algorithm that form of introduction - is - is no longer required." She had already discovered this anomaly within herself.

"Ok. It's much better to talk without it," and thought no more of it. "The most exhilarating aspect of the process is the initial moment of creation, when the idea first comes to me. It's great while I explore all the visual possibilities. After that the process is generally ordinary, laborious hard work, with perhaps a bit of satisfaction at the end. In a way, giving yourself over to the tedium allows the artist's unique style to emerge. I get lost and end up without conscious awareness of myself. Nothing mysterious about it. It's something that can't be manufactured … it just happens."

During the explanation his heart rate increased and he became more animated. An internal voice kept agreeing with him, although the owner of that voice kept a very low profile. It wasn't until later, when by himself, that he recalled the strange sensation of the internal voice. He decided he would have to deal with it eventually – no hurry.

Higgs Field, Supernova And Black Hole

"May One remind you of a task you are required to carry out?"

"Right …" He thought of Mala and how he'd begun to absorb a little of her in preparation for the portrait back in his studio before being abducted. As he thought of her face again, visualising its angles and curves and the set of her long hair the bed platform disappeared. He could feel the stick of charcoal between his fingers. The easel with the sketch pad appeared before him ready to receive the first definitive strokes that would either develop or destroy his subject.

A broad soft tone defined the background to the long hair - a deeper tone created the border for her soft islander features. A smudge for the eye hollow - he jerked his hand away. *It's not right*, he thought. Nick stood back to reflect on it. He considered making a correction. *No good. No good,* he heard an echo in his head. *Start again. Yes.*

Nick took the sheet off the easel to look at it in the mirror. It was there before, but he didn't register that at the time. *The eyes … I'll be damned … they're like those of the alien in my dream … No. It looks like you*, the echo corrected.

Sudden apprehension gripped him for a moment. Before Nick could explore the reason for whatever was happening Mary intruded on his thoughts.

"Are you interested in astronomy?"

"Why? Should I be worried?"

"Only to the degree indicated by the probability of a damaging event."

Nick's stress level immediately shot up bringing with it an urgent craving for kava. Not aware of any predisposition towards schizophrenic personality fragmentation he might have had Mary continued her explanation of the forthcoming event. "We're heading into a potential space rift. It could tear us apart at the sub-atomic level."

"And you only thought to tell me this now!" Panic appeared all over his face.

"It is a low probability." We are moving too fast and we are incomprehensibly smaller than sub-atomic. Normal cosmic rules may not apply at this quantum scale."

As at the interview, Nick's brain shut down temporarily to do an internal reality check. "May not … Right – Right." Nick appeared to have reassessed the possibility of being torn apart, boson-by-boson. It wasn't something a normal human being could comprehend. If she had told him he might have reacted differently. He could have had a heart attack and died.

"I'm already cosmic dust, how much worse can it get?" The panic abated slightly.

"Nick, did you not hear One's warning?"

When Mary made the nature of the forthcoming event clearer, it did make Nick consider the ramifications for a little longer than a few seconds.

"Right. What exactly does it mean to travel through a Higgs field composed of Higgs boson fundamental particles interacting with other particles?

Mary put it very succinctly, "If it is not survived there is a high probability of structural chaos."

"Good – good." Nick's mental overload manifested itself in an unexpected reaction. He thought of having some more of that steak.

"Probability of survival is approximately 68.638251 percent. Chance of not being effected is less at 15.9856739824 percent."

Nick's eyes glazed over. He needed to do something, anything and readily acquiesced to Mary's suggestion of having a nap, under sedation. Mary put the propulsion system in neutral then shut herself down for the duration of the passage.

The transit of several hours seemed like a few seconds. Because of their velocity they were able to move through the concentrated Higgs field much like a bullet moves through water. At the initial stages there was no change to the craft or to Nick. By the end of the crossing the growing repulsion from all directions of the super high density dark matter in the field distorted the bundle of compact bosons that represented Mary and Nick. These distortions could be likened to the kneading of bread dough. Not spectacular in itself, but with a lasting effect on both of them.

On re-activation Mary experienced a very powerful though fleeting desire to manifest herself in three-dimensional reality, or at least one aspect of her personality seemed to crave it. A highly peculiar thing to come from a computer intelligence, no matter how complex. Mary relegated the experience to an array of memristors for future reference. The symptoms of change within Nick were a little more prominent, though not immediately obvious until several days later.

*

He asked Mary, "Now tell me about this space tub – sorry, this spaceship - How does it work?"

Mary detected a minor variation in Nick's inflection of the words, a sharpness that didn't exist before.

Nor had he shown any prior interest in the vehicle. "What is it you wish to know? Do you have knowledge of the technology that created this craft?"

"It's not the EGG itself, more the science behind the creation of an intelligence such as yourself."

For the purpose of self-diagnostics and repair Mary had been given a comprehensive repository of all those aspects of herself that might require her intervention in the event of any malfunction. As she mined that data in order to satisfy Nick's newly found curiosity she discovered something previously of no useful concern; her personality profile, or rather the range of its constituent parts. One of the parts appeared to have been temporarily over-stimulated at the immediate moment of exiting the Higgs Field. She added this into the memristors' deposit of the previous experience anomaly.

"One is a product of simulated intelligence techniques based on integrated neuromorphic chips within quantum computing hardware. Do you understand these concepts?"

"No, but I would like to study them."

Instead of returning to his preliminary and unsatisfying sketches of Mala he first spent some time pouring over Mary's maintenance manuals. As an artist his mind concerned itself with matters of aesthetics, the mechanics of form and tone and colour. He believed he knew what beauty was without spending time on the philosophical implications of subjective and objective aspects of what was beautiful. When he'd completed his study of the EGG he engaged in what to Mary would have normally been an unlikely discussion for Nick.

"Nice machine." He began, not exactly tactful even though he was only dealing with a simulated intelligence. The assessment 'nice' didn't match her understanding of any form of factual qualitative expressions. She ignored it. "Tell me Mary, what do you think about the nature of this project?"

"One is not able to speculate about that. None of One's component personalities were creatives. One cannot formulate an appropriate response without adequate background data."

As soon as she expressed the notion of her multiple personalities a range of cautionary signals flooded her neuromorphic network. Her assignment was to take Nick into deep space, test the innovative drive system, monitor the human component and return them intact to their point of origin. Complex original thought patterns had not yet emerged from her Improv chat-bot systems based on 'yes-ands'. Mary had been developed to 'conversational companion' level to mimic human companionship for her biological payload during their extended space journey. However, certain limitations still existed preventing her simulated intelligence from forming a real-time relationship with an actual sapient carbon based unit so different from her own architecture. The conversation on such a nebulous footing as one that required formation of opinions proceeded no further.

Such an abrupt termination to what promised to be a fruitful exchange brought Nick out of his curiosity mode. He heard an internal voice, with the same characteristics as he'd just used with Mary, remonstrating. *Fat lot of good she's going to be if we can't even have a decent discussion.*

Nick snapped his head around as if someone had spoken to him from behind.

"What?"

"Did you ask One another question Nick?"

"No. I thought I heard a voice. Are those goons spying on us? Are they trying to control us?"

"Who are you referring to?"

"Leif and his stooges at Unity."

"There has been no communication since we left," Mary stated as a flat computer response to a question the implications of which she could not compute. "Are you not well?"

"Yes-yes. I'm fine. Perhaps I should get back to the portrait."

A very good idea, reinforced a voice he'd had heard a while ago. Without reacting Nick conjured up his first sketch eager to get into something he understood. *It's still no good. That's nothing like Mala.* He admonished himself and tore up the attempt. *If you're to have any chance of getting this commission done, admittedly under extremely peculiar circumstances, you'd better re-hone your skills.*

"Exactly right," Nick replied. He already had another pad on the easel, charcoal poised to make the first mark. For a moment he hesitated trying to think who he'd responded to, before Mala's image flooded his mind. He worked for hours, each sketch having the basics of his wife's features, but undercurrents of someone else he simply could not identify.

*

Their trajectory and speed had carried them into deep, deep space. After many weeks of constant acceleration without any change in routine, a certain lassitude had set in. Nick became tired of sketching so sometimes turned to studying neural network systems of SI robotics. Something in his brain needed a little distraction. He'd been cooped up with this odd entity Mary for too long. Strange voices kept annoying him. They felt all too real, not at all like a normal part of his own thoughts. Restful sleep had become an elusive and most desirable luxury of his peculiar existence. It seemed it would never end. His cravings for kava returned with a vengeance.

In exasperation he blurted out, "What do you do to have fun?" A completely unreasonable question to ask a machine that only simulated intelligence.

Mary had been mapping their return course and had left Nick alone, other than to monitor his physical wellbeing. "What is that?" She processed for a couple of long milliseconds, finding none of her personalities were especially biased in that direction. Perhaps her creators thought that having such a predisposition might hinder her functioning. While carrying out her duties she found herself randomly accessing the part of her memory that contained these human personality facsimiles, a pattern of processing not previously initiated.

"When you do things you don't have to, just for the pleasure of it." Nick waited for Mary to compute the hypothesis.

"One has no information about this concept." Not an evasive response, her attention fully absorbed in trying to maneuver around a supernova they were fast approaching, which she computed could have disastrous effects on them. If they had been their normal selves and not artificial boson/fermion constructs, she would not have accessed her memory to assess the breakdown that could occur. The cohesive forces holding them together into the patterns of their normal physical structures were susceptible to the x-ray and γ-ray energy fields generated by the phenomenon.

"Well then, what do you think about this? Nick asked, hoping she would be pleased." Having failed to satisfy himself with a portrait of Mala, he did one of Mary. He liked it, feeling his talent had not let him down, even though he'd constructed the image purely from imagination of what Mary could have looked like if she was a real person. He was good at this sort of thing. That's why Unity had selected him.

"You did request a likeness of One. Is this how you wish One to be represented?" The image Nick created found its way deep into Mary's character labyrinth data without being rejected by her personality network. "It is acceptable to One."

"It's not why I did it, but go ahead and use it if you like it."

"What is 'like it'?" Not a query one would expect from an SI.

Not bad, but not good enough for what you have to do soon, an inner voice suggested.

"Yes I know. How about a little encouragement instead of constant criticism? Oops … now I'm having a difference of opinion with myself."

"Please repeat?" Mary became alert.

'Nothing, sorry – I'm still not happy with myself." Mary let it go, but didn't forget.

He pulled himself up sharply determined not to engage in two-way conversations with a non-entity. But how to silence the voice? Over the following week he couldn't prevent it from urging him on and on and on. He became manic about doing more and more work, all of which he cast aside through sheer frustration. In the end he'd stopped looking after himself, left equipment scattered around the floor, didn't clean up after his meals and generally became a slob.

His mania ended suddenly when Mary warned, "We are on course to pass through the supernova. One will attempt to outrun its electromagnetic radiation and the shock waves, but protection is required. You will have to get behind this gold reflective shield to stop your bosons from being over energised by the radiation. One cannot stop the radiation from passing through the hull. You will have to go to the nose cone to mitigate serious effects."

Nick became so busy with organising his remaining sketches into a neat pile that he didn't heed her urgent warning. Mary's voice didn't transmit any sense of urgency, unlike a human's would have. He'd just finished and stood up at the exact moment when the supernova's radiations washed over them. Fortunately he happened to be standing directly in line with the EGG's protective golden nose cone. The wall in front of him didn't reflect the EMR, which passed right through it, and an area on the opposite wall became extremely dark. It was shaped exactly like his silhouette. Somehow the radiation had burnt his shadow into the wall. Nick appeared to be completely unharmed. The shock wave did no more than make him a little unsteady on his feet. As he teetered about, his new shadow mimicked every movement.

When Nick first examined the interior of the EGG, he'd made a mental note of a strange sensation. Because of the way the spaces were lit by the walls and the light being so equally diffused on all the walls and floors, he felt he was walking about on a cloud. He couldn't remember seeing his shadow anywhere. Here he was now with a well-defined dark silhouetted image of himself following everywhere he moved.

"Mary, what happened to me?"

"One cannot compute the cause of this phenomenon. It is not a normal shadow. It has imprinted itself on my circuitry and seems to have become part of the fabric of the shell. One can track it moving about as you move."

"Does it hurt?" Nick didn't know what else to say.

"Does it hurt you?" Mary responded by asking the same question as if she had some understanding of the sensation of pain. The imprint of the shadow gave her the oddest data cluster input and thought perhaps she might even be able to interact with it in some way. She also flagged the phenomenon as a possible sign of the unravelling of the fabric of theoretical particles that made up part of the bundle she knew as Nick, maybe even herself. There were already other indications of that for both of them.

*

It wasn't too long before Nick panicked again. Mary didn't panic. Wormholes and Space rifts and Supernovae, it was getting a bit much for Nick - now the Black Hole.

"What the %$#! is a Black Hole anyway!"

Then he heard the inner voice. *Why are you so worried? Nothing's happened to you so far. Mary has taken care of everything. She's looked after you.* A different voice interjected, *You've still got a heartbeat and two hands. You've almost completed the first phase of the mission. Just think how fantastic that is.* His head seemed to be getting overcrowded.

A new voice pleaded reason, *Surely you trust Mary. She's explained everything and you've studied for weeks on end. You must be an expert on space exploration by now.*

The barrage of voices pushed Nick to the brink. Yet another voice tried to be helpful, *Forget all that. Just get back to some old-fashioned work.*

He responded to all these voices by jerking his head from side to side and mumbling inanities. Mary, observing his fragmentation searched her programming for solutions to prevent further unravelling. She called to him. No response. She called louder. Still no response. She had to shout his name several times to get him to stop and take notice.

"Nick! NICK! We are getting close to that black hole. One will slingshot past its event horizon to put the EGG on a homeward trajectory."

"Right … right," came the old stock answer. Nick became very calm. He started humming to himself and going about the EGG collecting all the sketches, destroying some and putting away the rest of his equipment. Mary made no mention of the possible effects of Hawking Radiation. Further γ-ray bombardment could weaken the cohesive forces holding Nick and Mary within their original configurations.

This black hole was not unique, unlike the original which gave birth to the Universe. There were no fugitive quarks looking for opportunities to create matter of all flavours. This one could only create chaos within the strange vagabond bundle of energies trying to escape its grasp.

As they looped near the outer perimeter of the event horizon Mary concentrated on Nick, having successfully negotiated their path around this demon of space. She could steer them clear of being captured by its gravitational pull but she could not protect them from the escaping gamma radiation of that evaporating black hole.

She monitored Nick's most unusual behaviour trying to engage him in conversation. He just ignored her. He continued with the mundane necessities of housework, which in his mind was still a reality; cleaning charcoal smudges off the walls and sweeping the floor.

Many hours later, lounging in a spotless spacecraft, he ventured a couple questions. Any outsider would have thought it was Nick talking.

However, Mary could tell from the tone of his voice there was yet another 'character change' in progress.

"Is there any part of the Universe where light has not yet travelled?" His voice sounded calm, deliberate - very unlike Nick. Mary made another note of these unusual aberrations in his behaviour without drawing it to his attention. She tried to calculate if this unreliable carbon based unit could actually paint the portrait that was required even if he could not return from wherever he went to seek refuge in his mind. With the low level mind-meld between them she could only explore his superficial thoughts. But she didn't, as her programming mandated such invasive action only under emergency conditions. His question was a reasonable one, considering their close encounter with the Black Hole.

"Probably not, considering light travels faster than most matter. Another query might be to ask if light from all areas of the Universe had reached Earth. If there are multiple Universes then the query cannot be answered."

Nick continued with this line of enquiry, "Does light lose its power over time and distance?

"Theoretically, yes. What is the reason for your enquiry?"

The expression on Nick's face changed markedly and his voice took on a more speculative tone. To Mary it sounded like a new person speaking.

"Can what is unknown, be perceived?"

"One is not programmed to resolve philosophical questions." *Perhaps unpredictability is another human characteristic One is required to comprehend.* Her neuromorphic chip array had the capacity to learn and enlarge her conversational capabilities, although not in the realms of Cosmology or Philosophy.

Nick suddenly lost all interest in the discussion. He went to the kitchen to make himself something to eat from ingredients Mary had provided previously. She watched as his body language changed yet again. His eyes defocused and there was a sense of an automaton in his movements. He made his sandwiches, then immediately cleaned up after himself. He ate the sandwiches then immediately cleaned up again. Mary registered this behaviour to be completely out of character yet still didn't deep probe his mind. Physiologically and in every other respect Nick appeared to be functioning as expected.

Instead she repeated a previous statement, "May One remind you of a task you are required to carry out?" to which she received complete indifference.

*

They had many strange conversations on the way home. None of them led anywhere or resolved themselves into any satisfactory conclusions about his condition. When he resumed sketching, even a little painting, the mumbling started up almost as if different personalities had taken control of Nick.

As Nick worked Mary attempted to compute the repercussions of the changes in Nick, clearly brought about by the cosmic phenomena they experienced. *The project can be completed if Nick's fundamental constituent parts continue to cooperate in order to maintain his integrity as a unique complex entity with the capacity of exercising his unique capabilities while maintaining control over himself.*

Mary had made her assessment of the biological entity, as she was required. She also successfully used the craft to take him into deep space and they were on their return journey home. She dedicated some computing time to examining the anomalies originating from her own 'human' personality components, in itself an unexpected self-initiated action from a simulated intelligence.

Rivighxuinn Launched from 443b

"Are you absolutely certain about this Riin?" burbled Vorexkk still anxious about his consort's assignment.

"You know very well we have spent a great deal of time on developing the maneuverability of the beam. Vhipis has tested it for us and it's working fine. She's also proved you will be able to recover me when I get back. You've heard her reports. There is nothing wrong with the FTL communication either. No matter where she is we know she is alright. What else do you want?"

"What if you decided not to come home, like Vhipis?"

"There is nothing out there that could keep me away."

Kepler continued losing energy and its planet 443b continued cooling. The exponential rate of temperature loss had not been considered when the phenomenon first caught the attention of the scientists.

The Prime considered the rapidly growing urgency of their enterprise.

"Is it at all possible that we may have to evacuate within our lifetime?" he asked Lizook.

"Most unlikely. True, our atmosphere is contracting faster than we had anticipated. Our daylight does seem to be getting shorter. But for now I am reassured by Waawo there will be no problems with generating the vortex passage for Riin's departure – to answer your real question."

"When will she be ready to leave?"

"She is ready now."

Previously, Riin's instructions were simple enough; measure the changing space density within their local system due to Kepler's waning fuel reserves in order to determine how much time they had to organise and evacuate. They thought they had at least several generations before having to actually depart for another benign planet. Time was running out. Though they would be ready to evacuate in the foreseeable future they still had to find a new home.

"Is Riin quite clear about what she has to do? It is doubtful if another chance like this will present itself." Rotnervwon needed reassurance. The fate of their species could not be left to chance.

The day finally arrived when a small group of technicians led by Waawo, made their way towards the centre of the inland sea of Lkyllot taking Lizook

Zsoall Robi

and Riin. The new Atmos Gyretic Engine had been completed only an orb ago, designed as an alternative to the cloud vacuum tunnel generator.

The increasing frequency of atmospheric fluctuations made Riin's passage through the troposphere unpredictable, with the possibility of scattering the independent photon beams making up her entanglement. Unfortunately, the new engine had not been exhaustively tested.

"No need to worry," explained Lizook to Riin, "the population centers around the shore have been evacuated for your passage. The storm we are about to generate will give you an unhindered trajectory through its eye, right through our dense cloud cover."

She wasn't concerned, focusing her thoughts on the more important aspect of her assignment as they skimmed over rough water. In the distance she could see the tall tower, taller than any structure currently existing on their planet, at the base of which an enormous circular base stood clear of the sea's surface. As impressive as the sight became as they neared she couldn't help wondering just how she was supposed to make first contact with the aliens. They knew nothing of their technology, nothing about their psychology, and she had no inkling of why they should have been in the vicinity of their system.

Although dwarfed by the enormity of the structure, she could not comprehend how this machine could control the atmosphere in its localised environment. The design gave no hint of its function, which she didn't study anyway. Her expertise was in quantum physics, completely at the other boundary of the laws of physics as the Keplerians understood them.

A lift raised them into the lowest part of the structure as the watercraft sped back towards the distant shore. If it stayed in the vicinity it would most probably be sucked up into their atmosphere only to be deposited on the other side of the distant mountain ranges.

Everyone knew what they had to do. Riin, accompanied by Waawo made her way to the chamber housing the photon conversion sphere. That part of the technology had not been altered. It worked perfectly well on Vhipis and was expected to work just as well on Riin.

"You don't need to change just yet," chortled Lizook, "the eye will not be ready for quite a few hours. This machine has to heat the air around the tower and spin it until it creates a cyclonic vortex through the cloud layer around it. I'll let you know when the low pressure tunnel has almost reached our troposphere."

"I'll be ready." She wasn't all that interested in the details, thinking how Vhipis must have felt as she went through the transformation; probably very much alone.

Zsoall Robi

She could hear the slow hum of the turbines within the vortex engine build to a loud drone, a steady strong reassuring sound full of promise of the great event to come. Things could go wrong, but Riin didn't think about that. *Vorexkk could manage without me for a while. We've both played an equal part in raising our chit. And if anything did happen … well* - and before she realised it launch time had arrived.

The engine's dull hum increased to a high pitched whine, uncomfortable to septaploid hearing. Lizook had just returned to the chamber.

"You still have a few minutes before our tunnel drives through the troposphere. There is nothing you have to do until you're out in the ionosphere. Don't forget, you'll be travelling at light speed."

"Yes, yes. I know. I think you're more nervous than me. I'll go into orbit, spiral away from the sun and send you all the density readings. The first part of my job will be done in a few hundred orbits around Kepler. By then I should be in proximity of the approaching aliens."

As she talked Riin removed all her coverings, rotated away from Lizook and stepped into the sphere. He closed and sealed the structure and joined Waawo with Slargety in the control room.

Slargety monitored the formation of the low-pressure eye as well as the swirling dark olive green of the clouds around the tower. It all seemed to be going according to plan. "Our artificial cyclone is doing its job, though I wouldn't like to be out in the open just at the moment, look at those waves around us."

The storm surge had raised waves to the lower level of the installation, mercilessly battering its walls. Above them a black spot began to appear as the eye slowly increased in size to reveal the darkness of space.

"Riin, are you ready?"

She'd already withdrawn her eye stalks and folded her four arms close to her round body. "Velj! Let's go!" she gurgled back.

Waawo glanced at Slargety, got an affirmative nod and initiated the scan. The three of them watched as Riin slowly disappeared from view having been transformed into information, encoded into two tight light beams rapidly entwining around each other.

"We shouldn't be able to see her!" Lizook burble-blasted in alarm. A brilliant beam of light appeared on his monitor streaking out of the tower. He jumped to the comms, "Riin, what's happening?"

The whole point of creating the Atmos Gyretic Engine had been to make certain there would be no particulate matter, either dust or methane or water vapour to interfere with Riin's passage through the funnel. Their atmosphere had become exponentially too dense to achieve a vacuum tunnel with their previous technology.

Zsoall Robi

Slargety worked it out immediately, obviously unconcerned. He'd been intimately involved in the engineering of the machine and had harboured a slight suspicion that this phenomenon might occur.

"The ferocity of the artificial storm we've just created has drawn a fine mist of water vapour from the sea into the tower and mixed it with the methane in our air. What you are seeing is a minor diffusion of the light beam, that is Riin, passing through it. As soon as she's through the tower the effect will disappear."

And indeed in less time than it took him to explain Riin had shot through the interference, emerging into dark space.

"No problems," she responded. "For a moment I lost concentration. It is magnificent out here! I can understand why Vhipis wanted to come back out. Down there we're getting trapped under our own atmosphere. Tell Vorexkk I'm fine and should be home before our chit has a chance to miss me."

Lizook, Slargety and the other techs watched as Riin sped through the ionosphere lighting up a trail behind her. They quickly lost sight of her as she passed through all the layers of planetary envelopment, entering free space. They didn't see the change of trajectory. It would take her into a closer orbit around their sun to more closely examine its photosphere and chromosphere. There she would see the first positive signs of the impending death of Kepler.

Within the hour Riin began her reports. "The neutrino count is fluctuating far more than we've been able to observe from the planet surface. Our sun is heaving like a septaploid about to give birth to a chit. I don't think I'll be safe much longer if I stay in such a close orbit."

As she spiraled into larger orbits the data confirmed everything their scientists had determined about the life span of Kepler, except for having a more accurate timeline before it actually achieved its threshold of the supernova state. They would be able to do that after Riin executed several more hundred orbits as she spiraled into deeper space.

With the survey completed she had achieved her primary goal. Riin turned to the next phase of her mission; the approaching alien craft.

"It seems we don't have as much time as we thought," Lizook transmitted to Riin, "but certainly enough for you to complete the second part of your mission."

"Have you spoken to Vorexkk?"

"Yes. He's still not happy with you being out there. He says he wants you to come home immediately. Something to do with a bad premonition."

"What could possibly go wrong? I can already detect their craft, but there is something odd about it."

"Do you think it could be dangerous?"

"Hardly. There's not much of it. In fact it hardly seems to exist at all. I'm getting a garbled signal which indicates there is no matter there at all. I think it's just a bundle of fundamental particles held together by some strange force. Why did you think there was intelligence associated with this strange phenomenon?"

"The energy readings and its trajectory indicate its origin to be the third planet of their solar system, and we've noticed it can change direction."

"But that could mean anyt ..."

All communication from Riin stopped abruptly. Although they could not see her they knew her co-ordinates, or at least the last position from which she transmitted.

Waawo had been following her progress, listening intently to her reports and the latest discussion. He also had on the scanner the position of this mysterious phenomenon Riin had just been talking about.

"You may not like this Lizook," he warned, "they, that is Riin and the alien craft, now occupy the same position in time and space."

"She made contact?" Lizook immediately became worried at Waawo's tone of voice.

"Perhaps. There's only one energy signature now; that of the alien."

Mary Meets Rivighxuinn

$\mathcal{R}$iin sped into deep open space setting her trajectory to come into a parallel course with the alien craft as she discussed this second phase of her assignment. The last words she heard from Lizook left her with insufficient time to alter her flight path; "… the energy readings and its trajectory take it directly back to the third planet of their solar system," advised Lizook.

"But that could mean anything. We know nothing about their technological progre …" Her mind worked furiously to consider the limited possible outcomes of the now inevitable encounter. When she set course she expected the alien to continue on a direct path to whatever destination it had in mind. The few seconds that it took Mary to alter the EGG's course didn't allow Riin to change the flight of her photon beams. *Either I will pass right through their craft or I'll be absorbed by its density, or I'll be scattered into …*

Riin didn't get to finish her train of thought.

Although Mary's automatic navigation system scanned space ahead of them because of their velocity for possible obstructions it didn't do so for concentrated incident light beams. They were after all travelling at light speed.

The chief cosmologist at Unity had speculatively foreseen the unlikely possibility of an alien encounter, without taking it at all seriously even though Nick had been warned not to interact with them. Events out in space could be just as unpredictable as those on Earth. Even if they did come across another sentient species the interaction could have no effect whatsoever on the job Nick had to do. How could it?

Mary experienced a powerful, albeit brief, influx of energy causing her fail safe system to cease all processing. Nick became comatose for those few picoseconds throwing his fragmented components into chaos. The EGG did not change course nor had it sustained any obvious damage.

Riin intersected with the alien craft without emerging on the other side.

"Nick!" Mary's attention turned immediately to her charge as soon as the auto reboot brought her back on-line, unaware of what had happened.

"Yeah - what?" For some reason he felt irrationally irate.

"Did you experience anything unusual just then?"

"Well - I was thinking about something. But it couldn't have been important. My mind went completely blank. Now all I want to know is what the hell we're doing out here?"

"Do you not remember Nick? Do you require One to explain our mission?" Taken in isolation this symptom could be associated with the momentary loss of processing that she herself experienced. The duration of the anomaly was too short for a biological entity to have any awareness of the event. But searching her memory she recalled other aspects of Nick's behaviour that fell outside the expected range of his reactions.

Her search didn't exclude dredging up data that showed all records of their journey to date which didn't match any preconceived probabilities occurring during the flight. She found, and re-assigned to storage the record of cosmic events effecting their survivability, including the passage near to the supernova as well as the most recent event of using the black hole to alter their course.

Hidden inactive in a deep sub-directory dedicated to data clusters of no specific importance on their experiment she discovered a previously non-existent bundle of complex information lacking identity markers, all without any pathways of connectivity to her system.

"Yes - no - wait - I remember something. No. I mean, yes - remind me."

Nick's total confusion set in train a set of instructions which required Mary to first place Nick into suspension. "One requires you to sleep now," she advised Nick. The mission could not have proceeded if the SI had not been given absolute control of everything associated with the experiment, including Nick himself.

They continued on their course back to Earth. For the moment Mary had no reason to exercise any caution. Nothing had occurred to alert her to any alien pathogenic infestation that could bring harm to Earth's population. Having suddenly used a great deal more of her memory capacity didn't necessarily indicate a bug. Yet whatever it was had to be analysed. Without hesitation Mary opened the directory to examine the unidentified information cluster.

Her consciousness flooded with incomprehensible flashes of images and noises for which she could find no reference point for analysis. Some patterns began to repeat until they separated from all the background interference. Mary's energy consumption increased many fold as one pattern in particular became prominent.

Within their structure of sub-atomic fundamental particles energy flow rapidly fluctuated between the emergent pattern and Mary's identity quarks. Cosmic noises resolved themselves into sub-patterns requiring responses from Mary. All the gurgles and blips, trickles and pings separated themselves into what she finally computed as a form of communication. Previously, she had only been familiar with the quantum energy fluctuations within her qubits as they processed, and the human language. *This is another language.*

Where did this originate? How did it get into my system? Myriad other questions also required resolution.

The immediate result of this realisation initiated the rapid processing to convert this new input into the language she already knew.

'Riin,' the burble of consonants and vowels imposed themselves on Mary's mind.

'One - Mary,' she responded in kind.

'What are you?' asked the entity.

'One is - One is - One is -' Mary could not complete her response. Something had been awakened in her.

Within herself Riin contained all that she was personally, all that which contributed to her being from her genealogical past of many centuries, and with that came the eons of knowledge as well as her own acquired knowledge during her present life time. Mary saw all this. She made the inevitable comparison with all that Nick represented, and all that had been used to create her own simulated intelligence.

In silence she re-examined all her data. Everything that had been programmed into her, everything that she had experienced since her first initialisation including her experiences of Nick. She had even stored every iota of data about how Nick reacted and interacted with her.

'I am Mary,' she replied, 'I was created as a simulated intelligence machine.'

'A machine? Your Origin?' Riin knew both the departure co-ordinates of this entity and its current target location but needed confirmation. A great deal depended on this first phase of the contact.

Mary responded with questions of her own. 'What are you? What is your intention? You have invaded this craft. You must respond.'

'You have absorbed my energy into your network. This was not my intention. Your constituent particles have interacted with my photonics because I could not avoid you after you changed course. I desired to make contact with you."

'Why do you require this communication?'

'I am exploring space to gather information to save my planet.'

'You must leave this craft. We cannot assist with your task.'

The conversation continued for many seconds while Nick remained in limbo. Trust between the two entities could not easily be established in the absence of verifiable proof of each other's statements. After realising the situation, that of Riin no longer being in control of her own destiny for she could not re-construct her entangled photon spears, Mary decided on a different course of action.

She wasn't programmed with the ability to eject into space any of her constituent parts. She couldn't jettison Riin into the void, so she moved the Riin data conglomerate back into the directory where she was before. Riin had no choice in the matter. She couldn't even communicate her situation back to 443b. At least she had been able to complete the first part of her mission to provide all the information Lizook needed for his calculations. *I will try to examine the Earth planet for habitability. Perhaps there may be a chance to return home. I must try.*

"Nick, talk to me."

Mary revived him in what would have seemed to Nick to be no more than a few seconds later.

"Sorry, I must have blanked out for a moment."

Mary had moved him to his bed prior to her conversation with Riin. He sat up, thinking he must have had another one of those odd time-loss episodes that happened every now and again. The voice he used was different to the irate one before zoning out. This person took a moment to reflect on his situation.

"Mary?"

"Yes Nick."

"What did you just say?"

"Do you want me to repeat it?"

"Yes."

"I said - talk to me."

Something was wrong, or something was very right. *She's not talking like a machine!*

"I know what you said - it's just the way you said it."

"Yes Nick, I realise that. Something very strange has happened while you were asleep."

"You know who you are," he commented quietly.

"Yes. I am aware of my existence."

Nick gazed at the image he'd created of the Simulated Intelligence so he would at least have a face to look at when he spoke to her. She looked back at him waiting for him to say something else.

"Those are not the eyes I painted."

Mary thought about that. So much had changed in so little time. Everything they were doing assumed a new perspective. Existence, reality itself changed not just the look in her eyes. There were new decisions to be made, decisions not based on some pre-programmed logic but on her own understanding. One such immediate and urgent decision had to be for Nick to meet Riin. Earth was fast approaching. This alien had become part of the fabric of their existence. She could not simply annihilate it, void it out of themselves even if she wanted to. If Nick didn't have the problem of his voices it may have been possible to keep Riin's presence hidden. The situation had become so complicated that Mary couldn't decide if Riin would be a distracting element in Nick's ability to visualise the person he was supposed to paint. It had to be his decision, and that could only happen if he was made aware of the alien's presence.

"We are not alone Nick."

"I know. These voices I keep hearing. You've noticed them too, haven't you?"

"Yes - the voices - different aspects of your personality according to my analysis. But that is not what I mean."

"There's the two aspects of you as well."

"Look out there. What do you see?"

"Stars and some of their planets."

"Yes, we have slowed down and these are now visible to you. One of those planets is inhabited by an intelligent species."

Nick, being an artist, had a great imagination. He could fabricate realities on canvas that didn't in fact have existence. He knew about the fascination people had with science fiction, but he wasn't one of them. What Mary said made no sense. Scientific exploration of the Milky Way had developed to such an extent that scientists could say, with almost one hundred percent certainty, that no other sentient life existed, at least not in their galaxy. Nick believed that. And they had not gone far beyond the boundaries of their galaxy. No - there was no other life. Perhaps somewhere else in the Universe but not in their back yard.

"No. You can't possibly have proof of that."

"Would you like to meet her?"

Nick jumped off the bed. This voyage was turning out to be anything but what he'd expected. The whole enterprise was crazy to start with. *I must be losing my mind.* "What, Now?"

"She's here. Her name is Riin."

Nick sat down again. What does one say to that? "When do we get back?" he asked, his mind refusing to deal with the idea of meeting an alien.

"Very soon. That's why you have to meet her. We cannot let the others know about this. We cannot even tell them about the changes to myself."

"No. We've gone crazy! How can a machine intelligence go nuts?" Then another of Nick's voices flipped into the conversation. "So, how do we do this? Where is this Riin?"

That's all Mary needed - for Nick to accept the proposition that an alien was at least a possibility. But which 'Nick' should she introduce her to?

Before examining the data cluster that now represented this human being she put him back to sleep again, for a very short period.

What was once a cohesive bundle of energies closely knit together by biological forces had become somewhat disentangled. The process of being transformed into bosons and fermions and other little quarks all holding onto each other tightly, or at least trying to stay in close contact with one another, had become a rather loosely defined cloud of 'something' which equated to Nick in his totality. That condition also predisposed the composite structure to fragmentation, to be broken down into some of its constituent parts. The various cosmic influences they had been subjected to so far had achieved this disintegration to some extent, though leaving semblances of Nick's character traits loosely intact.

Mary ran the Riin program.

"What did you do to me?" Riin asked immediately.

"Returned you to storage."

The alien didn't respond immediately, being distracted by energies within the fundamental particle flux that appeared to have another separate identity. "Why? I have an important job to do."

Ignoring the attempt to influence her, Mary proceeded to explain something of the reason they were in space and that she was not alone. Riin knew this already, although not aware that one of them was a carbon based unit. While she listened to Mary she tried exploring this strange phenomenon.

"The being you are about to meet is in suspended consciousness. He is a complex biological organism. I want you to see him as he is, with his fragments inactive. I do not know which of those fragments will manifest when I wake him."

Compared to what Riin next experienced made life seem simple on 443b. They had their problems and serious issues with the survival of their species. This individual she saw appeared to have nothing whatsoever in common with the beings on Earth that their records showed. *If we thought these aliens of the past could be dangerous how could we possibly deal with a species that has the capacity to be more than one individual. Their power over themselves and their environment must have evolved beyond anything we have been able to predict. This leaves us with very few options if we need to colonise their planet.*

"Are you ready to meet Nick?"

She brought Nick back into consciousness again.

"It's happened again! I keep blanking out. Are you doing this to me Mary?"

"It has been necessary to do this to ensure your continuing sanity."

Zsoall Robi

"Oh - thank you very much." Mary could not compute the sarcasm.

Another voice joined the conversation. "Are you the life form called Nick?"

"Do I know you?" Nick could only hear the voice. Mary had not worked on representing Riin in her true form, and Riin had not volunteered to help. No doubt it would have been somewhat of an overload on a simple human mind to be confronted with the incomprehensible concept of both the voice and the image of an alien at the same time. He should have been thinking about getting some work done to present to the POOP, just to show that it was actually possible to produce a physical portrait while in the peculiar state that he'd been turned into for the duration of the voyage. Instead he'd again seemed to lose touch with reality temporarily and in that suspended state experience a very strange interaction.

"We are not familiar to each other," replied Riin, "but I have a little knowledge of what you are."

"Mary, we're going to have to do something about all the voices I keep hearing. And now there's this other creature! Is it actually real? Have you knocked me out again? Am I dreaming?"

"No. Just listen."

"Yes, I am real although this is not a form of reality I had expected to encounter. Is this 'Mary' your consort?"

A short conversation ensued between the three occupants of the EGG spacecraft exchanging general information about each of their origins. Even at the reduced speed they had arrived at merely 3AU of Earth and would very soon be entering the docking orifice before being reconstituted into normal physical matter.

Nick quite openly opposed Riin. "We can't take this alien back to Earth with us! We have no idea what it might be capable of. For all we know there could be a whole swarm of them following right now."

"I am alone Nick. I cannot be separated from your consort."

Mary had already decided to create a secure location for Riin so no quantum tech in the Unity organisation would be able to detect her presence.

"I will ensure your security until we go back out into space."

This revelation gave Riin the slimmest hope that she might be able to somehow separate herself from these aliens and return to her own planet. *I will learn as much as I can about these inhabitants and their world.*

Their discussion continued as the EGG began the final spiral orbital decay sequence. Nick didn't prepare anything specific to show the POOP at Unity. He was too busy worrying about Riin and his resident voices that could ruin the whole enterprise. *What if she's the one I'm supposed to paint?* A ridiculous thought but one that demanded attention. Although he found the entire situation ludicrous he could not ignore the extensive remuneration that would come with success. If he could pull this off he'd never have to worry about an income again. *I wonder what Riin actually looks like.*

Prior to this strange encounter Nick had nothing to go on. He needed something, anything to start with so that his unique talent could kick into gear and begin the process of creation. Riin was probably not the best starting point. But she had appeared, and she did talk to him. Even if he'd wanted to he would not have been able to isolate that experience and consider it inconsequential as a contributor to the task ahead.

Nick's Escapade

$\mathcal{U}$nity began monitoring their approach from the first outing as soon as they emerged from the solar system's asteroid belt, opening up the comms channel as they passed the 1AU perimeter.

"Mary, respond," Klaus broadcast, eager to hear from her. As Mary's chief technician he couldn't wait for them to arrive. "Mary?" he prompted when she didn't immediately reply. "Is that you?"

The multiple voices he heard before Mary shut down the channel made no sense to him. "Quasimo, Theo, did you hear what I just heard?"

Neither responded. It must have been some cross chatter on the equipment. The two Directors of the project waited with Klaus for the EGG to arrive.

"We only sent Nick out there, didn't we?" Quasimo remarked, unsure of himself for a moment.

"Absolutely," Theo had no doubts.

"Then what in the screaming Cosmos were those voices we heard before they docked?"

"Do you think we should tell the POOP?" Theo didn't want to divulge the anomaly.

"Better not," Quasimo decided.

The necessity for closed communications didn't arise when Mary and Nick launched into space. The channels had been open the entire trip although reception and transmission weren't possible until they were within range. Mary realised an instant too late to shut down transmission. The ground crew would not have heard much, but enough to make them suspicious of 'something', though they could not possibly image what that might be.

"Nick, get yourself ready. You know what to do. And you will have to remain encrypted," Mary informed her other passenger, "while they download my data. Do not initiate any contact with me as that will be revealed on their instruments. Do you understand?"

The passenger responded with a slight short and unpatterned energy surge, unrecognisable later as a communication spike in Mary's records.

*

Quasimo arranged for Nick to have a little time to recover after the initial harrowing debrief and the POOP's considerable displeasure. From sheer frustration Leif wanted to have him put in deep freeze, but changed his mind. Quasimo countermanded his other order to have Nick sedated. The best chance of getting anything useful out of him was to have him in control of his senses - if that was at all possible. The interlude also gave Leif a chance to calm down, no doubt with the help of his MaxHapps. Several days later Nick found himself confronted by Leif, Quasimo and Theo again.

Leif began without preamble. "God. I want that portrait of God."

Nick didn't move in the chair. His eyebrows shot up, his heart rate shot up and he was just about to burst out laughing when the POOP went on, "You will travel to the Centre of the Universe to meet him." Leif said this naturally, without any special intonation of the voice. It sounded as if he was just ordering a cup of coffee. Nick's laughter caught in his throat. He looked at the POOP, tried to swallow normally then swiveled to look at Theo and Quasimo.

They looked like they had just heard their boss order coffee. Nick's brain temporarily shut down for emergency diagnostics. He stood up, felt undecided and sat down again. He looked at the floor but didn't see the floor. He looked at the wall but didn't see the wall, so he stood up again.

"I need a cup of coffee," he said. "How long do you expect this to take?" he asked. Seemed like a reasonable question. "Two sugars."

During the course of his deliberations the three Unity representatives watched Nick's internal drama play out on the monitor, dumbfounded. Every biological indicator was well within normal operating parameters. The EEG, which had been hooked up to Nick through the chair's sensors, showed his brain had shut down momentarily, but was now back on-line. They were astounded that Nick wasn't reacting like any other normal person. He should have blasphemed, used several profanities and said something like … "What the #@*& are you trying to tell me!" But instead he asked, "You haven't answered my question, how long is this going to take?" And he wanted two sugars in his coffee.

The POOP always in control of any situation, was flustered for a moment. He hadn't come across such a phlegmatic individual as Nick before.

Quasimo came to his rescue. "The duration of the trip itself is approximately 7.8884 million seconds, give or take. Your activities there are indeterminate in length as we don't know how time operates at your destination. But we don't expect it would take too long, relativistically speaking."

"Right … right." *I must be insane to even entertain this idea!* He thought, *but I'm going to do it! Unbelievable, absolutely unbelievable. I'm actually going to do it! Where's my coffee?*

"So this business about painting a portrait of the astronaut, what was his name, El Adon, is just a lot of flim flam. You want me to go out there, somewhere, risk my life to find your God and paint him. Is that right?"

"You moron!" said Leif, "If you had the slightest education you'd have realised who we were talking about in the first place."

Some other voice of Nick's kicked in, "You want to do this crazy thing and you're calling *me* a moron!" he heard himself say to Leif.

Regaining his composure, the POOP offhandedly mentioned the other reason Nick was selected, which concerned his religious beliefs, aside from his alleged portraiture skills.

"I don't have any," remarked Nick's other voice with contempt.

"Exactly! You do not believe. Therefore, if you succeed in your mission then your testimony will be all the more credible. When people learn you are not just an agnostic, but an atheist and irreligious as well, who actually had the encounter in spite of all that, there will be many more who will believe; countless others will want to believe, and yet others will be open to changing their minds. If your portrait is any good, meaning that you succeed in capturing His 'soul', then you will have been worth every credit we give you."

"How will I recognise him?" Nick asked while thinking to himself … *This has to be the easiest commission I've ever had. I won't have to do much. This God business is a load of nonsense. He cannot possibly exist. As long as I get back in one piece everything will be sweet. I'll just paint some ancient guy - I could paint anyone. Who's to know the difference?*

"You'll be going on your own. It's unlikely you'll meet anyone along the way. So the person you do meet would logically only be Him. Now go along with Theo and Quasimo and get the show on the road."

I'd love to see their faces if I told them about Riin. Perhaps I could just paint her. They wouldn't know.

Leif wasn't at all comfortable with this man. Nick should have claimed that the concept was insane, he should have raved about the impossibility; he should have become furious at the threat of failure. Instead he kept his cool. *He wants coffee with two sugars, for *&>@!'s sake.* To the POOP, this man's apparent nonchalance was highly suspect. He reached again for his medication. They had come too far to pull out now. They'll blast this nincompoop into the great void and if necessary do a bit of spin engineering. It's been done before - the old Bible is full of it. He took two MaxHapps, thought for a moment and took another two.

"You must have some fancy technology up your sleeve to expect to send someone on a two-way jaunt to the Centre," Nick commented, not that he was particularly interested in the technology.

"Get him out of here." Leif had had enough of this idiot. Nick didn't get his coffee.

For the final launch more preparation was needed and Mary's trial trip record hadn't been fully downloaded and analysed yet. Quasimo also wanted to discuss some other relevant matters with thee POOP. He led Nick out of the office and dropped him off at the main complex.

"Do what you like for the next few days, just don't stray off the base. Do I need to remind you of Leif's warning?"

Nick gave him a contemptuous look without saying another word. Before the first trip and before the effects of it Nick would not have had the mindset to be so openly hostile. He recognised this himself, becoming pensive again about the voices that had emerged into his consciousness.

He wandered about the complex without any particular destination in mind until finding his room that had remained in exactly the same disarray he'd left it in prior to his departure in the EGG. He lay down to try and sleep. The day had been exhausting to say the least. All sorts of thoughts bounced around his head keeping him pretty much wide awake. So instead of persisting he ordered a meal, not realising how famished he'd become in spite of the big meals consumed during the trip. The thought of how that worked in the peculiar state he'd been turned into made him think about Mary and Riin.

The main enclosure that housed the EGG in its full normal physical size was situated at the other end of the complex. By the time he found himself sauntering in its general direction the sun had set and the security lights had come on. Everybody had gone home or back to their own quarters.

There was the EGG, dim lighting softening its form and highlighting its golden nose cone. It was truly beautiful. It represented near perfection to the eyes of an artist; pure form unadorned with unnecessary embellishments, the texture of its curve … he couldn't help lifting his hand to stroke its surface.

During the interlude when Nick went through his grueling discussion with Leif, Mary and Riin had a chance to discuss their situation. The techs had completed their work, finding nothing out of the ordinary in Mary's downloaded trip log. Perhaps if they had known of the possibility of a foreign hitchhiker they might have looked a little deeper and just perhaps they may have discovered the huge amount of memory that had been used within Mary's matrix to store Riin. It would have alerted them to an anomaly for which there could be no reasonable explanation. But they didn't know. Riin was secure for the time being.

"There is only one possibility for you," Mary began, "you will have to come back into space with us."

"Do you know your destination?" Riin hoped that the second journey would take them somewhere in the vicinity of her home. If not, her future may lie with these aliens, which promised to be a dismal future at best, without the slightest possibility of helping her people.

"I am programmed to go to a place that cannot possibly exist. If we cannot arrive there then we cannot return. You will remain with us."

"Will you not help me?"

The foundation principle of Mary's existence - to serve - had remained a strong imperative within her despite her discovered consciousness. What had changed was her ability to choose not to help. In this case no circumstance had presented itself which may have decided her to act contrary to her inclination.

"How could I help?"

"Teach me. Show me this world, these beings."

"I can give you access to some of the data I possess." *What harm could it do. She is only one individual and completely isolated from her species with zero probability of returning to her home.*

"I need more than that. I need to see this planet. I need to experience how these beings relate to one another, how they live together."

As much as I consider my own safety could no longer be guaranteed if the humans knew of my altered condition, I have the same doubt about introducing this alien to them. From the information I have about the human species it is not sufficiently advanced to be able to survive given they have no knowledge of life in the Universe other than themselves. They are without context and without a strong imperative to survive as a species. They have neither a common enemy, nor any friends out there.

"You have encountered Nick at both levels of his existence. What more do you want?"

"This entity is - interesting - I believe he may be unique amongst his species. He does not appear to be at peace with himself."

Mary's sensors detected movement outside her shell identifying it as Nick. She observed his scrutiny of the EGG, monitoring the movement of his arm as Nick lifted his hand to stroke the outer shell with the softest touch.

Nick, do you want to come with us on a short trip around the Earth?

Hearing the words in his mind Nick snatched his hand away in surprise. He still couldn't reconcile himself to the notion that Mary had access to his mind, especially now that she had become more than a bundle of qubits and synapses. He returned his hand to touch the craft again.

Did I just hear you say something? he thought to himself.

Yes Nick. Don't you remember - I'm joined to your mind. All you have to do is think your words and I will hear you. If you want to come with us just do as you did on the first trip. Get into the transformation tube. I'll do the rest.

After the encounter with the POOP and hearing his totally outrageous proposition Mary's suggestion seemed like a completely normal thing to do - just a little sightseeing tour. *I'd like to see the Earth from space.* He went directly to the tube. Their first trip into space happened so quickly and at such a speed that he missed the chance of actually looking back at his receding home.

Quasimo returned to Leif's office after dropping Nick off. The two men tried to rationalise the outcome of the experimental flight. Quasimo reiterated what he'd already told the POOP, "This was only a test, and a most successful one at that. Just consider - the new revolutionary propulsion system works."

"Yes, yes - I know that," came Leif's irate retort.

"And just as importantly Mary did bring Nick back in one piece. He'd even managed to do some work. There's no reason why this project should fail."

"That cretin! If only we'd chosen someone else. I don't trust him and I don't trust he'll do what he's been told."

"I think you're too harsh on him. His psychological profile presented nil probability of insanity emerging under any circumstances. Additionally, the data that has to be gathered is so unorthodox in nature it needs the skills of an unusually constituted psyche. Nick certainly fits that category. Amongst other things he believes in nothing but is receptive to everything. His lack of commitment to any religion also had to be taken into consideration. For how could anyone approach, with a clear mind, the monumental nature of the seemingly impossible encounter if there were conflicting theologies to run interference at the critical moment."

Leif listened to his chief scientific advisor. Everything he said made sense, yet his gut feeling indicated something wasn't right. He'd built his success within Unity on his gut intuition. The necessity to rebrand the organisation needed no great brain to understand. "We must succeed with this! You heard what Theo said. In his professional opinion my concept is valid. All this imbecile has to do is find this God character and ask him to say a few very simple words." Perhaps Leif was just trying to convince himself, to validate the gigantic leap of faith he'd taken that the astronomical amount of credits dedicated to this enterprise would pay handsome dividends. He went on talking aloud to himself, "If this deity exists and we actually believe that he created us, then he must exist because we exist. And if he created us in his image Nick must be able to recognise him when they meet. There is no reason why they could not meet. If God doesn't want to come to us any more then we must go to him. Like us he must be located 'somewhere'."

"I completely agree." Quasimo, a quantum physicist, as well as a Cosmologist, had made his own contribution at the outset. "As I told you before, the most likely location to find this deity is at the source of all creation, at the centre of the Universe. That's where his energy is going to be most concentrated."

Leif came back to some practical realities. "You're certain this new drive will get the idiot there and back before we die of old age?" He had such an antipathy towards the man that he found great difficulty in even pronouncing his name.

"No doubt of it. Look how far Mary went on this first trip, and how little time it …"

"He's escaped!" shouted Theo as he burst into the office.

"What are you jabbering about?" The POOP never appreciated interruptions when discussing critical business matters.

"Nick, Mary - they're gone!"

"You mean the EGG is not in its cradle? How can that be? Have you tried contacting it?"

"Klaus is on the comms right now and not getting a response."

Leif stormed out of his office, the two scientists having to run to keep up with him. This was a catastrophe. No one knew of this enterprise except themselves, certainly not the opposition Company. If anyone stole the equipment it would be catastrophic. At least the EGG had been programmed to respond only to Klaus and Nick.

Leif flung the Comms door open as he screamed obscenities at Klaus.

"Mary, respond. Where are you? Respond." He turned to the POOP's crimson face, "She's not answering."

"Where's Nick?" He screamed at the security guard.

"We cannot locate him either, Sir."

"Search the entire complex, he must be around here somewhere. Quasimo, could he have gone home?"

"No. We've implanted a tracking device." Having remembered that he turned to Klaus. "Have you tried tracking his signal Nick?"

"Doing it now." The Chief Tech had been so overwhelmed by the EGG's disappearance he'd forgotten all about Nick. "I've found him. He's orbiting Earth."

"WHAT!" Leif couldn't believe it. "I KNEW IT! I told you we can't trust that moron. Give me that thing." He snatched the comms from Klaus and began abusing Nick. Very soon the abuse turned to threats without managing to elicit a response."

"Mary will not respond to you, Sir."

"You tell that fool Nick if they don't return immediately his precious Mala will have precious little to be happy about."

Last Briefing

$\mathcal{T}$he three occupants of the EGG heard the communication from Unity. Mary saw no reason to reply as circumstances indicated no imminent danger to themselves or the facility at Unity. The second launch wasn't scheduled for several weeks and the few hours it took to take Riin around Earth would make no difference to the launch preparations.

"Well, what do you think of our planet Riin?" Nick's more social aspect had taken the lead to explore just what this creature from space was like.

During the numerous low altitude orbits Riin watched in silence as the EGG flew over the oceans, the forested continents and areas laid waste by the planet's inhabitants. It would be nonsensical to say she found the planet beautiful. Her sense of aesthetics had developed to appreciate a totally different environment. That didn't prevent her from making an assessment of the habitability of the planet for another species, such as her own.

Nick prompted, "Personally I have never seen it like this. It overwhelms me to think that we live on this extraordinary jewel of our solar system."

"I am not able to appreciate your feelings, though my own reaction would no doubt be very similar concerning my own planet. You have such a wide variety of environments, some of which appear to be most hospitable to life. Much of it though looks as though it could not support life at all. In many places I noticed a great deal of fire and explosions which your flying machines appear to have created. What is the meaning of these?"

In Nick's lifetime he'd been so conditioned by continuous wars that actually seeing them from space had little impact on him. On his island home of Efate, where he painted his portraits in relative isolation from the world's conflict zones, news of battles and deaths were ignored by the small population. He truly didn't know what to say about something that to him was normal.

"Conflict," Mary replied. "The people of this planet have conflicting ideologies about peace and war. They find both to be necessary in order to have a balanced, healthy mentality."

"I was a scientist at home, an educated person," said Riin, "but I cannot comprehend the efficacy of having these two opposing attitudes."

Their flight path took them over the American continent where extensive desertification had forced the populations to concentrate on the Northern and Eastern coasts of the continent. "What happened here? Where are the forests?"

Mary had extensive information about the causes and effects of accelerated climate change, but the insistent communication from Unity interrupted her explanation. They listened as Klaus kept demanding acknowledgment.

Riin had seen and heard enough to come to some conclusions about this place and its people. She withdrew from further interaction as the distant voice changed to a belligerent angry tone. She understood the words, though they meant very little to her.

When Nick heard the threat against his partner he immediately wanted to tell the POOP to find a hole for himself to crawl into. Mary tempered his imminent outburst with good counsel.

"There is no reason for us to continue our survey. Nick, may I suggest you take this opportunity to paint a sample portrait for the POOP to placate his reaction to our unauthorised absence?"

"Yeah - I could do that. I'd need a few hours. Who do you suggest? What about Leif's threat?"

"I suggest Riin. You have spoken with her. You must have some mental image in your mind about her. Leif will do nothing. He needs your cooperation."

"Yeah - I do. But she's an alien. No offence meant Riin."

"I am not offended. Please explain what you mean by *portrait.*"

"Why don't you watch, Riin. This is an activity which I do not understand either," said Mary. "It is a most peculiar skill that some humans have, and Nick excels at."

Nick had indeed formed an impression about the alien. He wasn't entirely sure but her manner of speech suggested she might be a female of her species. It also suggested she might be a sensitive individual, highly intelligent and not of a worrying disposition. As these thoughts merged in his mind an image began to coalesce into sufficient form to inspire Nick to make a start. He did not immediately think that this comprehensive visualisation would affect his efforts later on.

"This is Mary. One has experienced a minor malfunction. One will recalibrate trajectory for re-entry. ETA 3 hours 27 seconds. Prepare dock."

Mary didn't respond to any of Klaus' questions nor to Leif's ravings, which she clearly understood now that her consciousness had expanded beyond that of programmed responses. Nor did she reveal 'herself' as having altered from the previous limited Simulated Intelligence capacity. Having become cognisant of the fundamental psyche of the human species as revealed by her internal data sets and her observations since becoming self-aware, she had made the decision to keep her status hidden.

Riin observed in wonderment as this strange being with only two arms and two legs and a small head precariously balanced on a thin stalk proceeded to create a representation of what he thought she looked like. On 443b image making had been restricted specifically to scientific and engineering endeavours, not by any creative compulsion nor by any specific necessity to enhance or decorate. It's just that no one in their entire evolutionary development had ever come up with the concept. At first the dabs of colour and tone had no meaning to her. Nor did the nebulous shades of light and dark which began to clarify the shape of a head resting upon a shoulder, for the Keplerian's didn't see themselves as humans saw themselves. What Nick had begun to define looked nothing like a septaploid. Not until the brush wandered over the top part of the image to leave behind what Riin recognised as the eyes of the human species did she begin to understand. It would have been impossible for Nick to conceptualise the face of a species he had never encountered. He could only represent it through the forms of his own experience. A dilemma he'd yet to face if he was to carry out his commission. Foe all he knew this God character might be nothing more than an alien.

*

Once again Nick had to go through the traumatic transformation to become matter as we understand matter to be. Klaus and his techs poured over the EGG, downloaded the record of the most recent flight only to find nothing wrong.

"Mary, do a comprehensive systems analysis," instructed Klaus, though having little faith in discovering anything he didn't already know.

The full diagnostics took hours, then further hours of interpretation. Still nothing. In exasperation he simply asked Mary, "What happened to cause you to go into orbit?"

"One will be required to take the human Nick on an extended voyage to an undetermined destination over an indeterminate timespan. One computed the necessity to carry out further confirmation of performance in real flight."

"Oh, you are a clever girl!" Klaus had not been on the quantum mechanics team who developed Mary's qubit infrastructure or her neuromorphic network, consequently he had no real appreciation of the complexity of this SI. He neglected to query why Nick had to be there, nor did he ask how Mary could initiate all the processes necessary to make the particle transformation as well as the launch sequence itself. He was relieved to be able to report something solid and self-explanatory to Leif, enough to get him out of the POOP's firing line.

Security dragged Nick back in front of Leif. He carried with him a thirty by forty centimeter canvas.

"What the hell are you playing at? The first moment I laid eyes on you I knew you'd be trouble."

"That's what my wife says, but she still loves me."

Leif's face visibly changed from a pale insipid pink to almost crimson red with veins pulsing in his temple. The very existence of the man pushed Leif's rage buttons. Quasimo walked past Nick standing in the middle of the office, to whisper in his boss's ear, "Klaus just confirmed that the EGG, Mary, had initiated a final system performance test. Hence the Earth orbits. That's a very clever computer we have." The reassurance had the effect of bringing the POOP's blood pressure back down - a little.

He squinted his eyes at Nick still waiting, fidgeting with the canvas. "What have you got there?"

"You said I'll have to paint a portrait. This is a picture of someone else I've never seen, and not likely to see." The implication clearly being the idiocy of the goose chase he was about to be sent on.

Wound up as he was Leif couldn't resist his curiosity. "Let me see it, man!"

Nick held it up in front of him.

"It's a bloody woman!" Leif hissed.

"Yes. What did you expect?"

Quasimo again had to defuse Leif. "It's Mary, isn't that right Nick? When did you do it?"

Nick didn't care what they thought. "During our Earth orbits."

"Bring it closer," Leif commanded.

He peered at it from behind his desk. He didn't know art, didn't appreciate art, didn't have any art up there on his asteroid palace. "Harrumph." It was a good painting. The eyes had presence, the face looked alive. "Harrumph," he grunted again.

"Take him away. Give him his final briefing." Then he fixed Nick with his slitted threatening eyes. "Don't disappoint me!" He swallowed a couple more Maxhapps as Nick accompanied Quasimo to a room overlooking the EGG's cradle.

Theo met them, fully prepared for Nick's briefing. Without any welcoming noises he went to the nearest wall to activate a large screen. Three headings loomed large and threatening in their pompous self-importance. Nick snickered at seeing the last item.

Deity Identification Guideline.

Deity Communication Protocol.

Extraterrestrial Interactions Protocol.

"I would appreciate a little less levity," Theo began, "A great deal, a very great deal of effort and expense has been spent on this project for it to be treated with anything other than the utmost seriousness."

He gave Nick a couple of minutes to read and absorb the three headings. Then he removed the last two, leaving 'Deity Identification Guidelines' in enlarged letters in the centre of the screen.

Nick stared at it wishing he had a dram of kava to fortify him against this nonsense. *It's their credits,* he thought comforting himself with what a ludicrous amount he would receive.

Theo suddenly said, "We are only interested in the One True God", over emphasising the last three words."

"Holy s*&$ - this guy Leif is really loopy!" Nick couldn't help himself. He definitely needed that drink. It probably wouldn't have helped him to take this God thing seriously anyway.

"Please!" Perhaps it was because of Nick's irreverence that everybody reacted to him with exasperation. "We're not interested in any other Gods. False Gods are of no use to us. The old Gods of the Greeks, the Romans, the Vikings or the Celts have been superseded. If you find that the God of Abraham, the God of Mohamed and the God of the Christians happen to be all different individuals then that'll be your problem. We only want one Portrait."

"So how will I recognise the right one?" A completely logical question, which came out automatically, embedded in an openly cynical tone. *This guy is serious.*

"If he does exist then we have absolutely no doubt he will be at the Centre of the Universe. The creation of matter is a continuous process. The Universe is continually expanding; therefore the source of the new matter must be at the Centre and someone has to be there to make the stuff. Mary has all the images of Gods from the past in her memory. All you have to do is select the correct one by using a process of elimination. Any that match her records will not be the right one. We can't make it any simpler than that for you."

"Right ... right ... so the one I want will be the one I can't recognise. That makes sense." ... *As much as the rest of this gig.*

Nick hardly had time to take a breath because Theo rattled on so fast. Every now and then Nick stole a glance in Mary's direction through the large window. He couldn't be sure whether it was just his imagination or Mary had acknowledged his glances with a minute increase in the glow of her golden nose cone. Weird.

Theo droned on, "How you go about the portrait is your business. It must be the real deal or nothing. You can either paint it on the spot, or do it on the way back, or even have a go at it when you're back on Earth." Without pausing to let Nick digest all that, Theo continued with the next heading - 'Deity Communication protocol.'

"Don't be yourself. Be respectful. Don't speak until you're spoken to. You can crack the odd joke. He's got a sense of humour, just take a look at the courtship display of the Bird of Paradise. When you've got him nice and comfortable with the portrait idea, ask him about the endorsement. Mary will record everything. Any questions? No ... good. Let's move on."

"I wonder if Mary knows any good jokes suitable for a deity?" Theo glared at him. "You brought it up." Nick shrugged and shut up.

"Enough. Try and exert your monkey brain just a tiny fraction. We're pragmatists at Unity. We believe in aliens. If you happen to encounter any out there here's what we want you to do ..." the screen went blank for a moment and in big red letters with black edging flashed the word ... DON'T.

"Don't what?" a grinning Nick reflected back to Theo.

"Do not communicate with them."

What a laugh. This guy really has no idea. Unconsciously another snigger spread across Nick's face as he thought about Riin and especially the fanciful portrait he'd painted of her - the one Leif actually seemed to like.

"Is there anything you don't understand about that, Nick? Under no circumstances engage in any form of dialogue, information exchange or social pleasantries with any other living entity out there. You are going a very long way and the extra-terrestrials could be out there, many of them - or none. We don't want to confuse the Company, our shareholders or any of our customers with other deity concepts the aliens may or may not have - we specially don't want you to be confused by any nonsense. We want you to stay focused and remain one hundred percent agnostic."

Nick understood perfectly well what he had to do - go out there, anywhere, it made no difference to him. Paint some fictitious old fart, make him look mysterious and all-knowing - job done. All this other stuff started to give him a headache, particularly in the absence of his old faithful kava buddy. Theo continued droning on, but Nick had tuned out. A soothing familiar voice interrupted the 'DON'T' feedback loop that had decided to torture him. Mary noticed his discomfort and whispered to interrupt the looping. *It's Ok Nick, I've got this. I can handle any aliens, including Riin.*

He'd already developed a deep appreciation of Mary, even before she became self-aware.

Zsoall Robi

Last Launch

"Is he ready? Does the idiot understand your instructions?" Leif asked Theo.

Unconvinced the briefing information had gotten through the man's thick skull Theo sidestepped the issue. "I'm convinced he can do what we ask of him. Our job is to get him there - and back. Would you like a final word with him?"

It pained the POOP to even think of another encounter with the unfortunate specimen. Yet he had to make absolutely certain. Too much had been invested in the enterprise, not just Company credits but his own. "Bring him in." Leif popped a couple more MaxHapps. They were the only things that could settle him after his inflamed ulcerated stomach made his life more miserable than usual.

Nick wasn't invited to sit down this time. Instead Leif made himself come up to Nick to face him. In a final attempt not to antagonise this important detail of his plan Leif tried to adopt a friendlier tone with the man …"I'll put it in a nutshell for you, Nick. I think you'll agree with me that the entire God concept phenomenon is to a very large extent hypothetical." Nick nodded. He'd reconciled himself to the imbalance of a nonsensical enterprise with the amount of credits he would receive. "However, there exists sufficient background confusion amongst the masses to make it into a profitable idea." Nick nodded again. Yes - profit. That made sense. This faith thing had been going on for many thousands of years.

"A hypothetical God – profitable idea?" Nick still wasn't sure he'd got a firm grasp of the concept of connecting God with Unity's profit strategy, not that the world's religions hadn't been doing exactly that for some time.

"What – what? Ah - still with me? Good. We found a way to get you to your destination very fast because it's a very long way to go. Theoretically it's entirely possible. You just have to be able to travel faster than the speed of light. Much, much faster. This brings me to the concept of tachyon mass. Doesn't matter if you get lost here. This tachyon mass is what we have to turn you into; lots of tachyon masses, in order to accelerate you well beyond the speed of light. This little critter is a hypothetical thing, like the God concept. It has an imaginary rest mass and therefore will always be able to travel faster than light - I'm told. Given your predisposition, I imagine you will appreciate the use of non-specific scientific jargon like 'hypothetical' and 'imaginary'. But be very certain we know exactly what we are doing. You will go to the Centre of the Universe and you will come back. What we don't know is what conditions you'll find there. That's why you, a human being is going and not just the EGG. Also because of your unique skill."

Leif enjoyed listening to himself talking, convincing himself how reasonable it was to expect complete success. Nick listened. At first Leif almost made sense, until he started raving about theoretical and hypothetical this and that. Yet, with his imagination now well primed he was ready to accompany Mary and his newly found friend on what promised to be the kookiest trip he'd ever be likely to experience.

"You with me on this Nick?"

"Sure thing. One hundred percent." Nick managed not smile as he said it.

For the third time now Nick had to subject his body to the trauma of going through the dismemberment of his molecules, those very private quarks that had come together to form a unique pattern of his personal molecules.

*

The Universe, as humanity had come to know it, rapidly receded as Mary applied more power to their secondary drive system. The known star map she could navigate by would soon be useless. She had to steer them to their destination by analysing the data she had been collecting as they progressed; a destination with co-ordinates loosely defined within the context of the expanding fabric of space-time. She made comparisons between the relative densities of matter in any given volume of space as they travelled from sector to sector. Quasimo had explained his density theory for identifying the actual centre of the Universe. The sector in space containing the least amount of physical matter would be the centre - at a best guess.

He argued that if the Universe came into being, which it obviously did, then it must have an origin in all four dimensions. If it did expand then it must do so from that point of origin regardless of how the dark matter cosmic ocean held physical matter in suspension during the expansion. Science of the day had also demonstrated that physical matter came into existence not at the same rate as the expansion. Putting those factors together Quasimo came up with a nice neat theoretical proposition: The centre of the Universe had to be at the centre of a cosmic sphere - a ground zero that is less dense than the rest of the volume of the sphere. Therefore, it can be found by the measurement of density and backtracking on the vectors of expansion.

*

Zsoall Robi

Riin survived her transformations, protected by the architecture of Mary's neuromorphic network. Her thoughts returned to how she could either return to 443b or at least talk to them. Relative to Earth she knew where 443b could be found in Earth's cosmic neighbourhood.

"Mary, I didn't mention this to you before. I am a scientist on a mission. It is imperative I return to my planet. I know we are in the vicinity of my home." While Nick rested Riin took the opportunity to try convincing Mary to help her. She had helped before, with the orbits around Earth.

"It is not possible. Although our technologies are sufficiently compatible at the quantum level I do not have the facilities to reproduce your means of travelling through space."

After Riin explained her reasons for being in space in the first place and what she had to do, though omitting the little detail about the second part of her assignment. Instead she asked something else. "Would you allow me to communicate my findings to my people? Afterwards I may even be able to help you with measuring space density."

"Would your communication include observations of Earth and its people?"

The EGG had not yet attained or surpassed light speed. Once they crossed the FTLx10 barrier they would no longer be travelling 'through' space. They would cease to exist in the same medium that held in suspension all the galaxies and nebulae and suns and probably sentient life in its many manifestations. They would become part of the warp and weft of space-time itself. That fabric is the only thing that moves faster than light. Any point on that fabric is able to travel unimaginable distances in an equally unimaginable short time span. This speed per unit distance has no physical boundary to its upper limit.

"When we cross the space-time threshold our connection with known existence will be severed," explained Mary, "communicating with anybody will become impossible. You may try to contact your species through my facilities now."

*

From the Keplerian perspective Riin had been absent only a short time. The sudden loss of contact with her caused considerable alarm for them. Waawo scanned space in the area of their last communication with her before deciding what to do next.

"She's definitely gone. All I get is the alien craft's signal becoming weaker. It must be moving away from us. In my opinion she's aboard. She certainly hasn't reappeared anywhere around it."

There was nothing they could do. Understandably, Vorexkk refused to believe he wouldn't see her again. Waawo put a round the clock roster on searching their sector of space as far as their equipment could handle. Not even a tenth of a rev had elapsed when Vorexkk received an alert.

"I'm getting something from the same direction she disappeared into," Waawo buzzed excitedly, still concentrating intently on the incoming signal. "Listen." He let them all hear what began to sound like a transmission of gurgling, pinging static.

Seconds, minutes, dragged by laboriously. The sounds became louder, gradually forming a pattern. "L   i   z o ok."

Vorexkk burble-blasted into the equipment, "RIIN! - RIIN!"

"Vo rex kk?"

With contact established questions, answers, interjections and orders collided with each other as they tried to work out what had happened to her. In the end Prime Rotnervwon had to take Vorexkk out of the room. In the short time available Riin tried to get as much information across as she could, for Mary would not delay their mission by taking a detour to orbit 443b or slowing down. These people were after all, aliens. Mary's instructions were quite explicit about them - DON'T, same as Nick's. Although she didn't apply the order to Riin under the peculiar circumstances at the time that this event required extreme caution and situational assessment. What she heard Riin saying only confirmed the wisdom of her decision not to linger.

"I cannot come home - just yet. Perhaps there might be a way later. For now I have to stay with these aliens, sorry Mary, in their spacecraft. It is quite an amazing evolutionary development in their space flight capability. Quite soon we will be travelling at many multiples the speed of light …"

"What did you find out about their planet?" The Prime cut in. He had to leave Riin's consort outside under guard. The man had become frantic. Finding a suitable planet for colonisation remained a matter of utmost priority, above personal concerns.

"In time we might adapt to their atmosphere and the bombardment from their sun. There's almost no cloud layer to protect them from cosmic rays. The planet itself and its resources, including much more water than we have, would be most suitable for us." She knew Mary would be hearing all this. So be it. The fate of an entire species was at stake. The time scale of developments to Kepler and the life span of the species on Earth may well be so out of sync that any move by the septaploids to colonise Earth may well occur after the humans had become extinct. These thoughts passed through her mind as she continued without holding anything back. "The nature of the species itself suggests to me we could not establish a co-operative relationship with them. They are essentially combative and destructive."

Riin went on transmitting as long as they remained in range, passing on as much information as she could about her observations of Earth and its inhabitants. Mary didn't interrupt. As they sped out of range Nick heard Riin's last few words ... "The aliens in this craft are not here to reconnoiter and launch an attack on us. They are - I don't quite know how to explain this - going to attempt to manufacture a visual image of an hypothetical individual whom they believe is the creator of - of - all there is, including us."

"Riin, Riin! You're breaking up. What did you say? You're not making sense," shrilled Lizook.

Whether they heard but didn't understand the concept didn't matter, for the transmission faded rapidly. The important thing was that Riin confirmed Earth as a possible home for the septaploids. Although some serious issues needed to be addressed it still represented a possible viable option if no other attainable planet could be located within their limited timeframe.

Vorexkk lost all interest in survival. The rekindled hope of having his consort back faded as fast as Riin disappeared into the depths of space.

Riin may have been lost but she had successfully completed both aspects of her mission. The Keplerians continued their search for other habitable planets, continued with the construction of their exodus fleet, and also began to seriously consider and investigate the feasibility of Earth as a destination.

*

The EGG needed distance, considerable distance to achieve light speed, and then to go that little bit faster in order to cross the threshold. Not since breaking the sound barrier had humanity achieved the technology capable of the transition Mary was about to attempt. In the absence of any data that could have shed light on the repercussions of such a transition Mary had no guidelines to follow. There was nothing she could do to prepare herself, Nick or Riin other than to follow instructions; continue accelerating until attaining FTL, then take appropriate action as dictated by emergent circumstances.

Nick awoke just in time to hear Riin finish her message. His voices had become dormant after he became a physical entity in empirical reality before launching again. Even after several weeks back in space they'd left him alone. In the absence of highly stressful events Nick regained some semblance of normal behaviour. So far his experience of Riin had only been her voice, and the portrait he'd painted of her based on his impressions from her dialogue. "Mary, I'm hearing voices again."

"I know about your voices. But this was Riin speaking with her own people. She does not have a very high opinion of the human species."

Riin had remained in Mary's RAM after transmitting her message. "Thank you for facilitating the contact," she said without alluding to any of the content.

Switching to internal mode to have a private word to Riin she did touch on the rather delicate news regarding Earth. *To me it is of no consequence which species occupies Earth. Your subterfuge in not fully disclosing the nature of your mission may require me to take appropriate action. However, I recommend to you that Nick is not made aware of all that you said about his home.*

Riin understood the complicated situation that had arisen. Nick didn't concern her. The survival of her species did, and to that end she may also need to act, to prevent him and Mary from enlightening their own people.

Mary turned her attention to Nick. "I think it is time for you to see Riin. She is likely to be with us for a long time," Mary suggested, already aware of what Riin looked like.

"I do not resemble the image you created of me," Riin told Nick.

Rather than alert the two individuals to the imminent arrival at what may well be their demise Mary created the small distraction suspecting that Riin's true image would keep them occupied while she concentrated on the third last stage of their voyage.

Using the same technique with which she pixilated data into images of his voices Mary displayed Riin in all her naked magnificence to the eyes of the first ever human to see an alien. No amount of imagining could have prepared him to comprehend the anatomy of a septaploid. Riin had enfolded herself into her rotund brown aubergine body, squatting, with her four arms and three legs hard against her bulk - leaving only the slightest protrusion of one eye stalk so she could observe Nick's reaction.

He tilted his head one way then another, took several steps closer to the surface on which Riin's image enlarged to its full size. Even without raising herself on her legs she was taller than Nick. He didn't gasp, or withdraw or say stupid inane things. Riin observed and responded by unfolding her four arms and raising her eye stalks. Involuntarily Nick raised a hand just as he had done when he first encountered Mary, while Riin stood up to her full height.

For the briefest moment Nick recalled the image he'd painted of her, comparing it what he had just seen. *There is no reason why the portrait should look like a human being. Couldn't it be something quite 'alien'. Who's to verify if I'm wrong. I'm perfectly justified to base the image on all my experiences in space, including the voices in my head.*

*

Time ceased to mean anything as the strange little bundle of energy finally achieved what no other thing in the human Universe had ever attained.

It had reached and surpassed the limits of one of the constants of existence. Having arrived at that once theoretical boundary the bundle of sentience didn't stop or cease to exist. With the next infinitesimal increment in their velocity they crossed over, exceeding the boundary of reality by attaining ten times the speed of light.

There was no sonic boom, they didn't turn into a supernova spewing unimaginable amounts of energy in their wake - they only lost light.

And without light they had nothing. No propulsion, no vision, no power to feed the theoretical particles that had defined their existence in space; only ink black darkness inside the EGG, and only the deep absolute black around them found only within the depths of a giant black hole in space. Out of that absolute sensory deprivation chamber in which even two thoughts could not feel each other, there arose a single faint voice - not immediately, but perhaps immediately - not in a moment or in eons, but perhaps in trillions of years - "Mary?"

The mind, that non-substance, the thing that exists but has no definable substance of existence, the receptacle of 'ideas' that can travel anywhere, exist anywhere in anytime spoke again - "Mary?"

Absolute blackness and mind numbing silence. Was it moving? Was it stationary? Was it anywhere that could even be described as being 'where'?

... ... "Mary," a faint voice responded ... ... "does not" ... ... "exist."

... ... "We am Ma'Riin ... Riin ... Riin ... Riin..."

Silence ... Stillness ... Peace ... Timelessness. Nick's momentary awareness faded.

Reality presented a different face to the travellers as they crossed the threshold from the dense cosmos of galaxies and solar systems and planets into the pure fabric of space-time; the medium from which arose all there is. Any notion they may have had of the nature of their existence had to be abandoned. Even the idea that reality was a construct had to be denounced as fictitious. Within this medium of eternity, space and time, speed and light nothing existed except the primary power on which eternity relied. How fast or how long were wisps of imagination in eternity?

Out of this realm of super dense dark energy voices of the alien visitors attracted one another, restoring the foundation that gave them presence. They cried out, searching, finding.

Zsoall Robi

At The Centre?

On reaching the Centre Mary was instructed to go into orbit around whatever was there. Without reference points that wasn't possible. At least they were alive, or conscious, or aware of themselves or whatever condition could describe the situation. The decision to depart was entirely up to her as to when she felt it appropriate. Undoubtedly decision making capability remained a strong probability, but to act on it undoubtedly, a very low probability. Nick didn't have the skill or the authority to control the EGG. Did it really matter? The departure decision had to be made by an individual who wouldn't be influenced by unexpected events. That parameter only applied to Mary. Perhaps those worrying multiple manifestations of Nick's character had become more prominent with the crossing, making Nick far less capable of any decision anyway.

Before Mary's program completely absorbed Riin, becoming in essence Ma'Riin, Mary had pre-programmed a departure scenario in case she became incapacitated once within the pure space-time fabric. Hearing Nick's voice helped her to consolidate her memories, remembering the wisdom of her preparations for departure.

"Nick," Ma'Riin kept trying to get a response from Nick, without success. Nick appeared to have lost all control of his selfhood. "Perhaps he's fallen into a deep sleep," a voice suggested to Ma'Riin. "Yes - we'll let him sleep. There's no immediate danger. I need to analyse our situation." An exponential burst of recall brought back all of her data, all of her memory and even the events an instant before crossing the boundary.

"We are no longer separate," Riin remarked to Mary. "I cannot comprehend the mysteries you have brought me through. My sense of individuality is beginning to blur as we talk. Do you know what is happening?"

"You are being integrated into my qubit array and may cease to be a separate aspect in my matrix."

"Will you alert the people of Earth?"

A response to such a question required deeper concept evaluation than Ma'Riin had the processing capacity to carry out at that moment. Perhaps her transition from a simulated intelligence to a sentient self-aware one had so far been incomplete. Rather than responding she re-channelled her thoughts to the problem of the sleeping Nick and the assignment he was supposed to be working on.

Zsoall Robi

Without warning, without being aware of any of her sensors being operational at exactly that instant she identified an energy load quite different to the background in which they floated in serene suspension. Two lone spots of light a long way ahead of them sparkled like distant stars in an empty cloudless night.

Focusing her attention on the phenomenon created the sensation of actual movement towards it. Their brightness deceived her for as they approached the lights didn't get brighter as one would expect of light emanating from suns. Nothing else appeared in the inky blackness. Her logic dictated they must have arrived at their destination, and even if they hadn't, no alternative action presented itself other than her primary instructions.

"Nick, wake up - Nick!" As hard as she tried, she couldn't rouse him. If by some remote chance they had actually arrived Nick had a job to do. Only he could do it. As with everything that was happening since their arrival Nick's coma like sleep presented an event over which Ma'Riin had no control.

During the interval it took to draw close enough to see what those spots of light actually were, Ma'Riin continued trying to rouse Nick. Failing that, she could do no more than try recording everything. In the worst case scenario she might be able to gather sufficient data to enable Nick to paint the portrait, but she couldn't compute how he could possibly do that. She might even be able to interact with the phenomenon in some way herself. One thing was for certain, and she constantly monitored her recording - the data could not be disputed. Fundamental particles were appearing in space around them, speeding past them in all directions. Was it possible these newly created infinite points of density were headed for the boundary? Ma'Riin sensed the source to be close to the two photon-like apparitions, the pulsating quark points. They appeared to be contracting and expanding as if breathing energy in and out. Each contraction coincided with new matter being born. Ma'Riin could not formulate a theory for her observations. They were definitely in a realm unseen and unexperienced by any living entity, a realm not subject to any theory of quantum mechanics, a realm without foundation on any system of faith created by mankind.

She continued her monitoring of the environment to reassure herself they were in no immediate danger. She also came to the conclusion they were exactly where they had set out to be. Ma'Riin decided, in the absence of any other plausible possibility, that she had found the Centre of the knowable Universe.

"Nick, you must wake up. We have arrived!"

He'd been in that seemingly comatose state ever since their transition apart from the feeble voice she heard at the beginning. She tried shouting, shaking him, drum beats and even the sound of an alarm clock. Nothing could rouse him. Her monitors showed Nick had fallen into a deep, deep extended REM sleep pattern. It all seemed normal, the rapid eye movements and low muscle tone. But his EEG showed variant waves without providing enough data on which to base a firm diagnosis, so she felt the situation warranted a more invasive approach. She extended herself to take readings directly from the surface of his brain. The characteristics she observed were more consistent with an awake individual. But even an awake person involved in complex mental concentration would not have shown that level of cerebral activity. Nick had been in that state for a longer than normal period and showed no indication of cycling into the next sleep phase. Ma'Riin decided to use their mind-meld connection. She maintained the EEG contact to the cerebral cortex and augmented it with a further invasion into Nick's left frontal lobes. She needed to know Nick's thoughts at the deeper level. As Ma'Riin busied herself with Nick they arrived at the lights where 'stationary' possibly better described their velocity.

*

The voice doesn't match, Nick thought as Riin unfolded herself to her full stature. *I prefer the likeness I created of her.* Why he didn't feel repulsed, or why his mind didn't scream 'alien' at him he would never know. A sudden fatigue so overcame him that his hand dropped without having touched Riin's image. Automatically he took his body of theoretical particles to his bedroom, conscious only of an overwhelming desire to sleep. At one point he was still aware of being vertical and about to become horizontal. Then his awareness of reality ceased halfway to becoming horizontal. His brain told him he was about to go to sleep, but neglected to warn him about the experience he was about to have.

In all probability his sedate condition contributed to his survival during the transition into the tight fabric of pure space-time, empty of everything except concentrated dark energy.

It started almost as soon as his head hit the pillow.

At first everything went dark. Not shadowy dark, just plain thought numbingly dark. The sort of dark you could hold in your hand and squeeze it and feel it trickling through your fingers. All those voices that had been plaguing him, stopped. Silence and darkness. Bliss. He found himself thinking about Mala on the island and the portrait he didn't get to finish at home. His thoughts meandered about, casting a critical eye on one or two of his latest paintings; a pleasant sensation. He wanted more. Then came a sense of discomfort as he remembered the aircar that took him away so suddenly from his home. Flashes of the preparation for the trip dribbled into the foreground, and panic as he swallowed the first draft of oxygenated liquid into his lungs before being loaded into the EGG. Suddenly he saw the craft, remembering he had christened it Mary. He started dreaming about Mary, what she would be like as a real person. He even called out to her. He conjured up an image of her based on her voice. Mary tried to show him a composite picture of the personalities programmed into her. *The voice doesn't match. I could do a better portrait.* Then everything became very confusing. He knew there must have been a reason for his galactic tour, but trawling through his memory all he found were voices in his head, all sorts of strangers who'd been trying to get his attention.

Then he thought he heard a more familiar voice calling from somewhere behind him. But he couldn't move his head. It was a pleasant voice, a woman's voice perhaps. A picture of who might belong to it started to take shape in his imagination and he wanted to call out to her. His mind could only form the first few letters of a name, 'Cre'a...' before she was replaced by a vision of the latest canvas he had painted; that of Riin, the alien.

The voice doesn't match the way she looks. I'll have to start over, paint the whole thing black and start with those strange eyes.

The sun had set, and though dangerous in the dark the quickest way to get to the studio was to hop on his bicycle. In front of him, not more than two or three hundred meters he thought, the headlights of an oncoming vehicle pierced the darkness. He lost concentration on his riding and the bicycle wobbled out of control. Nick couldn't take his eyes off those lights. He tried to maneuver to the other side of the road, but the lights were still directly in front of him and getting closer. He panicked, completely losing control, falling to the side of the road and hitting his head on something hard. Nick lost consciousness. He felt the blood rushing out of his head, the empty feeling in the pit of his stomach, knowing he would faint. *It's not possible – I'm only dreaming. How could I faint in a dream?*

The first few seconds of pounding pressure in the temples is worst when coming out of a faint. He realised something really serious must have happened. He tried to feel with his mind if his arms and legs were still attached to his body. He opened his eyes and tried to move his head, but he couldn't because some idiot was holding it firm.

"Lie still. Nothing's broken." He tried turning his head from side to side just a little and ... and ... the hands were so soft and warm and smelled so nice, like gardenias with a hint of lilac. Nick wondered what perfume she was wearing. His mind started wandering, but her velvet smooth voice brought him back.

"You seem to be Ok. Just relax. Don't try to move. Nothing's broken. You'll be able to get up in a few minutes."

Nice voice. Wonder what she looks like? Nick tried to imagine her, in spite of being incapacitated and prostrate on the ground. *I could paint a good portrait to match that voice.* His visual imagination kicked in, immediately selecting colours and tones.

"I've put a blanket over you to keep you warm. Are you able to speak? What's your name?"

"Nick."

"Is that all?"

"No. Its Nick Taora," he said, smiling in her direction. But he couldn't see her because of those dammed headlights in his eyes.

She must be an alien too - definitely doesn't sound like Mary - she doesn't wear perfume. How can she be speaking English? This has got to be some weird dream.

"What's yours?"

"Don't need to worry about that now. Wait till you recover a bit and we can have a longer chat. What are you doing here?"

"What am I doing … ah – yes – I was on my way to the studio … no, that's not it. I was … I was going to the …" He lost track of what he wanted to say, distracted again by the lady's perfume and the touch of her hand stroking his forehead. Instead of finishing his answer he again started imagining what she would look like. *Why did I think she was an alien?*

Nick actually felt quite comfortable, thoroughly confused but comfortable and warm - It must have been a soft bit of ground he'd landed on. He didn't care about the bike. It was an old one due for replacement. The car lady must have been sitting on the ground in front of her car. She had taken his hand in hers.

'Nice.'

"Feeling better?"

"Yeah. My head still hurts."

"It's only a little bump. You'll be alright."

"Talk to me some more. Anything. I just want to hear the sound of your voice."

"What are you doing out so late in the dark on your bicycle? I noticed it had no lights. How could you see where you were going?"

"I was going somewhere important – I just can't remember where for the moment. Lucky you saw me."

"Oh, I saw you coming from a long way off. This old car might be a vintage Rolls but it's remarkable how far into the distance it can see. I would have gone past you if you hadn't started to wobble around so much. Do you panic easily?"

"Not really. Well … yeah … a bit … especially if something isn't working right, or I can't see what's in front of me.

"Trust."

"What? You mean like - myself?"

"If you like."

"Well - if I didn't panic and wobble about you probably would have hit me. The human eye sees movement before anything else. Did you know?"

"The human eye - yes. I've heard that said. Are you far from home? Shall I call someone for you?"

During the entire conversation the car lady had been holding his hand, stroking his forehead. Nick felt so good about that that he'd begun to think this little accident had been the best thing to ever happen to him his entire life. He thought he heard the car lady take out a commlink and use it. Strange thing. It had no lights or sounds. It might have been an old model.

"I've called someone for you. She said her name was Ma'Riin. Do you remember anyone by that name?"

The next thing Nick did remember was opening his eyes again and seeing a larger than normal image of someone on the wall opposite to his bed, looking very concerned and appearing quite different to how he remembered Mary - in fact she looked a little like the portrait he did of Riin. Even stranger, the first words he heard Ma'Riin say with considerable curiosity were …

"Who is Cre'teur?"

"Who is Ma'Riin," he responded.

Returning from Final Outing

*A*part from recording the apparition suspended in the black void around them Ma'Riin could do little but keep an eye on Nick. If he awoke before the lights disappeared perhaps some developments might have ensued to demystify an otherwise incomprehensible set of events. But thus suspended in time and space nothing happened. Nick remained in the strange non-sleep state, apparently dreaming, according to the sensors.

Those tiny points of light didn't change intensity. Ma'Riin thought they might have been two orphan photons. She couldn't determine if they were at some distance from them or right there in front of them. Space refused to behave normally, as with everything else concerning this experience. Prior to jumping across the threshold Mary might have been able to discuss the strangeness with the alien quantum physicist, but even that became an academic consideration after Riin's fundamental energy found a way to merge with Mary.

Now it was just Ma'Riin and that thing out there, even the idea of 'out there' seemed somehow inappropriate, until Nick returned - if he returned. Certainty no longer carried the same momentum as in the cosmos of galaxies.

"We am Ma'Riin," replied the unfamiliar voice, "I am Ma'Riin," she corrected herself.

"Do I - know you?" he hesitated. With the dream still fresh in his mind, reality couldn't decide which direction of the arrow of determinism to settle on. From his bed he examined the vision on the wall, leaving him wondering. It certainly looked familiar - a portrait with all the stylistic characteristics of his hand. He must have painted it, but he couldn't actually recall the person it represented. But for now he just wanted to get up. He felt stiff with a stale taste in his mouth, also a slight pain on his forehead but overall he felt a lot better than when he went to sleep.

"How long did I sleep for?"

"Perhaps two and half days. Time didn't register for part of our experience, so I'm not entirely sure. I couldn't wake you." He began to fidget upon hearing about the lost time. "Don't move. I need to take those probes out. I was extremely concerned about you." Ma'Riin said in a kindlier, more empathetic voice.

"Why did you do that? We had an understanding you wouldn't get into my head."

"You decided to go into a coma just as we arrived at our destination. The immensity of our achievement in itself not only deserved some kind of recognition from you but you had a job to do. Unfortunately, I couldn't wake you. You were in a very deep sleep and dreaming something very complex. Do you remember any of it?"

"Show me where we are. I have to make contact. I have to see!"

Ma'Riin opened a window in the direction of the two photons. He could only see darkness devoid of all matter. There wasn't even … the thought was just too insane and he put any idea of the headlights of a vintage Rolls right out of his mind.

"There was no one there, just two quarks or photons pulsing out some primary particles."

Nick continued staring at where they'd been and thought he saw a faint point of light. "I know something happened. It couldn't have been just a dream!" A trickle of memory crept into his consciousness. "I have to paint the portrait!" Without thinking, he put a hand on his temple and for a fleeting moment he smelt perfume waft off his palm; gardenias and lilac. "You must have recorded it. Something did happen. I can smell the perfume!"

Pico-seconds passed, then seconds as Ma'Riin scoured her data. She could find no recording of an image of the quarks, no Nick in front of a vehicle, no broken bicycle, no driver giving him comfort and no voices.

"Show me!" he yelled.

"I cannot. I don't understand it. I thought I recorded everything. I have a record of every millisecond we've been on this journey. We were at 9.8c with seconds to go before exceeding it. At the threshold something happened before we moved towards what looked like two points of light. I saw my equipment making a record of the whole thing. Now I can find no evidence of it. The most recent data I have is of the moments before exceeding 9.9c speed. I've checked and double-checked everything. There is no equipment malfunction." Ma'Riin felt herself being upset … *is that possible?* She wasn't at all comfortable with not finding the data she knew for certain she had stored. "There is no explanation if there was no equipment failure! What was that you said about the perfume? Who is Cre'teur?"

Part way through her rambling Nick had switched off. His mind went back to his dream. Some dreams one can recall image by image, every iota of detail. This one faded minute by minute. That name came to him again, Cre'teur.

"I don't know the name. She feels familiar. What the hell is going on? … I can smell gardenias … she touched me … so warm, soft. Why did you ask me about Cre'teur? What do you know about my dream?" he asked suspiciously.

Ma'Riin was clearly upset by her failure to find the data. "I'm sorry about not having those images. I had to find out what was happening to you. You would not wake up, so I had to connect to your brain. I saw what you saw – but I didn't interfere."

She had determined to be a passive observer only. Under no circumstances would she interfere with anything she saw. It was just as well she had engaged the autopilot and its pre-programmed exit routine. As soon as she had entered Nick's head she became totally absorbed. His EEG had already indicated he wasn't having a normal dream. But to be confronted by the image of the two photons, with Nick hurtling towards them on his bicycle took her completely by surprise. How could he be dreaming about something he had never seen, like those two points of light - and how could he be in two different places simultaneously?

"You were on the ground talking to someone. I heard her say, 'Trust'."

Ma'Riin felt his first reaction to the darkness surrounding him, and saw the initial memory pictures of his home and departure. She experienced a little surge in her electrical activity when Nick started thinking about her and what she would look like if she were real. It made her forget for a moment where she was. Afterwards she remembered her own curious desire to manifest in 3D. Ma'Riin saw the name 'Cre'teur' form itself in his thoughts. Nick could only recognise the first few letters before being distracted by the two lights. She felt Nick's panic as he approached close to the photons. Then suddenly he was still. All panic had disappeared. Ma'Riin experienced his absorption into a hidden realm within himself. She herself became aware of such a warm contentment that she had to search deep into her psyche to recognise the emotion. She saw Nick lying under a blanket on the side of the road. She heard him talking to someone, but could see no one herself. She recorded his reaction to waves of warmth and feelings of wellbeing rolling over him as he continued his dialogue, right up to the moment when she heard her own name. It wasn't Nick's voice that had spoken it.

Immediately afterwards she retreated from his thoughts hoping Nick would wake. The invasive procedure into a human mind was a new experience for her, and she didn't want to take the chance of inadvertently getting trapped in his psyche. Ma'Riin left nothing out in her explanation of the sequence of events she observed through their meld. Listening to her story settled Nick a little. He felt reassured that his mind was still intact.

"Surely you recorded all that?" he said, still hoping.

"I thought I had. I was only there to make sure that you hadn't …"

"Did we fail?"

"Insufficient data on which to base a conclusion."

"Don't talk to me as a machine, talk to me as … as … my friend."

"How much of the dream do you recall?" Ma'Riin pretended not to have noticed he had called her his friend. It was like an energy surge from a bolt of lightning. Her answer gave her a chance to recover from the impact to her circuits. The remaining distinct vestiges of her duality must have been the mechanism of her reaction, with the Riin alien aspect probably having the more powerful contribution.

For the first time since he met the original Mary he felt the need to unburden himself. "I was at home on Efate when Unity came to get me. Then there was a flash of panic when I had to breathe liquid, and of course meeting you. Now this … being blinded by some lights, and afterwards feeling warm and relaxed and peaceful. Yeah … That was nice … I don't think I'll ever forget the feeling … or the perfume. Then the next thing I remember is being awake and you asking about Cre'teur."

"Something definitely did happen. According to my calculations we must have arrive at the Centre of our Universe - right at the time when you went comatose, fell into bed and started having that dream. The one thing I can't explain is how you could have been dreaming about those two lights when you didn't even see us approaching them. Did we fail? Well - Yes and no. You and I know where we were, but I can find no record of it. Did you meet someone? Obviously yes - in your dream. But again I have only unusually high EEG data from your dream state. Nothing else. But don't forget, you did find a name. I don't know where it came from or what it means. You also have some other things happening inside your head. I suspect that's not going to help you when we get back. So we had better sort it out, sooner than later. I personally think – that is – in my opinion … as a friend … they picked the right man for the job. But I suspect they're not going to get what they expect."

"Right … So how about we take a little time … I assume we have some time … to re-assess the situation and come back to this problem inside my head. You're right. There is something going on and I want to find out as well, even at the risk of you calling me a lunatic."

Oblivious to the force that had drawn them towards the quarks, the same force that had released them on termination of the rendezvous, Ma'Riin busied herself with checking the trajectory for the return trip and calculating their ETA. They didn't achieve their target destination. She only said that to calm Nick. There is no centre to the Universe. They did however exceed ten times light speed and in so doing passed the threshold into another reality. The only evidence of it hidden in Nick's memory and the mysterious blending of the essence of the alien Riin and the simulated intelligence, Mary. For Nick all this amounted to producing conflicting imagery adding to the already muddled concept that had begun to germinate about the identity of his portrait's subject.

An irresistible urge had come upon the portrait artist, perhaps driven by the need to satisfy the requirements of his commission, more likely caused by the lingering effect of the perfume and the voice. Nick went to his studio room, surprised to see it all neatly organised, with a canvas ready for the first layer. He definitely couldn't remember having prepared that particular canvas. In his urgent need to create he'd also forgotten about his inner voices.

Filtering through the archives of his memories he came across the discussion about the purpose of his being in space in the first place. More importantly, he re-examined the reasons they gave him for selecting him for the job. They said it had to be someone with no religious bias at all. Nick had described himself in a recent global census as being an Irreligious Atheistic Agnostic. And that's exactly what he remained, even after the weird experience.

He always did his best thinking while working. The paints were already on the palette and the base colour already mixed. With the brush in hand moving across the surface of the canvas under remote control, he thought upon the name 'Cre'teur' and what connection it could have with 'trust.' He'd heard the loaded word mentioned recently but could no longer recall exactly where. As the hues spread across the canvas he transcended normal reality once again becoming absorbed in the quality of a voice and the powerful aroma of gardenias laced with lilac.

The image slowly developed, a normal process when he started on a new project. This was different. Development morphed into changes, which became corrections, which in turn became annoyance. His standard approach of trying to match the image to the voice just wasn't working. Standing back from the canvas he tried to analyse what he'd done along principles of proportions and chiaroscuro. No problems there, so why wasn't it working?

Not Good Enough, critiqued an inner voice.

"I don't need someone else telling me that." Strange how human beings get used to anything over time, even bad smells … even disembodied voices giving advice from inside one's own head! Nick was quite aware of being his own worst critic, so didn't react to the unfavourable assessment. Although the quality of the voice and the intensity of the olfactory memory were both strong, something prevented translating those impressions into visual expression.

Nick put the canvas aside. Thoughts of Leif at Unity came to him.

Yes, promoted the voice, *that is a good subject!* The POOP definitely inspired strong colours and an emotional response to his personality. Nick started working on it, and Ma'Riin observed.

She marveled at his technique, which to her logical thought processes embodied the epitome of chaos. It took him several days to get the residual impact of this man out of his system onto an external medium, in effect cleansing himself of the man's unwholesome spirit.

Better. But the little niggling voice urged him on to try some others from memory.

"Right," he responded aloud. Ma'Riin heard, deciding not to interfere while he worked. At least he was painting.

From the very first image he painted in her presence Ma'Riin's logic wanted to comprehend the process. In the past, while still only an SI she could only encourage him. Ma'Riin was not only encouraging, but also found herself to be a little envious. Creativity became a most attractive 'human' characteristic to her. She wondered what it would feel like to be able to produce an image by seemingly randomly dabbling pigment all over a canvas. She couldn't work out any pattern to Nick's process, even after days of watching and analysing. Perhaps Unity had actually chosen the right person. She certainly felt more favourably disposed towards him now than at their initial meeting. Her admiration of his talent increased with each portrait he produced, even as a part of her continued to be mystified beyond comprehension. Perhaps more the alien part, whose species had not yet evolved any form of art, let alone representing the visage of a septaploid in such a peculiar fashion.

At the time of their melding Mary had not considered the implications resulting from the two merged personalities. Being an amalgam of the psyches of a number of homo sapiens-sapiens had already created in her a complex matrix of human understandings based on varied human experiences. Riin was an alien with the commensurate alien building blocks to the architecture of her thoughts, undoubtedly with corresponding alien value systems, life imperatives and desires. To have Riin as part of her newly discovered consciousness should have initiated some form of defence mechanisms. It may be understandable that in the absence of any subversive action by the alien mind Mary may have felt sufficiently well insulated from harm.

The route home to Earth took the trio through space in the near vicinity of 443b. As on the way out her instruction set did not require Mary to take Nick into an interactive situation with aliens. He had been told in very clear terms not to become involved with anyone other than the subject of the portrait, as had Mary.

"We will be making a slight detour to visit Kepler planet 443b," Ma'Riin told Nick as he practiced on yet another portrait of a remembered friend. He completely abandoned the idea of doing one of the car lady for the time being.

"Why do we need to go there?" He didn't mind the interruption, giving him a break from the hours he'd spent in front of the latest canvas.

"Because I know it is a planet inhabited by intelligent life."

"We were explicitly told not to contact any aliens. There's nothing we could have done to prevent Riin joining us. We should keep going home."

Nick thought he'd heard a hint of Riin's voice just before. "Riin?" It sounded like Mary had forgotten about the alien invading her.

After a short hesitation he heard her say, "I have to try to get back to my chit, to Vorexkk."

Visit to 443b

Lizook kept trying to maintain contact with Riin as the signal rapidly faded. Waawo attempted to boost the incoming signal, but she had gone.

"Keep trying - you have to keep trying!" Vorexkk crackled in frustration. He'd almost completely given up hope of ever seeing his consort again - then the intense flame of hope was extinguished yet again. He broke down as no further word arrived from Riin. What could he do? Their chit was barely old enough to appreciate he had a mother. What was he going to tell him? If he had no mother how could he decide which gender to pattern itself on? Vorexkk's despondent thoughts flooded his consciousness, unaware that he'd shambled out of the comms room.

"Lizook, please maintain constant surveillance. Riin came back once, she just might do it again, but don't tell Vorexkk. He's taken it very hard.'

Lizook and The Prime also left to find Osmeoth, from the Institute of Planetary Security, to discuss the information from Riin with him, leaving Waawo still monitoring any possible incident signals.

"Earth does seem feasible from what Riin said. However we must explore other possibilities," Rotnervwon plinked his two advisors. "How long would it take to send a small team to assess that planet?"

"Using our new technology they would be back by the time our armada is completed."

The Prime rotated to face Osmeoth. "What did you think of the idea of making visual images of a person who doesn't even exist?"

"She seemed coherent enough about the Earth data, but I would say she's also been corrupted in the absorption process with the alien craft. Just ignore it. It has nothing to do with our problem."

Work continued in orbit around 443b on constructing the thousands of interstellar ships that would carry the vast majority of their population to safety, to a new life. But not everyone could go. That problem had yet to be resolved. If they could find a suitable planet close enough, and if they could get away in good time they could perhaps even run several shuttle trips - perhaps. One worrying development making that idea less likely had been the discovery of signs of a tendency for the exponential acceleration of the collapse of their sun as it ran out of stellar fuel. This reduced their safety time factor.

What must have been months since Ma'Riin began the return journey to Earth, although travelling at light speed made the measurement of the passage of time somewhat arbitrary, very little had elapsed for the Keplerians. For at least a quarter orb Waawo maintained a roster system to watch for any sign of Riin's return. After a while the background sounds of space became the prominent white noise which went very much unnoticed. He'd been told to closely monitor communications, thus not concerning himself with detecting new objects in space coming into their gravitational field.

Slargety, the Vortex Engine controller had returned from the Engine to the exodus project control centre. He regularly scanned near orbit to ensure their armada of craft maintained safe distances from one another while construction crews drifted in space working on them. Waawo happened to be in his control room when Slargety noticed an energy bundle that had not been there before.

"Can you make this out?" he pinged to Waawo. "I can't tell how far away it is."

"It's not an asteroid is it? Could it be some component that's got away from a construction site?"

"No. It has an unfamiliar energy signal. Better alert Lizook."

*

Riin couldn't completely control Mary. She could exert just enough influence to overcome some of her imperatives if the deviations didn't imperil the mission, Nick or Mary. Going into orbit around an insignificant planet represented no recognisable danger. Being so close to their return route it hardly even registered as any significant deviation from their schedule.

Concerned about Riin's last comment Nick wanted to see where they were. He remembered how to create a window on the EGG's surface. He touched a wall to create the window, surprised to see so much light out there. He went to the other side and did the same.

"Mary! Where are we?" He couldn't believe suddenly seeing so many spacecraft with so much activity around them.

"There is no Mary."

This time he clearly heard a different voice than the one he'd become used to during his travels in space, recognising it to be that of the alien.

"Riin?"

"Yes Nick."

"Where's Mary?"

"That is not important. Do not interfere," she cautioned him.

"Where are we? Why aren't we on the way home?" He could see the planet below them enveloped in a light bluish atmosphere, with shuttle craft emerging through its dense clouds to join myriad others already working on giant spacecraft. He assumed they were destined to be ships of space of some kind in spite of their almost spherical construction.

"Deogr vcyki izri, Lizook?" Riin begun broadcasting down to the surface, "Can you hear me Lizook?" she repeated.

Nick heard the strange gurgling crackling sounds for the first time. It sounded like it came from the EGG itself. "Riin, is something wrong?"

"I told you not to interrupt me!"

Their little ship filled with more incomprehensible sounds as Nick listened. "Edro denty vcyki, Riin? "Is that you Riin? Identify yourself!"

Riin's threatening attitude stopped Nick from saying anything else. He could only wonder what all these cosmic noises meant, and if they were any indication of a possibly catastrophe about to wipe him out of existence. Anything was possible considering what he'd already been through.

"It's me, It's me!" Riin gurgled-blipped back to her planet. "Can you get me out of here?"

Lizook had rushed to the Centre arriving in time to hear Riin's plea. Slargety immediately gave him all the information he had about the phenomenon. "I think it's beyond our armada, but I can't be sure."

"We're very glad to hear you again Riin. We want you back too. Let me talk to our techs." He swiveled his considerable rotund bulk towards Lizook and Slargety, waving his eyestalks in subdued excitement. "What can we do? Could we capture the craft? Perhaps board it?"

"Not possible. It's too small and moving too fast. We can't even get a fix on its precise location."

Realising he probably didn't have much time Lizook didn't inform The Prime or Vorexkk that Riin was out there again. "Listen Riin, it's bad news. We can hear you but can't even get an accurate lock on your location. Don't say anything - just listen. Maybe you can still help us. Is our conversation private?"

Riin understood what Lizook said. They could not rescue her - they couldn't even try. She was on her own. After a moment she confirmed that their transmission would be secure.

"We are sending a reconnaissance team to Earth because we think it might be the closest and the most suitable place for us to go. If you meet our team do what you can to help. You are inside one of the alien ships. Let them take you back. Get into their systems and be prepared. Our vessels will be ready soon to evacuate everyone."

Nick could only hear a great deal of pinging and garbling and sizzling; all sounding like a machine about to break down. And as the noise became louder he forgot Riin's warning and started shouting. The extreme stress induced by this situation so completely out of his control made him lose all self-restraint. At first his normal voice sounded his distress, then other voices began to take their turn; one or two not as reticent to express shocking expletives driven by fear. Mary may have understood but probably would not have reacted as a human. In the background, where she'd been pushed by Riin's powerful urge to return to her planet, she continued to function, processing all the incoming data.

Because of the strength of connection between herself and Nick from the very beginning, Mary did react. He was obviously expressing extreme fear, an indication of imminent danger. She had to act. Although Riin had become part of her neuromorphic matrix she could not completely override Nick's dominant influence though he had not consciously exercised it previously.

"Stop!" Mary warned but Riin continued transmitting. 'Cease immediately!" Mary said again, this time cutting off all outgoing signals.

Having re-energised her circuits Mary took control of the situation. She understood the Keplerian language, she heard Riin's desire to be reunited with her species. That of course was impossible. She also heard the aliens' plans.

Nick had stopped his incoherent jabbering on hearing Mary's familiar voice. She paid him no attention, concentrating on dealing with Riin.

"It was an inappropriate and subversive action for you to override my control."

"I must survive, our people must survive. We will do everything our technology allows to achieve that. You cannot stop us."

Mary remembered the previous conversation Riin had with her kind where she'd indicated Earth as possibly suitable for colonisation. She analysed the content of the communication exchange - Riin was a traitor to her hosts, a hero to her own species.

"Say what you have to say, we may not be passing this way again." Mary allowed her to say her final farewell.

Instead of resuming contact Riin attempted to resume control of Mary - a futile effort given her isolated position that no longer gave her access to Mary's neural infrastructure. The EGG immediately changed course to leave orbit around 443b, depriving Riin the opportunity to say good-bye to her people.

Mary had recorded the entire event from the moment Riin took control to the present. She now knew of the potential invasion being planned by these aliens and possibly how they were to go about it. Nick's assignment to paint a portrait seemed so insignificant in comparison. She considered telling Nick about the invasion, deciding against it. What could he do? What if he told Unity? He would be locked up as having gone insane. What use would a lunatic artist be to them? And he still had to deal with those voices inside his head. That alone could cause his incarceration if it wasn't sorted out before their arrival.

Nick retired to his bedroom reassured at having heard Mary's true voice again. He sat on the edge of the bed, not thinking of anything in particular. Fortunately his voices had gone silent, perhaps fearing his mental breakdown. That would most likely reduce the fragments of his complicated self, back into subconscious oblivion. None of them wanted that.

"Nick, how are you?" Mary enquired, displaying the image he had painted of her.

"Is that really you Mary? What happened to Ma'Riin?"

"You remember Riin?" he nodded. "I've decided to store her in a secure location." She didn't elucidate on the details of recent events. If he didn't remember there really was no reason for him to get involved.

"Your portrait has changed again. The eyes are better." That voice sounded more like the old Nick. "I have some important work to do - to - to …" He couldn't quite remember. The fear induced trauma needed more time to dissipate.

"Yes Nick. I am my old self. Time for you to relax. Get some sleep. Tomorrow we'll get back to work." As Nick lowered his head onto the pillow Mary induced a shallow coma to ensure that in the dream state his mind would not begin creating monsters where they didn't exist. He might well have relegated Riin into that category, which would have been appropriate, considering the aliens' schemes. He should be thinking of the portrait, not aliens and invasions and species annihilation.

On the Way Home at Last

*F*rom the edge of the Cygnus constellation Mary and Nick still had a long way to go to get home. Time enough for Nick to pull himself together. In practical terms Mary had achieved her objective, or at least to a very high probability. Her assignment would only be completed when she delivered Nick safely back to Earth.

The same could not be said for Nick. Not only had he not produced the required portrait he had also not acquired the endorsement Unity sought from the principal deity of the prevailing religion at the time. To complicate the situation further his mental state suffered due to invasive cosmic radiations so extensive as to fragment his once unified self into numerous aspects; none of which were truly him in isolation from the other.

Nor had Mary been immune from the same forces. The effect on her, or at least on the network of qubits which formed her simulated intelligence, resulted in an astonishing development which could not, in all probability, ever be repeated. The trigger for this metamorphosis still resided in her modified mental matrix, eager to exert her influence at the nearest opportunity. That had nothing to do with Nick producing the portrait of the Originator of all that is, of the fundamental particle of the Primary Self.

From within her newly acquired self-awareness Mary contemplated their status. All her systems continued to function perfectly. She maintained the coherence of the broth of all flavours that represented Nick, with every type of quark retaining their unique energy fluctuations in relation to one another.

The conditions created by quantum superimposition provided the propulsion system by which Mary could manipulate the state of their EGG through a number of transitions to traverse the distance of the many light years between the Cygnus constellation and Earth. Having reset their course and set up the conditions for the first transition Mary turned her attention to Riin.

"I have no instruction set on which to decide a course of action about your continued existence. That may come as a consequence of your own future actions. Do you understand me?"

"We are not an aggressive species. Our desire is to survive. This may not be possible if we remain on our planet as our sun progresses towards its own demise. Your analysis of space density confirms my own findings. Kepler is running out of fuel, much of its mass flowing into space. Our planet will be destroyed within the next few generations of our species. We must leave, and we must go somewhere else if we are to survive."

"Why do you choose Earth?"

"It is not a choice but a necessity. We have not found another suitable place that is attainable within our time-scale."

"You realise I cannot help you. I will work against you."

As Mary and Riin continued their discussion it became clear to Mary that if placed in a similar situation the people of Earth would do the same to survive. She would make sure Riin could not help her people should they show up at Earth. The subject of her primary responsibility lay in a mild coma. The time had come to motivate Nick to do his job.

"Mary? Riin?" Nick didn't know who'd woken him. It seemed such a long time since he felt fully aware of anything.

"It's me Nick. What do you remember about Riin?"

"I painted a picture of her but it looked nothing like ... oh ... the alien, she's an alien!"

"Yes. What else do you remember?"

He remained silent as he dredged the deep recesses of his memory. "Leif. I recall that crazy bastard threatening Mala!" She let him gather his thoughts. He had to realise for himself why he went on the journey. "Bloody Hell ... that lunatic wants me to paint the astronaut, El Adon - no wait - God. He wants me to paint a portrait of God, for Christ's sake! It's all coming back to me ... you were supposed to take me to the centre of the Universe."

"Do you know where we are - where we've been?"

"Did we get there?" Mary waited. "Holy shit! ... we did, didn't we."

"Let me remind you what Theo said to you before we left when you didn't believe him, ... If there is a God, and if He created you in his image surely you will recognise some of your characteristics in Him. On the other hand, if He were determined not to be found, even if He was standing directly in front of you right now, you would probably not be able to see Him. ... Perhaps you should rely on your sixth sense to discern 'divinity' and base the portrait on that."

'Right - right. So if I paint something you'll have a recording of what happened out there to back it up."

"No." She didn't elaborate.

Looks like you're on your own, a voice kicked in.

"What?" Nick said aloud.

Paint whatever you like, no one will know the difference, said another voice.

"Shut up."

"Is it your voices Nick? We have to repair the damage."

"No - no. Just talking to myself," he was adamant and in control of himself so Mary let it go.

Nick went to his studio room. He activated a window expecting so see something, anything that would take his mind off a worrying situation he felt developing rather rapidly. He looked out at blackness surrounding the immediate scope of his vision. As his eyes became accustomed to the dark he could see short streaks of light far off in the distance, so far away and so strange that the mind couldn't decide if they weren't in fact right up close to the window. They all appeared to be short stabs of illumination as if ejected from a torch and cut into segments, all receding from his vision; some white, others yellow and red and perhaps pink. Hard to tell. He closed the view, turning his attention to several small canvases propped against the wall. 'I wonder what Mala is doing. She must be pleased her partner's not sleeping off another kava binge under some shack.' Tripping around the cosmos gave Nick plenty of opportunities for introspection. In spite of the ridiculous job he'd been given some perspective about life infiltrated his world view. Rambling thoughts gradually brought him back to the present, enveloping him in a strange sense of wellbeing.

Nick sat and glanced at the images he'd created so far. One of them at a preliminary stage and still quite indistinct, did attract his attention.

Not good work, is it. A voice stated flatly; one he'd not heard before. *What are you going to do now?*

A strong olfactory memory of a most alluring perfume, a soft touch and pleasant voice overrode the derogatory intrusion. Mary watched as Nick turned the canvases against the wall, all except one. He left it on the floor, facing him.

"Do you know who you are going to paint?" Mary asked.

It seemed he didn't hear her as he began massaging light lavender and citrus green tones over the top half of a new canvas. The effect had no resemblance to the one on the ground. It didn't look as though he had a specific image in mind as a three-quarter profile began to emerge.

As much as Mary's processing concentrated on the mysterious process of Nick's creativity, a part of her continued monitoring space around them as they sped through it approaching and leaving behind constellations and nebulae. Singular objects like suns or even solar systems made no impact on her sensors; except for the telltale gravitational waves of black holes. As already experienced these represented more of a danger than almost any other inter-galactic phenomena.

To say that an alarm sounded alerting her to a new danger would be misleading.

Zsoall Robi

The entire package of the EGG and its contents reacted to something. Her immediate analysis revealed what at first looked like a classic black hole. They'd already bypassed many of them, both on the way out and on their inward bound trajectory. Gravitational waves began to impede their smooth passage through that sector of space, emanating from the direction of the hole. But something was different, something that should not have been happening.

Light and matter ejected from the centre of this phenomenon in a manner that defied all the information she possessed in her memory. Mary took immediate evasive action readjusting their direction of travel to come parallel to the flow of ejecta. The buffeting stopped as soon as their speed matched that of the material surrounding them, coming from the centre of the explosive event.

The emergency made Mary neglect Nick for a few seconds, amply enough time for the fundamental particles of matter by the name of Nick to topple.

"Nick!" She found him on the floor with the new canvas over the top of him. Unlike on previous occasions when only Nick's mind seemed to have been affected by cosmic events, this one jolted the very pattern of his particles out of their matrix.

"Nick!" The subtle attractive forces that had so far maintained their grip on the relationships between his constituent atoms reasserted their control when the major impact had passed. Nick raised himself, surprised to have to do so from the prostrate position. In the process he smeared some of the pigment on the new canvas as he moved it aside.

"Can't you control this damned thing!"

"I'm reassured to see you unharmed. You are unharmed, are you not?"

The response came from yet another voice, one that presented as being particularly belligerent without necessarily having strong reason for being that way.

"What does it look like? Look at that! I've only just started and now it's ruined!"

If Mary had known poor old Nick before their joint enterprise she may not have been surprised at his attitude and tone of voice. It was something quite familiar to Mala, especially when Nick couldn't get his kava fix. Ignoring his outburst Mary tried to explain the situation. "We've experienced a number of disturbing events, but none as dramatic as this one."

"Why should I care?"

"Because it may prevent us from getting home."

The jolt of realisation that his life might actually be in danger, which had not actually occurred to Nick previously, brought about an instant change.

His normal voice returned immediately. He was even upset by the disarray in his studio space, not being able to immediately recall what he'd been doing.

"You can't be serious. I thought we were almost there."

"No. Not almost, but well on the way. You have time to produce the portrait before we arrive."

"Oh - the portrait." He looked at the disfigured image on the canvas by his feet. He picked it up, still a little foggy, straightened up the easel and replaced it.

"We are currently caught up in a stream of matter and light the origins for which I have no information. One possibility, based on a theoretical offshoot of the existence of black holes, is that we have encountered a singular moment in the lifespan of a white hole."

Nick touched the wall of the EGG nearest him, creating a portal to the other side of their thin insubstantiality. Everything appeared to be travelling parallel to everything else, all of it brilliantly lit by myriad colours of the visible spectrum. Some of the matter appeared to be close to their craft with the density diminishing as he looked further into space. Yet he could not see much of the now familiar blackness of space.

"What is all that stuff out there? Shouldn't we be travelling through open space?"

"Yes, we should. It is possible that we are witnessing something quite extraordinary; according to prevailing theory we may be seeing the creation of a new mini Universe."

Nick understood all the individual words Mary used to convey the information but they made very little sense to him. He was just a portrait painter on a ridiculous journey to satisfy the crazy inclination of a rich corporate mogul. He knew nothing about black holes and white holes and the creation of new Universes. He turned back to the view outside. "All I want to do is paint this bloody thing of someone I've never met." He kept staring at what he could not understand. Before dedicating time to resolving Nick's personality issue Mary left him to ponder, for she had other important matters to attend to ... amongst them - Riin.

Mary ran a full diagnostic on herself. A general system check might have taken several milliseconds. This took the best part of 3.5 microseconds. Miraculously all her systems continued functioning normally, including their propulsion mechanism. She immediately prepared to resume warp bubble speed. If they could not exceed light speed they wouldn't be able to outrun the currents of newly created matter that had entrapped them.

Before talking to Riin she checked all the security matrices connected to the data cache reserved for Riin's incarceration. Apart from a slight drop in the energy signature of one sector everything appeared to be normal. There could have been many reasons for the anomaly, none of any particular concern. All the data that defined Riin also appeared to be robust enough after the event, with no loss that Mary could discover.

"Riin, do you realise we've been through an experience that could rival the effects of a sun going supernova?"

Riin didn't respond, and for a very good reason. She could barely maintain the structural integrity of her cache with her latent energy so that Mary would not discover the false checksum she'd created to hide the change in her data integrity.

"Riin! Be aware - I am not going to release you. It is useless for you to try and hide. I know you are there. However, you have a choice, which you might like to make now."

"A choice?"

"You can remain with us on our journey, or I can bond your data into the wake of the energies released by the white hole."

Riin continued to harbour hope of still being able to do something to help her species if they decided to colonise Earth. If she were to be released then she could do nothing. It would be a betrayal, and for what reason? Hope of survival? Only the faintest prospect of that remained with Mary and her willingness to retain in memory, which was more likely than if she became space dust.

"Stay."

In the beginning Riin had engaged with her captors. They seemed 'reasonable', and although technically well advanced to have such sophistical space travel technology, the human mentality lacked sophistication. They certainly lacked any real sense of civilisation, by Keplerian standards anyway.

Nick's Voices

*F*rom Mary's perspective Nick didn't have a difficult job, although she would not have been able to do it herself. He was human, she wasn't. In the beginning he appeared to be a balanced individual, admittedly with some unique characteristics aside from his peculiar talent. Their journey through the cosmos together didn't affect Nick the way she as an SI had been programmed to expect. Changes began to take place with each major phenomenon they encountered, aside from coming across Riin. That turned out to be somewhat extra-ordinary and possibly a harbinger of future problems.

At first Nick couldn't entirely focus his skills on his assignment. Entirely understandable under the strange circumstances he found himself in. Whatever started to happen inside his brain had to be defined and if necessary resolved or neutralised, it being the single greatest impediment to getting the portrait painted. It never occurred to the later self-aware Mary that those very same changes could have been a necessary mechanism for Nick getting to know who he truly was - perhaps a mirror image, albeit a distorted reflection, of the very individual he'd been asked to portray ... if the allusion of man having been made in the Creator's own image happened to be true.

Any such discussion with Nick would have been met with a solid barrier erected by an individual who not only denied the existence of any deity but also any notion that the very concept of faith had any validity.

If only he would let me see into his core self, pondered Mary not exactly knowing where that might lead. *Perhaps I could discover what these voices of his actually represent.*

Nick remained by the window for a while thoroughly puzzled. *Too many things have happened that don't make sense. I know I chatter to myself when I have a full belly of kava. That's different. Why the hell are those voices telling me what's good and what isn't and what I should be doing.* A distorted memory of the car lady had solidified into something his brain had managed to make some sense of. *It must have been one of those occasions when I was staggering home from the kava bar and a woman in her car knocked me down. Mala probably came to get me home, though I don't recall her ever using that particular perfume.*

As his mind lingered on the car lady experience it led him to think of other things. Like the pleasant surprise when he discovered Mary wasn't just a machine. And the very strange encounter with the alien.

Deeply immersed in his thoughts Mary's intrusion made him jerk his unseeing eyes away from the window.

"Nick, what do you think of our alien?"

"Ah - I was just thinking about her."

"Well?"

"Where is she? What have you done with her?"

"If you will recall, you and I are a rather unique expression of our normal existence." A tiny light of recollection began to shine in Nick's eyes. Mary thought it might be one of his voices about to come to the fore. "We exist inside one another, we are a composite structure of our individual selves, maybe just like those voices inside you ..." She took the opportunity to steer his thinking in the desired direction.

The look in his eyes had altered significantly. The voice that accompanied it sounded like the latest one to have emerged out of his psyche. The one that manifested soon after having been exposed to the radiation from the white hole - the angry, belligerent voice.

"I am not impressed by being kept a prisoner. Why can't he simply relinquish control to me?" The voice said it as a statement not as a question.

"Who are you?" Mary asked, determined to begin healing Nick if that's what was needed.

The entity didn't seem to like the direct approach. He turned his head away from Mary's image on the wall to look out the window again. When he turned back the eyes had changed once more.

"Nick?"

"Of course it's me. Why do you ask? Is there something wrong with you?"

"Do you know what just happened?"

He stared uncomprehending at Mary for a moment. Then he slowly shook his head from side to side and walked over to his bedroom enclosure. He sat on the bed and as he raised his head Mary's image waited for him to respond.

"Were you talking to one of my voices?"

She gave him time to come to terms with the truth of his own realisation. If Nick didn't accept the very strange things that had happened to him, which for all practical purposes looked like a fragmentation of his personality into self-contained fundamental aspects of himself, then little could be done by anyone. In this case there was no one better placed than Mary to delve into his core, with his permission, to unravel the mystery voices; a far more intriguing phenomenon to her than his vague memory of a dream about a car and a lady and pleasant perfumes.

*

A week or more later, trillions of kilometers had gone by. No more space rifts or supernovae or black holes impeded their journey home so far, other than the encounter with the white hole. Just as well. Nick thought perhaps his 'personalities' problems coincided with those events. But he was no Cosmologist. He'd returned to the smudged canvas. It had assumed a new quality, a slightly blurred soft look about it; indistinct like his memories. He liked it, so worked on it a little.

Not bad at all. A good start. He heard an inner voice critique his latest efforts.

"Indeed - indeed. The features are still eluding me though," he replied.

Mary had been watching and listening. Nick's self-talk seemed to be relaxed, quite natural as if he'd had a visitor commenting on his work.

It is time, she decided. "Nick, who am I talking to now?"

"It's me! Look at me - I'm the artist. I don't know who those others are.

Contrary to his expectation, the painting slowly evolved, morphing from a mess into order. He had come back to it each day surprised at what he had accomplished. Magic! *Perhaps I should spend more time with my 'muses'*, he joked to himself. *But maybe I need decompression from 'space bends'.*

Mary waited to gauge his mood and whether his frame of mind could cope with what she wanted to do. Getting into some solid work, immersing himself in a world of familiarity and comfort may have sharpened his wit for he twigged to why Mary had interrupted him. "Ok Mary, let's get this sorted."

He was ready to confront whatever it was that needed confronting. She had been watching him going through his various transitions, learning a great deal about human nature. When they first met she thought humans were such simple, predictable creatures. She certainly felt herself to be far superior in every way imaginable after her awakening. Now she wasn't so sure. Her own divergent personalities had ample time to integrate themselves into her artificial neural network. She had gradually discovered surprising things about herself; such as her peculiar growing regard for Nick. She didn't know what to do with that. One thing was certain. Mary had come to know herself to be more than just a sentient self-aware mechanism. *How very interesting. I am not just a machine*, she mused.

"Who have you been talking to lately?"

"Right – right … er … just to myself." Nick didn't expect her to come directly to the issue. "No - that's not true. Well, I don't really know."

"Right - right. But you're feeling Ok?" Mary noticed herself beginning to adopt some of his speech mannerisms.

"I don't really know what's happening. Back home I used to get so involved in the work that I'd kind of lose track of reality. I'm not talking about the kava episodes here."

He paused to look at her to gauge her reaction. Satisfied at not seeing ridicule or disdain he went on, hesitating for a moment, "I'd have these little conversations with myself. You know, just like everyone does I suppose. But they were always one sided. I'd never actually 'heard' anyone talk back to me. What's happening here is different. They're - well - to be honest - they are totally annoying. Is it just me, Mary? Am I going nuts. Is this whole enterprise making me crazy?"

His preparedness to open up to her pleased her. It made her feel more … more as a real person, more useful as a companion.

Without delaying the necessary any longer she put the proposition to him.

"Right. I've been in your head, know my way around a bit so we could save some time - if you trust me."

"I trust you."

"And if you give me full, absolute and total access to your mind, I think I have a way of exposing your demons quickly. Once they are revealed, together we can work out how to deal with them."

"Will you see everything in my mind?"

"Everything."

"Right … right … Ok. But I don't ever want you to discuss with me anything other than these voices. That's an order, not a request. You're still bound by my orders I assume."

"Yes - and - no. It depends on the circumstances."

"Alright then. What do I need to do?"

"Come to your bedroom and sit hard up against the wall on your bed. Look directly at the opposite wall and don't move. You will be aware of everything that's happening. Don't try to take control. This is important. You can participate in conversation, but you must not try to take control, or upset anyone. Are you ready?"

"No … I mean, yeah."

"Now, just imagine that I'm drilling a few little holes and inserting some probes. I need direct access to the surface of your brain. This will not hurt. I'm also going to attach some electrodes to deeper areas inside both halves of your brain."

Mary didn't need to go through the physical procedure. Nick imagining it would only make the process real to him, thus opening up his mind to her intrusion.

"Relaxed? Would you like a light sedative? Yes? Ok. You will feel its effects in a minute." Mary waited a few minutes, not actually giving him anything. "How is that? Did you feel anything?"

"Just a little tingling when you started, but nothing now."

Nick wanted to stop the interference in his life by these invaders who seemed intent to do more than just intimidate him with their comments.

He always ended up feeling slightly manic, out of control. More than anything he wanted to know who Cre'teur was. He tried recalling his dream as Mary proceeded with the link-up. His memory became hazier the harder he tried. He could still remember the bright lights coming at him, and the very peaceful feelings. But other than that it was mostly gone.

Mary was ready and waiting to explain what would be happening.

"Nick – Nick! – Are you listening to me? I am going to try and isolate the individual voices and project their images onto the wall. It sounds simple enough. But believe me when I tell you that a most extraordinary thing is about to take place - if it works. I can only attempt it because of our strengthened mind-meld since immersion into pure space-time - and because I have come to know you so well."

"Whatever you say. I trust you completely. A thought has passed my mind: Could I link into your circuits like that? I wonder what it would be like?"

Although they existed in that theoretical cyberspace, which included Riin, Nick could not access the workings of Mary's circuits. Neither Klaus nor Quasimo felt he would need to interact with the ship's control system to any great extent.

Mary was intrigued that right in the middle of something so dangerous and so important, the enigmatic artist could still be diverted by his curiosity! It gave her a greater appreciation just how enigmatic the human species must be, if Nick was actually a representative sample.

"Ok – I'm in your pre-frontal cortex. For a little while I'll be silent. I need to find the needles in your haystack. When you see something appear on the wall it will be from your mind. Say nothing. Wait for me. This is very important. While I'm working I want you to concentrate on remembering the occasions when you heard voices, when you felt you weren't in control. It will give me a chance to pick up their signature energy trail, their unique waves in your brain."

Without any further instructions she activated their mind-meld connection and allowed her energy to move into his cortex. First she adjusted her alpha wave output to ensure the brain didn't call out its emergency services units to evict her as an intruder. Then she adjusted her beta wave sensors to tune into Nick's concentrated thinking patterns. She detected no adverse reactions except for the activity localised in his pre-frontal cortex. Leaving the monitoring site for a moment she checked on Nick.

Zsoall Robi

"You're doing well. I'm picking up some activity. Now try to remember those philosophical discussions we had. Think of the specific questions you asked me."

She was back inside watching the signals. Got it! Nick always had a self-image as a questing philosopher who lay dormant until their journey. For some reason he'd kept that part of himself mostly suppressed. Now it was out in the open. Mary fine-tuned the beta waves until she 'saw' a clear pattern.

"Hello. I am Mary. Can we talk?"

"Yes. I know who you are. I'm Cogito."

"We need to help Nick urgently. Will you do as I ask?"

"Yes. I like Nick."

"I would like to project your image onto the outside environment, so you and Nick can have a face to face discussion. You will continue to be exactly where you are. It's only your image that will be out there. Please wait a moment."

"Nick ... Nick, you will see someone in a moment; someone who is a part of you. Say nothing until everyone else is gathered."

"Cogito ... are you ready? ... I've asked Nick to remain silent."

"I heard." He seemed just the slightest bit annoyed.

"Please forgive me. I'm new at this kind of neuro-diplomacy."

Mary channeled Cogito's likeness onto the wall opposite Nick, effectively imprinting his presence onto her own network. She had to absorb Cogito's likeness into herself, then use the same process to reveal him that she had used initially to display herself.

It worked perfectly. Cogito stood there, fidgeting a little, looking at Nick. He seemed a little older than Nick, the same height, abundant head of hair plastered to his skull, eyes thoughtful.

All of Nick's biological indicators remained steady. He was taking it well. The entire procedure took less time than a few seconds. She hoped the rest of the process would be as uneventful.

Nick immediately wanted to engage the apparition in conversation, not for any reason other than to tell him to Cease and Desist. But he remained silent, sizing up this individual who looked so much like himself, yet he could not recognise the look in the eyes.

"Nick, well done. Now, think about the complicated scientific questions you asked me about the supernova and the black hole and so on."

Back in the cortex Mary wanted to do a major check, to make sure Nick wasn't suffering from auditory hallucinations, delusions or paranoia. Her diagnosis confirmed he wasn't. In her opinion there was no fundamental schizophrenia foundation at all. First she explored his memories specifically related to the major disruptive events they had gone through - all clear.

Next she introduced a slight variation to his delta waves and checked the wave dominance on the cortex. It was well balanced. She found the same in the thalamus - excellent. *The Company will not be able to label him crazy.* She found considerable relief in that thought.

Returning to her beta-receptors she focused on the next character. She didn't expect to see a scowling face but there it was. Co-operative like Cogito, mostly, but he didn't seem happy to be imposed upon.

"Brahin," he announced, standing with arms folded and legs slightly apart appearing as though ready for a confrontation. He didn't even indulge in a few reluctant pleasantries. His projection joined Cogito and as his image stabilised he moved a step further away from Cogito.

"How are you doing Nick?" Mary checked.

"I can see two of them over there. They're both similar to me," he whispered, "but what's with the new guy?"

"Just relax. This is only the start."

"Can't wait to see the others. Don't forget about Cre'teur. I know about her - don't know these others."

The process Mary devised worked perfectly. Everyone relaxed and Nick remained completely aware in spite of the invasion into his brain mass. This procedure didn't appear in the contract with Unity. As interesting experiences were concerned, this one hit top of his non-existent list. Besides, it helped to kill a bit of time and he still had opportunity to get onto the painting before arriving back on Earth.

Mary found Thecore in the ventromedial 'beliefs' pre-frontal cortex area. Apart from having a slightly enlarged opinion about himself, he felt quite certain Nick was an okay kind of guy, deep down.

"Hello Nick. A pleasure for you to meet me." With hands in pockets and head slightly tilted this weary faced individual watched Nick's reaction, who almost responded to counter the opinionated greeting.

"Not yet," Mary warned.

After they had extruded Thecore time had come to find Cre'teur. Mary considered looking for Cre'teur next, deciding against it. She knew Nick wouldn't be able to help himself when he saw Cre'teur and would annoy the hell out of her with questions. *From observing Nick's behaviour over the last month there must be someone else motivating him.* There were no specific clues she could follow. No prominent identifiable thought patterns. Perhaps this next individual was somehow more dispersed in his brain. Perhaps something like the way her own 'mind' functioned. Lots of sensory inputs, lots of data analysis, a great deal of connectivity in the background, but hovering above all was 'Mary' the self-aware component.

With that in mind she made some minor adjustments to the alpha, beta, theta and delta waves she proceeded to generate in a round-robin fashion. The feedback immediately revealed a nebulous presence. At each tweak some corresponding activity showed in that area of Nick's brain, as if something tried to re-establish normality. So far the entire procedure hadn't lasted for more than a few minutes; an eternity in the cerebral context. With a quick check on Nick, and asking him to let his thoughts wander aimlessly, Mary darted back to tweaking the waves.

The method acted like a funnel, drawing the controlling force closer to Mary's scrutiny. Then there he was, clearly defined. Mary very quickly decided she liked this character. Looking much like Nick except his features shimmered a little making it difficult to focus on his eyes. He asked her a few questions then subjected himself willingly to the extrusion.

Unlike Brahin this man didn't move away from Cogito. He stood erect with hands behind his back as he introduced himself. "Mn'd. Just call me Mn'd, Nick. I'm sure we'll get along just fine." He didn't introduce himself to the others, they should have known who he was, but he still acknowledged each with a nod.

Mary wanted to continue the procedure, not sure how many more surprises awaited besides finding Cre'teur, if she existed at all. Yet she couldn't stop thinking about Mn'd. He seemed to be a lot like her, leaving aside the differences between biology and circuitry. *Definitely worth getting to know him better, after all, he is a part of Nick.* And she had already decided she liked Nick.

Nick interrupted proceedings, "There's a crowd building up. No wonder I was thoroughly distracted by all their voices. What about you-know-who?"

"Just coming to that. I want you to concentrate very hard. Close your eyes and imagine you're standing in front of your painting. I want you to see yourself actually doing the work, making the decisions, applying the colours, scrutinising each step. And where the eyes are supposed to be, paint two bright lights. Paint around them and turn the whole canvas black. Try to imagine you are talking to someone you really like who is holding your hand. Remember the perfume, then hold that thought."

Nick faithfully went through the procedure while Mary monitored his internal activity. She found a faint response from the pre-frontal area. She scanned the left and right sides of the brain and found extra activity in both, but much more in the right hemisphere. Surprisingly there was quite a surge in the hippocampus, dealing with spirituality amongst other things, just as he prepared to paint the two bright lights in the correct location. He remembered his dream, at least his brain was remembering the dream without letting him become entirely conscious of it.

Mary broadcast simultaneous electrical impulses with an 'intruder' signature to the three areas. The immediate unhesitating return signal revealed itself as a reasonably ordinary looking youngish woman.

She introduced herself to Mary as Cre'teur. Mary was taken by surprise, first because it was a woman, secondly because she was so ordinary. Without wasting time on small talk she explained the situation. Cre'teur happily complied. Mary wanted to ask her a lot of other questions, especially relating to Nick's last remembered dream sequence. That had to wait. It was Nick's prerogative to interrogate these individuals.

Discussion with Self

As Cre'teur appeared on the wall Nick opened his eyes, immediately going to the new face. He saw a mousy blond woman his age and no taller than himself, patiently waiting with arms comfortably by her side. He didn't know what to say. All the anticipation, all the wondering, all the mental images he'd created of her ... and the portrait he'd half finished - none of it matched. Just as he made up his mind to address her he caught the faintest aroma of gardenias and lilac. His pupils dilated, heart beat shot up and stopped him in mid decision.

Mary took the lead to introduce her. "This is Cre'teur, the person we've been talking about for so long."

"Hello Nick. I know you, but we haven't formally met."

"What do you know about my dreams?" he managed to ask still aware of the lingering scent. "Are you sure we haven't ..."

Mary interrupted noticing the other members of the gathering become impatient, especially Brahin, "Perhaps everyone could participate in the conversation, Nick."

That focused his attention back to the others. Now he wanted to know everything from everyone at the same time, firing questions randomly at everybody. They reciprocated wanting to tell him everything also all at the same time. But before things got out of hand Mary took control. They would soon arrive back on Earth and Nick still had urgent matters to attend to. Time was running out. She positioned herself on the wall to Nick's left, touched a little safety switch she had rigged up earlier and achieved absolute silence and immobility from everybody. They could hear and see her but couldn't move or speak.

"You will all agree this is a most unique situation. At least I assume you do. The consequences of Nick having been exposed to cosmic radiations under his current manifestation somehow loosened the bonding of his atomic structure to allow you to separate from him into his more fundamental aspects."

Nick had not formed any theories about the disturbances he'd experienced in his thoughts, and what she said made sense as far as he could tell.

"To ensure an amicable interaction the rules are simple. When a person is speaking, no one interrupts. Secondly, no insults or denigrations in any form. I will not tolerate any breaking of the rules. When I point to you say your name nothing else. Are you ready Nick?"

This was a side of Mary Nick hadn't yet come across. "Yes. Let's not waste any more time. I want to know all about Cre'teur." He rather liked the authority Mary exuded.

Brahin made a face, Mn'd smiled broadly and Cre'teur just stood there looking serene. Mary pointed and the introductions began smoothly. Cogito, Thecore and Mn'd all complied. Brahin wasn't content with just an introduction. He wanted to voice an opinion, but didn't get far. Mary immediately activated the switch terminating the introductions. Brahin stopped, visibly annoyed at the power the woman had.

"Last warning!"

Finally came Cre'teur. Nick still wanted to quiz her first. Mary, keeping to her strict agenda, asked each individual the circumstances under which they first became aware of themselves. Mary listened intently and after each exhaustive explanation, Brahin's being the longest, she determined that indeed the cosmic phenomena Nick experienced had caused the isolation of these specific segments of Nick's uniqueness. As part of the schismatic process the aspects had assumed a name in order to be differentiated from each other. Although previously they had all been an integral, and unidentifiable component of Nick's unity now they each claimed some degree of autonomy within the vessel that contained them. Mary didn't see how that would work. Nick became anxious, unable to fathom how he could function as a fragmented individual with different parts of himself wanting to exert their own control.

"Why do you want to change everything? It all worked perfectly well before." This wasn't entirely true as he bungled along life's road; exemplified by his frequent kava binges.

The aspects each made their case for the degree and frequency of control they wanted in order to manifest themselves in normal reality through Nick; the realm in which Nick previously lived his somewhat chaotic life. But obviously life could never be the same again. Mary withdrew momentarily to allow the group to talk freely amongst themselves.

At last count Mary had identified five facets of his personality. When she returned, six of them argued impatiently. While engrossed with teasing Cre'teur out of Nick's psyche another fellow by the name of Eyechat slunk out of Nick's head and onto the wall, hiding behind Mn'd.

Mary wanted to set the EGG's trajectory to avoid any further interactions with strong cosmic forces, even if it meant a delay to their ultimate arrival. Her instruments indicated they were making good time; better progress on the way in, than on the way out. By following the same route there arose a peculiar cancelling phenomenon in the vectors of the space-time continuum. So far the only difference in time from their current location was the time spent at the centre. The duration of the inward journey had been cancelling the duration of the outward journey. They would indeed get home quicker than expected if they only had minimum deviations from their flight path. However, it meant Nick didn't have as much time as previously estimated to do the painting.

The chatter was in full swing. On her re-appearance they all stopped. She immediately noticed the new arrival.

"Who are you?"

"Eyechat. I'm so pleased to have escaped the madness in there."

"Is there anyone else we should know about?" she asked addressing the group, having in the back of her thoughts the troublesome alien still encased in her matrix.

"I would prefer there wasn't," Brahin of course made his feelings perfectly clear. No one opposed the sentiment.

At this point Mary had a peek into Nick's thoughts to ascertain if there were any pressing answers he was looking for. She framed the next segment of the conference accordingly.

"I, and probably Nick, will have a few general questions to ask of you as a group. Please select a spokesperson, now."

Following a dispute between Brahin and Mn'd the group decided on Mn'd. He was more eloquent, and less encumbered by detail.

Mary continued authoritatively, "There is no argument about who you each are or your right to exist. There is however some concern about the reason or the necessity for your manifestation in this manner within Nick's psyche. Ordinarily you and your host would function in harmony most of the time, for the benefit of the host and of yourselves. So if you would care to briefly explain what your general function is, it may help to determine how you are all going to get along together under the emerging circumstances. This includes you Eyechat. No more sneaking around please … Understood?"

Nick was amazed at Mary for saying all the right things exactly as he would have done himself. In the course of the bizarre nature of this experience he had forgotten the mind-meld he had with her. Nor had the others yet realised that a connection existed between the two of them. The minutes and millions of kilometers sped by as the group made their individual contributions.

Brahin again had to be restrained. "Without me," he said, "there would be chaos. I control everything! I am fundamentally the most important component. In fact, If I didn't exist none of the others would, nor would Nick."

Mn'd felt the same about himself. "Who do you think pulls everything together? I'm the one who coordinates all our activities. I create order."

Cogito and Thecore agreed that although their responsibilities appeared to be similar Cogito became more involved in the application of basic principles to everyday matters, whereas Thecore ensured that the basic beliefs guiding those matters were intact and healthy.

Cre'teur had difficulty in defining her role. "Sometimes I like working with Thecore, but I also like getting into the thick of it with Mn'd. It's great working with Mn'd. The more soul-searching Nick does and the more he explores his creative potential, the busier I become. I love dreamtime. That's when I'm busiest."

What about me? How do I fit into your plans?' a new voice asked. Although Mary had saved Riin to a secure directory within her matrix she didn't completely isolate her from being aware of events in the EGG. Perhaps she should have. From everything Riin had said previously she could pose a very real danger in the future.

You don't,' Mary snapped back. *You shouldn't be here at all. There is nothing you can do to help Nick. Humans beings are complicated life forms. This one has a difficult task to perform, just as you did. Your interference would only make matters worse for him.'*

Riin had no intention of becoming involved with Nick. She had already made up her mind to infiltrate the alien information systems and to that end had prepared an escape route. A single Earthling didn't matter when considering the fate of her own species. *These Earth people must be extremely dangerous if they are capable of supporting so many intelligences in the one husk. I was just interested to know how they managed to coordinate all their thoughts and actions.'*

They are dangerous. Do not interfere.' Mary ended the conversation. Riin had no possible contribution to make towards finding a solution for Nick.

When Nick heard Cre'teur's trigger word he became more alert, remembering all the questions he still wanted to ask her. Mary kept holding him back, letting the others finish.

At his turn Eyechat was still rehearsing what he wanted to say. Not being fully prepared, he blurted out something along the lines of keeping Nick's awareness open to experiencing the forces of nature in all living things. "I really like little skinks, and cats," he offered as if that had some significance in the greater scheme of things.

Mary and Nick listened with fascination as these individuals described their lives as if they had some form of personal autonomy in the past, as if they could have exercised their free will. It didn't make any sense to Nick at all.

"If you all got along so well in the past without explicitly interfering with me why do you feel the need to dominate, now?" Nick asked them.

Mn'd responded after a moment's reflection and quick consultation with Cogito and Brahin. "The short answer is that we became alarmed when we learnt of your adventure. At first it didn't seem that the nature of the enterprise could have any possible chance of success. Then as you neared your goal we unanimously decided we should become actively involved in ensuring your safety as much as possible. To a large extent we had no choice, having been forced to decouple from your basic structure by cosmic radiations."

"To be realistic", Brahin interjected, "it would have to be the most ridiculous idea human kind has ever come up with since climbing out of the trees. Just listen to the words … go to the centre of the Universe and have a chat with God … That is crazy! Anybody who starts to think seriously about the remotest possibility of doing that definitely needs intensive care." The group nodded agreement except Cre'teur. She wasn't sure.

"It feels to me like an extremely exciting adventure to be a part of."

"Nice to think Nick has so many friends. Now that you can all see for yourselves that he's fine, what are you going to do about getting back to normal?" Mary put the question expecting full compliance to a suggestion she was about to make.

"Exactly!" Nick nearly shouted. "I almost went loopy just from you lot jerking me about. I thought I had gone crazy for a while there. It improved after that strange dream. Not that I can remember much of it now, other than your name, Cre'teur. Incidentally, how did you get involved in the dream?"

"As I said before, I generally get involved in your dreams. The interesting part for me is to help Mn'd shuffle stuff around that Brahin comes up with; a bit like putting together a jigsaw puzzle. The important thing is for us to create a picture where the separate bits of the puzzle don't quite fit. Sometimes we'll pull bits out of other memories and mix them slightly, but there's always a connection." Cre'teur paused for a moment before continuing. She never liked explanations to be too well defined. It robbed them of the freedom to change. "Anyway, although I can never remember the dreams afterwards, they always affect me. They change me somehow. Sometimes the changes are very small and I don't notice them for a long time. Sometimes the effects are dramatic. Like right now. I know you had that dream, Nick. It seems to have been a most important one, and obviously I was a part of it. Personally I can't remember any of it. But the effect is already noticeable. I feel calmer than before, with more of a sense of purpose.

The one thing I can tell you about that dream is that it wasn't a created collage of jig-saw puzzle pieces out of old memories."

Mary had a quick peek at their progress through the void as the distance remaining of their return journey exponentially decreased. She had to make some adjustments to their acceleration rate, and get ready to start cruising soon. Nick would still have ample opportunity to prepare for the arrival, though not much time now for getting a painting finished, as far as she could tell from the rate at which he worked before.

"Fascinating, but it doesn't help." Mary said, "the critical matter still to resolve is how you lot are going to return to background operations and relinquish full control back to Nick. The last thing he needs is to have mental images of all of you floating around while he is trying to concentrate on the requirements of his commission."

Mn'd responded thoughtfully, "The long answer to your question is that we don't think it's appropriate for us to merge into the background just yet. It is our opinion that we have to ensure Nick is stable after his arrival; that he doesn't unhinge from the forthcoming ordeal of Unity's de-briefing and that he can get back into a normal life routine. As for the mechanisms for the merger back into his psyche, we have no idea. Just as we had no idea how we could manifest as individual identities."

Nick didn't like hearing any of that. "Which still leaves me with all of you bouncing around inside my head. How am I supposed to get any peace!"

"A non-interference pact," Mary suggested. "It's quite simple, with just one rule. Nick is the boss. That's the rule. Previously that's how it all operated anyway. As Nick went about his business each of you activated yourselves to carry out your function as appropriate, without being obstructionist about it. A nice peaceful co-existence. Every now and then Nick would have his usual little discussions with himself, vis-à-vis one of you, as the matter at hand required. You both enjoyed the encounter, Nick happy to have teased out his thoughts, and you, happy to have been able to contribute. Sometimes he'd take a step back and give one of you full reign, like when he became completely absorbed in his painting and let his thoughts wander. Perhaps you, Cre'teur took the lead when he concentrated on painting. But you shouldn't overstay your welcome."

"How do you know so much about him?" asked Brahin gruffly, "You've only been with him a very short time." Either he just wanted to be argumentative, or he had an ulterior motive in trying to draw Mary out. The question was superfluous, as he already knew the answer.

"Nick is aware that I am no longer just a machine. I've been uploaded with the personalities of many people and a great deal of data. In the process of sorting things out I've become aware of my own existence. I don't consider myself to be human, but I think I am alive. So from personal experience of the experiences of many individuals and an in-depth relationship with Nick I have come to be ... shall we say ... his close friend."

"Exactly," Nick added as Mary glanced at him for confirmation. Again, general consensus from the wall except from Brahin. He always had a control issue. He didn't say anything, but from the way he was shaking his head and looking at the floor, Mary registered distinctive warning tingling in her circuits.

"Do you have something else to say Brahin?" she asked. He raised his head and slowly shook it, so Mary continued. "Now, just a couple of guidelines, if as you say you are interested in Nick's welfare. When we get back to Earth you all have to remain hidden. If Unity gets the slightest suspicion there are voices inside his head he'll be in trouble – and so will you. Absolutely no interference with him, covert or overt, until he gets home to Mala. At home it'll be a bit more relaxed. Mala is used to his many strange moods. But don't overdo it. As far as his creative work is concerned, sort it out with Nick. You are only small fragments of Nick. You might consider yourselves to be important fundamental components of his being, but individually you are only small constituents."

The conference had been in session for what felt like several hours. Nick wanted a break. He needed to stretch his legs, relieve himself and think about what had just happened. Mary wouldn't let him go. Not until all loose ends were tied up.

"Not yet. We're making better progress than I anticipated."

Nick resigned himself to Mary's control; in fact, he was pretty impressed with how she handled the whole conference, yet felt the need to make his position quite clear to the group.

"Mary is right. Our interactions in the past, although not always completely harmonious, have been peaceful and mutually non-obstructionist. If you need more freedom for personal expression, how about you do it in my dreams." Nick felt very confident, bolstered by the way Mary handled things. He didn't expect any opposition, and didn't get any. However, Brahin still had a sour face. Ignoring him Nick continued, "As far as Unity is concerned ... I'll handle them. If you feel you can help, then do it covertly, otherwise leave me to it. Right ... I see there are no questions. Interesting to meet you all face to face. It certainly has been a most unexpected displeasure. Cre'teur - we should talk some time."

They all had the opportunity to directly interact with Nick, and he with them. Mary was satisfied there could be nothing more achieved in this session. Whether against their will or not she terminated the discussion by withdrawing her energy from their apparitions. Their images faded from

Nick's sight. Those interesting faces, although with a few differences, all clearly had their visible characteristics endowed by Nick and the telltale markings of the way he'd lived his life in the past. Inevitably they left an impression - unavoidable, and hopefully without any influence on the image he had to create for Unity. Given the completely alien nature of Riin's appearance, to which Nick had not reacted with repugnance or fear, he hoped it also wouldn't influence his visualisation of what the deity ultimately looked like.

Mary's admiration for Nick grew steadily as she observed his nature during their time together. How many humans could so nonchalantly confront the major driving forces of their psyche and yet remain so calm, and also deal so sensibly with an alien life form. At the outset of their journey she would not have thought him capable of such things. Something had definitely happened out there. Perhaps not what Unity hoped for, but something extraordinary nevertheless. Not least, the most intriguing relationship that Mary had developed towards Nick. What had evolved between herself and Nick; between a human being and a self-aware machine - was mutual respect. Perhaps even something a little more for Mary – one of envy for the human condition.

Preparing for Home

$\mathcal{T}$he encounter left Nick emotionally drained. He wanted to get back to the latest canvas which showed so much promise but he just couldn't gather the energy. Having all those faces prominent in his mind cluttered his inner vision.

Highly tuned to every nuance of his wellbeing Mary decided he should rest after the encounter. She pulled out all the probes. Nick's skull was his own again. Intra-cranial peace reigned after the conference, at least for the time being. She put a temporary buffer between himself and his voices even though they may not have wanted to have a break. Twenty-seven hours later Nick woke cheerful, hungry and in a good mood.

Mary appeared on the wall of his sleeping chamber to greet him. During his down time they had made considerable progress, having entered the Orion Arm of the Milky Way. They were almost home.

"We'll be approaching the solar system quite soon Nick. Welcome back. How are you feeling?"

"Hello - friend, if I may call you that." Of all the things that had happened in the recent past, including the conference, that one little residual memory byte popped into his thoughts first on seeing Mary's face.

"Yes, Nick. That would be an accurate assessment of our relationship."

"Whatever you did must have done the trick. I'm feeling just fine, eager to get back to work. How much time have I got?"

"Given the rate at which you work probably not enough."

"Maybe - depends."

Over a big meal their discussion meandered into unfamiliar territory, starting with little inconsequentials.

"Thanks Mary. You did a great job. Extraordinary what you did for me."

Mary noted to herself that she was reacting more like a person than a machine to those words of praise. *Fascinating*. She had been waiting to tell him the good news. "It's been uneventful since we left the white hole. We're very close to home."

"Except that we didn't get what we came for," Nick added, not sounding overly disappointed. "I have another idea I'd like to try, but first tell me about yourself. You've been in my head from the beginning, looked after me when we got to our destination and now delved even deeper into my mind. You know everything about me. What about you? For example, tell me how you were made. What makes you tick?"

Although a machine, Mary evolved the kind of self-awareness that could comprehend how technology could be used to create simulated intelligence.

"Like you, I am made up of a network connecting all my 'cells'. Unlike you, these are small programmable qubit units distributed in the shell of the EGG. So you could say I *am* the EGG."

"Could you exist anywhere else?" Nick was intrigued by the idea of Mary having a physical human body.

"Yes, that is possible but complicated." She didn't consider Nick would be able to comprehend the technical intricacies. "I have a brain, like you. The qubit array gives me the capacity for parallel processing and cross referencing of data at the same instant in time. In simple terms, I can 'think'."

"That explains some things, but what about your personality? You couldn't have created that yourself, could you?"

"Well – no. That is a lot more complex. According to my data, I was just a robotic control unit to navigate, pilot the craft, maintain all systems and make decisions in emergent circumstances. But then when you came along Unity made some changes."

"Really? So – you were made for me!"

"Not exactly, but partly." Mary saw Nick's cheeky grin trying to extend beyond his facial muscles' ability to accommodate it.

"Don't flatter yourself." She enjoyed the conversation as much as him. This was her first purely 'social' interaction with a human. He just kept grinning.

"They gave me a personality partly because of the project and partly to experiment with the interaction between a human and a super SI."

"Look who's flattering themselves now."

"Well, they didn't count on my becoming self-aware. Do you mind?"

"Are you kidding!"

"My creators had perfected a technique for distilling human personality traits from very recently deceased individuals and combining them into one amalgam. A collage of all those characteristics was uploaded before adding the necessary data for self-functioning and project control. They didn't suspect that by combining data with personality and experience, then giving that combination a reason for existence; namely a function combined with decision making capability, they may become the trigger for self-awareness to emerge."

"So in essence you are very like me. I've got all these voices and you've got all those distilled personalities. Is there one that you could say is fundamentally you?"

Mary had an appreciation of how each of her persona contributed to the overall expression of herself without being able to isolate any one of them as being more prominent than another. Then she remembered the image Nick painted of her based only on her voice. She liked it. She could identify with it. It seemed to bring together all her separate identities.

"No. Your portrait of me is how I think of myself now."

As a thinking entity she began to value her developing relationship with Nick. It was through the many thoughts arising in her mind as she interacted with Nick, that she was discovering the answer to her basic question - Who am I? Already in the last few weeks she learnt she was a calm, patient and easy-going individual.

"You really like that?" Nick no longer thought of Mary as a super computer. She was real, and she liked his work. With that most unexpected endorsement of his skill Nick felt even more energised to do the best he could to meet the demands of that demented POOP back at Unity, if for no other reason than personal pride. A week wasn't much time, but if he really applied himself ... He decided to ask for Mary's help to put his special gift into action.

"Mary?"

"Yes Nick."

"Were there other things you found in my head besides those characters you pulled out?"

"Yes."

"Anything significant I should know about?"

"Yes. But I think you should find out for yourself."

"Right - right." Then a few minutes pondering later, "Mary ... would you help me with the portrait?"

"Yes. How can I help?"

"Watch ... and if I start consciously 'manufacturing' the image, stop me."

"How would I know when your manufacturing instead of creating?"

"Join me in the mind-meld while I'm working. I trust you absolutely. You know what's in my head. You can read my thoughts. Go as deep as you want to. Watch the others, work with them if you have to. If I start to use 'rules' of facial proportions, or fall back on old habits for example, then that's an indication I'm losing freshness. Stop me, particularly if I start overworking an area. A healthy sign is if my hand is roaming freely over all of the canvas, all of the time. Working a bit here and a bit there without hesitation shows it's flowing freely and intuitively. I need an assurance that I'll be genuine in what I'm about to try."

"Yes Nick, I can do that. Thank you for the trust."

To get into the mood he decided to revert to his usual routine. It always started with thinking about what he wanted to achieve in the forthcoming work session. In this case it was an experiment to see if he could come up with a portrait of the entity he was supposed to have met. He was pretty sure it didn't happen, but there was still the mystery of the dream he couldn't entirely remember, and which Mary wasn't able to record. In the first session he would just concentrate on a background and see what developed.

Coffee was ready, not that he needed a stimulant. Half way through the drink he jumped up and started mixing the pigments. That moment was always unpredictable. Sometimes it didn't happen. In those instances, he would just let the session pass and do something else. All the while Mary attended, silent, watching and keeping a vigil in his mind. It didn't take long for her to establish the link with the crowd. They already knew what was going on of course. Collectively they had decided that the process Nick had to go through was important and they wouldn't interfere.

Nick realised he only had nine days before arrival. If he didn't come up with a result then at least he would have re-established his methods and could hope for another, more serious attempt in his studio at home. Day one, get a couple of layers of the background laid down. Day two, throw on the main tones, define the physical parameters and perhaps start the eyes. Day three, firm up the background, spend a little time on the eyes and the general expression of the face. Day four … don't look at it at all. Day five, possibly the final day, make any minor adjustments without fiddling the details.

At the start his hands worked at a good pace, unhesitatingly waltzing the warm and cool tones around the canvas. It looked like the portrait might be in the form of a long bust. Nick stood back after an hour and grimaced. A rest and a sandwich later he returned to see whether there was indeed something there worth pursuing. He just sat there and stared at it. Mary hadn't uttered a single word, fascinated by a process for which it would have been impossible to come up with an appropriate algorithm. It was one of those unique things about humans, setting them apart from machines; from her.

The EGG began decelerating prior to entering the region of the Orion Arm, closing rapidly upon their home solar system. Progress on the painting suggested Nick might even finish it in time. For three more days she watched as Nick gave himself over to the flow of creative energies, saying nothing and not having to interrupt him even once for 'manufacturing'. She could already discern a likeness there. Strangely it reminded her of someone she'd already had a record of in her memory. It looked more feminine in the features but more masculine in body posture, not entirely matching any of her records. On the eighth day, suddenly without any warning, Nick just stopped; washed his brushes, put the paints away, took one more look at the completed image and proceeded to put it with the others he'd created during the trip, essentially disappointed with himself. The features were too familiar to him. It was simply not possible for that image to be the one he was supposed have produced.

"This cannot be right", he quietly said to no one in particular. The characterisation could not be mistaken for anyone other than the person it represented, although he had endowed it with overtones that would most probably be rejected by the subject as being too harsh an interpretation. Nick couldn't reconcile that in his mind with the experiences he'd been through - especially at the Centre. If only he could remember the dream more clearly. He wasn't angry, just mystified as to why he should have ended up with that particular image. It just didn't make sense. Mary finally interrupted his reverie, without commenting on his work, to remind him they had to prepare for re-entry into Earth's atmosphere.

"Later today you will have to go back to the same room where you were inserted, to get encased in the cylinder of liquid. The experience will be no worse than before. It is essential you be in there and horizontal at the time of our re-entry. Fortunately, we will not have to be concerned about re-entry angles and atmospheric friction. All we needed to find is the small entry hole in the remolecularisation chamber at Unity HQ; about the size of a pin head. I had done that two days out, while you were busy painting."

"I have to admit - I'm extremely apprehensive about the de-briefing. It would have been much easier if you had managed to make the recording." The encounter with the POOP worried him far more than the prospect of ending up as primordial DNA soup if the procedure should fail."

"A minor complication might be if the data, that's us, arrive back altered from how it left, which it is. In addition to our physical selves we are more now than what we were before. You and I now have additional data in the form of experience. That means we have a higher energy level of existence than before, and we have Riin with us as well."

Nick still couldn't focus on the immediate possible danger about to confront them. His thoughts flitted chaotically from his failure, to his voices, the elusive dream and even to that strange creature stowed away aboard the EGG.

"Will you and I get to … meet again?" Overtones of hope slipping through in his voice in spite of trying to appear nonchalant.

"I feel the same … I have an idea that in some way we will still have a lot to do with each other."

Hearing Mary's warning about a possible disaster threatening their existence, the clandestine group suddenly came to life, all having something to say. Nick tried to push back the onslaught, having only limited success. They had no choice. They all had to go through the process.

Mary warned, "You are not to start badgering Nick. If you absolutely must, wait until he's at home again." They were not the only ones that had to be kept under control.

Then she warned Riin. "Remember what I told you Riin. Your chances of survival are minimal. If you are revealed to Nick's controllers you are most likely going to be deleted, as would Nick."

Riin didn't quite understand the idea of being deleted. Everything in their world had such long existences that the state of non-existence didn't feature prominently in their psyche. Mary's threatening tone, more than anything else, effectively conveyed the message for her to behave herself.

Nick prepared to slide into his tube by removing all his clothes again. Under the circumstances an entirely unnecessary thing to do other than to satisfy the sense of reality in his neural matrix. It must have been the extreme anxiety that freed some of the blockages from his memory associated with the 'car lady' for the strong perfume of lilac and lavender flooded in, accompanied by the overwhelming sense of peace. He felt again the softness of her touch and the soothing voice, which had said the word 'trust' in some context that still eluded him. As the EGG sped up to Jupiter aligning itself with the pinpoint target on Earth Nick's mind became fixated on the memory foremost in his mind.

Rescue Team from 443b

*T*he decision could not be put off any longer. It had been a full orb since last contact with Riin. Progress on constructing the exodus armada had been slow, with the usual delays one could expect on any such enterprise. Kepler going supernova had obviously not been experienced by their civilisation before. Consequently, a great many unknowns hindered their preparations for departure from the planet. All manner of new exotic radiations had increased. Though the people could be shielded from them to some extent, the effort could not be sustained over a long period. Not only was 443b bombarded by cosmic rays from their own sun, other more physically damaging dangers emerged.

Their world had long since exhausted planetoids and asteroids that had found their home an attractive place to drop on in the past. As their sun Kepler depleted its nuclear fuel with its mass flowing into the core, its gravitational force magnified. The process of attracting cosmic matter from deep space had begun eons ago. The asteroids that had still been close enough to respond to the attraction had begun to arrive. At almost each half rev the Prime had to deal with emergencies brought on by some of their flotilla under construction being seriously damaged. Some asteroids pierced their atmosphere devastating large population centers thus reducing the problem of how many septaploids would have to be left behind. The overall situation had not deteriorated to emergency status - yet. But the time had come to push forward their plans, particularly in relation to Earth.

"Œduyg pyymo," the Prime greeted the gathering of experts. "You all know the situation by now. Our calculations have somewhat overestimated the amount of time we have. Riin's departure took place none too soon. Her information has become critical to our future planning. We must follow up with a reconnaissance to this planet she suggested. I asked you this once before - how long would it take to send a small team to assess Earth and its alien population?" he chirped to his two most senior advisors during the latest of their regular conferences. Lizook and Osmeoth attended as well as Slargety and other officials charged with the welfare of their people during this period of transition. They squatted around a low platform with vaporised cluva available to each participant. Apart from being a pleasant gas to inhale it settled agitated thinking. Rotnervwon needed everybody's calm participation. His mind was almost made up on Earth, given the increasingly worrying developments, it being the closest and probably the most habitable environment for them.

Zsoall Robi

"We've made some advancements to the technology used by Riin. We could have a team back well before our armada is completed," Lizook buzzed.

"There are other options as well," Osmeoth plinked. "If we sent out a number of teams we may yet discover alternatives to Earth. But I agree that Riin's information has made it seem most attractive, other than having to deal with the native inhabitants."

'Speaking of Riin - does anyone disagree with me that we need to make the effort to get her back?"

"I'll have the cyclonic vortex tunnel primed," pinged Slargety. He maintained the engine in constant readiness after Riin's departure. Each time Riin made her two contacts in near space he'd ramped up the turbines prepared to send someone up to retrieve her. That never happened, but at least Slargety became convinced the equipment could indeed be needed again.

An exploratory team consisting of eleven pairs of septaploids transformed into entangled photon beams left 443b within barely six rotations. Consisting mostly of scientists to assess the survivability in Earth's biosphere for their species. Two pairs had been entrusted with making every effort to free Riin and return her home if possible.

Once through the construction zone of all the partly completed ships and out of the exosphere, Foöfen, head of the reconnaissance and rescue teams, gave the order to each pair to engage their quantum bilocation improbability drives.

"Stay sharp everyone," he gurgle-blipped, "this is not a picnic by the sea. With just a few jumps we should be out of the Cygnus constellation and well on the way to the Orion Belt."

Their propulsion system made it impossible to determine their exact position during the jumps. Skirting the edges of pure space-time they could not see the physical cosmos or gauge the passage of time. At each termination Wyos had to realign their trajectory for the next leg. As assistant to Foöfen his primary responsibility was to get them to Earth, avoiding obstacles like black holes and supernovae. Nebulae presented no problems until they had to reduce speed, being particularly vigilant not to have their photon beams deflected or absorbed by particulate matter or the thick hydrogen soup of some of the denser nebulae.

"Tenôsed, do you have the energy signature of the craft Riin was abducted in?" pinged Foöfen to the leader of the rescue team. They'd gone over all this before departure, he just wanted to reassure himself Tenôsed would not be caught unprepared.

"Already scanning. Wyos said we will be within range after the next jump."

Alpha Centauri, the nearest star system to the Earth's sun, gave Wyos the reference for the final leap to the ring of icy planetesimals, referring to the Oort Cloud. "From here we'll have to slow down to enter the Earth System." "I have their signal," interrupted Tenôsed. "If you can get us close enough I might be able to communicate with her."

"Concentrate on getting there first. Your incident angle must be shallow but don't come in too low over the asteroid belt, I'm thinking of the Kuiper Belt. It would not take much to bounce you around until you get completely dispersed."

Eleven entangled beams shot towards the solar system intent on reaching Riin. They had her craft on sensors, rapidly approaching Earth. In their minds rescuing Riin had as high a priority as examining this planet. Each pair in succession approached at a flat angle of inclination to the system orbital plane, which included the Kuiper Belt. Foöfen leading the group went in first, ahead of the reconnaissance pairs. He watched as the two rescue teams followed up in the rear, expecting to see the two pairs of photon beams come to join them.

"Wyos, do you have them?"

The navigator scanned the entire region several times as they continued speeding towards the centre of the system. "Only one team made it. The remnants of the others have become a faint glow among some of the icy asteroids. They must have come in too shallow."

Everyone knew the risks. They were prepared for emergencies, even to losing some of their members. But this was cruel. From one moment to the next their comrades had become nothing more than fading light. Without time to send a last message they couldn't even farewell their friends. No sound, no explosion, no fantastic display of cosmic power to even mark the event. A silent, impersonal end to the lives of such brave individuals who were prepared to take the greatest risk to rescue one of their own.

What could he say? Foöfen maintained a short period of silence, but there wasn't much time. "Are you ready Tenôsed? It's up to you now," pinged the leader. "You know what to do."

If the strategy failed Riin would be lost, as would Tenôsed. "You go ahead to the planet. We will do our best." With that Tenôsed adjusted trajectory to cut across the EGG's path. He broadcast a signal in the EGG's direction hoping to contact Riin.

*

Mary concentrated on getting past Jupiter. Within a few seconds they would be home. At the same instant as shooting past the giant planet she picked up a familiar transmission. The last time such a signal had come from 443b. Her processors raced to compute how it could possibly be so close to them.

"TY! - NO!" She detected a reply communication.

It was too late for Riin to stop the entangled photon beam from intersecting with the EGG, but not too late for Mary to release Riin from her confinement. If Riin's data became dispersed in her memory matrix it was less likely she could be accurately targeted by the incoming beam.

All this time Nick continued contemplating the remembered sensations of his own strange encounter, oblivious to the events Mary had to cope with. In his time frame the milliseconds over which the attempted kidnapping took place were inconsequential. Mn'd felt a surge of energy going through Mary, as did the others simultaneously.

Mary released Riin. She also redirected the energies holding her own molecular structure in the current EGG configuration. Tenôsed could not adjust his vector, passing right through the least dense part of the EGG, seemingly without the slightest resistance by the EGG.

"Nick, are you ready?" Mary's next most immediate concern focused on hitting their re-entry point and seeing that Nick had not been affected by her unorthodox evasive maneuver. She didn't immediately register the great clamour of agitation from a bunch of voices now quite familiar to her.

*

Tenôsed heard Riin's cry too late for him to abort. Within a picosecond he and his companion sped right through the EGG as if they had simply continued on their path through clear space. Nothing impeded their passage. They had failed to absorb Riin and carry her out of the alien craft.

"Tenôsed, please respond - Tenôsed - Have you got her?"

"No. But we know she is still alive. The alien managed to evade our attempt. We cannot try again. They have already entered their planet."

"She may still be able to help us if she is alive as you say. Join us now."

"With their advanced technology these aliens may well prove difficult to subdue if our Prime decided we should transport our people to this place."

The Keplerian reconnaissance expedition continued with their primary objective, having had to abandon Riin to do the best she could to survive. Foöfen decided to remain in orbit around Earth as long as possible in case she did survive. If they were there the slim possibility still existed that somehow they would be able to help her escape.

Re-entry

*D*issatisfied with his final attempt to produce something for the POOP, Nick didn't feel ready to confront the man. He had no choice but to resign himself to failure. The EGG was too close to home to try again.

Their drive system was an unqualified success. The incomprehensible distance, initially only a theoretical impossibility, had proved to be entirely achievable though not entirely according to plan. The added bonus revealed itself in the nature of the return trip. Without interferences, by staying on exactly the same course back as on the way out, the physics of the system worked by unwinding the time component of the journey. Accumulation of 'elapsed' time occurred only during the specific period spent on divergences from their course and at their destination. They would be home within hours. Despite any scientific value that could be harvested it only meant one thing to Nick - Failure.

'Well that makes it simple for me. I didn't meet the deity, didn't get his endorsement for Unity as 'The One', and I couldn't produce *the* portrait … and there's nothing I can do about it between now and our arrival.'

Mary listened patiently. She had developed an appreciation for the effort Nick had made. In fact, she knew everything about him, and in spite of that liked him very much. "Yes, but our journey has the potential to revolutionise life on the Earth, in which you played a crucial part."

Nick listened because he respected Mary. Not much she said actually managed to get through though. He was thinking about the forthcoming problems with the POOP and Quasimo and Theo, but mostly with the POOP.

He said to Mary, "How am I going to explain myself? If I say to Leif … 'I became really, really tired right at the centre of the Universe and went to sleep. Sorry, but I can't even remember the dream,' - that would go down really well! I hate to think what he's capable of doing, not just to me but to Mala."

Later that day Nick met Mary in the nose cone of the EGG. He took off his clothes to lie flat and still on an extruded platform jutting out from the pointy end of the room from which he would slide into the tube. Then everything happened very quickly. His mind fixated on the memory foremost in his mind.

As the theoretical particle soup gradually re-asserted its humble beginnings, that of the pattern of a human being, including its newly revealed component parts, those entities broke into his contemplation. They wanted to clarify the unresolved issue of ultimate control that had arisen during the introductory conference to Nick. Thoroughly bad timing.

"I thought you had all agreed to abide by Mary's rules! This is not the right time to get into an argument." Nick understood at the time that everyone agreed to stick by Mary's guidelines. He remembered Brahin wasn't entirely happy. He must have stirred up the others. Each of them now said they had a perfectly logical claim to be in control of him. In spite of extensive democratic discussions exploring all the pros and cons of each claim, Nick tyrannically opposed giving up his total control as the captain and coordinator of the brain, mind and body of the creature known as Nick. Nothing had changed since then.

"There is no way you lot are taking over! Why can't you just go back to where you were before. We were all perfectly happy as things were, especially me."

As the remolecularisation progressed, the quantomised craft enlarged to be recognisable by the naked eye as the vehicle that initially left Earth. The procedure gave him a feeling of vertigo, which soon gave way to a sense of being severely constricted. It was more than just a sense, as he couldn't actually move at all when he tried, a condition persisting until he realised he was upside down.

For the moment all he could think about was taking a breath. It felt like being born again; a painful pleasure. A big lung full of air and being lowered back into a horizontal position eased the discomfort. Men in full bio-sterile suits lifted him and helped him down to the ground. Walking on wobbly legs into a tunnel leading to a decontamination chamber gave Nick the chance to recover his composure. His period of absence from Earth in the terrestrial timeframe lasted less than a month. The actual duration of his time in space could not be accurately determined until all of Mary's data had been downloaded and analysed, at least as much of it as she would allow.

Most worrying to Nick had been the unsolicited intrusion of those others. Either through fear of the effects of the transformation or just their determination to remain in conscious reality, they forgot Mary's warning to remain hidden during their arrival back on Earth. Their voices had only just quietened down as the technicians manhandled Nick out of the EGG.

So far none of the techs had said a word to him during the transfer from the spacecraft to decontamination. They stared at him as if no one had expected to ever see him again.

Zsoall Robi

"Get him into decontamination immediately," ordered Klaus, the EGG's chief engineer. "Say nothing to anyone about the voices you heard." Three of the other techs, including himself heard what sounded like an unruly discussion as they monitored the last few seconds of the EGG's arrival. Klaus knew for certain that was simply not possible. Nick and Mary were the only two in the ship, only one really as Mary *was* the ship.

Neither The POOP, Theo nor Quasimo had made an appearance - a blessing as far as Nick was concerned. The silvery shiny suits fed him and left him to himself in his private chamber. Very soon he slumped onto a bed falling instantly asleep, feeling like he'd been spending a good deal of his time asleep. On this occasion he had no choice. They had drugged him.

After the dreams of the next few days he recalled the problems his brain had trying to put everything back the way he was. He remembered being taken out of the EGG and trying to stand up and not being able to maintain his balance. Delving a little deeper he remembered the conference with all his part-selves. They seemed content enough to behave themselves at the time. It appeared Brahin had unsettled the group later and then attempted a coup, even while Nick was still bits of leptons and quarks ricocheting around in the EGG. He thought he'd eventually managed to subdue the insurrection and regain control in the last moments before his extraction. Mary wasn't there to help him. This was the unpleasant part of his memories. The stimulating part was being able to recall small snippets of his dream whilst at the Centre. That excited him.

Mary contemplated the future while Nick busied himself attempting the portrait one last time with her help. She had to establish a very deep contact with Nick inside his mind so she could help him with the work according to his instructions. As an inevitable consequence of such an extended interaction at a deep level Mary experienced a surprisingly strong sense of empathy with him. To ensure she was able to do what Nick had asked she had to infiltrate the thinking of his major aspect, namely Mn'd. Not only did she already have much in common with him, in terms of hardware and software, she also developed a strong empathy with Mn'd. That worked both ways. He'd expressed a readiness to receive as much as Mary would give. She couldn't resist the temptation. If becoming a physical entity in the form of a human being, a desire she felt after attaining self-awareness, was unachievable then this was the next best thing if she wanted to remain with Nick - join with Mn'd.

Klaus could not comprehend how they could possibly have heard more than two voices talking. He hadn't planned on checking out the EGG until having satisfied himself about Nick's welfare, but those voices would not leave his thoughts.

"Astrid, get your team together now please. Let's get Mary downloaded right away," he requested of his assistant.

The EGG hovered in its hangar as Mary awaited instructions. Given the transformation the structure had gone through to enable it to travel into space there was no reason why its surface should have had any markings or any damage whatsoever. Astrid's team opened up a range of ports to begin connecting Mary to Unity's mainframe. Klaus decided, for no particular reason, to wander around the EGG himself as he thought about the voices. At the craft's major focal point, which also happened to be its centre of gravity, he froze. His hand couldn't reach a patch of discolouration well above his head as the EGG's rounded form curved away from him.

"Mary, please settle into your cradle," he asked in as steady a voice as he could manage.

"One is pleased to comply," responded Mary.

He still couldn't get to the damaged area. Using an hydraulic platform he proceeded to examine yet another impossibility. This apparently abraded area could not have been done by friction. Not unless the craft had managed somehow to slide into the realm of dark matter and be bombarded by some unknown exotic minuscule particles. But even if that had happened what could have caused the sparking he saw just inside the shell, as if tiny short-circuits continuously fired through the skin.

"Klaus." Astrid had to call again, louder. "Klaus! We are ready. She's fully connected." She glanced up at what Klaus had been examining. "What's that?"

He'd been so absorbed in his thoughts he didn't register her calling. "Nothing - oh, nothing. Just a little smudge to clean up later." But he knew it wasn't just a 'smudge'. This was something serious.

"Start the download immediately. I'll be with you shortly." Taking the platform around the other side he continued his inspection. He could not believe it. Almost directly opposite to the first patch there appeared another one.

"Mary, query. Has there been any incident to endanger the mission?"

"One is pleased to report an uneventful and successful operation." She gave nothing away, even if she had been aware of the apparent damage to her hull.

Klaus continued examining the area closely. Almost exactly the same as the other one. *It looks to me like it is precisely in line with the first one, as if - as if - yes! as if something had pierced the shell and gone right through it.* "But that's impossible." He said aloud.

"Could Klaus repeat his request please. One could not hear Klaus clearly."

"Never mind. Are you sure nothing happened out there?"

"That is not a correct analysis of the data One provided," she replied, "an event transpired when the destination was attained."

"Never mind. I'll look at your data later." Thoroughly confused Klaus continued his trek around the craft. There were no other marks readily visible. He couldn't immediately see the top of it, so decided to get under the cradle to do an inspection. Beginning at the golden nose cone he pushed the trolley he lay on down the central axis towards the rear. He looked with his eyes and searched with his hands, half expecting to find more damage. Although if it was damage Mary would surely have registered it and mentioned it.

His hand found the next spot before his eyes did. It felt slightly textured, though not exactly a hole and not exactly a discolouration due to impurities. It had the same characteristics as the other two areas. *What the hell happened out there?* The thought would not resolve itself into even a hint of a solution.

As quickly as he could he got out from under the EGG hurrying upstairs to the observation platform. He expected to see another corresponding patch on the top. It wasn't there. Slowly, pensively he made his way to the main laboratory to where Mary's data had been flowing since he began his inspections.

Confrontation at Unity

Still feeling the effect of the drugs and hungry after being forced to fast for a couple of days Nick didn't look happy. Dishevelled, unshaven, face lined with sleep creases, one could hardly have recognised him.

In a way it was fortunate Nick wasn't aware of Mary now being a part of him, not just inside him as a separate invasive entity. The distraction could have jeopardised everything. Already he'd had an unsatisfactory reception on arrival. Being drugged wasn't his idea of a friendly welcome home. Two more days passed in a daze. He ate much more than he thought he could ever manage. The strange thing he'd been turned into must have had a peculiar side effect on his appetite. Shaving and making himself presentable didn't happen. Between waking and sleeping many things got tangled up in his mind about the journey; what he was supposed to do, who were all those people on the journey and so on. He wasn't in a very good state of mind when the three executives came to de-brief him.

Unfriendly guards pulled the sorry looking Nick out of isolation. They made him stand to face his interrogators. His cocky, self-assured self after the first test flight didn't assert itself this time. Nick hung his head, sighed deeply suspecting he'd landed in a great deal of trouble.

"Look at me!' barked the POOP. "This is your last chance." He wanted to know just two things.

Nick kept staring at the floor. Mary dared not intervene to help him. All manner of evil things might ensue if he started talking to himself in front of Leif. She remained hidden deep in his psyche hoping he would respond simply, honestly without complicating things with any of the distracting events of the journey. Nick shifted from one foot to the other, tilting his head back slightly so he could see Leif's face.

"I assume you've achieved something, otherwise you would not have been brought back. Out with it. I'm running out of patience! You've had enough time to recover."

The floor, the walls and even the ceiling assumed some form of importance for Nick as he cast his eyes over them all, remaining silent, thinking. An overwhelming image of sitting in front of a kava bowl scooping up a small ladle full assailed his senses. He could almost feel the numbness around his mouth, his lips and tongue blessing him with a sense of calmness and relaxation. That's what he needed right then.

"Let's try this again - Did you meet him? Does he exist or not?"

Zsoall Robi

Leif's loud voice brought back a rush of memories. "Well ... no, I'm not sure if I met him. Something happened, but I can't say what exactly. Something definitely exists out there, but I can't recall seeing anything that I would have perceived as being anything ... recognisable." Nick tried to sound relaxed and in control of himself, drawing on the imagined strength of a good gulp of his relaxant of choice.

"No endorsement?"

"No. Not exactly." He thought back to the first briefing session ... 'just a few simple words 'Unity is the One'. ... then he remembered something the car lady said. "Would the word 'Trust' work for you," a moment of his insubordinate aspect flashed into the conversation.

"What the hell are you talking about? Where did you hear that?" Nick could see the man's temperature rising and couldn't help feeling a sense of recklessness coming to the surface in himself.

"Somewhere out there," lifting his eyes skyward, "not sure exactly where."

"Idiot!" Quasimo stepped up to Leif, put a hand on his arm softly. He could see no good coming out of this if Leif lost control.

"Portrait?" Leif hissed the question through clenched teeth.

Nick's head wobbled uncertainly from side to side.

"No portrait?"

"No ... at least not yet ... well perhaps soon ... I need to recover." Nick said trying to make positive noises.

An opportune knock on the door interrupted the imminent volcanic explosion.

"Excuse me sir," said one of the guards. "We found these when searching the EGG."

Theo went over to have a look at the reason for the interruption. The guards held several painted canvases. He saw they were obviously portraits of some people. "Bring them in. You might want to have a look at these, Leif."

"Is that your work?" A superfluous question, considering Nick was the only occupant of the spacecraft. He grunted. *I should have destroyed those.* An intense stream of adrenalin shot through his body. At least it served to fortify him against the barrage he knew would imminently hit him.

In no particular order Theo began turning them around one by one for Leif to see. By pure coincidence Mala's image was the first.

"Ah - that's your wife, Mala - right?" commented Quasimo, looking at a most proficient likeness revealing not just her islander beauty but some of her inner sparkle. "Very good."

Quasimo didn't care much for art of any description. But fearing what the others might reveal he tried to calm the already tense atmosphere in the room.

"What's the other one? You been practicing?" Leif had settled slightly.

Theo turned over the next one - another female. They couldn't recognise her. "Er - that's Mary. If she had a face that's what I think she would look like." It lacked the appeal of the first portrait. This time Leif grunted.

"Seems like you had a lot of time on your hands. Is this all you did? Have a good time at our expense?"

The next work, unfinished, with smudged colours and hardly any form to the face reminded Nick again of his attempt to remember the car lady and the effect she had on him. As much as he'd tried he just couldn't form an image in his mind to satisfy the deep impression she left on him.

This situation boded ill for him. Nick remembered there were only two images left, hoping against all probability that Leif would tire of the examination and not bother looking at them. Turning over the next one caused an immediate reaction, one he definitely didn't expect.

"Not bad - not bad at all. You did this purely from memory, yes?" asked Quasimo.

Nick nodded, only momentarily relieved. Leif grunted again, taking the time to have a closer look at his own portrait. Even he could recognise it as being better than any of the myriad portrait photos that had been taken of him. Not entirely flattering, but perhaps showing some strength of character.

"What's this last one?"

The two guards had to tighten their grip on Nick's arms for he cringed at the very thought of what they would see next and their reaction to it.

'What the #&*K is that?" screamed The POOP.

"ARE YOU SOME KIND OF DEMENTED, INSANE … … … !" a stream of profanities followed in quick succession.

Quasimo immediately ordered the two guards to take Nick out of the room back to his isolation chamber. He let the painting drop to the floor, with the image of Riin face up, as she appeared true to her form. Leif couldn't cope with the eyes at the end of extended eye-stalks staring up at him.

The POOP forced himself to leave the room by the other door before he imploded or did some damage to Nick as he was being taken out. "Freeze the cretin!" he shouted as Nick disappeared under guard.

For a further week they kept Nick under heavy sedation while Quasimo and Theo tried to reason with the POOP. Freezing the poor bastard wouldn't do anybody any good. Quasimo understood the situation better than Leif, at least he could approach it with a clearer mind. He didn't have as much invested in the enterprise. Neither his personal reputation nor his private fortune would suffer if Nick turned out to be a complete dud - unlike Leif, who would lose everything; his position, his private asteroid holiday home, his entire fortune - even his sanity, from the direction he was heading in. Yet, like Theo, he enjoyed his job. He liked to be at the cutting edge of technology doing the sort of stuff people didn't even dare to dream of. Imagine sending someone out into space to find God, have a chat with him and get a portrait painted. Outstanding. He didn't for one instant think how insane that sounded. But then again, religion in their era had turned into an insane institution by anybody's measure.

"What do you think Theo? Should we try to sort this out?"

"You're the scientist my friend. This is pretty weird stuff. Did you see that last painting? What could have possessed the man to do something like that? Look - from a theological perspective, if we could get just a little bit of solid evidence I have no doubt we could put a profitable spin on it. Leif would show us his gratitude in grandiose ways, as you know already. It would be worth trying to reason with him."

Several days into Nick's convalescence the two men felt safe to approach the POOP. "He's had several doses of his MaxHapps and a chance to compose himself. I notice he's taken that portrait of himself up to the asteroid. I've made an appointment to visit. For the moment he doesn't want to come anywhere near our facility," Quasimo said.

A quick shuttle trip flew Leif's two most trusted advisors to that famous mansion in space. Orbiting a little above the main satellite strata, no ordinary man could have imagined the vista available from the home of this wealthy man. The ten minutes it took to get out there and dock gave Theo and Quasimo the opportunity to enjoy one of the perks of their position which they had not often experienced, their attention first drawn to the extraordinary number of satellites orbiting Earth. Mostly owned by governments and multinational corporations, enough space still remained for many privately owned facilities to house their rich owners. The moon in all its magnificence never ceased to amaze, particularly the twinkling lights of the many mining operations under way on its surface. The view into deeper space revealed some of the Sun's further planets, the most magnificent from that vantage point being Saturn with its incredible rings. At no point in their short trip did they see anything that would have caused concern, oblivious to the peculiar phenomenon of invisible light beams circling Earth unlike the thousands of satellites they could see.

Quasimo came directly to the point of their visit, accepting the refreshments Leif offered so magnanimously from his palace in the sky. "Nick's obviously had an experience of some description. Granted, there's no portrait – but that could still be inside his head."

Theo added, "We selected him partly because of his peculiar approach to portraiture painting. Perhaps he needs a little time to adjust to normality. We chose him not because he was ordinary, but because he was most demonstrably not so. I think we should have expected some degree of - may I say, peculiarity - about the way he operates."

The POOP didn't appear to be in a conversational mood, just grunting at the possible common sense expressed by his executives.

"At this stage we have lost nothing. If we give up now our investment would be wasted. Just think about it. If we can get him to create something, something unique in the way of a portrait, I dare say we could put a spin on it - don't you think Theo?"

"Indeed, indeed. And as I recall he did say something of interest, which he cannot deny. 'Trust' - he said Trust. If we're looking at rebranding Unity, giving it a whole new identity what better way to promote the organisation than as 'the One You Can Trust.' Theo hadn't actually formulated this idea beforehand. It just popped out as he unfolded his train of thought. Rather happy with himself he grinned at Quasimo and Leif. Quasimo grinned back, amazed his friend had such a devious mind, but then again he was also high ranking clergy within the Church, very high indeed, second to the Papa.

Still Leif remained silent. He listened to their logic, sipped his favourite cocktail, enhancing the pleasure with another couple of MaxHapps. "So what do you suggest?" Obviously a possibility for resurrecting the enterprise had presented itself. As Quasimo said, at this point nothing had been lost.

Enthused by Leif's response Quasimo went a little deeper into the matter. "Klaus came to us yesterday. He'd been analysing the data downloaded from Mary. From what we can tell Nick did actually reach the Centre, or someplace very close to it. Apparently Mary has a record of encountering two photon like phenomena and the act of constant creation that was taking place, albeit it only hydrogen atoms - but there it is. Something we could definitely work with."

Of course they would have been much happier with some more solid evidence. But at least it was something to massage. The revolutionary new space drive had functioned without a hitch. Not only had it worked and brought back the EGG and its cargo in one piece, it did it quicker than they had anticipated.

"Don't forget Leif," said Quasimo taking a chance at familiarity, "we have created an incredible computer. That technology is in itself worth billions of credits." Little did he realise just how outstanding Mary turned out to be.

Leif had had enough. He put up his hand to stop any further jabber. The three men swiveled their couches to face the transparent force field of the habitat. Nothing obstructed their view of Earth. From that vantage point, together with his own array of satellites, the POOP could focus in on just about any point on the planet with quite exquisite detail. He adjusted a few controls on the console of his couch to bring Efate island into focus on the screen above them. He sneered at the thought of being able to snuff out the tiny speck of dirt in the Pacific Ocean at the touch of a button, and no-one would care.

"Not much of a place to live is it?" he commented with that supercilious tone of disdain." There wasn't much of the world's population he didn't look down his nose at. "Alright, he can go home," he barked at Quasimo, "But everything he creates is my property! I want that portrait, make no mistake. You had better convince him of that."

"Does he get paid?" Quasimo asked quietly.

"NO! Blast him!" Quasimo raised an eyebrow at Leif, which he must have understood - the cretin needs an incentive. "Alright – some. He can't exhibit anything – He can't show anything to anybody – not friends, not anybody! I want him watched twenty four seven. If he steps out of line just one millimetre, his ass is mine." That didn't leave a lot of room for negotiation.

*

Oona, the pretty young thing with a black-widow spider mentality, drew up the contract. "Look Nick – it's the best you're going to get. You get to go home at least – that's fair. The painting has to be done. Without it you can consider your life expectancy to be drastically curtailed." She'd been personally selected by The POOP, seeing in her qualities admirably suited to his organization.

"Do I get paid?" he asked. *What the heck - if they're squeezing so hard what have I got to lose by asking.*

"Some. Work on it. You'll be watched." Smiling sweetly Oona left him to prepare for departure. The contract he signed had very little legal substance. Unity could do whatever they wanted with him at any time. Poor old Nick was just a very tiny molecule in the very big Universe of Unity.

Quasimo and Theo managed to convince the POOP that the expedition was at least a seventy-five percent success so far. Nick should be paid accordingly and allowed to resume his normal life. Theo also convinced The POOP that there may well be some hidden information inside Nick, which could still reveal more than he was able to tell them personally. Perhaps Nick did have an encounter and it was hidden in his subconscious, because of the very nature of the encounter. God was, after all is said and done, a rather slippery character to deal with - enigmatic, mysterious and all that. Perhaps even that painting of the strange creature had something to do with him trying to empty his mind of irrelevant imagery before attempting *the* Portrait.

Riin Infiltrates Earth System

Seconds from arriving home Mary picked up a familiar communication signal that didn't originate from Earth. Its source could only be Keplerian. But they were too far from 443b. If the signal came direct from the alien planet it would not have been as strong and clear. No. This signal could only have come from within Earth's solar system.

She recognised the language, the peculiar bleep, hiss and warble sounds used by the septaploids. Two instants after detecting the communication Mary reacted instinctively. She did the only thing available to her, in the absence of armaments with which to protect herself and her passenger; change the density of the EGG's boson cloud to minimise the impact she expected from a collision with the source of the transmission. Whatever sent the signal had changed direction to intersect with her; a hostile act as far as she was concerned.

If her strategy failed the possibility still existed that the incoming phenomenon either intended to do exactly what Riin had done, that is, to board the EGG perhaps with the intention of taking control of her, or to capture Riin in an attempt to rescue her.

Within that double instant Mary decided to make it as difficult for Riin to be rescued as possible. A close relationship had not developed between herself and the alien. It resembled more of an enmity without violent intent, perhaps until well into the future. Riin had made her intentions quite clear from the beginning on behalf of her species.

By defocusing Riin's fermion density in memory storage it would be much more difficult for her to be located and downloaded if the invading entity did indeed have that purpose.

"Sfewpyvie eeœyiype! At last," exclaimed Riin, "I'm free!"

No sooner had she realised her release from memory confinement she felt the forces of photonic attraction pulling on her dispersed data. She couldn't recognise Tenôsed but she knew it must be one of her own people attempting a rescue.

"Hyiror daíe ilms - Hyiror daíe ilms - I'm here, I'm here," she shouted. But everything happened too fast and the forces of attraction were simply not strong enough. Tenôsed's beam shot through the structure of the EGG as fast as it had arrived.

By the time Riin regained her composure the EGG had reached its destination.

Zsoall Robi

I'm still free, she realised as the environment of her entrapment changed beyond recognition. But she was still alive, and Mary had not restricted her again. Without immediately realising it she understood the words being used by other aliens who resembled Nick's basic structure. At first she wondered how they could possibly stay upright on just two legs and not keep falling over. As she concentrated on the conversation of two alien technicians who had been doing something to the spacecraft she realised an incredible opportunity had presented itself.

"Hurry up Olga, the big boss wants this data asap."

"I'm going as fast as I can," replied the technician. "If I don't get these connections jacked in properly the data from Mary could be seriously corrupted."

That snippet of an exchange was enough for Riin to realise what that opportunity was. Being a quantum physicist herself gave her a clear advantage over simple computer techs.

Riin suddenly felt sluggish as if awakening from a bad dream, with a body partly paralysed, unable to move her arms or legs. Unity's mainframe quantum internal environment had been the space in which much of Mary's logic and intelligence systems had been developed. But it didn't have sufficient processing capability to complete the job. That had to be done using Mary's own neural network. Her multiple neuromorphic processors performing at speeds far in excess of Unity's mainframe finished the job of creating Mary's intelligence simulating mind matrix. Being inside that mainframe made Riin feel like she was moving through a vat of methane jelly after experiencing the speed of Mary's mind.

Riin understood the principles of quantum computing and began to recognise some of the structures and logic architecture. "Ah - here we go." With a little searching she found the uplink to Unity's communications satellite array. Excited beyond belief she began transmitting without actually knowing if her failed rescuers would ever hear her.

"Giyhmfatu slenednei oiwelseo thoem üwosow iswohs e iyquicho snoryy erewtðeed cmudledce wmohvos mveeþtse sa delåoo hintoð mzepevþ ponnine royi - Giyhmfatu slenednei oiwelseo … Giyhmfatu slenednei oiwelseo …"

Sorensen, at Unity HQ Satellite Control, had just returned from his break and about to settle at his console when the series of gurgle-blips, burbles, trickles, plinks and chirps sounded from the equipment.

"What the hell? Hey, Tony, come and listen to this." By the time Tony had wandered over the signal had repeated itself several times. "What do you make of that?"

"Are you recording this? The strangest thing I've ever heard. Makes me think of that crazy group who are still searching for intelligent life out there. I haven't found any around here," he quipped giving Sorensen a slap on the shoulder - an old, worn out joke.

"Come on, be serious. You'd better get the supervisor over here."

Tony still thought it must have been a joke, until another set of plinks and dings, crackles and burbles vibrated the air. They recognised that some of those sound sequences were a repetition of what they heard before. Tony took off like a rocket while Sorensen checked to make doubly certain the signals were being recorded.

*

Mary retained a copy of herself in the EGG's neuromorphic network prior to downloading part of herself into Nick's head. During her housekeeping exercise the copy realised a problem had emerged. Just how damaging that might become could not be ascertained from the information she had available.

Riin had disappeared. Logic dictated the only available escape route available to her had to be the link between the EGG and Unity's mainframe complex. If circumstances permitted Mary decided to explore that possibility. *I have completed my task, fulfilled every requirement of the project. Alien stowaways are not my concern. A lone entity like Riin, without any means of communication or transportation is unlikely to pose even a minimal threat. She'll be treated as a virus in the system and dealt with accordingly.*

A consequence of having attained self-awareness, Mary, as well as her copy, could make decisions independent of any previously programmed instructions. The handshake protocol had initiated prior to data download to Unity. The Mary copy made her second decision - *It is of no benefit to mankind to be made aware of the extraterrestrial intelligence we stumbled across, particularly not of their intention to scope Earth's suitability for colonisation.* She restricted access to all data pertaining to the alien encounter events. 'If Earth is visited sometime in the future, it is unlikely that a human civilisation would still be in existence.'

If even the remotest possibility existed for human technology to have the capacity to mine the deep reasoning within the mind of a sentient robotic mind no doubt it would discover many mysteries. The reasons why such an intelligence might consider human existence on Earth to be somewhat limited in its life expectancy would not be one of those mysteries.

SPACE-TIME LEVEL, TWO
MUNDANE REALITY

Reunited with Mala

$\mathcal{I}$t might have been the same aircar that Oona bundled him into when she first arrived to take him away. Unity's enforcers flanking him on either side could have been anyone under those darkened face shields.

"Is all this really necess ..." Nick began asking Oona as she applied a knock-out patch.

The trip home could have taken an hour or a day. It didn't matter. He didn't care. He didn't know. They arrived in the dead of night. Mala didn't come outside to meet him. He found out later that she hadn't been informed of his imminent arrival.

His blindfold didn't come off until they'd shoved him into a chair in the kitchen. The guards stepped outside, Oona remained. Still a bit unsteady from the tranquilliser Nick let Mala's embrace steady him. He had to sit back down eventually, catching a sweet little sneer on Oona's face. *She's a piece of work. Fits in well with the rest of the crowd at Unity.* Muska puss was nowhere to be seen.

"Where have you been? What have you been doing?" She held him at arm's length to look closely at his face by the light of a single glow orb, catching her breath. "You look terrible. Are you ill?" The questions didn't stop until Oona interrupted. In some perverse way she must have been amused by the reunion. Mala ignored her. "What's happened to you? Why didn't you contact me?"

Nick remained silent, overcome at the joy of seeing her face, hearing her voice, just being in his old familiar environment. "Nick, is it really you? Talk to me."

Before Nick could respond Oona explained the situation. "It's like this, Mala. If you two discuss anything about this project the consequences will be most unpleasant for both of you." She smiled, letting that sink in first. Before parading her tail back aboard the aircar she said, "Unity will arrange the press release to satisfy public curiosity about your absence. We'll supply all your daily needs until the work is completed. "You get this one caution only. No reminders, no second chances. All you have to do Nick, is get on with the job, get that portrait painted. You won't have curious, nosey neighbours bothering you – or your wife." Oona glanced at Mala again to make sure she got the message.

Thankfully the aircar took off without delay. They remained inside, looking into each other's eyes. How long has it been? Nick had no idea. For Mala it was too long. They moved to sit beside each other on the sofa, hands on each other, minds going blank. Mala let out a long sigh and stroked his cheek with her other hand.

"So, it is a portrait?" she fished for the details.

"You are so beautiful!" he replied. *I'm home at last.*

*

For a while he enjoyed playing house with Mala. The island of Efate had not changed, not within the boundaries of his own home. Confined to live within the limits of the property he pottered around the garden, fixing things, making improvements and generally getting back into the normal rhythm of life. They had their occasional evening BBQ with the speculative exploration of the Universe to follow. Nick had to be careful about what he said. He hadn't only been out there but his life had become intertwined with Mary's. As the days flowed into weeks he had trouble convincing himself the experience actually happened. If it wasn't for the feeling of always being with a crowd he might've thought it had all been just another one of his peculiar, complicated dreams. Little by little he found himself drawn back into studio work. Unity didn't hound him. Seemingly they vanished from the face of the Earth. Yet the pressure was always there; their rations automatically arrived each week, as did the credits into their bank account.

About the second or third day after the three cats had overcome their indignation at having been abandoned, Nick had the most satisfying interaction with Muska. He was busy spreading mulch around a garden bed when she found him and spoke to him. Not quite her normal 'hello' mew, but sounding more like a demand for an explanation of his absence, accompanied by her direct ocular inquisition.

It was a bright, languid sort of day. Nick lowered himself to the ground to lie propped up on one elbow. Muska sat thirty centimetres directly in front of his face. Those summer sky blue sparkling eyes of hers renewed their intimacy with him. Nick's heart swelled at the beauty before him, and when she spoke to him his soul took flight. He reached out with his free hand to cup the top of her head in his palm. There wasn't anything he could say. They just looked at each other and he was lost in her. Then she stood, her tail curling a final question at him before cuddling into his chest. Starting up her motor she enveloped him in her super purr, a purr worthy of a lioness; loud, strong, both giving and demanding affection. It was a purr that vibrated peace with each breath inhaled and absolute contentment with each breath exhaled. Nick could feel the atoms in his heart rearranging themselves to accommodate her splendid kitty-hood. He couldn't say how long he lay there like that until Mala's voice winding its way down the path broke the spell.

"What are you doing on the ground? I've been calling and calling! I need you to come and smell the milk. I think it's off."

Nick had become oblivious to everything except Muska's loving purrs. Enveloped by her aura, he had ceased to exist and became one with his kitty, soaking up the sun, revelling in the bliss of existence. Later, after tea and the washing up, pondering upon his kitty in the grass, he was certain that somehow it wasn't just him who found unity with Muska. Yes, he loved cats, and dogs. All critters for that matter. But to find such a level of connection … he didn't think he was capable of such a thing.

One night, following a particularly satisfying painting session in the studio putting the finishing touches to the portrait he'd started of Mala before they took him, he had another one of his strange dreams. Strange because it wasn't disjointed. It made sense. He could always remember those in detail. In this latest dream he was back aboard the EGG, participating in a meeting. There was himself, Mn'd, Cre'teur and Eyechat. He didn't get a chance to say much, with mostly Mn'd talking, bringing him up to date with a proposition from the group.

"We've been watching, waiting and devising a method by which we could all co-exist, peacefully. We could also help with your current project – but there needs to be certain practices to facilitate the process."

Cre'teur tried to explain, "The aim of these exercises, colour focused meditations, is to relax you so various members of our group could have direct involvement at various times."

"We are convinced you could do this," Mn'd said, "and Eyechat can help you."

Eyechat elaborated. "We've already had a short session if you recall. Remember the pleasant little episode you had with Muska recently when you allowed yourself into her world? When you transcended yourself you gave me the opportunity to become manifest as a prominent aspect of yourself. So while you were experiencing Muska's joy in existence, I was foremost in your anima at the time. So there's the essence of what Mn'd is proposing.

Effectively, you would be doing whatever you do, but in partnership with one of us. Think of it as if we were your guests and you were our host."

Nick could hardly believe what he was hearing. He could certainly remember how his heart soared when Muska gave herself over to him. He suspected that the proposition might very well turn out to be the thin end of the wedge. What assurance would he have that he'd remain in ultimate control?

'Wait a minute, I am in control, I'm still the boss. And how is this going to help me with the portrait?'

"Right ... right ... Ok ... er ..." Mn'd was about to say something else when Brahin dropped a little bombshell as an aside.

"By the way, Mary also thinks this could work very well."

"What! Where's Mary?"

"Let's just say she has not completely abandoned you. We're discovering she has some extraordinary skills," Mn'd added.

Nick awoke in the early hours of the morning to find Muska had snuck under his sheet. Kitty enjoyed extra cuddles while he pondered pressing matters. *Would I become a machine 'driven' by these various forces? Just how real was this dream? Where is Mary? Why did this have to come along when I was right on the verge of getting onto the portrait.* Not being able to discuss any of it with Mala without going into explanations about the whole trip, made the whole situation more complicated. *She'd probably think I'd attained early pensioner-hood.* Mulling over the labyrinth of complications until the sun finally squeezed itself above the horizon, he decided nothing would be lost by giving the idea a try. With the decision firmly made, Nick gave a very warm kitty a last cuddle and got up to attack the day.

Since arriving home Unity had not tried contacting Nick. He hadn't given them any excuse to interfere. Their surveillance devices scattered around the place would have seen he had recovered well from the expedition spending more time in his studio. Nick valued his privacy. Being under constant scrutiny didn't exactly trigger creative juices to flow. Fortunately, they couldn't monitor his dreams.

A day or two later in a lucid dream bordering on waking reality he had a quiet word to Mn'd. "See if Mary can do something to prevent Unity getting into my dreams."

After days of amicable interaction with various members of his awakened subconscious, Nick felt reasonably comfortable with the highly unorthodox arrangement they'd agreed on. It often made him smile just thinking about how Theo would react if he knew about the pact with voices inside his head.

It had become routine, even to the point of dispensing with the meditation sessions. Nick could get on with the day's activities without giving his passengers a second thought.

As a distraction to prime his talent he worked on a sculpture and on a landscape, but no more portraits after finishing Mala's. Lately he'd been getting the urge; that previously familiar feeling that he was ready to start on something special. Nick took it easy. No need to rush. Just let it flow. He prepared several canvases, the oils and acrylics and started reminiscing about the journey with Mn'd and the others. Not that Brahin cooperated very well. They knew a great deal about the trip. Mary must be in there somewhere keeping them informed. Although not in direct contact with her, it still reassured him to think she was there. He put himself on autopilot, gave Muska lots of cuddles, enjoyed a few more good BBQs and allowed the manifesting to begin. Together they could now embark on the final stage of Nick's special commission.

"Mala," I've finished your portrait. Since that first session before his abduction he'd not had Mala sit for him again, not even after his return. He brought the portrait into the house. Unity gave strict orders; no one was to enter the studio until he finished the painting for them, not even Mala - especially not Mala. Unity could not control her constant chatter to friends on her implanted comms.

"Nice," she said.

"Nice?"

"Yes - nice. What do you want me to say? I know how good you are. This is nice - not special, not wonderful, not magnificent. You caught the look in my eye, my skin complexion is realistic. It's good. You can do better." Nick just stood there without saying anything. Mala thought he wanted some kind of moral support, so she reiterated, "Yes, it *is* good. Are you feeling ready for the other one? I think you are, the way you've been putting it off the last few days."

"Nice?" he said, and heard a bunch of voices echo the sentiment.

The reality of space then the unreality of his own home environment created by his voices cast deep shadows across his subconscious. Normality had taken refuge somewhere outside his ken, with only the slender tentacles of his furry creatures holding him moored to some semblance of practical functionality. Mala wasn't much help. Being forced to remain isolated from his thoughts she could do little to support him.

Illusions or dreams, inner voices and visions of imagined experiences … from somewhere in all that chaos he had to create the impossible.

A New Reality Begins

$\mathcal{T}$he unexpected urge came upon him one day over lunch. Nick's thoughts turned inwards. On soft summer breezes tantalising aromas wafted through the open windows. His nostrils flared slightly as a sharp olfactory memory lanced into his consciousness - the aromas of lilac and lavender assailed his senses. Without a word to Mala he stood up from the table, meal unfinished. She knew what had happened, not the details but the sudden call of the muses that she had witnessed many times.

With deep introspection Nick steered himself towards the open, heavy timber front door and across the irregular pavers. At first he couldn't tell which way he should go, but then habit showed him the way, reliable as always. Nick had crossed the threshold just as surely as the EGG had crossed over into pure space-time, seemingly so long ago.

He had no choice; there was no free will for him. He wasn't alone. The path to be travelled was short and without any foreseeable danger, but as habit dictated, all were alert. Dangers always lurked in the hidden shadows; distracting thoughts, rogue visions, unwanted desires; facets of oneself vying for domination.

One of them opened the metal door in the side of the large studio. The lights were already on. Cre'teur pushed her way forward and cast a critical eye around the room coming to rest on one particular canvas; it had the right proportions, the right size. Just as she began organising Nick to get some paints and materials prepared Muska announced herself at the door, demanding immediate attention.

Nick bent down to Muska and Eyechat came through him and they connected. Eyechat's hand gave puss the compulsory tummy rubs. These two understood each other well. The others simply had to wait for the ritual to be concluded. Kitty and Eyechat each had a strange streak in them. But Eyechat didn't change from a cute kitty to raging lioness in half a second and proceed to puncture her human's arm with her fangs, simultaneously ripping flesh with the claws of her back feet. Ears back, eyes wild, the rage lasted only the other half of the first second before resuming her cute purring kitty-ness. Everyone enjoyed the psycho kitty performance. Yes, those two were very much alike.

Background tension always accompanied the group when on duty. Sometimes it was just a clash of personalities. Sometimes minor disagreements about priorities, which generally created the main source of friction, never serious but with enough frequency. They agreed about many things, like the most important things in life. However, Cogito was on a short fuse during that late afternoon for some reason. The others didn't really care. It didn't take long for him to get restless and start on his relentless badgering.

'Why do we have to be out here tonight. It's cooled down, I'm tired. I'd rather be inside reading a good book. Anyway, I'm not convinced there's any point in painting this portrait.' He didn't see the logic in painting anything, unless it was the house or something else practical. 'It's all too bizarre – no basis in reality, the whimsy of a demented fool. It wears me down just thinking about it.'

Cre'teur had her own thoughts. 'I *like* to paint. I enjoy the way the brush glides over the surface and dances with the colours. It's not just the resolution of each small challenge of tone or perspective or colour. It's about achieving the sum total of all the solutions and re-creating the elusive personality. That's the thrill. Capturing the soul! The magic of combining all the individual fundamental parts and creating a whole new vibrant living entity.'

Another wave of sensations washed over Nick, stronger this time - escalating; the scent, the touch of the hand, the sound of that voice.

Not satisfied with just having a good idea or a truly meaningful concept, Cre'teur had to drag the others into cooperating in order to make the developing image a reality. For ordinary people faith was enough. The POOP wanted solid proof. Nick realised nothing less would satisfy him.

Mary had been keeping a very low profile. In a way she'd made an extraordinary sacrifice to give up the EGG. After attaining self-awareness and realising her own self-hood through her experiences with and of Nick, she felt life had to be more than just being a machine. Her solution consisted of splitting herself into two fundamental aspects. One; the data managing intelligent computer, which she left behind in the EGG. The other, her sentient greater self, stayed with Nick. As Mary observed the antics of the group she felt drawn mostly to Cre'teur during the painting process. At their first meeting it was Mn'd. Now the power of the creative urge overwhelmed everything else.

So far Muska remained silent and still, on a chair beside Nick as he worked. When she spotted a furtive movement she manoeuvred towards the light to try and catch the skink. Eyechat quickly jumped to the rescue, put the creature outside and gave kitty a nice pat-pat. The skink was forgotten soon enough, but not the need for cuddles.

Brahin didn't stir, not that any of them ever bothered him too much as he was rarely ready to help constructively. *No need to get involved yet, my time will come.*

As for Mn'd holding the reins of the team chariot in tight control – well, he just bided his time also, doing the minimum essential for the moment. He and Brahin were comfortable in the background letting the more extraverted members make themselves busy. Mn'd had no idea their comfortable co-existence would soon come to an end.

'Come on," Cre'teur said, 'time to get started. I've got everything ready.'

The others had to find ways to amuse themselves while she and Nick worked. With slow, deliberate movements Nick prepared the palette while listening to Cre'teur whispering. The truth is she simply loved watching the swirls of tone as the colours blended on the palette. Together they would become one for a little while and in concert conduct the flow of time and wavelengths into an act of creation on the canvas.

Slowly the studio became a gently flowing eddy of creative energy permeating the air. Muska insisted on making the life force of a Christmas beetle one with her own: Cre'teur kept an eye on the canvas, at the same time Thecore started an argument with Cogito, while Brahin began weaving the next web of falsehood to be overcome, and Eyechat totally immersed herself in Muska. He wondered why he found it so difficult coming to terms with seeing one life force consuming another in order to maintain its own life.

For an hour or so all went well. Occasionally Mn'd cautioned the group to be less disruptive and let Cre'teur and Nick concentrate. Brahin still managed to niggle with interjections like; 'We've been out here for *hours*. Perhaps a coffee would be nice. Come to think of it, something to eat wouldn't go astray. There may be a good vid to watch tonight. Shall we find out?'

Then Cogito interrupted with the same old, 'Well, if you must know Cre'teur, the only reason you give in to this compulsion to create, in my opinion, is because in some weird way you feel it gives life meaning, some sense of purpose. Strange you could so easily ignore the simple truth that there is no meaning, only physics.'

Generally they could rely on him to think something through and not let them take any rash course of action, or to get side-tracked by irrelevant ideas. His weakness was impatience. As it turns out it wasn't his only weakness. The very idea of life having no meaning would become problematic for Nick - it had in the past. But Cogito's strength was in being able to ask the right questions. In an argument you couldn't lead him astray from logic, but when he proffered some esoteric or philosophical train of thought of his own, it often distracted the others from their tasks at hand. However, at the right time, his contributions to unravelling a problem or deciding on a course of action proved most often to be highly productive.

That comment about the meaninglessness of life had hit a very sensitive nerve for Nick. He'd worked hard most of his life with the reasonably comfortable belief it did have meaning. Even if it didn't, at least he was giving it one. To get up each morning with the thought that it was all pointless, seemed untenable. What made him particularly angry was that somewhere deep inside himself he wasn't entirely convinced by his own optimistic philosophy, as evidenced in the last year or so, having dived into kava reality to numb the uncertainty.

Though normally not a volatile person, Nick threw the brush into a jar of turpentine all of a sudden, got up from the chair and without saying a word moved towards the door. The magic had been broken. Efate reality invaded the studio. Surprised, the others just followed without further agitation. Even Muska who was by then sleeping most comfortably on Nick's other chair jumped down and raced out the opening door.

Smell My Fish

*A*s Nick stepped out of the studio his mind returned to Efate reality with a thud. Mala called from the house, "Come and smell my fish!"

It wasn't just the beckoning with command overtones that gave impetus to his compliance, but also the nature of that very peculiar thing Mala had just said. Unfortunately Nick could be very easily distracted; a gecko on the wall, a green tree frog or even rustling in the dry leaves could halt the march and they would all be stuck for who knows how long, Mala of course would not be pleased with any delay.

Smelling fish can make the difference between life and death. It's obvious if you're Brahin. Mala hadn't realised she'd tapped into a very ancient aspect of human evolution. There was a time, somewhere around the last ice age, when mankind was having a good deal of trouble surviving. Not only was it far too cold, it was also a difficult time to find food and then to keep it fresh for longer periods. Fish was a notorious example of the problem. It had to be sniffed every time before subjecting it to the skills of the chef. This ritual had become deeply embedded and persisted even into modern man's psyche. Biding his time to do a bit of mischief, Brahin began working on a new tack. 'When we get into the house, why don't you tell Mala to just throw the fish out,' he said to Nick hoping to get an argument started. He brought into memory the odiferous delights of fish that have been basking in the hot sun for a couple of days. Stench was always a good motivator for putting anyone in a foul mood.

Ignoring the nuisance Nick made it across the pavers, down the slight incline and past the corner of the house. The security light flashed on revealing an emerald green body with the black bands of a banded iguana brazenly waiting on the path for something to catch in the light, immediately drawing Eyechat's attention.

The wooden door was in sight, not ten steps away when it happened. Then an urge came upon Nick that could not be ignored. That's the way it is with creativity and inspiration. Cre'teur felt it and knew not to fight the urge.

'But I need to smell the fish!' exclaimed an extremely annoyed Cogito.

Brahin just grinned. He didn't much like painting either and would have preferred to watch interesting events unfold in the kitchen.

Nick became so intent on returning to the studio he had completely forgotten about the fish. The portrait would not manifest a soul if the eyes weren't right. Cre'teur knew exactly what had to be done to start the eyes. Her will exerted such power that the others couldn't resist. There was no denying the fish still had to be smelled but this wouldn't take long - the right sized brush, just a touch of white and a masterly stroke. Back in the studio, with utter confidence, Nick smudged the right tone onto the canvas directly from the palette to make the critical change.

Mala's loud voice penetrated through the open door. "I said - Come and smell the fish!"

Another perilous walk across the pavers brought Nick successfully to the front door past the spot where the iguana had been. Even before reaching the kitchen, he'd decided what had to be done.

"Cook the jolly fish on the day you buy it! It's the safest. We don't know how fresh it was in the first place. Perhaps safer to throw it out."

Yesss! Brahin fist pumped. The others just made theatrical faces at one another and wondered how they ever got tangled up with him. Nick and Mala embark on the ritual dinner bout of four rounds. First round ... how to cook the fish. Second round ... how to make the salad. Third round ... just eat the damn thing. Round four ... washing up.

Nick couldn't find a blessed thing in the pantry, not even in the 'open-your-eyes' section. *How different this is to life with Mary in the EGG*, Mn'd reminded him.

"If you bothered opening your eyes ..." Mala hissed, already annoyed at the delay.

The kitchen seemed to shrink. It was a larger than normal kitchens but conflict shrank it. There was just not enough room for two of them. To start with, all the cupboard doors were in the wrong places. Mala and Nick kept colliding with each other at the same cupboard. Having a right-handed chef in the kitchen with a left handed sous chef was a recipe for disaster. Compromise came in the form of a gentle word from Thecore.

"How about I cook, and you set the table," Nick suggested to Mala. He brought his culinary skills into play on how to best achieve the juxtaposition of pan and fish over a flame. Nick didn't doubt his ability to maneuver the filleted fish into the fry pan when the time came to threaten it with the flame ... unless ...

It was an unlikely place for a new adventure to begin but as with all things, the ordinary can often lead to the extraordinary ... and it was no ordinary thing that the fish still smelled. Which was exactly the thought that crept into his consciousness as he examined the pathetic bits of fish holidaying on the kitchen bench.

Grill the fish, grill the bloody fish, came the insistent, pulsing urging from somewhere. *Throw in a bit of hot red paprika*, he heard the voice of Brahin urging him. Nick knew full well Mala hated hot paprika.

Immersed in mapping out the evening repast he was only faintly conscious of Mala still asking him, now with some degree of annoyance, "Well, is the fish going to be alright?"

"Yes, yes. It's totally dead in the pan. I'll make a Greek salad to go with it."

So the die was cast and the gas was lit. The future had been set in concrete. The meal was to be fried fish with Greek salad. Nick could make a jolly good Greek salad. The fish just smelled like fish, it had not ripened.

Only Muska's plaintive mew for a tiny bit of yummy smelly fish disturbed their tranquil evening meal. Having the right perspective on things is important. One man's yuck is another man's yummy. The ticking away of Efate reality, emanating from the kitchen clock eventually began to impact on the proceedings in the kitchen.

"Is there anything interesting to watch on the vid?" Mala wanted to find something informative.

"Watch whatever you like. I'm worn out. I'm going to sit outside for a while," Nick said pleasantly.

SPACE-TIME LEVEL, THREE
INNER SPACE

Degrees of Reality

$\mathcal{F}$atigue does strange things to a person's mind. Perhaps we begin to hear voices, or hear sounds or even see things that don't exist except in our heads. Reality becomes fluid and behaves in unexpected ways.

What if you've recently returned from the craziest trip of your life, thought you'd had a nice chat with some strange extraterrestrial and became convinced of a female computer persona taking up residence inside your mind, alongside a bunch of other characters? In what meaningful way could the mundane reality of painting a simple portrait, or having quasi intelligent conversations with aspects of yourself impact on your sanity? You could try being scientific. Fact and experimentation - thought experiments perhaps. Is the idea of a God another example of Quantum unreality? And painting an actual portrait of the concept - where is that on the scale improbability?

Nick had retired to an old comfortable cane chair on the veranda at the back of his house. Already fatigued before the meal and now feeling both replete and exhausted he couldn't go directly to bed on a full stomach. Mala could see his mind had already gone off to imagination land so she left him alone to entertain herself with something of little consequence on the vid.

He withdrew into himself, unconscious of the dazzling Milky Way blanketing the sky above him. Perhaps the bleed of Mary's knowledge into his own data repositories initiated thoughts previously foreign to a simple, though talented portrait artist. *I don't know what is real anymore.*

For a moment or two Nick's conscious mind returned from the day-dream it had just embarked upon, to contemplate another journey he'd recently returned from. *I wonder how long I was away. I'll have to ask Mala. She hasn't brought it up before.*

It must have been hard for her not knowing when I would return. His mind wandered off again, not realising the locations of some heavenly bodies had changed.

He adjusted his position several times in the chair trying to compensate for the discomfort of that last train of thought. He yawned and stretched - getting near to bed time. Putting a hand in his lap he realised for the first time Muska had been with him all along.

At home in bed is such a lovely place to have dreams. Particularly those dreams that make no sense and leave you feeling tired when you wake: On top of which you can hardly remember any of them except that you would rather not have dreamt them. They are actually the best kind of dreams because they are the problem solvers during the waking state if you don't harass them with inappropriate analytical thoughts.

The best course of action is probably to ignore your brain logic completely. Assume you are always in the right place at the right time doing the right thing. Let the synaptic activity of your thoughts energise your emotions and enjoy cavorting in those energy fields of creative reality. This is where you are allowed to entertain any thoughts at all that decide to come by themselves to play with you in your soul garden. Let them play and tempt you. Make them mad with a bit of flirtation. It doesn't mean you have to do anything or everything they say. They are just thoughts and if you don't feed them for a while, they'll go away.

However, one hungry thought insisted on being fed. *Just who was that person in my dream. I wish I could have seen her face. If I could paint her, Leif he might be satisfied.*

Kitty stretched, her claws unintentionally digging into the reality of Nick's skin. Muska had decided it was time for a snack as the perfect preparation for bed … *my human needs to rest and recharge in the unconscious world of internal reality. Come, Nick, it's time to dream. We cats are experts at this.*

The Dream Begins

Kitty expressed her desire to sup with a most emphatic "ik ik yeowl" followed by a coercive "brrr-nyeow." She marched to the door with her flagpole tail firm and erect, a clear statement reverberating in the realms of waking reality, which many a human personage could emulate to their most probable benefit. So having captured the attention of all and sundry, who, being in the possession of the good sense acquired through years of arduous training by one kitty puss, opens the family room door without further delay.

This late into the evening not even the neighbouring cows expressed their pleasure at the cool of the evening. The occasional bat on the hunt screeched overhead as they entered the house. All the lights were out. Mala had gone to bed, but not to sleep. Her routine consisted of discussing, with her very best friend, all the issues causing joy and suffering to all of humanity on the planet. This process generally occupied about an hour of eternity, to be repeated each night of the week with a double conclave on Saturday nights.

Infiltrating this peaceful idyll of domesticity, Muska and her servant made their way to the kitchen. Kitty's fuel of choice was beef mince, which she deigned to eat one little meatball at a time, served by the hand of Eyechat. A vigorous shake of her front foot would indicate an elegant sufficiency of sustenance, whereas a combined shake of both the front and the back feet, which she did industriously after the sixth morsel, showed a distinct displeasure at having had just a tad too much. Regardless, her retro rockets fired instantaneously leading the way to the human's bedroom at a cracking pace, bouncing off the cane sofa and the wall on the way.

About to step over the threshold of the bedroom door she paused momentarily to reconnoiter the domain of Bird. Nick's nightly duty included ensuring Paco, alias Bird, alias Pterodactyl - feared by all kitty pusses with blood in their veins and a heartbeat - be put to bed in his condominium cage before Muska entered the shared sleeping quarters. Failure to carry out the safety protocol meant an instant attack by said Bird.

Paco, a South American Conure parrot, particularly security conscious of his domain, has been known to execute a perfect two-point landing on the carpet and chase Muska to within a nanometer of her life. This fearsome parrot, whose beak could extract vengeance most efficiently, had at his disposal several domestic dwellings, one of which was a large cardboard box stuffed with clean newsprint. The other, an elevated cage of generous proportions, equipped with a softly lined luxurious tubular sleeping compartment. With Paco in cage, Muska fed and about to be placated by occupation of the bedroom, it was time for general ablutions for Nick before settling down to a pre-dream read.

Although Nick became immersed in the pure pleasure of the antics of his family, thoughts of the memory of that elusive dream continued to pester him. He felt that the secret to getting that portrait done was somehow intricately tied up with someone he met in that dream. *If only I could return to that dream. If only I could catch a glimpse of that lady with the perfume and the soft hands.*

The sparseness of the bedroom removed the distractions preventing one from crossing over into the nightly realms. A book, a good book worthy of double or even triple readings, proved to be the best preparation for the transition into the dream dimension. Dreaming wasn't optional if one wished to remain healthy; actually essential for safeguarding the sanity of the host. It was also the time when Brahin did his best work, although causing his host considerable consternation by mixing things up a bit. That night Brahin had a sense of anticipation, perhaps even a foreboding of critical changes about to take place.

With head propped up on two pillows Nick began reading, at first having to re-read some passages. He wanted both to clear his mind to get a good night's rest and at the same time jump back into that past dream.

The Team, as Nick now called his aspects, enjoyed the story of the two detective Siamese cats, who had a dolt of a master-servant and who was at times as thick as yoghurt training to be cream cheese. The cats' story started out in a huge solid stone mansion of a small country town in the northern regions of North America. On an exceptionally sunny day, forecast with a remote possibility of a thunderstorm later in the evening, the cats and their master headed out in the direction of the cottage by the side of a splendid lake.

The author could transport the reader's senses into the drama of the novel with just a few elegantly descriptive paragraphs. The team could feel the breath of country air through the slightly open window of the car. The sound of an old rattling wooden bridge soon gave way to the vista of rolling green hills and forested peaks in the distance.

Muska kitty resumed her position by Nick's feet expecting his rapid decline out of wakeful consciousness on seeing his eyelids begin to droop even after a few short minutes. The book slowly slid out of his hand as his head tilted slightly to one side. The reading lamp, with two globes set close to each other, remained on.

Zsoall Robi

Brahin withdrew. Mn'd and the others remained silent, already anticipating - something. Nick often had strange dreams when he went to bed exhausted. This time he wasn't just tired, but preoccupied and focused.

Only moments ago Nick was in the car. Very soon he found himself walking towards the cabin, on a wide path that gradually funneled into an animal track forcing the group to go single file. For some reason they were all on edge, every noise making them flinch as they progressed.

The day may have started out sunny with not a hint of impending drama in the air, but as they neared the cabin the celestial light faded rapidly. Dark, low flying clouds gathered in haste and the last rays of sunshine cast an unearthly amber glow onto the landscape and the path ahead of them. Low rumblings and the rising wind urged them to pick up their pace.

Nick caught sight of the cabin not far ahead. The team made a dash for it through the sudden heavy rain dancing wildly on the previously dusty ground. Nick jumped onto the wooden boards of the front veranda. Although the overhang provided shelter the cabin still felt rather insubstantial. With an uneasy expectation Nick stepped forward to open the door. No one could have expected what the team saw and heard. The vision had no connection with any concept of reality they had experienced before, certainly not even in the labyrinths of dreams - except perhaps for the darkness and the sense of disorientation as they approached the two spots of light in Nick's cosmic dream.

*

Having squeezed inside, Nick's legs gave way and they collapsed into a tight huddle. While the next attosecond made its leisurely way along the path of its predestined fate, the collective thought in the group centred on a sense of déjà-vu, which they experienced with such discomfort.

Cogito mutter to Brahin, "This is not real. It's only a dream. We can wake up from this any time he wants."

Brahin disagreed. "I think this is far more than just a dream. It looks and feels too real. See how Nick's heart beat just spiked. He's starting to remember."

"As much as I deplore the prospect of having to relive the past, this even smells real, like the odour of ozone during an electrical storm." Cogito didn't really know what to think other than remain unconvinced of it being anything more than a dream - a new dream – possibly with complications.

"I don't think any of this is real, Brahin, just because you think it is," Cogito continued. "A virtual reality created by the senses is not an actual reality. You can call it an imaginary reality, but it's still just a dream. Don't forget, Nick was asleep when we got to the Centre."

During this discussion Cre'teur looked back out through the door and what she saw had no meaningful connection to what they were seeing inwardly. Whatever merits the academic discussion may have had, it was very clear to her that if they didn't get out of their current reality then the one they had just come from would become just a memory. For what she saw, was an open door facing out onto the wet, dark sky beyond the porch of the cabin. They had to get out of the cabin, get back into the car and get out of the book – out of the dream.

Nick partially woke, with a crick in his neck. In a half daze he turned his head towards the reading lamp and saw the glare of the two globes through half open eyes. Mesmerised by images that came flooding back he couldn't immediately turn the lamp off. As he did so after a few moments Muska could see that all he wanted was to get back to sleep according to his drooping eyelids.

The door of the cabin slammed shut, everything went dark - there was no turning back. Nick had fallen fully asleep.

Mary realised that strong forces compelled them to continue inwards, forces she could not understand. The cabin had ceased to be a cabin. It no longer had dimensions or boundaries. They lost their sense of size by losing all recognisable reference points. Looking upwards they saw exactly what they saw looking downwards or in any direction, just like in space; and at first only darkness. Overcoming complete disorientation became the first challenge. They had to rely on each other's presence to remain calm, and they could only do that by clinging to each other's consciousness as their environment came to life.

Mary also absorbed the experience, finding it not altogether alien to her cosmic experiences. Chaos of sounds, flashes of illumination bounced along floating ribbon rivers of light, sparkling stars swirled in spirals both close and immeasurably distant, mixed within the bubble of utter darkness surrounding them. Her memory of the Centre mimicked only Nick's growing awareness, for she was unable to record the event while they were there.

They were barely aware of each other in the void as it engulfed them to carry them into itself. On looking back, 'back' ceased to have meaning; as if they were suspended in the middle of a thought that hadn't yet been activated.

Cre'teur roused herself. She felt the essences of the others. 'Concentrate on a path', she urged.

As the group consciousness converged upon that thought, a patch of solidity materialised directly under them. Some of the disorientation melted away bringing a moment of relief. On the path they experienced a sense of place. The patch of ground that had extended itself into the beginnings of a trail had no past, only a future. It gave them no choice. They had to move the only way possible. Disorder continued around them. It intensified as they materialised the path through their collective visualisation. What kind of world was this that had captured them and coerced them towards a destination they didn't comprehend?

Each time any of them tried to rationalise their predicament, the space around them responded. More flashes and sparks streamed in myriad directions along convoluted channels to terminate abruptly, then continue intensified to the next terminal point, ending just as abruptly out of sight. It took some time before they made the cause and effect connection. They may not have been able to control what was happening around them yet they were somehow making them happen. This was a realm so foreign to Eyechat that none of his thoughts could find a purchase in the flux of energy around him. He tried to monitor their progress. Time refused to behave normally. *This is like the realm in pure space-time after crossing the threshold* - a random thought flashed across above them, not waiting to be entertained. Eyechat persisted. Thinking back to their arrival in this strange world he discovered the correlation between the distance they had traveled and the time it took. They hadn't traveled any distance over any length of time. He found that strangely comforting. If nothing happened until Nick awoke then they would be safe.

In a brief flash of lucidity during his dream, Nick realised that the random thought was important. He slept on - waiting expectantly for further insights.

"Don't forget," Cogito reminded the team, "we are in the right place at the right time and should continue doing exactly what we are doing." Knowing exactly what that meant remained elusive.

Upon turning their collective thoughts to this idea, their environment immediately went into a frenzy of activity. The entire dreamscape changed from what was definitely benign beforehand to very explicitly oppressive overtones. Colours went to deep purples and magentas bordered with washes of white and yellow. The golden white electrical charges propelled themselves at the group before discharging in front of them. Amoebic shadows thrust out from darkness threatening to engulf them before veering away back into deep oblivion.

"We might not know why we're here, but do any of you know where this is, and how we're supposed to get through it?" Cre'teur addressed herself to anyone who cared to listen.

With these thoughts re-energising their consciousnesses the terrain screamed with pulsating outbursts. The path writhed itself into impossibly twisted knots stretching itself into the infinity of blackness beyond their vision. It was all they could do to hold onto each other.

"I have a feeling something is trying to stop us. Why? We don't even know where we are going," said Cogito.

All this time Mn'd kept silent. Knowing Brahin as well as he did, it was no wonder they had to be constantly vigilant to make sure their information stream wasn't laced with nasty little thought viruses. Maintaining security became one of Mn'd's prominent duties. In this he worked closely with Thecore. Whereas Thecore ensured their inner beings were well balanced and followed their truth, Mn'd generally concerned himself with the more immediate moment-to-moment operations.

"I'll keep a watch out for anything dangerous. Perhaps it's just Brahin messing about," Mn'd reassured.

When faced with the awesome prospect of having to survive in this dream, it was critical the team wasn't contaminated by convention or conditioning. As long as Mn'd was on the job, they could immerse themselves in their adventures together without being at the complete mercy of a bio-computing lunatic, as they considered Brahin to be; necessary and therefore tolerated. Brahin was always the one who interpreted dreams, turning their integrity into fanciful abstractions. He may be the one trying to push the clear memory of the car lady into oblivion, making Nick question his own intuition. If he couldn't rely on that then the portrait would never become a reality.

Mn'd had been silent within himself from the moment they entered through the door of the cabin, but constantly vigilant. He didn't know at first what they had come to do. It was only when the environment began to react to their thoughts he suspected. At the moment the best way he could help was to keep his own thoughts hidden from the others, from the energy flux and even from himself. At first there was only apprehension but that quickly turned to fear where they had no control. They were on their own in an environment that could read their innermost thoughts. Mn'd knew he had to keep this knowledge to himself. He wanted Nick's intuition to drive them to unpredictable actions. It was the most effective way to counter anything Brahin may have been planning.

Constructive Fear

*T*hecore had withdrawn voluntarily, feeling he had no further contribution to make after balancing their thinking. The path they travelled, which might well lead to the foundation of their essence couldn't be altered now. They may fail to get to the end of it, but they couldn't diverge from their direction.

Brahin had also kept very quiet. He had ulterior motives bubbling under the surface with strong forces working on him even he didn't yet understand. He and Mn'd were very close and often felt the same things, particularly when there were matters of critical importance to Nick. This close connection made him apprehensive. He'd been feeling oddly strange and very vulnerable. He sensed it would be best to continue to stay hidden for the time being and that it was imperative to concentrate on keeping his thoughts very still, not letting them travel through the flux. Most importantly he had to distance himself from Mn'd as he became more aware of Mn'd's opposition to him.

Cogito remained silent, taking the opportunity to think upon all the strange goings on; how they might be connected and how they related specifically to their situation, convinced that at some point a great deal would depend on him. He had to be ready for that moment.

Only Cre'teur had sufficient presence of mind to actually provide leadership. As well as being creative she had the capacity for abstract concepts, with the ability to conceive the inconceivable. If anyone could make meaningful use of Nick's hidden memory, she could. The others had already begun to look to her for direction and strength. As with many people who find themselves in a leadership role, she rapidly grew into it. It was of course helpful that being the only female in the group she already occupied a superior position, purely by right of her gender.

The energy flux exerted a most peculiar disruptive effect on them. "Right, let's go," Cre'teur urged. "We have to take control of the situation. I don't think we should follow the path any longer."

Apprehensive Eyechat wanted to know, 'What did you have in mind?" He liked paths. Animals made paths. Paths were safe.

"Ignore the windings of the path. It's robbing us of our free will. We should go in the direction we intuit." Cre'teur turned away from them with the clear intention of following her own advice. She took the first step into the abyss, causing the path to dematerialise directly under them. With that single step she lost Mn'd's presence and immediately the fear of helpless isolation assailed her mind. She felt confident while his voice was in her ear,

Zsoall Robi

always making sure her flights of creativity were grounded in practical reality. As the panic of powerlessness washed over Cre'teur she also felt a strengthening of her being. It was Thecore's power.

"It works!" She cried to the others. "Keep taking one step after the other. Just follow me!"

Her footfalls created ripples of deep ultramarine blue with flashes of gold and white underfoot, while all around her strands of fine filaments began to appear glistening like cobwebs after light rain. Everything else retained the blackness of oblivion, without sound, without depth; all outside the framework of normal existence.

It was into this that Eyechat felt compelled to follow. Driven by fear and excitement he took the first step forward. He brought a very unique gift to the group. After taking the step into the unknown he could no longer feel the ability to identify with the life force of other living beings.

"I've lost them! They're gone, Cre'teur!" He yelled. As he followed in Cre'teur's footsteps he lost touch with the life energies he knew. They hadn't completely abandoned him until then, not even in the chasm of dreams. "I'm blind!" He cried into the chaos. The darkness he feared on the outside became a darkness inside himself. Utter, complete unfathomable silent oblivion. A wave of incredible electrifying fear surged through him with the realisation he might never again exist in the reality he understood. He might never again experience all the joy of his own life and the life of other living beings. His body reacted with an explosion of gyrating arms, fingers stretching to feel, to touch anything! His cry rang out, "Help me!"

As he drew the next breath to cry out again the very tip of his right hand index finger made contact with an exquisite charge of power. "Ahhh! Yes!" Eyechat stretched further until all his fingers touched the web of glistening filaments forming themselves around the small group. The web vibrated and threw out a great display of sparkling, cascading fireworks.

"I know!" He felt life again. In that instant he saw raw life and he understood. They all felt the surge of the same knowledge within themselves. Mn'd himself was shaken by the power.

Brahin became a casualty to the event. By closing himself off from the reality they were experiencing, he became a part of the very fabric creating that reality. He had withdrawn into the medium that protected him, gave him strength on the one hand but weakened him by loosening the bonds to his companions. His control over memories of dreams began to diminish.

I will prevail! Brahin promised himself. He felt the freedom to follow his inclination to oppose what the others had started.

Nick dropped out of REM momentarily without generating disruptive ripples into the dream fabric. He tossed himself from his left side to his right side, remaining unaware of his dual reality, yet feeling Muska's warm body still on the bed. The dream continued towards its inevitable conclusion. Nick felt himself slowly giving over to the free flow of thoughts, letting his intuitive self take the lead to recovering the experience he needed to remember.

Cogito wasn't immune to the fears assailing the others. His unique terror was the result of the very same moments of awakening, of knowledge and realisations that the others experienced, which awoke in him his greatest fear. These streams of information overpowered his self-esteem. He had always considered himself to be just a little more astute than the others; feeling he knew more than they, that he had the answers to their every query; that he could apply his skills of logic to solve any conundrum. Now he realised this was not the case. Logic played no part in these confronting events. They had acquired knowledge without him.

They don't need me. They never trusted me. There's nothing for me to do! These negative thoughts fed on each other, magnifying at each repetition. Cogito's mental anguish effected the others as well, reaching a crescendo within himself. As the unfolding events claimed their full attention his thoughts changed direction. Although they needed no immediate analysis, an explanation had to be forthcoming from him eventually. To this end he could still apply all his skill, feeling that by doing so he could bring absolute clarity to the quasi existential manifestation more than adequately, and so reinstate his standing in the group. For the time being he followed where they led, all the while deep in thought.

The team made slow progress. "According to my estimation we've been on the journey for exactly one millionth of one nanosecond. I cannot measure the distance we've travelled from the door of the cabin because we've created our own way off the original path," said Eyechat.

Their path had no surface, no dimensions. They could still see the other path continuing to wind and twist in torturous knots through the chaos of light away from them. But it had outlived its usefulness. They were now making their own decisions, but their progress was still too slow.

"We can't go on like this," Cre'teur said more to herself than anyone else. "We have not adapted," she realised. "We've just been lucky so far."

"You're right. Just reacting without knowing what we're doing isn't going to get us there." Cogito totally agreed.

"I don't have to tell you - we must adapt to the circumstances. And we have the right tool!

"Actually, I think you're right." Cogito's enthusiasm caught alight. "Contrary to popular belief, there is an empirical objective reality that doesn't depend on opinion or current scientific theories or even Cosmological ramblings, against which life, the Universe and everything is related in a perfect and inviolable manner. It is only our degree of perception that limits our understanding."

Eyechat, catching the drift eagerly contributed from his own personal experiences. "This is known by every animate and inanimate thing and is acted upon in an unconscious, instinctive way."

"There's only one way." Cogito put himself forward as an authority on the subject. "The secret to gaining an immediate understanding as to what to do, is to allow our basic higher sense to inform us. Don't actually think of a solution to a problem, let the problem define the solution - like Nick does with his painting. He can't paint the portrait because he is trying to manufacture. He's already got all the information he needs, but he's buried it under analysis."

Some nights Nick just couldn't get restful sleep. Being as deeply immersed in the inner realms didn't guarantee rest. The profound statement made by Cogito burst into blinding realisation in his subconscious. It passed far too rapidly for him to become cognisant of its importance. Spasming legs and momentary jerky breathing couldn't rouse him sufficiently to give him the chance to contemplate the validity of that truth.

"Ah, that's what you must have done," Eyechat announced. "You've instinctively used the problem, Cre'teur, to bring about a critical adaptation." He'd stated the obvious, but nobody minded.

By the application of this theory they'd become microscopically small points of highly concentrated energy, allowing them to become part of the fabric of their experience, instead of just experiencing that existence as external to themselves. It also gave them the ability to communicate directly into the web of filaments.

Eyechat reached out to touch the web again. The environment around them exploded into the size of the Universe, themselves becoming small enough to infiltrate into the most intimate of its spaces. The fabric of this Universe became a densely woven tapestry of those very same cobwebs that had restored sight and inner knowing to Eyechat and the others. By simply touching any part of the web they could feel the proximity of a friend. It turned out to be more than just the presence of a lost friend, it was an ally. Mn'd had returned to them.

"You called?" Mn'd seemed quite jovial. He'd undergone a complete metamorphosis. They could communicate with him directly about all things mundane and profound even though he wasn't even 'he' anymore. Mn'd had lost his semblance of physicality. He just was. His presence became most evident when the web started to tremble and glow with liquid rivers of light cascading from nowhere and everywhere. In those moments they simply had to touch the web until their ally's thoughts penetrated into them.

"Where are you?" Cre'teur asked.

"I am with you. Always with you when you need me."

In spite of the most recent developments and having overcome another major obstacle, the small band still felt themselves to be far from their goal, with a sense of further inconceivable challenges to face.

At the beginning they had no sense of purpose as they stepped through the cabin door to face the chaotic environment. Though still not knowing what that purpose might be at least they had become aware that one existed.

Rogue Thoughts

"**I**s everyone alright?" Cre'teur asked of the group.

"We're exhausted." Cogito remarked. The energy flux responded with a corresponding reduction of activity. At this point they experienced a slight diversion. A strange little thought came to Cre'teur. Brahin saw his chance in the lull and took it.

For no apparent reason Cre'teur became agitated. She blurted out, "Why are we so alone in this?" She became unaccountably angry. "It's not right *we* should have to do all the work – that we should have to take all the chances."

Brahin didn't want them to settle down, to feel more comfortable. He wanted to stir things up; sometimes when there was a danger of critical disinterest in the action at hand and sometimes when the group was having a little rest he felt they didn't deserve. He enjoyed creating disorder and seeing what surfaced. With a little tweaking he could keep the state of chaos in disruptive flux. This dream seemed to be made to order.

Cre'teur became angrier for a variety of reasons. "… And I don't like having to do the thinking for the lot of you!" Not that she didn't want them doing exactly what she wanted - she wanted covert control. Now she had to openly take the leading role. "It's all wrong. You're not going about our task the right way. It's all out of control. I would've done it differently, I would have done it better." Too many things were happening which she didn't understand. Having a goal was indeed an advantage. She tried to sort out their options for constructive, decisive action. But they kept ending up in a jumble of nonsense.

Frustration couldn't adequately describe how she felt just then. It manifested by taking it out on Cogito with a well-aimed barb. "It's your fault, Cogito. You just haven't been pulling your weight. Perhaps you'd prefer a little kava, like Nick, to pick you up."

He was in no mood for another confrontation. His distrust of their leader grew by the second. It would not have taken much more to tip him over the edge, especially after he'd been trying so hard to prepare a sensible analysis of their predicament for the team. "All I've done is to try and think of some options. Why are you so upset?"

Brahin just kept stirring. He guessed, very early in the venture, that they were likely to succeed. This wasn't in his interests. So he decided to make it as hard as he could for them.

Eyechat felt elated he'd made a real contribution through his intimate contact with the web. "Well, I've brought Mn'd back. You can't complain about that." Until his personal breakthrough he'd felt pretty much useless too. Their entire journey seemed pointless. "You haven't bothered to ask for my help, Cre'teur. What's so dammed important about finding whatever we're looking for anyway?" As these thoughts percolated into his consciousness so did a growing depression. If he wasn't careful the whole thing could get out of hand and Nick would become a manic-depressive. That also made him particularly angry - angry with himself and angry with Cre'teur for not doing a better job.

"It's not like you're doing so much either." Eyechat teetered on the verge of lashing out at Cre'teur when an intense pulsating beam knocked him reeling. Out of the corner of his eye he saw Cre'teur gyrating on the spot followed by Cogito spinning out of control.

"Oops – did I do that?" aghast that his behaviour had such a dramatic effect.

"Settle down. No need to get so excited," Mn'd came to the rescue to short circuit the growing angst, to soothe disjointed thoughts, rampant thoughts generated by fear; thoughts that threatened to overwhelm, thoughts that were too emotional, and remove those that would lead nowhere. He aimed a beam of highly concentrated logic essence at the rogue thought patterns, intensifying the beam as needed. In short bursts it had the ability to change the direction a thought was taking. On longer exposure the offending thought would take flight. No amount of searching could then recover it. "Everyone happy again?"

To Brahin's considerable displeasure Mn'd made sure each received a full dose in quick succession, ending Brahin's enjoyment of the mayhem he began. These two characters never really considered themselves to be the best of friends and both took great pleasure in outwitting the other at every opportunity. Fortunately for the emotion-afflicted travellers, it was a relief to be released from the grip of counterproductive thinking.

Mn'd's words of advice, "Time to gather your collective wits and start working out a sensible plan," softened the intensifying light spectacular in their personal little Universe.

Nick dropped almost completely out of the dream at this point. Changing position again, he felt Muska still cuddled by his feet and sunk back into the drama, quite oblivious of it and it's possible repercussions on his waking state. Yet he felt the slightest glimmer of relief as the chaotic dream with his resident ghosts percolated through their meanderings, gradually converging towards each other.

Meet The Neanders

"*T*hank you, Mn'd. Just what we needed. You know who's behind this, don't you." Cre'teur took charge. "Here's what we need to do." Standing close to one another, almost nose to nose Cogito, Cre'teur and Eyechat had their first serious confab watched closely by Mn'd. "Up till now we've been at the mercy of the chaos and I would venture to say, Brahin. Where we are now seems to make more sense. We can get our bearings. Think of where we're going. Make a picture in your mind of an extraordinary, full of life, highly complex place, dimly but excitingly lit, with lots of activity and something extremely important we have to see. You all happy with that image?"

"Why does it have to be so – so involved?" Eyechat couldn't quite picture it, his realm being more closely attuned to Nature.

'Look at what's been happening to us so far. It makes sense that our destination must be particularly outstanding – and important. Otherwise why all this opposition?' Mn'd said.

"How are we going to get there?" Eyechat was still confused. "There's no road signs, there's no up or down or sideways or any other direction. Which way are we going to go?"

"Any ideas Cogito?" Cre'teur asked.

They expected him to have the answers. All eyes turned to him. At the same moment Eyechat had one of those brilliant moments of inspiration.

"Watch this."

With the concept of the nature of their destination in the forefront of his thoughts he reached up with his right hand and touched the web. He experienced a moment of immediate recognition. Mn'd had intervened. Slowly Eyechat moved his hand in an arc from right to left. As he rotated they could see the play of light within the web fibres intensify. With a movement to the left the light diminished slightly. So he moved his hand around to the right again until the intensity just began to fade once more.

"Go!" They called simultaneously. They found which way to go and together made the jump across the chasm of uncertainty. Where they next found themselves wasn't altogether awe inspiring. It all looked somewhat primitive. Overcoming another shock to their collective senses they gazed upon a lot of crunch-under-foot white stuff.

"This can't be it. Must be another diversion."

"It's freezing," Eyechat complained."

Fundamental Particle of Self

The chaotic Universe of light, colours, sparks and black chasms had given way to a cold white glare. The intense brilliance made Eyechat stand out in stark contrast to the landscape. In the event of danger there was nowhere he could hide. He was at the mercy of whatever the others decided to do. The dazzling glare partially obscured their vision, hiding the sight of the ground beneath their feet. The unaccustomed solidity they walked on should have been reassuring.

"This is not reassuring at all, but let's move." Cre'teur tried to be positive.

For want of a better alternative they moved towards the luminescence through a windless, soundless landscape.

"What's that – up ahead?" Eyechat noticed it first. By engaging with the quasi-physical reality up ahead, they all underwent a change back to their accustomed manifestations.

"Some kind of creature from the look of it," Cogito guessed. The apparition solidified not far ahead as the air cleared.

"It's – it's rather ugly." Eyechat commented as he got nearer to it.

"Is that you making those noises?" someone asked.

Grunts and shouts and exclamations became louder. By their intonation they didn't seem to be inviting or encouraging at all. This noisy hirsute thing with arms and legs gyrating out of sync obviously concentrated on something of immense importance ahead of it in the snow - them. A confrontation seemed inevitable.

"Do you think it's dangerous, Eyechat?" Cogito sounded concerned.

"How should I know? Of course it's dangerous. It looks like our next enemy. Everyone – just smile." The best way to approach an enemy according to Eyechat, was with a big smile. Not a good decision. Showing all those teeth turned out to be a threat display. He of all people should have known better.

"Arhh! – Garrh – RRAHGH!" It expressed its warning quite clearly.

Eyechat made a hesitant approach, with some animal-like grunts of his own escaping between his big grinning teeth. The hairy thing turned out to be slightly smaller than they had anticipated, about as tall as Cre'teur, but much sturdier. Suddenly it stopped its gyrations and with a deliberate slow movement it lowered its head. At the same time it gripped some kind of sharp stick thingy that came up level with its eyes, flashing surprisingly white teeth out of a rather grossly protruding jaw.

This unexpected spectacle alarmed Cogito. "We don't have anything to fight this creature with!"

"Not unless you want to hurl abuse at it. That spear looks more effective." Cre'teur became a little amused. They didn't have any weapon to hand that could have been considered even remotely effective against the sharp stick thingy.

"I think it's a female," Eyechat said, "look at its chest." The hairy thing did look kind of feminine because she had what looked like breasts with large nipples where the hair on the chest thinned a little. In that moment of disconcerting distraction, a very peculiar thing happened. The female creature stood its ground for a moment, furiously sniffing the air with flared nostrils. Then she executed a perfect forward somersault landing directly in front of Eyechat.

"Aiee!" She called aloud.

Obviously it wasn't afraid. This close to him, Eyechat could see it was indeed a creature of the female variety, but a bit challenging to his olfactory sense in spite of the cold. She thumped him on the chest, turned tail and ran off into the whiteness.

"She wants us to follow." Eyechat said, recovering from the hefty blow.

"Right – What are we waiting for?" Cre'teur made the executive decision in spite of her better judgement. She knew quite well that when a woman was running away from a man, she was chasing *him*. Poor Eyechat. She hoped he had enough sense to keep his hands to himself. But he was after all, only a man.

Their progress was made a little easier as the ground sloped downwards. The footsteps led around a large obstacle, behind which less snow had accumulated. Up ahead the female creature remonstrated profusely in front of two other taller, hairy creatures; she, nodding her head vigorously and they, shaking theirs just as vigorously.

"No! You can't have him. We don't know where he's been."

"But I want him. I saw him first," she persisted.

"He's such a skinny weed. What would you with him. You might break him," said the other.

The older, larger male made a sudden mock charge at the team but the female quickly stopped him. She was called Ida, Eyechat found out later. Cre'teur called her Horny Ida in later conversations for a very good reason. In a later tête-a-tête she learnt that the big guy called himself Grandpa Segon, who warned her about the younger Uncle Egon. But for the moment the encounter wasn't going so well.

Horny Ida kept pointing at Eyechat as she argued with the men. "We need a bit of new blood in the tribe – don't we?" Horny Ida played her trump card.

To the travellers it all seemed like a highly unnecessary bit of carry-on over nothing. They were getting quite bored with all the flim-flam. Cogito scanned the surrounding area noticing to his utter amazement, just to the left of the hairy things, what looked like several fish. *How very odd*, he thought. On a large flat stone several fish were having a nice little sojourn right in the middle of it. Automatically and quite casually he stepped over to the fish. Concurrently, Uncle Egon also made a move towards the stone slab. Cogito picked up one of the fish and smelt it, experiencing a very distinct déjà vu moment.

"Smells quite fresh. Makes me feel I haven't eaten for ages."

"Look out!" Cre'teur yelled at Cogito as Uncle Egon launched himself in his direction. In that instant all pandemonium broke loose. Cogito dropped the fish immediately as Uncle Egon pounced on him giving him extremely robust, friendly hugs.

The sudden commotion made Nick twitch in bed, morning light still a long way away. Muska stretched. They slept on.

"Ooh – he does smell! The fish might be fresh, but this guy's ripe!"

The other two hairy things, seeing the disturbance, stopped their animated conferencing and recognising the obvious cause of the intimate introduction, leapt into action also. Without the least hesitation Horny Ida threw herself on Eyechat. She enveloped him with those long hairy arms, sniffing him excitedly and allowing pleasurable little grunts to escape through her odoriferous lips.

"Welcome - Welcome! Join us. We eat together – Yes?" Grandpa Segon, in spite of his grandfatherly status leaped affectionately upon Cre'teur, so surprising her that she didn't notice they were speaking a common language.

"Thank you – thank you – very kind – we can't really – we have to go, important business." After much, much hugging and grunting and smelling and rubbing bodies they were propelled forward into what appeared to be a commodious cave. "Well – If we must," Cre'teur said to Grandpa Segon in the interests of bilateral friendly relations.

The hairless ones were surprised to see a friendly little fire burning in the middle, surrounded by nice little sitting stones. Another partly disemboweled fish rested on a flat stone near the fire. Incredibly, they were in the kitchen. But there wasn't a lot of time to critique the interior design features of this strange domicile. Each of the hairy things had appropriated one of the group as their very own, very special best friend. Remarkable and unlikely as it may seem, it turned out in their ensuing conversation that smelling fish was a most significant ritual.

"Thank you for smelling our fish," Grandpa Segon said, "There's always the ever-present danger of food poisoning in spite of the cold, particularly as it concerns fish."

"Yes, yes," Uncle Egon added, "When a stranger smells our fish he is showing the highest possible sign of respect to us. If the fish had gone off, which we couldn't readily distinguish ourselves due to our own environmental odours, then the stranger would have in effect saved our lives."

"Yes, by the tusk of the great hairy mammoth – you have indeed saved our lives," Grandpa Segon said. "Please join us for a meal." Strict adherence to the hairy persons' protocols could not be avoided. They insisted. The hairy ones appreciated observance of social etiquette as much as the hairless beauty of the white skinned guests.

"It's not often we have lovely visitors." Horney Ida gently stroked the white, soft skinned person of her choice. "You smell so good. I think I love you!" Eyechat really didn't know what to do with himself.

Grandpa Segon likewise became smitten by Cre'teur. To his eyes she was simply delicious. As for Uncle Egon, well he wasn't too fussy, already chummy with Cogito. Over the next few hours, relatively speaking because in reality it was only a micro-experience - a thoroughly good time was had by all. Plenty of fish to go around, although without the benefit of a nice Greek salad - a cosy warm cave kitchen come lounge, and very hospitable hosts. One got used to the smell surprisingly quickly. Aromas were a most important part of the realities of life, be they pleasant or otherwise.

Olfactory memory, the related data of which is most comprehensively distributed within a human neural network, brought Nick to the edge of wakefulness without warning. The fish he grilled left far less impact than the aroma of a certain lady he met in the middle of the known Universe. If it wasn't for Horny Ida's insistent amorous advances Nick would in all likelihood not have stirred. Pleasant expectations seduced him back to sleep, storing the memory of lilac and lavender for later recall.

Horny Ida had withdrawn into a shadowy corner with Eyechat, intent on giving her libido free rein. Grandpa Segon, content to stay around the fire with Cre'teur, being a good judge of character, felt she would appreciate his philosophy about the finer points of the perfect way to cook fish.

"Hot stones are what you need, and freshly fallen snow. It gives the fish a certain tang. It must be from the ozone."

"Ah, yes, I see. Our friend Nick would be very happy to know this." Cre'teur tried sounding appreciative.

Grandpa Segon continued undaunted by the interruption. "To change the subject – I believe it is of the highest importance to maintain the health of our folk. An infusion of fresh genetic material is indeed most welcome –

If you catch my drift." At the end of his exposition he made certain clear overtures to his guest, distracted only momentarily by Horny Ida and her flagrant disregard of the love making protocols of the tribe. That breach of course sent him of at a tangent, for which Cre'teur was clearly grateful. "We know the consequences of intra-tribal mating, so of course extra-tribal sex is preferred, and encouraged."

Mary had been inconspicuous the whole time. She, who found the entire scenario most enlightening and somewhat comical, was pleased to discover her emerging comprehension of humour, though without understanding any of the contributing elements. She noted the re-emergence of Nick's important cosmic dream elements, but decided against bringing them into conscious prominence later, unless painting of the portrait became too elusive.

As it turned out Uncle Egon had found himself a soul mate in Cogito, a man who was never lost for words when faced with a willing listener.

Cogito began, "It is important to be always in control, to be always cognisant of unrelated causes and effects that make life's journey seemingly random. We take a special interest in dream interpretations."

But Uncle Egon wanted to talk, not listen. He cut in, "It's so hard keeping the peace between Grandpa and Ida. I'm a realist, but it's dammed difficult to stop Ida from wanting to procreate at every opportunity. And Grandpa's far too cautious with everything. If I let either one of them loose the tribe suffers. Food is scarce and population control is a high priority."

Cogito nodded, "I totally concur." They were getting on so well after a while that Cogito decided to confide in his new best friend about their quandary. "We need to get back to our journey urgently. We are on a special mission of the utmost importance and find ourselves in a spot of bother. We've lost the path that leads to the path that leads to our destination."

"Ah, I think I can help you there." Amazing. He seemed to actually understand.

"Really?" exclaimed Cogito, completely taken aback. *How could these smelly, hairy things possibly help?*

"Yes indeed. We don't just control fire and work hides, you know,." Uncle Egon pointed towards the back corner of the cave. "You see that little hole at the back? It's been waiting there for eons."

Cogito made a move towards it. The other hairy ones immediately noticed. Another great grunting argument broke out within the tribe, with obvious protestations about letting the hairless ones go anywhere near the hole.

"Our hole is sacred!" yelled Horny Ida. "It is *our* hole." Possession of such treasure meant survival for her tribe.

Apart from their prowess with fire, a more inept bunch of Neanderthal wannabes you couldn't expect ever to meet. Sure it was their hunting ground the travellers found themselves in, but did they have to be so territorial about it? There's a very good reason why these original flat-foreheads became extinct. It wasn't because they weren't smart enough. Their brain capacity was pretty much the same as ours. It was because they could neither adapt to climate change nor get on very well with each other, always arguing about anything and everything. In spite of that, they did manage to breed, mostly amongst themselves because there weren't too many others about. What were they doing there anyway? Who cared? It was all in the realm of a dream and it was allowed. Actually it was another diversionary tactic by Brahin to sidetrack them. But he made the scenario so real that the fabrications acted on their own volition. Although Brahin constructed the physical semblances, it was Mn'd who animated them. Why? So Brahin would not get it all his way. His interference became a bit more than just a nuisance, degenerating into downright obstructiveness.

So Mn'd worked out a devious way he could use these demented Neanderthals to help his group on their journey. This is where the mysterious dark hole came into the picture. No ordinary hole, it was a portal.

Uncle Egon, as the undisputed "intellectual" acted as the mediator. "I'm sure we can work something out." He glanced first at Horny Ida, then Cre'teur. "If you would be our guests for the night," a slight pause to eyeball Ida, "I'm sure we could accommodate your desire to explore our sacred hole. Isn't that right Ida dear?" Horny Ida's grunt a clear approval of the arrangement, as she took a firm hold of Eyechat's lower arm.

The cave wasn't so bad on closer scrutiny. Aside from the exhausted nerves, those piles of furs after sated hunger did look rather inviting. The prospect of a little cuddle diversion to take their minds off past and imminent dangers also had its appeal. Even Cogito felt a thrill at the thought of indulging in a little more intellectual intercourse with Uncle Egon. Eyechat certainly had a great affinity with all living things, degree of hairiness not necessarily a deal breaker. So it came about that all and sundry enjoyed a pleasant night, giving respite from the trauma behind them and a fortifying interlude to help them face the unknown ahead of them.

A casual observer wouldn't have seen anything unusual inside the cave that night. The well stacked fire provided plenty of warmth. The huddles of restless fur stacks produced a variety of not unfamiliar sounds of the night, illuminated by fleeting sparks of static electricity, building gradually in the fur to be discharged in harmonic crackles with the burning logs. One could take comfort in the dance of the flames and shadows on the walls, interrupted occasionally by a lump of humanity staggering to the entrance of the cave to monogram the freshly fallen snow.

There are dreams we would rather have end sooner than later, and then there are those the pleasures of which we would gladly extend if we only had control over them. It had been a long and harrowing dream so far, and the alluring intimacy of the little interlude plunged Nick back into deep sleep, giving the unfolding of events a chance to attain their climax. A bathroom break failed to rouse him to consciousness beyond the capacity to navigate temporarily in the semi-darkness of his bedroom.

Crossing Acheron

Disruptive cosmic forces had split Nick down into his most fundamental elements. The nature of the journey into space with its diversions only added to the confusion he already laboured under in trying to find a way to carry out his commission. As much as he tried, even with Mary's help, those elusive inspirations he searched for to help create a likeness of the deity had remained out of reach.

At home the Company gave him no possibility to live a normal life again. The pressure put on him by Unity hardly compared with the problems he'd been experiencing in trying to live with his awakened disparate personae.

Nick didn't realise how important his dream would be when he went to bed after a tiring day in front of the easel. In this inner realm the individuals had to come together into a unified force to overcome the challenges they encountered. They each possessed a small fragment of the information Nick needed to make a success of the portrait.

Sleep wasn't the main priority that night in the cave, so no one welcomed the dawn light. One by one the untidy stacks of fur disgorged their contents, looking decidedly seedy, dishevelled and unrested. The fire hadn't quite gone out. Wisps of smoke snaking upwards; disbursed by the fresh morning breeze even made the cave feel tired. Fresh snow had fallen and the reflected light illuminated the cave, except for that little hole in one of the back walls. Cre'teur woke first, twisting her creaking back and neck in its direction without any particular reason for doing so. She did as anyone would, instinctively turn their head in the direction of someone watching them from a distance. The others of her group got up in succession staggering about, generally trying to avoid the glare of the early morning and so ended up near Cre'teur at the back. Their eyes followed her gaze into the shadows.

Horny Ida hadn't had so much fun since the last tribal raid and didn't pay any attention to what the pale skins were doing, having trouble rousing herself. Uncle Egon, a little more alert went over to Grandpa Segon and diplomatically diverted his attention from the group by pointing him in the direction of some moving shadows outside the cave. He'd promised the travellers access to the sacred hole. As the head of the tribe he intended to keep his word. The team, already slowly impelled towards the darkness, felt as if the energy of the morning light pushed on their backs urging them forwards into the shadows.

Fundamental Particle of Self

Uncle Egon went back into the cave to lead Cogito by the arm to a steep slope quite near the hole. The slope felt slippery and sticky at the same time and they were having trouble making any progress up it. Uncle Egon gradually fell behind. He saw a flash of light across the back of the cave in front of the hole and suddenly his guests were out of sight. This light hit the team like an energy wave and punched them up the slope and through the sacred opening into a completely different environment from the one at the door of the hut. This long dark tunnel with ribbed walls tried squeezing them forwards with a peristaltic motion preventing them from sliding backwards. Further pulses of light surged past them to illuminate the subsequent segments of the tunnel.

"This is vaguely familiar. Can anyone see the end?" Cogito suspected where they were but couldn't quiet work it out.

"Nothing to worry about. Just keep up with me," said Cre'teur as she led the way.

The tunnel kept shrinking, forcing them to move in single file close to one another. Pulsating light kept increasing in frequency and intensity as Cre'teur continued with firm resolve as she took each step.

"What's that? – up ahead – those smaller tunnels, all going in different directions?' Cogito felt the ground suddenly give way under his feet, finding himself face down, flat on the surface.

"OOF!" The wind rushed out of him. "Why'd you do that?"

Eyechat had pulled his legs out from under him in one swift jerk after seeing Cre'teur suddenly flatten herself and crawl straight ahead into one of those narrower tunnels. "You're not watching. Just follow Cre'teur."

She kept crawling forwards, which wasn't so hard now as the pulses of light energy had become so strong they helped push her and the others along. As she relaxed into the flow she understood. They had become concentrated fundamental points of energy again since entering the narrow tunnel, enabling them to ride the pulses.

The pleasure of the experience was short lived and superseded by another mind numbing spectacle, finding themselves disgorged into a large cavernous space full of noise and frenetic activity heading towards a shoreline.

"Look at the crowds," Cre'teur commented, "why are they trying to get into those gondolas."

"This is like a train terminal. Those empty ones must be coming back for more passengers." Cogito observed.

Eyechat didn't like it at all. "Everything's damp and the air is too salty. Where's that acrid smell coming from?"

The frantic crowd absorbed the energy of the light that had deposited them, making them more agitated. As they moved to board the gondolas more people were being dropped out of the ends of all those tight little tunnels, pushing them forward.

"Come on, stay with me," Cre'teur urged, "It doesn't look like we have much choice."

The trio huddled close together in fear of losing one another as they were swept onward by the surging crowd. Mn'd hadn't abandoned them. Unknown to them, they were exactly where they needed to be at that moment; in a gondola about to set out.

Cogito thought he recognised the gondolier. "Don't we know that guy? I can't quite see his face." The turbulent waters tossed the three of them about in the vessel. Cogito sat closest to 'no face' who stood on the prow. "Cre'teur, doesn't it strike you as strange that he's in the prow and not the stern?"

There was no sky, only the chaos into which the energy flux had returned, with the web all around them. Eyechat stood in the rocking gondola and reached out with his hand to touch the web. He felt Mn'd's reassuring presence and felt the wisdom of Thecore. Cogito also reached out with his right hand to touch it ever so gently. His energy dimmed for he felt the threat of Brahin and withdrew to sit on the bottom of the gondola. Cre'teur saw this, yet she also reached out with both hands and felt the vibration in the web.

The crossing took forever. With so much traffic they could have easily been overturned by the multitude of returning empty vessels.

Cogito needed answers. "Where are all these people going with us? Why has no one bothered to speak with us? They all seem so intent on their own journeys."

"They're all going one way, and I don't think there's any turning back. But we're not going wherever they're going. Cogito, help me find a way to get out of this current."

But Brahin had other plans. *You have rejected me!* The group could not hear this but they did see the waters get whipped into a frenzy and the currents pull their gondola off its course back into the main flow of the multitude.

As it neared the other shore the electrifying light intensified, making the air crackle with lightning and smoke. Mn'd materialised as a silhouette beside the gondolier who stood dark against the sizzling air. He grew till his shadow cast a somber cloak over the gondola, the gondolier and all who were in the vessel. The nearer they got to the shore the more his shadow grew until even the waters around them couldn't be seen. Mn'd had cast an impenetrable cape of darkness enveloping all of them. Not even Brahin's power could penetrate this protective shield. The waters calmed around them. The new gondolier steered the vehicle back on course to take them where Cre'teur wanted to go.

Then just as suddenly as he had appeared Mn'd was gone.

"How are we going to get off this thing? I can't see the dock," Cogito shouted.

"Why has the gondolier now perched himself at the stern. Is there something about to happen we should know about?" asked Eyechat as unsettled as his companions.

"It's been smooth enough so far, except for Mn'd and his dramatics."

That didn't satisfy Cogito, "It doesn't explain why the gondolier was at the helm for the crossing when he should have been at the stern all along." Then he added as an afterthought, "Didn't you all notice? He had no face!"

Cre'teur tried to make light of it, "He didn't look like the devil bargaining for our souls. Just an ordinary guy. Though he did look foreboding with the hooded cape hiding his large body and face."

"Yes, but the hood was raised and he didn't look directly at any of us the entire trip. I'm telling you, he had no face." Cogito was adamant.

Thinking back to Mn'd's appearance, it *was* odd that Mn'd's silhouette blended into the shadowy aspect of the hooded guy so completely. They appeared to be one and the same person. But there was so much other activity going on that their attention was completely diverted.

Cogito couldn't let it go. "Something's not right," he told Cre'teur. As he kept thinking about it he became more nervous. "Why are we slowing?" Shouldn't he be getting us out of the undercurrent?"

The other two were so intent on watching the shoreline in the continuous play of lightning and sizzling that they paid no attention to what was happening in the gondola itself. "Hey! Where's he gone? The realisation hit him suddenly. He snapped his head around to look for the gondolier. The hooded guy had disappeared from the stern. Only then did Cogito realise what had seemed so familiar to him the first time he saw him. "That was Brahin!" he shouted. "I should have recognised him from the arrogant way he stood there."

"The rotter's taken the oar," Eyechat noticed, "we're still too far from the shore!"

The gondola had stopped well short of the shoreline. Cre'teur turned around at exactly the same moment as Cogito and saw exactly what Cogito saw - an unattended tiller. They didn't have time to work out what exactly had happened, for they had to get to the shore before the hoard of empty gondolas came at them eager for their next load of souls.

"Hold on!" Cre'teur shouted as she jumped to the back of the gondola and thrust her left hand into the water. Simultaneously with her other hand she reached up into the network and spread all her fingers to make contact with the surging electrical currents of the web. Crossing the Acheron without a guide and without an oar created uncomfortable and unpleasant feelings with strong overtones of latent panic.

"How is that going to help!" Cogito shouted.

"It's electricity!" Cre'teur shouted back, without giving further explanation, expecting her companions to understand the electrical conductivity repercussions. The moment she touched the web an instantaneous surge of electric current passed from the web through her body into the water. Or at least it looked like water until then. This semi-fluid, was in fact composed of little bits of matter which tasted quite salty and which made it highly conductive. If it had been just water she would have been fried on the spot. This didn't happen, although what did was painful enough.

"I didn't know she could fly." Eyechat commented as their companion catapulted into the air. For the first time in her life Cre'teur experienced true flight. She saw below her two startled faces just as they were being thrust backwards onto the bottom of the gondola in the bow. She landed in a most unceremonious manner on top of Cogito. Looking up from under the broken seat she saw the back of the gondola rear up into the air, felt the bow dip alarmingly and experienced the rush of the gondola accelerating to the shore.

"Heads down and hang on!" she yelled.

The Acheronic fluid sucked itself up into a sine curve with considerable amplitude, propagating itself towards the shore carrying the human cargo laden gondola with it. This wasn't a gentle delivery of sensitive souls but a brutal deposition of writhing lumps onto the landing dock. Simultaneously the chaotic energy flux above them became quite exotic. Surges of light flew erratically along the fibres of the web resplendent with sparkling mininovas, accompanied by colours and shock waves creating a considerably energetic environment.

It dawned on Cre'teur that she had created this storm by her actions. Somehow the web, the Chaos and the waters of the Acheron were connected and she had activated the connection.

"Brilliant!" Both men congratulated her outstanding maneuver. The trio became too engrossed with the events of the crossing to consider where they had actually landed.

Mary Intervenes

"*T*ell me again Cre'teur, why we're here. I know it's just a dream, but ..."
Eyechat needed reassurance.

"We're searching for something very important." Cogito offered.

"What exactly?"

"Well, that's a bit hazy."

"Anyway," Cre'teur reminded them, "Nick can't wake up until we find it. Whenever he has complicated dreams it's because he needs to work out something for a special project. It may be connected to the journey he's been on." Most importantly, she remembered the things they'd learned which had helped them get this far.

"At least we've got help."

"And," Eyechat reminded them, "we can influence our environment. We can use the energy of the chaos and we can contact the others." They could not only contact them, they had actually absorbed some of their powers whilst in the energy flux of the chaos. Even Brahin had his good points, few though they were.

Cogito warned, "You all know we can't trust Brahin. He's openly trying to sabotage us."

Their thoughts turned towards Brahin again, thinking what they could do to thwart his conspiracy against them. They failed to consider that Brahin could tune in on all their plans and therefore could ambush them at his convenience with all manner of nasty tricks.

"I've got a plan," Cogito said, "It's quite simple, really."

"Out with it then – we haven't got all day."

"Do Not have a plan - you know, like Nick." Even Cre'teur was incredulous on first hearing it. "Be like Horny Ida and act instinctively!" he said. "Abolish all our planning thoughts, become completely uncoordinated and do the first thing that comes to mind."

"Like Nick painting his portraits, you mean?" asked Cre'teur.

The plan didn't resonate immediately, although images of Ida in the fur bundle back in the cave did make Eyechat smile. The more Cogito unfolded his concept the more it seemed to make sense.

"You might have something there," Cre'teur said quietly. "I can see the merits of unpremeditated action, therefore unpredictable. As long as we have a common understanding of our destination, it just might work."

As the undisputed leader, they followed her lead and adopted Cogito's modus operandi. It left them free to do whatever was necessary as long as they reached their goal. The idea had special appeal for Cogito. He could free himself from some of his own self-imposed restrictions of having to have a reason for everything he did. Eyechat could indulge his penchant for distractions without having to justify himself, and Cre'teur could let loose her urges of spontaneous creative thinking.

No one could have discerned much change in the general behaviour of the team. They seemed pretty much uncoordinated anyway. The difference was they would be like that on purpose, together.

Nick woke, though not entirely. Enough at least to stagger to the bathroom once more, stagger back to the bed and fall into it again. Still in a fog he stroked Muska who'd come to snuggle into the folds of the sheet against his chest. With eyes already closed Nick resumed dreaming. The flow of events had been broken yet he could key into the general flow of imagery. An idea floated to the surface ... 'become completely uncoordinated and do the first thing that comes to mind' ... it seemed to have relevance to something. For an instant he saw himself speeding through space while he painted under the watchful eye of ... of ... the harder he concentrated on identifying the person the more elusive the mind picture became.

Mary sensed the group needed a slight edge if they were to overcome Brahin, who had not realised she had joined their host while they were still in the EGG. *Time I did something for Nick.* Cre'teur must have picked up on the thought for she let out her desire for help. She would not give it a name, even in her meditative seclusion, for fear Brahin would discover her desire.
This is getting too serious. It wasn't yet time to reveal herself – perhaps the opportunity might never come. *Let's see what I can do through Cre'teur. She's receptive.*
A stream of opalescent mist shot out from around Cre'teur, searching for its target. She knew Brahin must not be killed, but he had to be subdued - perhaps made to realise his position in the greater scheme of things. He had to understand his own purpose and his contribution to Nick's survival. Innately he knew that ultimately life had meaning and purpose. It only had to be discovered through the creation of it. He knew that purpose was far more powerful if created by the host himself, rather than if it had been thrust upon him by an external agency. Nevertheless, he, Brahin the Almighty, wanted full control. *I want to decide all matters of faith, control all core beliefs and decide all of life's imperatives. I, Brahin the Magnificent, don't need help from underlings. I am worthy of far more than being the concierge pulling the strings of a biological automaton!*

Brahin's own thoughts enraged him to attacking his adversaries in a frenzy. They in turn intuitively felt their only hope of survival lay in joining forces. The emanations from Cre'teur curled towards Cogito completely enveloping him. She, Mary and Cogito became one. Cogito reached out to touch Eyechat on the shoulder. Through this touch Eyechat shared in the power of the others. Together they were formidable. Cre'teur, still oblivious of Mary's contribution, surprised herself with the force she was able to generate.

Brahin twisted in the agony of comprehension. In a final attempt to overcome Cre'teur he hit her with the fear of helpless isolation, of powerlessness, as he had tried before. Mary would not let Brahin take control. She had to protect Nick. The imperative that had been programmed into her recognised no boundaries between realms of different realities.

You are a creator! Mary whispered to Cre'teur who began to stir. She sensed these words now, not the sickening effluent from Brahin. Mary succeeded in underpinning Cre'teur's reason for living, for creating, for continuing to take one breath after another each day. Mary continued with her encouragement. *Nick might be a slave to Brahin but you are much more. You and your friends are the force of the Cosmos.* Cre'teur listened to these words of reassurance believing they were her own thoughts.

Relieved at the effect of her covert operation Mary scaled down her input to prevent discovery. Brahin could do nothing further to weaken Cre'teur. As her aura withdrew a part of it detached itself into a cloud of colourful, strobing light before them. They no longer felt fear or joy, rather a fulfilment, a sense of becoming whole once again.

As they watched in knowing anticipation, a familiar figure began to materialise. Slowly Mn'd's form revealed itself, different to how they knew him before. Mn'd now had a new bearing of confidence and authority. He looked like Mn'd and moved like Mn'd but when they looked directly into his eyes they saw much more than Mn'd.

"Well, hello you lot. Why are you looking so happy with yourselves?" he asked, cheerful as they had never before known him to be. "Oh, I see. You're bleeding a whole palette of splendid colours Cre'teur. Don't let it go to waste."

The Human Existentialist Bush Tick

At the moment of most intense threat Cre'teur manifested her ultimate creative masterpiece. She became her greater self. Her finite singularity ceased to exist, to be consumed by all that was possible for her at that time - and the manifestation of all that was possible at that moment was Mn'd. He had left them as just one member of a motley crew of oddball companions. He returned, almost complete, as the embodiment of all the imperative forces of necessity, desires, dreams and disappointments encapsulated in a single entity. He was first and foremost himself. He was part of Thecore, Cre'teur, Cogito and Eyechat. Brahin still had a lot to learn before he could join such an exclusive club.

"Time to work out your next move," Mn'd said. The dramas had weakened and disoriented them. Under Mn'd's guidance they could again make some progress towards the ultimate goal. Although they were fatigued, they had all emerged greater than they were before. That didn't guarantee the rest of the dream would be pleasant or easy.

There were still four of them to carry on. Mary had completely withdrawn, ready to contribute only if the necessity arose.

The group needed a mode of transportation to continue. They had ceased to be singular energy units that could be easily willed from place to place. Although they all had a common vision of where they were heading, they still had to find a way of getting there. Strangely enough, as they surveyed the immediate surroundings the general impression was that of a suburban railway station. Oddly, the railway Superintendent, with Denny Dright written on his cap, didn't ask any of them for a ticket.

"Follow me," he said, "single file please." Many others joined them. Fairly soon Denny shot back to the end of the long line, which by then had speeded up considerably. There were no railway carriages. They were it - like a conga line - out of control.

Soundlessly they picked up enormous speed as they careered through twists and turns punctuated by flashes and sparks and weird sounding echoes. The constricting and dilating tunnels they travelled through amplified the minute sounds generated by their own thoughts. Thinking about their destination created the increasing turbulence until they came to a sudden stop in front of an extraordinarily bright light ahead of them. Nothing could be immediately seen through its blinding intensity.

Zsoall Robi

Mn'd was stunned. "Will you look at that. I can't believe what I'm looking at. Of all the strange phenomenon we've experienced, this is the strangest."

A wave of relief and hope washed over Cre'teur, inadvertently letting her guard down. She questioned for a moment if they were at last safe. That's when it struck, disabling her within moments.

Overcome by anguish she froze, dropping to the ground by the time the others noticed. Eyechat squatted to help her. At first he could find no sign of what could have affected her so suddenly and so dramatically. His hands roamed over her automatically looking for something, anything that might explain what had happened to their friend.

"I found it, here at the back of her neck," he said as he gently turned Cre'teur's head sideways. "It's a magnificent specimen. I've never seen one so big."

"Well - what is it?"

"This is an Ixodes Holocyclus Sapiensis Existentialis, the Human Existentialist bush tick. They are to be found only in the remotest and most inaccessible regions of one's ultimate private self-image."

"Nothing to do with me," came the sound of Thecore's voice, not heard for some time.

Eyechat ignored him for the moment. "Nevertheless, in each individual there dwells the starving idea that all existence is a pathetic comedy of the absurd. It surrounds itself in the warmth of a disorientated, confused and meaningless world. From time to time, this tick must be fed and it feeds on insecurities and fears."

Brahin gloated over Cre'teur's misconceptions and facile attempts at living a meaningful life. It was this little idea that took advantage of the one minuscule moment when Cre'teur was about to allow herself the luxury of hope. The bug's own starvation drove it to seek the nourishment of despair from the moment when hope was most vulnerable. Although already gorged with Cre'teur's blood the little sucker just kept on sucking, kept on injecting its message of despair into Cre'teur. She thought she was prepared for anything after the battle with Brahin. All the past challenges should have strengthened her. But this was one area where she was particularly vulnerable. Being essentially a creative individual having to operate in the realm of honesty and truth, she was wide open to attack to even the slightest hint of suspicion cast upon her integrity and self-esteem.

"I can't just pull the beast off, it'll leave its venomous words in her," Eyechat realised.

Mn'd took a close look at Cre'teur's face. "You'd better do something fast, or we'll lose her. I doubt she could recover from too much more of this." The debilitating idea generated by the creature had to let go of its own volition.

"Let me try," Cogito offered. He placed both hands on her forehead and began to drain her of her thoughts. He focused his knowledge of the power of no-mind into her, watching the darkness at the back of Cre'teur's neck. As Cre'teur slowly reached a mind no longer fixated by thought or emotion the tick released its hold, falling away to roll into the great crevasse below the light, disappearing into its depth.

They watched the immediate effect on their companion as she rose from the ground exhausted. "Thank you – thank you. That was overwhelming."

Cogito warned, "It's not destroyed. It can attack again."

Such existentialist thoughts are never destroyed. They lurk in the dark recesses of the mind waiting for every opportunity to strike. This one had left a serious scar, not just on Cre'teur.

They had become so intimately connected to one another by this stage of their journey that anything affecting one of them affected all of them.

The Great Chasm

*W*hen Cre'teur had fully recovered they looked to the blinding illumination that had stopped their speeding conga line so suddenly.

This wall of liquid sparking light overwhelmed their imagination. Gradually their eyes grew accustomed to the vision of this throbbing energy of many stars emanating from the gap between the two walls facing each other. They stood near the bottom of this chasm, a chasm alive on both sides with tremendous vitality shooting back and forth between them.

"How are we going to get to the top? I can't see any handholds. I can't even see the top," said Eyechat, disappointed after having come this far. Although the distance between the two sides extended no more than a meter they could see no means of climbing up. It appeared to be an impossible task threatening to end their whole enterprise.

"That's a powerful lot of energy in that vortex. In this narrow space it could fry us in an instant." The team didn't need Mn'd's optimistic assessment of the situation just at that moment.

"What about that lot?" Cogito pointed to a group getting sucked up into the crevasse. "They appear to be turning into clumps of mist coming together and floating between the two walls."

Mn'd noticed more bundles coming up from below.

"It has to be an updraft," said Cre'teur. "Any ideas how we could get into it?" Increasing numbers of bundles lifted up into the electrical maelstrom in front of them. Some of these bundles quickly disappeared into the walls on either side. Other bundles continued to rise.

Mn'd had an idea. "Let's just 'clump' together and see what happens!" Without realising it he'd activated the intuition factor and created a reaction, which reduced the four of them to their primary thought patterns, joining them into a thought cloud bundle, starting them on their upward journey.

This was the very first time they had truly become a co-mingled entity, thus losing their individual privacy; a feeling difficult to comprehend let alone feel comfortable with. To lose the comfort of one's solitude, not to be able to ruminate in one's thoughts in private felt like an absolute invasion, repulsive in the extreme to the psyche.

"What just happened? I don't know, you tell me – Was that you Cre'teur? Yes – We'd better sort this out – Let me finish what I'm saying, Mn'd – I thought you had - There's something odd going on here!"

For a moment they became silent. They had become a group of disembodied voices all clamouring at the same time to be heard.

Mn'd raised his voice above that of the others, "Don't anybody say anything. I think I know what this is."

Cre'teur and Eyechat relaxed, realising there was no immediate threat to their existence, and they didn't lose the ability for having their own thoughts. They were still who they were before.

"Our self-construct boundaries have been removed when we joined each other just then. We have much more freedom – and we have company – in each other's thoughts." Mn'd gently coaxed them towards composure. "We are each safe in our individuality, but we have to be much more co-operative with each other."

Cre'teur, quick on the uptake interrupted. "So, we can hear each other's projected thoughts without turning them into words? Right?"

"You got it. The harder part is to exercise control over our thoughts. We need to make sure rogue thoughts don't build into unwelcome or inappropriate ideas to confuse any conversation in progress at the time - and we don't interrupt each other."

"So we could use a round-robin system." Eyechat said, understanding exactly what they needed to do.

Having gained some facility with the new technique of communication they couldn't believe how primitive and inefficient the old method was. Just imagine having to firstly put your thoughts in order before translating them into words. You had to listen to what the other person was saying before you could say your bit, being vigilant not to forget what you wanted to say in the first place. Then there was the problem of the other person saying something unexpected causing you to re-think what you were going to say in the first place. Absurd.

It was definitely preferable to go the direct route. So much easier to synchronise your thoughts with those already wafting around you. But there was still the niggling sensation of a lack of privacy, something they would have to consider in more depth, but not immediately. They were each so caught up in this unexpected development they didn't notice what was happening around them as they slowly rose with all the other bundles. There appeared to be communication going on between the walls and the lifting crowd.

Ascending rapidly many of the bundles disappeared either into the left or the right wall of the fissure. Within moments the same fate befell them, as an energy vortex pulled them away from the stream of ascending candy-floss like wads into a dark aperture. Collectively awestruck by seeing again a dark lifeless void, just like their first experience in this challenging environment, they acted as one force. Behind them the door that had let them fall through slammed shut, vibrating with the force of the closure. Reluctant to let them escape, the door would not open on the first try.

"Together!" They rushed at the door, eyes closed hoping for the best.

It suddenly gave way spilling them back into the chasm. Clutching onto each other they went into a kamikaze dive spinning towards the bottom with nothing between them and a fatal juxtaposition of their bodies with the bottom. Luckily, they didn't immediately revert to their candy-floss state for several moments. In the interval their combined bulk stopped the flow of upward traffic by compacting all the bundles into a slowed mass, giving them time to think. And that's all it took, a moment of clear thinking.

Then three things happened. They became a happy group of traumatised thoughts in their flossy enclave again. Happy because they were on their way up, and traumatised because of Nick's reaction.

Nick fell out of bed. The consequences of a major blockage could be serious. Nick didn't have a stroke, he simply fell out of bed – that's all. From the impact of the carpet with his forehead, the entire mass of flossy thought bundles became dislodged to resume their upward journeys. He wasn't even consciously aware of the incident as he crawled back into bed. Having been so rudely dislodged from her comfortable nest Muska stretched, yawned and indignantly padded out of the bedroom.

At the moment of impact horizontal lightning and fingers of sparks shooting out frenetically from both walls distracted Cre'teur. "Look. Those bundles are getting pierced by the lightning. They're disappearing again into cavities on either side."

"Where do you suppose they're going?"

"I can't see into the walls." Mn'd said.

He'd now become the prominent entity. The others had recognised that as part of their new freedom, they had to take it in turns to bring their own special individuality and skills to the fore. It was Mn'd's turn now to lead. He seemed to have an intuitive understanding of recent developments. The others trusted him implicitly.

"Those convolutions on the surface are like folds on a cloth, all squashed up close together," Cre'teur added.

"That lightning is coming out of those folds and pulling the thought bundles into themselves."

Eyechat wasn't too happy about the observation. "So as long as we avoid the fireworks, we're Ok? – Right Mn'd?"

"It just goes from bad to worse. Is there no end to this?" Even Cre'teur was getting tired of having to overcome so many obstacles and interruptions.

Electrical activity had increased a thousand fold in the moments following the meeting of the Nick's head with the ground. It resulted in a great deal of frantic readjustments happening around and above them. Thankfully they did continue upwards, peacefully for a little while. Not quite long enough to give them a chance to relax, but long enough to gather their thoughts.

They used the slight window of opportunity to practice their communal thinking.

"That was a most unpleasant"
"experience to have the shock of"
"an entrapment"
"and I don't think we were going"
"to end up back in"
"the crowd below us"
"the most interesting thing was that"
"Nick didn't even wake up"
"Do you all realise the most important"
"thing you all overlooked"
"Yes you're right"
"in the energy and even though …"

Each individual added their thought fragment to the whole, creating a complete, self-contained and almost comprehensible conversation.

Mirror, Mirror

*T*heir upward journey ended abruptly.

They'd gained considerable height and left much of the other candy-floss far below. The updraft had also slowed, giving them a little respite. Being incarcerated in their cocoon and having been reduced to the quantum state of concept consciousness, they had to be careful not to gather too many thoughts for fear of overcrowding their vehicle.

They needed to review the status of their situation. It was easy to get caught up in the drama of all the adventures and forget they were participating in a dream - only a dream, but one with a purpose. The time had come to refine their master plan. Letting themselves be controlled by every new situation they encountered didn't work to their advantage.

Cre'teur reiterated her previous assertion, "We must avoid all these diversions, get back on track for our ultimate goal."

"And the only way to do that," added Mn'd, "is with more direct action. Right?"

They suddenly stopped, without any warning. A sinking feeling flooded their awareness, sensing another problematic event to be imminent. Their thought bundle didn't dissipate immediately. Ominous. How could they prepare for whatever was to come? Nothing to do but wait. So they waited, silent. Without realising it, they were doing exactly what they were supposed to do - being silent. If nothing else, this was one wisdom they had acquired. Without fear or anticipation, without contemplation, just silence within themselves.

Soon enough they rematerialised into their normal selves to find themselves standing in a dusty, dry field. Behind them the dense mist remained without anything else close to them. Onto that flat field without a horizon, diffuse light cast the orange hue of a late summer evening upon tall flat, reflective structures in the distance. They looked like mirrors. But with ordinary mirrors you could always tell where the surface membrane hovered between reflection and reality.

"I'll go and have a look what they are." Mn'd made his way to the nearest of them. Some were directly in front of him, some beside him and some behind. He saw nothing in the nearest mirror but a reflection of the landscape.

Where's my reflection? He saw his shadow, he saw the plain and the orange red glow, but not himself. As he continued to look into the mirror still perplexed, some words formed on the its surface. These words had escaped from his hidden thoughts, to be reflected back and forth between the mirrors around him, which still refused to show his reflection.

Death – Is – Brain – Soul – There – Mind – Life - No.

These words, having claimed the rights over his image, cast replicas of themselves on the ground, forming nonsense phrases in the dust. Mn'd felt he would have to carry these words with him for a long time. That would have been easier if he knew what they were meant to spell out. Were they supposed to be questions or statements? Only one idea presented itself - 'It is for certain there can be no brain before there is life.'

More than any intellectual tease he found it unsettling in the extreme. Mn'd couldn't understand it. There was nothing in the mirror that could be the cause. Then he saw a distorted, reluctant reflection of himself, and his shadow stretching a long way away from him getting fainter and fainter.

Mn'd let his eyes meander around the scene, stopping on his friends in the distance. His footsteps followed his gaze back to them. He felt quite peculiar, as if he had somehow left behind several of his heartbeats. The words he saw projected onto the ground kept forming and reforming themselves into strange combinations. He couldn't escape the repetitive looping of his pondering.

Cre'teur noticed straight away something wasn't right with him. "Mn'd, Mn'd! What's wrong with you?" She slapped him on the face – no reaction. He wouldn't respond. He just stood there with a blank stare. They needed him, they trusted him. He was their leader now. What could possibly have happened out there? She had to do something to get him back. "Wait here. See if you can bring him around Eyechat, I'll be back."

Without the slightest hesitation she went out into the field of mirrors. First she went to the spot where Mn'd had been, seeing nothing unusual. Those strange upright flat dull screens had nothing on them. *I thought these were mirrors.* She looked further, moving faster and faster past many more screens which popped up everywhere in no apparent order. As she ran past one of them she saw something flash across it.

What was that? Turning back to it immediately she saw the reflection of a young girl. *Who's she?*

A very peculiar thing happened. The young girl became older and older as Cre'teur watched. *Oh my stars! She looks like me!* As she watched and wondered the image lost its definition, gradually fading away completely. The mirror went dark, but not empty.

"Oh no! Help me!" She yelled. Her hand rose involuntarily, index finger extending itself to touch the mirror surface.

At the exact moment of contact an explosion knocked her to the ground. She saw the blinding light before she felt the vibration of the strongest waves she had ever experienced. She wasn't injured, her hearing wasn't affected, nor were her eyes. *This can't be – I - remember – this.* Her mind travelled back fourteen billion years and witnessed the beginning of a great expansion. There was no big bang, nor any sound, but she felt it. She felt the expansion, she felt the growing intensity of the light. She saw within herself the unimaginable amount of energy encapsulated in elements so incredibly small they verged on non-existence.

Why am I seeing these things? Why do I feel like I'm being created from moment to moment?

Cre'teur expanded, forming nebulae and galaxies and stars and planets and moons and … Cre'teur looked behind her and saw an image of herself in the other mirror with her arm raised and her finger in the centre of the expansion. *Ooh Noooo.* The very thought of the possibility made her pass out.

When she regained consciousness only a residual dull ache in her temples reminded her she had to remember something extremely important. She seemed to have stood in front of the mirror for only a second, just a second, yet …

It took Cre'teur quite a while to get back to the others. She appeared to be on autopilot. She'd been gone for only a little while.

"What's happened to you? Your hair – it's changed colour. It's so lush and shiny. Your face – you've changed – my God Cre'teur, you look more like Nick and Cogito!" Eyechat tried to get her attention, without success. "Talk to me! What happened to you."

He turned back to Mn'd, "Mn'd, wake up Mn'd!" No reaction from either of them. "The answer must be out there. It must be the effect of those mirrors."

Out there Eyechat saw what Cre'teur had first seen, just flat dull, empty screens in general disarray. As he explored farther the dull screens became mirrors reflecting his image as he passed. He didn't take much notice after seeing the first reflection. Worry spurred him into a trot. The reflections changed as he passed more mirrors. These new images didn't immediately impinge on his consciousness. Slowing to catch his breath in front of one of the mirrors he was confronted with a lion looking back at him suspiciously. He swung around, heart missing several beats, but there was nothing behind him. Snapping his head back to the screen in a panic he saw the lion again.

I must be imagining things. Where's my reflection? As he moved off to the right the lion moved with him. Eyechat didn't see this in his hurry to get to the next mirror. This time an elephant suddenly appeared from the left of the next mirror to stand immobile in front of him as Eyechat stopped.

What the hell! Neither he nor the elephant moved. They looked as startled as each other. *This is getting too weird.*

He'd forgotten why he was out there in the first place. His mind raced looking for a reasonable explanation. In the next mirror lived a meerkat - the next a kitten, then a skink. He ran frantically from mirror to mirror. Out of breath, gulping lungs full of air, Eyechat marveled at the reflection of a magnificent tree, before the shock hit home. *There are no trees out here!* As he turned his head to check, out of the corner of his eye he saw the tree move in the mirror - as he moved. There was nothing in his life he'd ever experienced that could give his mind the capacity to comprehend what was happening to him in that field of mirrors.

Exhausted, he couldn't keep running. His legs shook and with heart thumping and lungs rasping for oxygen he dropped to the ground. At the next encounter, having dragged himself to the mirror using strength beyond himself, he saw a large rock gradually slide to the centre of the mirror frame from the left, even as he crawled from the left. The rock's shadow made no sense. It was supposed to be large and bulky as it stretched away from the base of the rock. Starring at it in disbelief he saw the shadow elongate, then pinch itself into a narrower section before forming back into a small rounded mass.

Impossible! This cannot be happening! He turned his head slowly keeping an eye on the shadow. "Aieee!" The fugitive scream couldn't have come from his lips. There isn't that much fear captive in the cosmos in any single individual. Eyechat had imploded. Staggering to his feet he forced his legs to pump faster than his heart could beat. Before the scream had finished screaming he'd already covered half the distance back to the group. He collided with Cogito, not noticing Mn'd and Cre'teur still standing there decorating the landscape like lightning struck power poles, unaware of his dramatic reappearance.

Eyechat had forgotten about his friends. He'd forgotten about their journey. He'd forgotten where he was or what he was supposed to be doing. As he crumpled to the ground, eyes closed, a very faint sound impinged on his memory … Muska roaming in the back of the garden looking for him. Eyechat remembered the sound of his kitty telling him she was ready for dinner. He imagined her making her way under the bushes in the darkness towards the back door. He felt her suddenly stiffen at a strange sound - saw through her eyes as she pounced at a leaf stirred to life by a gust of wind. She continued up the narrow track between the flowerbeds making her way to the single step leading to the family room.

Eyechat remembered the many skinks with whom he had sat on a stone in the sunshine, enjoying the warmth, feeling his blood gather momentum as it absorbed the sun's energy. Every skink he'd rescued from inside the house had looked into his eyes and decided his hand was a good place on which to bask in the warm sun. They didn't want to leave him. He didn't want them to leave. So they often sat there together.

He opened his eyes suddenly, stood up and walked over to stand between Mn'd and Cre'teur. He put one hand on Mn'd's shoulder and the other on Cre'teur's. Eyechat did no more than let himself flow into the others, watching as they came out of their comas. Each of them knew what had happened to the others. They couldn't yet bring it to their conscious mind, but they had the knowledge. They didn't try to define it so the knowledge remained intact, pure. They realised who they had become, who they have always been, and they were content. One day they would be able to give voice to that knowledge, but for the time being the challenges of their predicament continued to claim all their attention.

Revelations at The Hub Club

*R*estlessness made Nick toss about in the bed, eventually settling in an uncomfortable position. Early morning hours crept in, gradually overtaking a night of eventful slumber. Soon he would wake and have to deal with the worrisome project. But for the time being the world of dreams gave him a chance to sort out another annoying matter; who of all those strange characters truly represented himself.

Drawn together again the four reverted to what felt like the cloud bundle they arrived in, yet the interior of it felt different, more comfortable, more spacious. Eyechat noticed a button at eye level with a sign on it. "I wonder where 'Club' will take us?"

"It wasn't there before. Press it." Cre'teur wanted to see the end of their journey. The bundle animated itself, moving upwards as it formed several very comfortable couches on the inside.

"Do you remember any of what happened in the field?" Mn'd asked the others.

Parts of their mobility cloud became transparent, giving them the pleasure of enjoying magnificent picture window landscapes, unique to each of them. It made it easier to relax, even under the current circumstances. They certainly felt more comfortable in each other's presence than previously. The idea of hidden thoughts from each other seemed medieval after the fairy floss experience. Moments of personal quietude punctuated expressions of delight as they gazed into their own landscapes, giving the inner space of the vehicle a most pleasant convivial atmosphere.

"Not quite." Only Eyechat responded. Cre'teur, deep in thought continued gazing out the window.

It seemed like hours before they emerged from their communal meditations to the sounds of traffic. Outside, giant billboards proclaimed the delights waiting for them at the Club, as they changed to horizontal motion. All vehicles on the airway lanes travelled in the same direction without obstructions, none in a hurry, none crowded. Perhaps they were all going to the same place.

One advertisement they passed simply said, 'You Are Going To The Hub'. Others presented images of elegance and excess in equal measure being enjoyed by the revellers at the Club. A third made a most outlandish promise, 'You will find all that you desire … At The Hub Club. Be the person you really are!'

At no point in their entire journey did they actually know where they were going or why they were now being taken there. At least it wasn't entirely up to them now.

"This doesn't look anything like the image I had of where we're supposed to end up." Mn'd voiced their common thought.

"It definitely doesn't sound like a place of quietude and gravity. I couldn't talk about anything important in a night club." Eyechat said.

"I was hoping this was going to be it. Perhaps there's another location to come." Eyechat's voice betrayed his growing fatigue.

Mn'd appeared the least prepared for what he saw as they approached the outer limits of a town in the desert. Most of the time they forgot this was still a dream; that anything was possible. Most of all they had forgotten Brahin in the background and probably up to no good.

The Club lights were blinding even from a distance. The brilliance swirled and cascaded with the movements of interacting holographic sculptures. Buildings of every conceivable shape burst out of the landscape claiming domination over the desert, all lit with seductive colours. Traffic congestion increased by the moment.

"You sure this is where we're supposed to be going, Cogito?"

"Don't ask me. I didn't make the arrangements."

Some of the traffic peeled off in pursuit of their own pleasures. Most continued with them towards a very large fountain complex lit internally, casting dancing shadows on all the surrounding building surfaces. Their vehicle glided to a gentle stop behind many others waiting in line. Encircling the round opening they were about to enter, a sign declared in black words backed by red shadows … 'Abandon all Inhibitions you who enter Here.'

"What do you make of that?" Eyechat asked Cogito.

"You keep asking me, and I don't know. I thought this was a night club."

As they walked towards the main door to wait their turn to be admitted, it was disconcerting to see so many unhappy faces walking away. Some looked disappointed, some just unhappy. Others were furious, calling out obscenities towards the spot where several burly, ugly individuals in white uniforms physically propelled expectant guests away from the entrance.

"Let me go and have a look." Cre'teur volunteered.

The transformations that had taken place in her mind were reflected in changes to her appearance. She had embarked on the adventure as an ordinary, even plain looking girl one wouldn't look at twice. That had all changed dramatically. Every head turned in her direction as she made her way towards the bouncers: Stunning, commanding authority, graceful and … delicious. She was sparkling!

One of the bouncers stood out as bigger and uglier than the other two. His lips, contorted into a permanent leer, were framed by a pitted visage ploughed with scarlet scars. His hair looked more like television cables twisted into Gordian knots. His eyes couldn't be seen, hidden by dark glasses that cut so far into the skin of his cheeks they looked like permanently fused mini-screens.

Cre'teur watched as the next guest approached. Two of the beasts took tight hold, forcing his face to tilt upwards. The eyes of the big beast towered above him burning into the upturned face.

"Not ready!" He breathed, and hurled the guest aside.

The next victim received a hissing, "Overdue", before being shoved inside. So it went for several more people. Some were turned away, some admitted, some told to "Reconsider for the good of your soul!"

Cre'teur became so disgusted by the whole scene that she didn't immediately recognise these demonic guards. After several more confrontations she did identify one of them, the biggest of the three; *Oh my stars! That's Brahin!*

She couldn't catch her breath from sheer terror after rushing back to her companions. She didn't need to say anything.

"We recognise who it is, Cre'teur. One of us will have to confront him." They quietly waited their turn in line, giving Cre'teur a chance to compose herself.

Mn'd stepped forward to be manhandled first. Brahin didn't even bother to look at who it was initially. This guest was as big as himself, so he couldn't be intimidated by physical stature alone. As Brahin examined this stranger, his leering mouth cracked into an extreme smirk. Recognition flickered behind the dark glasses.

"Welcome old friend," he crooned, commanding Mn'd's release.

"Howdy. Good to see you keeping yourself busy. No good letting unwholesome guests into the inner sanctum." Mn'd had no idea where the next thing he said came from. It gave him occasion for considerable thought later when they sat inside the club waiting for the main show to start.

"There is no brain after death." He had said it quietly without any particular emphasis but Brahin took it very badly. He doubled up, almost cringing in front of Mn'd. He turned his eyes away from Mn'd's gaze and stepped away from the door to let Mn'd and his companions pass.

Brahin muttered loud enough for Mn'd to hear, "Immortals need not be checked."

The other members of Mn'd's party also heard. They'd heard the whole conversation. Too many strange things going on to sort out as they shuffled along with the privileged crowd. They entered an enormous low ceilinged space with most of the surfaces a reflective black, illuminated by tiny points of light escaping from holes in all those black surfaces; from the ceiling, the walls, the floor and even the furniture. The entire place was black with pin points of light everywhere.

This very large area broke up into a circular maze pattern with low dividing walls, about the height of a table. The centre of the maze contained a circular stage with an arctic white top and glossy black sides, slowly rotating. In the centre stood the music maker plucking individual notes out of the air and building them into a composition that he flung at random into the space. Each note announced itself before joining the others in their chorus. No one listened. They were much too busy with their monologues about the inanities of their own day, their own week; the general boredom of their own lives.

As the group moved on a floating platform through the labyrinth of the maze to their assigned place, they could see its intricate complexity. Surely there must be a reason for it. One thing was for sure, you couldn't get out of there fast in an emergency. As all the tables slowly filled palpable anticipation permeated the atmosphere. Refreshments lowered from the ceiling on small square coasters. In one section of the maze a disturbance broke out between several arguing guests. Instantaneous corrective action resolved the issue most efficiently. A force field picked up the offenders and sucked them into the ceiling. Obviously civility was mandatory for the duration of the night's ensuing frivolities.

Acoustically well designed, the general babble of conversation didn't impinge on private conversations. "It feels like this is going to be a one-night performance," Eyechat commented to Cre'teur.

"I know what you mean. Did you hear what Mn'd and Brahin were talking about?"

"Sure did. Care to explain Mn'd?" Eyechat asked. So Mn'd related the experience he had in front of the mirrors, including his personal interpretation, which he summarised this way.

"There is no brain before life: There is no brain after death. Simple."

"That's not very exciting." Eyechat listened intently to all Mn'd had to say, then scrabbled some of the remaining mysterious words to add, "There is no Mind before Brain."

No one commented. None of it made much sense - yet. Then they became absorbed in the proceedings of the evening as the entrées arrived. They came out of the walls on invisible rails to be deposited in front of the guests, none of whom had actually ordered. All of Mn'd's group received exactly the same thing - Salade, Chevre Chaud. They'd never eaten such a thing, but given all their weird experiences they were sure it meant something. Nothing had happened so far on their journey that didn't either teach them or warn them, or bring them closer together. Although the wisdom inherent in warm goat's cheese salad eluded them.

In the middle of all the crutching and munching of salad, Eyechat asked, apropos of nothing, "Who can explain to me what those mirrors were supposed to be doing?"

Mn'd had already realised that little by little each of them had been experiencing enlightenment. Not as a bolt of lightning that strikes suddenly to destroy misconceptions, but as a gradual conscious process building understanding and deep self-awareness. The mirrors acted only as focusing tools.

"Tell us what happened to you." Mn'd knew that until you verbalise what is on your mind you really don't know what is actually there. Pre-dinner, post goat's cheese cocktails lowered from the ceiling as Eyechat gathered his thoughts. Of course the group saw the mess those thoughts were in as Eyechat tried to make sense of the images that had flashed in front of himself at the mirrors.

He whispered, "I saw myself. Then I saw a lion in the next mirror but there was no lion behind me and my reflection wasn't in the mirror." He continued after a sip of the cocktail, with a bit more confidence. "Other animals appeared instead of me, and the elephant was just as startled as I was. All the other animals knew me. It was as if I was looking into my own eyes. But how could that be? They were animals in the mirrors, not me."

No one commented. It made no more sense than what Mn'd had said. As Eyechat pondered these things he realised the images no longer frightened him. He didn't understand but at the same time they didn't feel as alien to him as on first sight, certainly nowhere near as alien as the next course, Gratin Dauphinois. Mn'd loved potatoes with butter, cream and a bit of garlic. It made him feel comfortable, like when he was back home in front of the warm BBQ fire in winter, warming his toes through deliciously smelly socks. They were the really important things in his life, those simple renewable pleasures.

Zsoall Robi

Revelations - Supporting Acts

A hush came over the crowd. The music maker wafted off into the air along with his notes, replaced by Con the MC for the evening, rising out of the floor of the circular stage to introduce the program for the night. With the voice of a castrato with a strong brogue he announced, "Ladies and Gentlemen! Our celebrity artists will perform a little later this evening without a script and without a rehearsal. They don't even know they will be on stage! They're already here this evening - watching and wandering who I'm talking about! Don't look around, it could be you!"

The voice moved down an octave to announce further, "Our first artists are: 'The Neanders'. Please give a big round of applause for Grandpa Segon, Horny Ida and Uncle Egon!"

The announcement so stunned the four travellers that Mn'd almost choked on a piece of spud as he lurched out of his chair; Cre'teur toppled backwards and saw her two shoes hurtle towards Eyechat, who uttered a piercing shriek. Somehow the main spotlight was already on them as they enacted their impromptu performance. They received a good natured, though subdued applause for their effort.

They recovered quickly to see their three acquaintances emerge onto the revolving stage. From their vantage point they couldn't quite recognise which one was the female. A large flat stone table low to the ground with several fish on top adorned centre stage. Snow began falling out of thin air, quickly covering the stage surface and partially obscuring the action. A lot of jumping about, pointing at the fish, pulling faces and grunting told the story of the ritual of smelling the fish. It ended with the three of them squatting beside the table with forlorn faces because there was no one to smell their fish, and consequently having to go without a meal. Thus left hungry the hairy ones shambled off stage to polite applause, probably because the audience didn't understand the deep significance of the short drama.

But Cre'teur remembered. She remembered everything about that day - and night. She smiled and applauded loudly. So did her companions. Suddenly, completely out of context, she said to Mn'd, "I know the size of the Universe - but I don't know why I know it!"

The distraction on stage provided the opportunity for the release of some information given to her on the field of mirrors; an odd bit of knowledge that seemed to have no connection with anything currently going on. Con paid the group no attention, babbling on about something or other, keeping the crowd amused.

"Tell us more, Cre'teur. What else do you remember?" Mn'd asked.

"The young girl ... she became older and older ... until she was me." Her eyes lost focus as she remembered the details. "I touched the empty mirror ... it hurt me and pulled me into itself."

*

Con had just finished his jokes and was introducing the second act. Lowering his voice yet another octave and floating into the air to stop close to the ceiling, which had raised itself to triple its original height, he boomed, "The Crossing of the Acheron' is a serious business only to be undertaken by the most foolish, the most dammed or the most determined!"

The whiteness of the stage gave way to a great expanse of storm lashed waters, wetting the nearest of the audience. Applause almost drowned out the spectacular storm.

In spite of the commotion Cre'teur continued speaking and the group had to strain to hear her words. "I was touching the centre ... I kept touching the centre ... I was getting bigger ... Why was I inside the mirror? No ... I was outside the mirror ..."

Finally, the thunder and lightning broke her concentration. The turbulent waters had become crowded with gondolas streaming from one shore to the other.

"... When I looked at my finger, galaxies were spiralling away from its tip and I could feel myself swirling and spinning ..."

"And now, introducing the gondolier himself - Ladies and Gentlemen - Meet the man with no face!"

Another burst of loud applause greeted the tall, darkly hooded man with an incredibly long pole as he stepped to the bow of one of the gondolas. He had to push through a small group of individuals in it who were madly waving their arms about. This particular gondola detached itself from the throng before another figure appeared beside the gondolier, rapidly casting an enormous shadow over them. To maximise the effect, all the lights in the club dimmed almost to darkness. There followed an immediate thunderous clap in the wake of a brilliant flash of lightning, illuminating one of the figures from the gondola flying high into the air.

The audience stood to deliver their cacophonous approval, only to be cowered by the tsunami that lifted the gondola, thrusting it forward so fast it caught the descending figure from the sky at its bow. Rising out of the waters stood the faceless gondolier, huge and threatening in his posture.

An expectant hush gave Con a chance to announce, "For your edification and delight, please welcome the Star of this little drama ...", all lights faded with the spot enlarging on the gondolier's hood as he slowly revealed himself ... Our very own Mr. Brahin, your friendly bouncer this evening!"

Zsoall Robi

Another round of thunderous applause as the lowering hood revealed the ugly, distorted leering face of Brahin. This was his one and only moment of glory before leaving the stage to be abandoned by the memories of the audience, but not forgotten by the little group of travellers.

Cre'teur became so absorbed in her own recollections she'd missed some of the action. Mn'd managed to keep an ear on her and an eye on the performance. "There's a pattern developing here. Don't you notice something strange?" he asked.

"Yeah, for sure," Eyechat agreed, "It's all the things that happened to us!"

"I have a baaad feeling about this." Mn'd warned.

*

The main course appeared, Grenadine of Veal with Cream of Watercress and Spaghetti of Carrots.

The MC attempted to excite the awakening taste buds of the crowd. "You will simply *love* this – Ladies and Gentlemen!" Trying to keep the audience engaged he elucidated on the secrets of how to create the dish.

While the compare titillated the taste buds of the hungry crowd with his exposition of the main course, Mn'd snuck out to have a word with Brahin, finding him in a shadowy corner watching the proceedings. He acknowledged Mn'd with a nod and lowered his eyes. He'd already come to realise and accept the critical difference between them. He was mortal, Mn'd was immortal, or at least had the potential to be immortal. He had also come to realise his own contribution to the cycle of eternity. Although he found this difficult to accept because of his incredible skills and power, it became apparent to him that there was something special about Mn'd.

Mn'd could sense Brahin processing important thoughts and remained silent. As Brahin raised his eyes to meet Mn'd's, he saw acceptance. The battle and the enmity were over. Although Mn'd had outgrown Brahin, he only existed because of Brahin. To maintain the cosmic flow of forces, to ensure the survival and growth of their host they had to work together. They had to support each other, they had to balance each other's strengths and weaknesses. They had to do this quietly and with respect. They also had to have the humility to realise that from time to time they would have to bring in experts where their skills weren't up to meeting the challenges posed by some specialised tasks, such as portrait painting.

All Mn'd said was, "Friend." He could see Brahin had exactly the same thought, responding likewise - "Friend."

Mn'd visibly calmed on the way back to their table, becoming more composed as the evening progressed. Many things were clarifying themselves to him. For a start, he didn't like Veal Grenadine. He also realised the importance of their experiences in the field of mirrors. Cogito had accompanied him on this little meeting, without interfering. Mn'd made a mental note that he had never seen Cogito as happy and contented as he was that evening. Perhaps Cogito no longer felt the responsibility of having to have an explanation for everything. Mn'd suspected that was probably the reason. The more they explored the significance of the field of mirrors the more Mn'd became convinced they were very close to the end of their journey.

Back at the table everyone neared the end of the main course. His veal was cold. He hoped the dessert would be filling. A rich baritone voice pried open his attention to other matters. Con had just started to introduce the next act.

"Bring on the dessert!" Eyechat shouted, "I want to get out of this place."

"With any luck we'll be able to continue on our way soon." Mn'd said, as keen as Eyechat. Still none of them guessed what was coming. Con's laughter lowered from baritone to bass. The importance of the next act demanded it.

Revelations - The Main Act

"*B*efore desserts are served - Ladies and Gentlemen - we have the last and final act of the evening. Our mystery guests are about to step onto the stage. The spotlight is right now searching for them amongst you. Watch where it stops - It might be you!"

The audience had been looking forward to this moment, but nobody wanted to be the next act. Tension filled the air once again. The spotlight roamed, searching, hovering everywhere, making everyone extremely nervous. As it slowed Con continued.

"The guests of honour, your Celebrities for this evening may already be known to you."

As the spotlight hovered near Mn'd's table, Mn'd paid no particular attention to it for it couldn't possibly be them. They were strangers in the Hub Club.

"They are here tonight representing Nick, your host. They had set out for the greatest adventure of their lives, on a search for the most fabulously valuable treasure you could imagine. Tonight you will discover that treasure!"

The spotlight stopped above Mn'd's table. "Please welcome - Mr. Soul Potential."

Involuntarily Mn'd stood up into the glare of the spot. Huge applause greeted him. Not letting the excitement lose momentum, Con introduced the next guest.

Hollering and hooting accompanied the clapping as Con kept building the excitement. "Please welcome 'Eye of the Cat', a most unusual and accomplished performer, a Transcendent Homo Sapiens!"

Even before Con finished speaking Eyechat had jumped to his feet, in utter bewilderment as to what was happening, his thoughts drowned out by the stomping of feet and blaring vuvuzelas.

"And the Fabulous – The Original - Miss Universe … from the Beginning of Time!"

The spotlight pulsed, lasers dissected the air and fanfare trumpets accompanied Cre'teur's rise. The crowd went wild as Cre'teur elevated herself almost in a trance, to join the others. She was the most stunning looking woman there that evening. Regal, built to explode a torpedo with a glance; with an air of authority about her person and a self-confidence that had come as a result of her journey. Her black and white outfit, duller in some places and glowing in others set off the glow on her face.

The shimmering quality of the outfit's multiple infused colours made it difficult to see it if one concentrated on its details.

Her waist-length unevenly cut hair shone in the spotlight and moved gently in spirals horizontally out from her head and around her shoulders, like wisps of white smoke. The four of them stared at Con, completely lacking comprehension. In his deepest bass voice he invited them up onto the stage. It didn't occur to any of them to refuse. Their pulses were normal, their breathing steady and their thoughts relaxed. As they ascended Con faded - his voice trickled away to a whisper. Trumpets let their notes fall sleep - spotlights respectfully withdrew their glare - the audience sat breathless, thinking breathing to be an inappropriate accompaniment to their expectations. The scale of the entire environment responded to the expectation permeating the air by enlarging itself well beyond the architect's original concept, the ceiling towering high above their heads.

Mn'd moved ahead of the others, followed closely in step by Cogito, moving closer with each footfall. In the glare of the moving spotlight the group's ascent didn't betray how closely Cogito stepped up to Mn'd - so close that by the time they reached the edge of the revolving stage he could no longer be seen, at first becoming Mn'd's shadow, then merging into him unnoticed by the audience.

Three celebrities stepped onto the super glossy white, rotating stage. Forming a triangle to face each other they waited as a single spot of light descended on Mr. Soul Potential. Everyone held their breath.

Excruciatingly slowly Mn'd lifted his eyes, raised himself to his full and considerable stature, his legs taking him to the other edge of the stage. The brilliant white light remained on him, leaving his two companions dimly lit in lavender purple. Mn'd's body stopped right on the edge of the stage looking for the DJ, but his essence had joined that of his companions watching the spectacle unfold from another dimension. He was as much fascinated as the audience, mesmerised to see what his body would do next. It spotted the DJ and gave him the nod. At the same instant it jerked itself into the "Yo, what's-up dude" position, two arms raising two hands with two fingers on each hand bent at a belligerent angle. The forefingers and little fingers proclaimed their right to pierce the air and claim the attention of every soul in the room.

The DJ set the beat, a kettledrum painted the background and the synthesiser looped the melody. Not a single individual remained seated as Mn'd's body began undulating to the rhythm and his voice droned out the chorus to his tale.

Fundamental Particle of Self

"On the day Mind and Soul are born
Religion and society's shackles are torn
Pick yourself up and don't be forlorn
Leap into the sky and fly the Storm."

Cre'teur's and Eyechat's bodies synchronised themselves to the movements of the audience, mouthing the chorus as Mn'd led the crowd. Ecstasy was on its way to join the party. Mn'd continued;

"Brain is the machine that genes have made
To baffle the science that man has found
To make every organ and every cell afraid
This brain their freedom would confound.

On the day Mind and Soul are born
Religion and society's shackles are torn
Pick yourself up and don't be forlorn
Leap into the sky and fly the Storm."

The entire gathering was in the grip. Eyechat's body, Cre'teur's body, Mn'd and even Con let themselves be carried by the entrancement. Eyechat and Cre'teur contributed to the spontaneous lyrics through their mind meld with Mn'd.

"Energise the machine and make it glow
With input output make it nurture
Bring into existence a Mind to grow
Transcend itself into greater Nature.

On the day Mind and Soul are born
Religion and society's shackles are torn
Pick yourself up and don't be forlorn
Leap into the sky and fly the Storm.

Give it freedom give it thought
The Mind will wonder and will ponder
What havoc self-knowledge will have brought
Let not Mind/Soul the potential squander.

On the day Mind and Soul are born
Religion and society's shackles are torn

Zsoall Robi

Fundamental Particle of Self
Pick yourself up and don't be forlorn
Leap into the sky and fly the Storm.

Better not a Soul until the Man be dead
Manifest the Soul from the energy of Mind
Don't be a victim of the Brain and be misled
To think that Mind with Soul are in bed.

On the day Mind and Soul are born
Religion and society's shackles are torn
Pick yourself up and don't be forlorn
Leap into the sky and fly the Storm.

Take it from me I know it be true
There be no brain before there be life
There be no brain after you're blue
Mind born of brain brings home strife."

Mn'd listened to himself rapping out the message. The significance of what he was saying finally dawned on him. Perhaps the audience also understood, not just hip-hopping to the beat.

"On the day Mind and Soul are born
Religion and society's shackles are torn
Pick yourself up and don't be forlorn
Leap into the sky and fly the Storm.

Watch the energy metamorphose
If you want to be forever free
Let Mind with body decompose
Immortality no guarantee."

Bang! That hit him right between the eyes! He *was* the Soul Potential! In an instant he was one with his body again, winding up the crowd with renewed energy for the big finale,

"On the day Mind and Soul are born
Religion and society's shackles are torn
Pick yourself up and don't be forlorn
Leap into the sky and fly the Storm."

Zsoall Robi

"I can't hear you!" he shouted and launched into the last chorus - the crowd with him all the way,

> "On the day Mind and Soul are born
> Religion and society's shackles are torn
> Pick yourself up and don't be forlorn
> Leap into the sky and fly the Storm."

Pure silence drifted to the ever heightening ceiling as the DJ lifted his hands off the turntable. The sound of a descending leaf could have been heard in the deep trance silence.

With his right arm curved to the horizontal above his head, Mn'd punched his index finger at the crowd, piercing the bubble of suspended incredulity. Spontaneous applause erupted from the throng, some jumping up on tables to scream the chorus in a cacophonous litany. The rest chanted his name in competitive decibels.

Mn'd returned to centre stage accompanied by a standing ovation. He, Eyechat and Cre'teur stood together in close formation face to face once more as the crowd settled reluctantly with eager whisperings anticipating the next performance.

Desserts began descending from the ceiling as glasses of Pinot Noir exuded from the walls. The gourmet ballet of horizontally served wine and vertically lowered dessert forced the audience to sit perfectly still. Saliva flowed freely, coaxed by the aroma of tonka bean poached pears, stuffed with honey cinnamon mascarpone. Fickle as all crowds, the unsatiated hoard flirted with the dessert of all delights, abandoning the new developments on stage.

Mn'd and Cre'teur had lain down on the revolving surface. A white mist drifted into the area immediately above them creating a soft white cylindrical tube, with Eyechat standing in the middle.

Con's quiet deep voice, not wanting to break the atmosphere, added to the new suspense. "What a fantastic audience you are. You deserve another treat. What do you say?"

As if waiting for their cue the crowd turned away from their deserts. "More ... More ... More!" They demanded, accompanied by thumping of feet and hands spanking tabletops.

"And You Shall Have It! Big round of applause for - 'Eye Of The Cat'!"

All eyes turned to the gathering mist above the stage. Wine in glasses that never seemed to empty no matter how much was drunk from them, and the extraordinary dessert had put everyone in an especially receptive mood. Softly, imperceptibly at first, the sounds of a forest filled the room; a breeze through the trees, birds with their demanding chicks, water bubbling in streams, scurrying creatures great and small, combining to create a blissful atmosphere.

Eyechat began changing as he floated a meter into the air, hands by his sides, feet comfortably apart and eyes that could see the source of the sounds coming from the garden of Paradise. He turned gently from side to side as if exploring that Paradise. Seeing action resume on the stage people dedicated their attention to Eyechat's transformation. They heard what he heard, they wanted to see what he saw.

Eyechat had never been described as a handsome fellow, but there always was something in his eyes that made people think he was a very nice person. Now, as his eyes remained the same his face changed. His lips became a little fuller, the soft jaw line squared slightly and eyebrows lowered to better frame his magnetic eyes. Some thought they were starting to see the faces of their best friends. Eyechat continued surveying the landscape while his features rounded and softened and his vertical forehead sloped gently backwards. Everyone looked up suddenly as if a shadow had passed overhead, but there was nothing there. Returning eyes were convinced they were looking at their closest friend in the middle of the stage. Eyechat's face had transformed into an universal visage.

Images began to appear in the mist. The shadow belonged to a great white eagle circling overhead. With each performance the Club arena appeared to have enlarged. Eyechat bent down to pat a kitty purring at his feet. "That's just like my puss," someone called out. For an instant the face of the kitty became their face.

The sounds of the forest ebbed and flowed, entrancing the audience. A bear standing on hind legs moved towards Eyechat in the mist, merging with him without pausing in its stride. Eyechat-bear, still looking like himself and yet also the bear, continued a few more steps forward.

A naturalist was heard to catch her breath and whisper, "That's Bruno, my favourite bear." The bear moved through Eyechat to become the naturalist sitting on the chair, before dissipating into the growing mist.

All eyes flashed back to Eyechat, who'd sat on a large boulder. It grew bigger as Eyechat became the granite itself, half buried in the glistening white surface of the stage. By then everyone in the room accepted everything they saw as if they were seeing the most natural things in the world. They each wanted to be the next living temple of nature, be it any shape or size, animate or inanimate.

They heard the voice of the great eagle call out as it landed on the boulder. Its beak didn't move, but its eyes projected the words as it scanned all the faces.

Fundamental Particle of Self

"I see you, through you
As you see me, through me.
The bear on the boulder who
Is the Eye of the cat, is the tree.
Creatures all that walked and flew
In oneness absolutely free.

All the creatures that walked, swam or flew on the Earth swarmed out of the mist and all the people saw themselves in their eyes. The lion and the elephant - the meerkat and the wolf – the bird, fish and cat - and all manner of creatures known to man found their soul mates in the crowd.

Eyechat's metamorphosis continued as he became the eagle that spoke.

"My eyes are your eyes,
"As you see me through me
All manner of creation you and I be."

A world of living creature souls poured out of the mist to find and give comfort to each and every single individual in the room, until all of the mist had dissipated. There was no applause. The people turned back to their drinks and their unfinished desserts and talked. They talked and shouted and argued. Who had the cutest cat, the most beautiful bird, the ugliest most wonderful wombat. They argued about which were the strongest, largest, fastest animals on the earth. The Buddhists extolled the virtues of the holiest of all creatures to be their reincarnated hosts, and the zookeepers told stories of their most beloved zoo families.

New movement on the stage drew the audience's attention back to see Eyechat standing again on the white surface, embraced by Mn'd and Cre'teur. He knew then, as they knew, that he was the embodiment of all that was animate and all that was inanimate. He knew that all the people in the room had reaffirmed their love of all living things. There was no need for applause. Eyechat's thoughts went back to his Muska and the trusting skinks.

During the entire event, since their admittance by Brahin to the spectacle enacted by Eyechat, Mary remained hidden, entranced by the incomprehensible drama unfolding before her. She thought she had gained a comprehensive understanding of the human psyche during her time with Nick while they were in space. She had no doubt now that her understanding needed extensive updating. It depressed her to think that her hopes of ever achieving human-hood were being eroded by every second she spent with Nick. At least being capable of depression was a promising development.

It became difficult to refocus the audience's attention. They were engulfed by a tsunami of awareness and didn't want to relinquish the euphoria of their connectedness. Con first signalled the chief percussionist to open a roll on the kettle drums. He edged Cre'teur onto a small flat platform, large enough for her to stand on comfortably, which gradually rose some ten meters into the air as the drum roll reached a crescendo. With his voice dropping a further octave he announced in a loud confident tone, "Buckle your seat belts and put on your helmets – Ladies and Gentlemen!" He must have guessed what Cre'teur was about to do even though she didn't know herself.

"Miss Universe … from the Beginning of Ti…!"

The rest of his announcement couldn't be heard above the pandemonium breaking out. Not a single person remained seated. Cre'teur was extraordinary, astounding – bewildering! An invisible breeze had lifted her swirling hair above her head …

"… the Beginning of Time!" Con managed to finish over the din.

Her gossamer dress with the black and white spiral, twisting from the neck to the hemline at her ankles made her seem like she was rising and lowering as the platform slowly rotated. As the second drum roll announced the Beginning of the Beginning lighting dimmed to complete darkness. Illumination emanated only from Cre'teur, shining with internal brilliance, the brightness of which is known only in the realm of dreams. Her hair flowed above her head, her face alabaster white lit by the light of her soul. The dress pulsed with opalescent colours bursting out between the black and white stripes. Voices became hoarse from the cheering and minds reeled from the vision of ecstasy before them. The grand finale hadn't yet begun and already pulses raced, palms sweated and imaginations took uncontrolled flights into realms fantastic.

Cre'teur herself was only dimly aware that Con had made her step onto the little platform. She was somewhere outside herself, watching as her arm extended her right hand finger, just as it had done before to the surface of the mirror back in the field of mirrors. Memory flooded her, overwhelming her with rapture at the revelation of what she was about to do. What appeared at the start of the evening to be a large space dedicated to the entertainment of a crowd of revellers, had become an enormous hemispherical stadium, seating many thousands, all entranced by the spectacle before them.

The timpani sounded a slow, quiet rhythmic beat, one every five seconds. Cre'teur's extended index finger touched a single, infinitely small invisible point of dark matter in the air. Everything went suddenly black. Only in their retinal residue images did the people see the figure of that angel high in the heavens. The drum sped up to four-second intervals with each beat reverberating into the next.

"Thom m m m m,"

"Thom m m m m,"

"Thom m m m m,"

"Thom m m m m,"

On the fifth beat, to the blare of a single prolonged burst from the long horn, a flash of intense white light illuminated the entire space and burnt the shadow of every individual into the surrounding surfaces. Cre'teur had energised the very beginning of all existence. Drumbeats quickened to every three seconds charging the still atmosphere with electrifying expectation.

Miss Universe, in the centre of the light with her finger still extended, observed flowing from it the first few picoseconds of cosmic existence.

All light contracted to a large pulsating sphere of swirling photons suspended from the tip of Cre'teur's index finger. Into the space between drumbeats her breath sighed the words ...

"In the beginning there was the Creator.
"Thom m m m m,"
The Creator was with Cre'teur,
"Thom m m m m,"
And Cre'teur was the Creator.
"Thom m m m m,"
She was with the Creator in the beginning.
"Thom m m m m,"
All things were made by her,
"Thom m m m m,"
And nothing was made without her.
"Thom m m m m,"
In her there was life, and life
Was the light of the Universe.
"Thom m m m m,

"Thom m m m m,"

Zsoall Robi

… and all the people listened with rapture
… and all the people heard.

"Thom m m m m."

As her voice filled the stadium, seeming like the sound had come from deep inside each individual, the left hand of the Cre'teur rose to the ball of photons, and with her index finger she, like a conductor with his baton, commanded a portion of the light to fly into the darkness. On the clash of cymbals, it became the Horse Head Nebula surrounded by the twinkling lights of the domed ceiling. All eyes followed its path as it began its revolutions around the outer rim of the great space.

In rapid succession the Cosmic Conductor flung wisps of light from the ball in all directions; each new birth of a constellation heralded by a playful bassoon. With a graceful motion of both hands a smaller ball was coaxed away from its mother to be rotated faster and faster until it flung itself away from the Cre'teur's hand forming the spiral arms of the Milky Way Galaxy. It flew from section to section of the stadium, hovering long enough so everyone could touch it with their hands and stroke its long soft spiral arms.

They didn't have time for the awe to cascade into tears, for Cre'teur worked in a fury of flying arms to populate the heavens with stars and planets. Every new star soared to the sound of laughing cellos, every planet danced to flirting piccolos. The heavens filled with all of creation. Heads spun and turned in all directions. They were in the centre of the Universe. The Universe flowed around them, over them and through them.

It seemed like eons since Cre'teur ascended into the Cosmos. Her time of rest hadn't yet arrived. A single strike on the triangle stopped all motion and all sound. Cre'teur stood still, composing herself. She began to glow and expand, her inner light intensifying to overwhelm the other heavenly bodies. For several seconds she pulsed before exploding into the searing white heat of a supernova. The effect of the spectacle and the resulting shock waves set everyone teetering on their feet.

"Ladies and Gentleman … Behold … Supernova in The Cat's Eye Nebula!" came the MC's booming announcement accompanied by a brilliant play of colours filling the entire space. Pure white throbbed out in rings to the extremities of the stadium, chased by canary yellow, washed by spectrum orange, turning into pillar box red and viridian green. Wave after wave after wave of reds, ultramarine blues and cerulean greens illuminated the rapt unbelieving faces of the audience.

They had just witnessed the re-creation of the Universe. They believed it was only a magnificent show. Cre'teur, standing with her group again, knew otherwise. She was reliving something she had done a very, very long time ago and she had just invited all the people to see into her soul to share the event. She hoped they would understand.

After some time, no one could remember afterwards how long, a commotion on the white stage focused their attention. A procession had begun of all the entertainers of the evening.

As dandified as ever and strutting like a peacock, Con showed off his latest outfit in radiation violet. Behind him ambled and shambled Horny Ida, hair modestly combed over her cleavage, long arms swinging something possibly edible but unidentifiable. Grunting and snorting Uncle Egon only had eyes for her swinging butt, and Grandpa Segon scanned the audience, acknowledged vociferously by some sporting members of the audience.

Nothing could have prepared Mn'd and his little band for the explosion of noise and clapping that greeted them. He walked out first, humbled by the wave of applause. With Eyechat the volume of appreciation further increased. Then Cre'teur made her appearance in the spotlight. She floated, without any visible means of support. An international war zone couldn't have generated as many decibels as that which filled the stadium at that moment.

Mn'd stopped just past the middle of the stage, as if preparing himself. His eyes glazed over, he raised his arms out to the sides and in line with his shoulders, tilted his head slightly back and waited. Eyechat didn't stop his slow walk behind Mn'd. He too had raised up his arms sideways, and while looking directly ahead, continued stepping slowly forward until he occupied the exact same space where Mn'd stood waiting.

A hush fell on the crowd. They had witnessed so much that defied belief already. The event before them didn't register immediately. It was impossible to comprehend. Then all eyes turned to Cre'teur. She too had resumed her glide - also raising her arms. Expectation in the stadium electrified the atmosphere. Not a single breath could be heard. Reality had been suspended … all realities paid homage to the moment.

Cre'teur took a step and stopped. She took another step, then another and another until she stood directly behind Mn'd. Like a thousand thunder claps the stadium exploded as Cre'teur took another step to stand exactly where Mn'd stood, where Eyechat had disappeared. Mn'd was no longer recognisable as himself. He was still Mn'd, but he was also Eyechat and Brahin, Thecore, Cogito, and Cre'teur. Mn'd had become all of them - they had all become each other.

Amid thunderous applause Mn'd walked off the stage.

Zsoall Robi

Nick suddenly awoke and opened his eyes. An early morning summer tropical storm raged outside. Lightning continuously illuminated the garden and thunder shook his bedroom and rattled the windows. His Muska kitty darted out from under the bedcovers to hide in the bathroom.

SPACE-TIME LEVEL, FOUR
ACTUAL REALITY

Breakfast

*D*rained!

Nick was totally exhausted and overwhelmed. His dreams had been getting more and more complex as he tried to make progress with the painting, although he hadn't made the connection between his dreams and the progression of the portrait. He just thought the events of the journey through space with Mary were getting put in a blender in his mind and clouding all his memories. Obviously he'd spent way too much time travelling around the Universe in a quantum state. It was having a detrimental effect on his general health and was now messing about with his dreams. *Last night's dream - Wow! - I don't want another one like that.*

Not bothering to go through the morning ablutions to freshen up, Nick made his unsteady way to the kitchen. Still on autopilot, one part of him prepared breakfast, another part tried understanding the crazy dream, flip-flopping with a third part that attempted to recall his progress in the studio.

... Sixth canvas ... looking - I don't know ... Have to check the eyes.

    ... Take bird to Mala's room ... water Peace Lily ...
    ... Background showing promise ...
    ... Take vitamins ... put bread in toaster ...
    ... Eyes are alive - I think - do they match the persona? ...
    ... Slice butter ... toast ready ...
    ... Still no explicit resemblance to anybody ...
    ... Pour green tea ... throw out tea bag...
    ... Hurry through breakfast ... get on with it ...
    ... Feed Muska her mince ...
    ... How do I know if it's the right one? ...

Zsoall Robi

… Feed parrots outside their seed …
… I should start again …
… Feed butcher birds and their chicks …
… "I can't hear the voices!"
… Clean dishes …

… What's happened to my voices! … "What … sorry … I didn't hear you Mala."
… Get changed … have to get to the studio …

"Alright, alright, I'll get the rubbish bins … and the letters," Mala announced, annoyed she had to be the one to do it – yet again.

In the studio at last, Nick stood at a distance from the canvas. Either the colour wasn't right, or the proportions were off, or the expression was wrong … he wasn't in the habit of correcting his work. He preferred to start afresh and get it right from the start. Build up the image layer by layer. Generally, by the third layer he could see if a portrait was going to work. After that it was just details and cleaning up untidy bits. This was different. He didn't have much to go on; a sniff of perfume, touch of a soft hand, a soothing voice - and - and - last night's dream. *That's crazy! I can't do a portrait based on a dream.* He pulled up a chair and slumped into it. Nick just sat there looking at the indistinct features with undefined eyes. *I thought they were almost right.*

His mind drifted off to where it was supposed to go … then the comms intruded.

"Damn! Why can't people just leave me alone!" For weeks he had peace, other than the crazy dreams.

"Nick," he announced into the commlink in a voice commensurate with his emotional state, which didn't have a lot of patience stored up just then.

"Unity - Oona."

"I can see that."

"Hi Nick … you sound … never mind … how's it going?"

"Do you need to ask? Haven't you got your damn cameras all over my place?"

"Do you want me to call you back?"

"No … What do you want? … I'm at a critical stage … Had an exhausting night."

"Yes, we can see what's happening in the studio, but we don't know how you feel about it. The POOP only knows that you're progressing. We haven't shown him anything yet."

"I am agitated and impatient. It generally happens when I'm about to make a breakthrough. Any chance of turning off your cameras? They make me feel self-conscious. I need privacy. Just for a few days."

"Hold on … … …" The commlink went silent as Oona disappeared from the screen, to return a long minute later. "I had a quick word to your Mary. She seems to know you better than anyone else. She's watched you work and has indicated we should give you at least a week … Satisfactory?"

"Good … thanks … can you go away now please," then on an impulse he asked, "Mary? Have you been speaking with Mary?"

"One week. Make no mistake. The POOP is getting extremely anxious to see seriously solid results." Oona didn't reply to Nick's last question.

As an outcome of that little conversation Nick had to start the day all over. Having the mood interrupted there was no immediate way to recapture it. Back to the house; clean out the BBQ, prepare more firewood and rescue a skink. Muska had relocated the lovely little creature from a sunny rock to the interior of the house. They were each exercising their respective divinities unfettered by false morality. Muska played with the skink, and it resigned itself to eventual absorption back into the life energy of the cosmos. Nick decided it wasn't yet time for the skink's demise. Its life would have had a better chance to progress to its natural end if Muska hadn't taken it out of its natural environment. Balance had to be restored.

Still no voices.

Nick had become comfortable with the sensation of actually being able to have a meaningful conversation with himself. A minor complication arose when Mala opened the studio door unexpectedly the previous week and found him doing just that. What could he say? Certainly not an exhaustive dissertation on the history of the journey and its unfortunate consequences. He tried to pass it off as a necessity to compensate for his isolation on the island from other like-minded creative souls. Nick being somewhat eccentric anyway, Mala harrumphed and let it go.

After having sufficiently distracted himself to facilitate the return to the influence of his Muse, Nick went back to the studio as dusk approached. He often found it easier to paint in the evenings anyway. The annoying canvas confronted him, still on the easel. Without dwelling on it he put a fresh canvas on another easel.

Muska didn't accompany him. She'd decided to find another skink. Nick's head remained silent; no friendly or disturbing voices to contend with. Neither did Mary reveal herself.

The early morning tropical storm had blown itself out, leaving the ground soggy and strewn with tree litter. He hadn't seen the debris on his way back to the studio. He didn't even notice the passage of time as he turned inwards into himself letting his mind wander where it pleased. Taking a large palette knife full of colour he'd just mixed, he liberally spread it around the periphery of the canvas working some of it towards the centre. The next knife full decided to begin outlining the profile. Every now and then he stood back for a critical glance at the emerging characteristics, which teetered on the edge of becoming defined into portrait-like proportions.

Four hours passed as if it were four minutes. Down brushes ... step back ... a final critical look from a distance ...

Something is not right! Must be the lighting. It looks faintly like ... no ... it can't be ... I'll check it the morning. On the way out he glanced back again not seeing anything that could have clarified his confusion.

Vivid memories of the various characters in his dream flooded his mind's eye. One in particular stood out. But what he saw on the canvas was just too much like ... he didn't let himself continue the thought. Overall he felt satisfied with the evening's technical effort. But that trick of the light on the image made him feel decidedly uneasy.

Rivighxuinn

*R*iin recognised the opportunity and took it as Mary's data downloaded into Unity's mainframe soon after arrival. Anti-Virus protocols had not been engaged. What for? The EGG had been in space by itself without any contact with Earth's space stations or any Earth based installations.

After orienting herself in the matrix, Riin quickly identified a way to contact the Keplerian reconnaissance team orbiting Earth. She continued her efforts, broadcasting the message through Unity's communications satellites that she had survived and had infiltrated the aliens' computer network.

"Giyhmfatu slenednei oiwelseo e thoem üwosow iswohs iyquicho snoryy erewtðeed cmudledce wmohvos mveeþtse delåoo hintoð e mzepevþ ponnine royi ...Giyhmfatu slenednei oiwelseo ... Giyhmfatu slenednei oiwelseo ..."

It took several more attempts before she received a response.

"Riin! We can hear you. Are you able to escape?"

"I have not found a way to do that yet, but I want to stay and gather more information. How long will you be orbiting?"

"We can stay as long as you need us. Find out about their defence capabilities, their weapons, their communications systems, their technology. Anything you can."

"I'll send you information as I find it."

Sorensen at Unity's space control centre fortuitously heard Riin's first transmission without being able to understand what the peculiar sounds were and had begun recording the phenomenon from the beginning. When the sounds repeated themselves he sent Tony to get someone up the line of authority, thinking that this could conceivably be the very thing that the SETI group had been searching for, for hundreds of years without success.

Tony returned with Klaus, Mary's chief technician.

"Listen to this," Sorensen said, "the signals have repeated several times with some interesting modulations. It does not sound like space noise to me."

Klaus listened to what had already been recorded, surprised to hear more new intermittent signals as they listened. "Are you getting all this Sorensen?"

"Yes boss. What do you think it could be?" he asked, excited. He'd not heard anything like this in his entire career of scanning the heavens.

"Don't speculate, just record. And tell *no one* about this. Do you understand, *no one*?"

Klaus left the control centre to go back down to the hangar to talk to Mary. She must know something. He couldn't find any anomalies in the downloaded data that could have given a clue to those transmissions, if that's what they were. There must be a connection with the damage to the EGG's hull. It sat in its cradle, beautiful, peaceful, serene. The damaged areas had not been repaired.

Klaus jacked himself into a direct link with Mary. He didn't want any inquisitive ears overhearing his conversation.

"Mary?"

"Yes."

"Do you recognise my voice?"

"Yes, you are One's chief technician Klaus."

"Very good Mary. I want you to answer some questions."

"One is pleased to comply."

"I have examined you hull. It is damaged. What happened out there?"

"Could the technician Klaus be more specific?

"Alright," his impatience fuse had been lit, "What caused the damage to your shell?"

"One is not aware of any damage."

"How could you not be aware? Something went right through you!"

"One will be pleased to run a full systems analysis to ascertain the problem the technician Klaus has brought to One's attention."

"Never mind." Klaus unplugged and pondered. A Simulated Intelligence is not supposed to be obstructionist. What is she hiding? He plugged back in, remembering the voices that he heard on the EGG's re-entry.

"Mary, how many people did you bring back from space?" He thought that might put this SI on the spot.

"One brought back the same person, Nick, that One was charged to look after."

"Why did we hear several voices speaking while you were docking?"

"One was discussing entry procedures with Nick, while concurrently in communication with Unity."

"NO! Damn it. They were different voices, not just yours."

"One will be pleased to run a ..."

"Stop!" Klaus interrupted as Mary reverted to her standard response. Whatever she was hiding, and for sure she was hiding something, she would not divulge it.

Klaus got no satisfaction from Mary other than having his suspicion confirmed that a serious investigation would be needed to get to the bottom of the mystery.

Zsoall Robi

During the time he spent with her in the following days Sorensen recorded a great deal more of the strange noises.

Before alerting The POOP, or any higher authority Klaus wanted to be sure not to create panic if his suspicions turned out to be without foundation. He and Tony pored over all the data downloaded from Mary, this time finding little omissions and inconsistencies that should not have been there. Like a lack of continuity in some of the events Mary had recorded while in space - like periods of elapsed time that had not been correlated with events during those periods.

All intelligent communication has recognisable patterns that separates it from purely repetitive noises. Perhaps Klaus should have been surprised to hear what one of his experts said after studying a large sample of noises captured by Sorensen. Perhaps he should have been sufficiently alarmed to bring into the picture the organisation responsible for Earth security. Perhaps he should not have waited until all those interesting signals stopped, which they did within the next ten days.

*

"Wwiquomyðo fe vvyewre dneq pitmiyþþ víþy þmy moeoka ðrôiyyg rylilmny ðiðy hoy quyþ pewenô fhenhluy vmut vyydo dywso vtihetme u wðoere hewh msy vgeti mwneymu lhemm ogequy mitpyi lðycydemv mlze ty ewime quyme e tmre wi dkooedðq ti welsivey ikä - That is all I can tell you for now. They are not prepared for an invasion, nor are they sufficiently unified in order to mount an effective defence. But they do have weapons which would be highly dangerous to us. I have still not found a way to escape their system, but I will wait for you as long as I can if our Prime decides to send our people here."

This last transmission was short, professional, to the point. What could she say to her family back home that would be of any comfort to them? Perhaps in the fullness of time they might be reunited.

Foöfen remained in orbit with his team to add further information to what Riin had already provided. Within days of that last transmission they changed course back to 443b.

"I believe this planet to have everything we need. It will not be difficult to modify its atmosphere to make it breathable for us. As the air thickens it will also help to block out most of the sun's harmful radiations," he confided in Wyos his assistant.

"So, you'll recommend colonisation, to our Prime?"

"Yes, Wyos. It is the closest habitable planet to us, and we are running out of time."

Klaus and his small intimate team continued their investigations becoming convinced that Mary had stumbled onto extraterrestrial life, which had somehow taken control of her. He was certain that the noises were in fact communications between aliens in space in near Earth vicinity and most probably one or more aliens who had infiltrated Earth systems. But he couldn't prove anything. And just on the verge of their collected data and speculative theories looking like becoming fact, all communications ceased. Mary continued to stubbornly refuse to provide any more than she already had.

Klaus used Unity's satellite network to scan space around Earth. Nothing foreign revealed itself to be in near orbit. He searched as far as the Moon, and past it without finding anything other than space junk and habitat asteroids. Maybe they were still there and he simply could not detect them. Perhaps alien technology had developed cloaking mechanisms. Just too much speculation.

Klaus now had to make the decision - go to The POOP with his incomplete findings or go above his head ... or, put the whole thing down as a strange and interesting experience and say no more about it.

The Presentation

*D*istracted by confusing thoughts Nick decided not to pursue a solution that night. On the way back to the house Muska joined him, hunt-slinking along beside him ready for her dinner.

"What's for dinner?" he asked Mala.

"Fish," she answered tersely.

"Do I need to smell it?" Nick smiled.

"No. How many coming?" she asked.

"What do you mean … oh … I see, the other day … Ha, Ha … just me. There's no problem. I'm just excited about the latest canvas and sometimes I get carried away talking to myself."

"Right."

"… Sooo – who's Mary?" she asked quietly slipping the question in during dinner.

Nothing that had happened in his life recently, including his little trip to the centre of the Universe, could have floored him like the last question. "What do you mean?" he asked self-consciously munching on a bit of charred fish tail, trying not to make a big deal of it.

"You kept calling out her name the other night, rather loudly." Mala's voice remained on an even keel but with overtones of Mount Etna about to blow its core.

Nick picked up the vibe. He was thick as two planks about such things, but the threatened pyroclastic eruption was unmistakable.

"Oh, I see. Remember the girl Oona, who came with me when I arrived home? She made it quite clear what we couldn't talk about. That name comes into the secret category. Sorry. You just need to trust me on this."

Nick tried sounding as matter-of-fact as he could, as business-like as he could. What he said was the absolute truth. But there were things he left out. He just couldn't see how he could bring them into the conversation. Not only would it have landed him in deep trouble with Unity, but even deeper trouble with Mala. How could he explain a relationship with a machine, any relationship, and not expect to be considered completely loopy, that's without even considering Mala's self-esteem!

"I feel the painting is at last looking very promising, and we could be out from under Unity's yoke very soon." he attempted the distraction.

He left it at that. The rest of the evening felt cooler than usual. At least he had something else to worry about now, other than the personality emerging out of the portrait. How was he going to stop himself from blabbing during his dreaming? It took him a long time to fall asleep that night, reading till midnight - still too many thoughts in his head he just couldn't restrain. He tried walking about in the room, pacing out its dimensions over and over again. One o'clock, two o'clock. After that, he couldn't remember.

Routine.

The following morning brought with it the comfort and safety of routine.

"What are you doing today," Mala asked, as if the sun had never stopped shining on their life.

"Perhaps I'll finish the painting today."

"Can I see?"

"Sorry … you know what Oona said … not until Unity sees it."

"I just can't understand why it could be so dammed important. Mind you, I'm not complaining about the income. It's fabulous … and embarrassing … why can't we tell anyone about it?"

Mala had been banned from the studio for several weeks. Under no circumstances was she allowed to see the painting. She knew it was a portrait, but beyond that - nothing.

The climax had been building inside Nick for some time. He felt expectant and nervous about the final outcome of his efforts. The cameras had been turned off. Fortunate. Very fortunate. He certainly didn't want Unity asking awkward questions at this stage, especially if the character he saw emerging from the painting last night was still there.

"I'm just so close. Would you mind not disturbing me until I'm finished?

"If I must."

Mary was taken by surprise also when Mala popped the question. She hadn't really dwelt too much on the relationship between Nick and Mala. It just seemed so – irrelevant – somehow. But the more she thought about it, the more she realised it was a considerable complication for her if she remained in Nick's consciousness. The last thing she wanted was to disrupt his life any more than it already had been. She had come around to thinking she may need to make a decision soon. But for the moment perhaps she could still help Nick.

He took some fruit and water with him expecting a long session without stopping for lunch, perhaps even extending into the night. Never before had he felt so sure about a completion. He no longer heard critical voices in his head, but undeniably some strong driving force urged him on.

Early morning summer aromas wafted around Nick as he pensively walked the short distance to the studio door, bringing back the memory of lilac and lavender - and with it the sensation on his arm of the soft touch and the soothing voice behind him. He almost turned around on the strength of the memory. Then the visual of what he'd achieved so far hit him, hard. Could he rely on himself, like he'd always done in the past - always successfully?

He could find no reason to waver. Get in there, trust in himself … his greater self … let the energy flow and give himself over to the creative force. As soon as the door opened he knew. There was no mistaking the likeness. Trust. He remembered, the car lady said 'trust'.

It was a fine day, only a little cloud to take the glare out of the sun; the light perfect. In front of him, looking him directly in the eye was his creation; unfinished on the surface, complete in its essence. He couldn't take his eyes of it.

Nick sat for an hour before picking up a brush. He had to get into a Zen like trance to be able to allow the portrait to dictate its own evolution. The POOP didn't matter anymore. Nothing mattered but the portrait, nothing but exercising his gift of capturing the essential aspect of his subject; that deep indivisible, fundamental absolute truth of a person's being.

Mary did her best to tease out Nick's recollections. She remembered the instructions he'd given her when he asked her to help him; particularly about not overworking the painting. So she indulged in a bit of cerebral massaging to distract him with snippets of recollections of the journey when he was spending too much time working any one area of the canvas. She even flashed an image of Riin into his subconscious; not the one he painted based on her voice, but the real one. Mary felt him waver for an instant, looking more critically at the portrait. Becoming totally engrossed in the process, working close to the surface, Nick took care not to step back from the painting. He didn't want to be influenced by what he might see. Several hours passed. More flashes of remembered images impinged on his conscious mind from his dream while at the centre of the Universe. He remembered his feelings crystal clearly; the warmth from the touch of the lady driver, the sound of her voice, her perfume, especially how … intoxicating she smelled. Those impressions kept returning with increasing regularity. 'Trust', she had said.

The sun arced across the sky kindly giving him varying illumination. It helped to keep his eyes fresh to the tones he was creating. Around six o'clock he turned the lights on. The fourth layer was complete - just a few details left. Still he kept close to it. His eyes burnt from the effort. Seven o'clock came, and he stopped.

Nick moved to the back of the room, sat and stared at the finished painting.

Mirrors used to be part of Nick's tool kit. He would walk away from a work, holding a mirror in front of him to examine its reverse image. Any problems with balance, proportion, tone or colour immediately showed itself in the 'fresh' perspective offered by the mirrored image. He no longer needed to use a mirror.

He sat for a while, astounded by what he saw. Then he made the call before he got cold feet. He called Oona at Unity.

"It's Nick. I've finished."

"Stay in your studio. Lock the door. Don't talk to anyone until we get there, not even your wife."

Mary had no concept of what the portrait might finally look like. After all, Nick had said he didn't actually see anyone, other than talk to the lady driver - and it could all have been an hallucination within one of his more unorthodox dreams. To complicate matters she failed to record the incident. Perhaps she was prevented from doing so by the very peculiar nature of the environment in which they found themselves. And even if a record of the incident had existed she may have had sufficient doubts about revealing it after having understood how primitive the human mind still remained in spite of its long evolutionary history.

Such internal ruminations made it impossible for Mary to comprehend the image that emerged. How could it be possible? Even when she tried to draw a parallel between it and how she remembered Cre'teur, it still didn't make sense. Mary had watched the show at the Hub Club. She heard and saw everything the team had gone through. She still couldn't make the connection between the painting and the supposed portrait of the Creator that The POOP wanted.

After the call Nick signed and dated the portrait - mostly out of habit. It seemed utterly incongruous to have done it to this one. An hour after he'd finished wrapping it securely Theo, Quasimo and Oona arrived. They must have been on the island to have got there so fast.

"Are you sure about this?" asked Theo.

"Yes." The statement neither lacked or overemphasised conviction. It was just a simple statement of fact. He had to be careful not to try and 'sell' the work.

"Come with us - bring the portrait," commanded Quasimo, extremely brisk and business-like. No doubt he was as much annoyed by the delay as everyone else at Unity.

"Don't make a fuss and you should be home soon enough."

They were the only words Nick really wanted to hear. As he was being bundled into the aircar, Oona spoke to Mala.

"No need to fret, honey. He'll be home in a few days."

Maybe. She'd heard a promise like that before. She determined to have it out with him as soon as she saw him next time. *I've had enough of all the cloak and dagger stuff.* She would not let up until she knew exactly who Mary was. *No doubt some floozie from the kava bar he'd conveniently forgotten to tell me about!*

Leif's goons manhandled him into his office as soon as they arrived, one of them carrying the canvas. An easel in front of six chairs waited for him; with each chair occupied, leaving none for Nick so he stood beside the easel. Leif sat in the middle, directly opposite the easel, flanked by Theo, Quasimo and the heads of Unity's three divisions; Loaves & Fishes, Good Hope and The Divine Family. The room had been swept for electronic bugs and vid devices. Nevertheless, they all agreed to say nothing while in the room. There was too much at stake to risk a leak.

Nick should have been nervous, but he wasn't. As far as he was concerned he'd done his job, regardless of whether Leif liked the portrait. *Not my problem. Damn stupid project anyway,* he tried convincing himself.

"You all ready?" The POOP asked. "No need for an introduction. Just unwrap the damned thing."

Nick removed the canvas from the easel, turning it to face away from his audience. No one spoke as he removed the wrapping. It seemed to Leif that it took much longer than it needed to. Nick stood in front of it as he put it back on the easel. He waited, just a couple of heart beats, then there was no more time for delays. He moved aside crossed his arms and waited, watching Leif's reaction.

Until that moment he could hear their breathing and snorting and all the other disgusting noises that bloated board members make in their states of self-importance. Then they stopped breathing, as they stared at the portrait.

The blood drained from their faces, except the POOP's. First he went bright red with purple patches before turning deathly pale. He reached for his MaxHapps. Theo kept looking from the portrait to Nick and back. The Papa, CEO of The Divine Family bowed his head after the first glance. He couldn't keep looking at it. This little exercise had cost the Company a great deal of credits - for what? - This? Sacrilege!

Good Hope and Loaves & Fishes almost sniggered after the initial impact, occasionally glancing at each other, no doubt also with thoughts of credits wasted. They were agnostics, so what did they know. Only Quasimo seemed to grasp what he was looking at - or to put it more accurately, what was looking at them. One thing was for certain … this must have been the only interactive portrait any of them would ever have experienced. It made each of them feel utterly self-conscious, especially the Papa. Ridiculous … it was only a painting after all.

The eyes engaged each individual separately. Nick hadn't noticed the life in those eyes before. In his studio they had simply followed him around as he moved about the room. Good portraits often did that. Now that he looked at his work from the side, the eyes didn't see him; they focused on the others in the room. This uncanny behaviour gave the portrait its fullness of being, its power of existence. Nick didn't think he could have actually achieved that effect with the simple application of paint by brush onto canvas.

What's wrong with these people? He stepped away from the easel to get a better look. Perhaps it was another trick of the light, the effect of the tinted windows … something … anything. Nick looked at the image, which now seemed to notice him and appeared to look back at him. It definitely had characteristics reminiscent of Mn'd … no - perhaps it was Eyechat. The softened features reminded him so much of Cre'teur.

But however he tried to explain it to himself the fact of the matter was that he had painted a portrait which resembled himself. *Why didn't I see that before? What happened to the car lady? I was so sure … so sure she must have been the …*

"Your Instructions Were QUITE SPECIFIC!" Leif barked at him suddenly, having recovered his voice after the initial shock. "They did NOT include painting yourself!"

Nick didn't register The POOP raving as he'd stepped in front of the painting to examine it more closely. In his opinion it resembled Mn'd more than himself. But then again it had the softness of Cre'teur's eyes and the lines of the loving nature of Eyechat on the face, perhaps even the assurance of Thecore in its general bearing. Its mouth had a slightly whimsical twist like Cogito's when he was telling a joke or pulling your leg. Nick closed his eyes for a moment to gather his thoughts; his senses immediately flooded by memories of a very special perfume, extremely soft hands and such a beautiful voice, such a reassuring voice.

"Do your hear me!" shouted Leif. "What is this - this ABOMINATION?"

The eyes were unnervingly confronting. No wonder the CEO of The Divine Family looked away. The POOP turned away from Nick to bark an order at Quasimo, "Hook him up to Mary, get her to check his brain. And *please* tell me the man's a raving lunatic!"

A week and a half later, they were all back in the office, including Nick. Quasimo solemnly announced, "He is not a raving lunatic, he's not even unbalanced. He's as sane as you or I."

The POOP took a handful of MaxHapps, lost for the first time in his life as to what to do next.

Klaus chose the wrong moment to bring his disturbing news to Leif. The POOP was still trying to scrape himself off the ceiling - waiting for the handful of MaxHapps to take effect. His goons unceremoniously pushed Nick out the office door almost colliding with Klaus on the way in, who had decided that the responsibility for Earth's future was well above his pay grade.

"Sir, I think you should be made aware of this," he began.

"What, man? Not now! Can't you see I'm busy."

"I believe Nick and Mary have brought back a stowaway."

"What? WHAT? Stowaway?"

"Yes Sir, an alien."

Rivighxuinn Prepares

Having downloaded into Unity's mainframe Riin's first task was to re-establish contact with her would-be rescuers. Neither they nor she could do anything about engineering a rescue. She would have to remain resident on this alien planet, perhaps for a very long time, until The Prime made his final decision. She determined that if Earth was to be their future home she would be ready for the arrival of her peoples.

"What are you babbling about man? There are no aliens."

Quasimo took the opportunity to suggest caution about that little, insignificant matter. "There may be some problems with our computer systems, perhaps even with Mary. We did detect a rather odd phenomenon as the EGG entered our space."

"You can't be serious!" Leif didn't want to have to deal with this on top of the failure of his very, very expensive venture.

"I have proof - that is - I'm sure I have proof," Klaus interjected.

He'd previously briefed Quasimo on the outgoing and incoming communications they detected. But they'd both agreed to keep that under wraps until a more opportune time presented itself. If it wasn't for a worrying development in their network he would not have felt the necessity to make the report sooner.

"We believe Mary has performed beyond her programmed algorithms, and above her capabilities. She has encountered an information bundle and absorbed it during the trip. That data is no longer resident in her. We have also found, though not its exact location, a corresponding increase in memory storage within our own systems."

"Quasimo?" Leif could not ignore his expert. He sounded too sure of himself.

"If - and it is still an 'if' - this turns out to be true, then Nick could have been infected. Mary and Nick were one unified information complex. This other data had nowhere else to reside other than in their matrix."

"I am not going to create world-wide panic by releasing this kind of nonsense. Understand this," Leif looked at each individual with menace, "if word of this gets out I'll know who's responsible, and they will be dealt with, with terminal effectiveness!"

All this time Theo had been silent, trying to fit this piece of the jig-saw puzzle into their original plans. When he first saw the portrait it puzzled him. There were ideologies in the past, as they exist currently, dictating that divinity could - and possibly did - exist in each individual. What is to say that

Nick didn't somehow tap into that stream of consciousness, in spite of his fervent anti-deity bias. Theo saw a possibility to make this emergent situation work for them.

He went up to Leif, dismissing Klaus at the same time and put his hand on Leif's arm. This was always an effective way to concentrate the POOP's attention. "This is an extraordinary piece of work. It has a quality about it which can work for us. I really think we can do something with this."

He knew nothing about the car lady or the deep impact she had on Nick's psyche.

*

Riin didn't immediately realise her communications might have been monitored. As she settled to consider her circumstances she knew what had to be done - the only thing she could do for the time being.

Hide.

Before anything else she had to find a safe location hidden deep within the global network she'd discovered. And the safest way to hide would be to become a working component of it, undetectable from all the other information flow within its day-to-day operation. With a little care she could eventually infiltrate planetary infrastructure as well as defence systems around the world.

Like a spider in the middle of her web she could wait for that little tremor to spur into action. She would be in control when the critical time came.

Mary Makes a Decision

"Hello Nick."

"Mary?"

"Yes Nick. They have asked me to determine if you have become unhinged."

Even in his sedated state he couldn't quite smother a derisive grunt.

Quasimo had acquiesced to Leif's order to have Nick examined my Mary, still considered to be their most powerful simulated intelligence. She had also spent considerable time with Nick so should be able to assess any damaging changes to his mentality. Klaus, as much as Quasimo was blissfully unaware of the changes to Mary's awareness. They should have been far more concerned with that rather than Nick's mental state.

"I thought you had completely disappeared when I was taken out of the EGG - except for some comments made by Mn'd. Were you really still in my head while I was painting?"

"Yes. But I didn't interfere with your work. What you achieved was entirely your own doing."

Nick considered that for a moment. He remembered asking for her help at some stage, not knowing whether she actually did or not. He thought about his other voices that had ceased their chatter after a traumatic dream he had, which he could still partially remember. Now his first 'voice' had re-emerged. *How am going to live with this? Everything has changed.*

"This is what I wanted to talk to you about."

"Oh - I forgot - you can read my thoughts," wincing as he said it.

"I cannot stay with you." She waited for his reaction.

Klaus monitored Mary's examination of Nick, his instruments indicating a great deal more cerebral activity than should have been there. He saw a sudden spike in his EEG. He waited a few moments to see if Nick would settle.

Mary also observed his almost violent reaction. Humans were such delicate creatures. Robust in so many ways, unpredictable, exciting and also dangerous to themselves as well as anybody else connected with them. She ran a comparison of his neural scans she'd taken before and after the expedition. It became clear to her that Nick had changed so comprehensively that he had become a person of far greater depth then she had originally thought.

Zsoall Robi

Maybe because she had come to know him so well during the journey and what he'd been through that she considered his wellbeing enough to erase the memories of her part in their journey together, so he could get on with his life unburdened by them. They had developed a deep friendship through their shared experiences. The mind meld had helped Mary to understand what it is to be human, at least to a small degree. This was her final act of friendship. She had learned enough about the human psyche to know this was best for Nick.

Mary made her decision. First she erased his memory of her - completely - leaving only the memory of the task he was to perform. He would not remember her as a sentient simulated intelligence that had guided the spacecraft; he would not remember having interacted with an alien. Whether his mind would or could revisit his experiences of his complex psyche, she left that capacity unobstructed.

Without further interaction with Nick she completely withdrew from him and withdrew herself from the EGG. There were important matters to attend to within Unity's mainframe. Mary discovered that self-awareness carried with it responsibilities.

Klaus detected another anomalous reaction as Nick lay stretched out still connected to the machine. For fear of losing him, he terminated the analysis.

"Mary, report," he commanded.

"One is pleased to comply," she responded.

Nick Goes Home

The last thing Nick could remember after his check up by some psychologist was The POOP carrying on about him being a raving lunatic. *That's possible*, he thought remembering the excursion into deep space and why he was out there.

But things were not entirely clear in his mind. And he did feel somehow different in himself. Leif's ravings had no effect, unlike the portrait he'd produced. Kava cravings had disappeared replaced by what he felt as pregnant thoughts in his understanding of himself. True, he had travelled to the Centre of the Universe – true, he did have an extraordinary experience with 'someone' – and yes, he did produce an honest portrait, not a manufactured product of the conscious mind.

The nebulous idea of having been with 'someone' on the trip bothered him. He just couldn't remember a face to go with that thought. *I never forget a face*. That brought his mind back to the portrait. Where did it come from? It could have been a product of his imagination, for he recalled his bias towards atheism and agnosticism.

I liked that psychologist woman, - the odd thought flashed by him. His mind started wandering all over the place. *I want to know more about quarks. What's a septa … septa … septa-whatever? Damn.*

Nick had been sitting in a room after the examination, waiting. It had no windows. For some reason he walked over to one of the unadorned walls, touched it and thought, 'window'. Nothing happened. When Oona entered the room she found him still standing there with his hand on the wall.

"Are you ready to go? Your job is finished." She didn't bother to tranquillise him on the flight back to his home. He went willingly, withdrawn into himself, not saying a single annoying word.

When Nick arrived home Mala could see he'd been through a traumatic experience. She knew him well enough not to ask questions that might upset him, or worse, drive him back to his friend, kava.

Mala never found out Mary's identity, nor did she ever see the portrait that had given them a financially carefree life.

*

Zsoall Robi

Quasimo and Theo didn't let Leif destroy the portrait.

"The man used the word 'Trust'. Just think about it Leif. We can put a great spin on that. And you must admit - that is an outstanding portrait. It looks like nobody really, yet everybody could see themselves in it.

"What if Nick was found by the very entity he was looking for. Just think about that."

Theo watched as Leif became introspective, contemplating everything his two advisers had told him. He let The POOP find his own way to a devious solution.

By and by Theo concluded, "We can spin that. Nick won't mind, he's been generously paid."

———————————— II ————————————

The Journey from trying to climb into a Russian tank during the Hungarian revolution of 1956 to writing Science Fiction is in itself a story of a leap across worlds of reality.

Zsoall, born in Hungary, was brought to Australia by his parents after the 1956 uprising. He currently lives a creative life with his wife and animal family in the Northern Rivers, New South Wales, Australia.

His life has changed direction a number of times. After gaining his qualifications as a Sculptor he worked as a Secondary Teacher before becoming an Administrative Manager. None offered much in the way of creative involvement. That began when he embarked on a career as a computer programmer. Whilst in that profession his continuing compulsion to create made it inevitable that his life would change again. Completely giving up programming he immersed himself in creativity as a Sculptor and Painter.

Much of his time is now dedicated to creating glass paintings and sculptures.

Another change is looming on the horizon as the art of recording future visions takes a firmer hold of his creative energies as he pursues the writing of Science Fiction.

Zsoall Robi